Love: Jerilyn
2019

A Place Called Hexie

A Novel Interspersed With Historical Facts

SAMUEL MILLER

authorHOUSE®

AuthorHouse™
1663 Liberty Drive
Bloomington, IN 47403
www.authorhouse.com
Phone: 1-800-839-8640

This is a work of fiction interspersed with historical facts, some autobiographical, and set in a specific geographical locale. Any similarity to persons living or dead in the fictional portion is purely coincidental. The names of living persons in the geographical locale have been changed. Public record places have not been changed.

First published by AuthorHouse 7/23/2010

ISBN: 978-1-4520-2753-1 (e)
ISBN: 978-1-4520-2751-7 (sc)
ISBN: 978-1-4520-2752-4 (hc)

Library of Congress Control Number: 2010910080

Printed in the United States of America
Bloomington, Indiana

This book is printed on acid-free paper.

To Clyde Miller, a great historian, genealogist, and engineer.
June 11, 1946 - December 16, 1995
And to his family, Justine, Todd and Heather

Foreword

Finally, it comes to fruition! A local history that mixes just enough fiction to keep you turning the pages. For years I have been reading Sam's articles about Hexie in the Somerset Historical Society's Laurel Messenger, and his privately published articles. I've heard the local folk stories about the witches and how Hexie got its name. I have felt the chills go up my spine when I had to drive through Hexie on a blood-red full moon, and was glad to get out alive! I don't believe all those tales, of course, but they do make for good reading and for adding cultural color to an area that my mother always referred to as "The Hollow." Impoverished economically, it's alive with the culture of the Northernmost Appalachian Mountains. Sam brings that heritage alive, and will keep it alive for generations to come. - Linda Marker

This story, loosely based on actual events, is an intriguing read for anyone with a love of history, mystery, a touch of satire, and vivid location descriptions. The author makes those familiar with the area feel like they are going home, and makes those who have never been there want to visit. Sit back, relax and let the story take you on a wonderful trip. - Brenda S. Frederick

Author's Note

Why this book?

It is said of genealogy, that it is an interest, that becomes a hobby and ends as an obsession. I can agree with that, but there is a sad side to it all. After you have gone through all the records in courthouses, churches and cemeteries, searched the LDS libraries and internet sites, after you have perused many family Bibles and talked to family members of all levels of relationships, and after you have entered it all into the various genealogical charts, who will read it?

That is what bothered my brother Clyde as he collected and documented data on many families in the Hexie area. He and I discussed it through an exchange of e-mails back in 1994. He decided he would publish a quarterly news letter about the families and individual he had documented; he called it, "The Hexie Gazette." The first issue came out in January 1995. It was very well received and the request for copies increased significantly after each publication. But, as the saying goes, Clyde had a major mountain to climb, he was battling the big "C" in the form of Leukemia. I went to visit him in Houston in the autumn of 1994 when he was undergoing treatment at the Anderson Cancer Treatment Center. We talked of the times and people we knew in Hexie and of some interesting characters who proceeded us and the untold stories they carried to their grave.

He came out of his first round of treatment at Anderson feeling pretty good, but it was a short lived reprieve, he was going to need a bone marrow transplant. All his siblings were screened and it seemed like providence when our oldest brother proved to be a perfect match. The transplant was done at the Baylor Medical Center and was a success, but other complications caused the battle to be lost on December 16, 1995. He had completed four issues of the Hexie Gazette.

I received all of Clyde's research work from my sister-in-law. It filled two long shelves with three ring binders and various other notebooks. The question remained, who is going to read them? You are talking about deceased people and times of long ago, nobody cares. My theory was that the only way others will read about this type of research is if you can tie the people, places and times together in an interesting fashion. To me the answer was a novel.

I have written some historical pieces, but I am not a novelist, however, I wanted to give it a try. My only hope is that a few people will read "A Place Called Hexie" and come to appreciate their own history and ancestry. There are a lot of places like Hexie in one way or another, someone just needs to tell the story.

Clyde believed there was a story to be told under most of the stones in any cemetery.

He is buried in the Old Bethel Church cemetery in Hexie. There is an engraving of a beech tree on the left side of his tombstone. The letters CM are engraved in the trunk. One hundred years from now when someone else passes by collecting data, they will surely wonder about the significance of the engraving. They will probably never know. His children will probably remember, maybe even his grandchildren, but his great grandchildren, probably not.

Acknowledgements

To Linda for taking a grammatical nightmare and turning it into a readable manuscript, and for her persistence in encouraging me to publish this book. Also for her good advice throughout the process.

To Brenda, a proofreader of Navy texts and publications who found some mistakes that Linda and I missed, and who chastised me for my "run-on" sentences.

To my wonderful grandchildren, Tim, Stacy, Maire and Ruairi for letting me use their personality traits.

To my lovely wife, Hannelore, who forgave me for killing off her character so I had a starting point for this book.

To my two Roses. My cousin, Rose Tressler who lives in Hexie and provided me with the pictures I have used in this book. It was difficult to make the choices. She may have even captured an apparition of Mary. And to my friend Rose Spencer of Southern Exposure for making me look so young in the portrait of the author. It shows what a good photographer can do even when working with limited material. Ha! Ha!

Prologue

Awaiting the Procession

W esley drove his car up the winding driveway from his house and parked it in the clearing at the top of the Barney Kreger hill. From here he could look out across the valley and see the country church on the distant plateau. It was in this cemetery where the deceased was to be interred alongside his wife. Many of his family also lay there, starting with his maternal great Grandparents.

After parking the car, he walked back across the road and started down the driveway toward the house. About fifty yards down the driveway was a path off to the left along the side of the hill. The path paralleled the narrow township road just above. He would sit here now and wait for the funeral procession to go by, but he knew he had plenty of time.

He had read the obituary in yesterday's newspaper and knew that the funeral procession would not be along for at least another hour. The service at the church was scheduled for 10:30, it was now just 9:15 but he wanted some time to be alone with his own thoughts. So much had happened since he first met this man just seven months ago. In retrospect, it seemed like just a few days ago, but he knew that all he had learned and experienced in that time was more than anyone could accomplish in a few days.

Where he was sitting was one of his two favorite spots to which he would repose and meditate. He had found it the first time he stopped to look at the land.

When the builder had started clearing the area for his house further down the slope of the hill, he would often come up here and sit on the trunk of a long ago fallen tree and watch the progress. Later, after the stonemason had finished extending the old foundation for the house, he had asked him to build a bench here using the fieldstones that lay in good supply all about. The field above the road had been cleared and first tilled over two hundred years ago. Each owner since then had seen fit to remove the large rocks that somehow seemed to grow anew each year, and they would then dump them below the road. There was an ample supply for this project.

He had cut away the brush along the path and covered it with wood chips. The construction company had brought in a chipper to dispose of the limbs from the trees that had to be felled to make way for the house. He had asked that only the minimum number of trees be cut, and that in no case should the old black walnut trees be cut. The builder had warned him that the walnut trees were very old, and in the event of a bad windstorm they could pose a serious risk to the house. He had told the builder he understood that, but he would accept the risk.

Sitting here now he could just see the top of the roof of his house, but he knew that in two or three more weeks the coming winter winds would rake the beautiful colored leaves from their branches and the house would be visible, even from the road.

It was a beautiful autumn day. He didn't know what the weather was like elsewhere in the world, but he guessed that the Good Lord might have made this beautiful day at this particular spot in the world as recognition to his departed servant, and some time adversary.

The first time he had met his recently departed friend, he thought him to be a bit sacrilegious, but he soon changed his mind. Perhaps, better than most, he understood the correlation between earthly father and heavenly Father. You could disagree without being obstinate, but you should always look for guidance from the higher authority. He knew that if he disagreed with his earthly father, then that father would try and show him the error of his way. It was he who could choose to accept or disregard the lesson, but it was also he who had to accept the results. He envisioned that it was not much different with the heavenly Father.

It was a day very similar to this in early spring when he first met the gentleman who would soon be passing by on his last ride. He thought about it and felt a deep emotional pull well up in his gut, but because of his vocation, he had taught himself to hold such emotions in check. There was much that he knew now, but in totality, there was much more that he didn't know, and perhaps never would.

It was very difficult for him to accept this man's death, even more so than when his parents had passed away. With his father, he could see it coming and he prepared himself for it. With his mother it was unexpected, but she went so peacefully. With Jacob Grant, it was so sudden and tragic. His thoughts went back to the first time he ever came to this area.

PART I

The Return

Chapter 1

They had just passed the Pittsburgh Interchange on the Pennsylvania Turnpike and his mother had not said a word since they left Youngstown a little over an hour ago. Wesley wasn't sure what to attribute this to; had the fact of losing her older sister finally become a reality, or was it simply the fact that she was going back after so many years?

She and her sister got along quite well, although the separation in miles kept them from being real close. However, by today's standards, the two hundred miles from Youngstown, Ohio to Confluence, Pennsylvania was not a great distance. And although her sister had come to Youngstown to visit her several times, his mother had never gone to visit her in Confluence. She had never gone back since the family moved to Ohio over fifty years ago.

He knew his mother had some unpleasant memories of the area, but when he queried her about it years ago, she had simply told him she had no real bad memories, and even a few good ones, but it was just a part of her life that she preferred not to discuss and she would leave it at that.

The way she had said it, Wesley decided he would respect her wishes and not pursue the matter any further, although he knew the reason for some of her feelings, or at least he thought he did. But at this moment, he just wanted to get her in a conversation, something she normally had no difficulty with.

"You know Mother, I have traveled a lot since I graduated from the seminary, but this is one of the few times that I have been further east than Pittsburgh. We are now starting to enter the hilly regions of Pennsylvania, and with the leaves on the trees in the full autumn spectrum; we should get some spectacular views. Do you remember much about it from when you were a young girl?"

"Of course I do. It has been a long time, but many of the things of your youth, you never forget. If you were born in the hills, you don't notice the hills in any special way, but I would say they are beautiful, especially this time of the year," his mother said.

"Considering the name, and of course looking at the map, Confluence, as the name implies, sits at the juncture of three rivers, so it has to be located in a valley," Wesley continued.

"Well obviously Son, if there are three rivers, there has to be more than one valley. There are three valleys that bring the rivers to the juncture, and one carrying them all away."

"Yes, I can surmise that, but what I am trying to visualize, is do you get the feeling of being in a large valley?"

"As a young girl, I never gave that much thought. And even as I try to recall it now, I don't get the picture of a large valley. I remember there were hills all around us, but all the streets in Confluence were perfectly flat. Not that there were that many streets; it was a very small town, and may be even smaller now."

"I suppose," Wesley continued, "if it is like most of the small towns in that area, or in this general region, it may indeed be smaller now than when you left."

"That could very well be the case," his mother said. "And since you mentioned visualizing, I recall that the widest valley outside of the town followed the smallest river."

"And which river would that be?"

"Laurel Hill Creek," his mother said. "A mile or so up river is another small town called Ursina, but between the two is a fairly large flat valley. We lived up another valley, the one that overlooked the Casselman River, but I remember when I was maybe ten years of age, there was a really bad rain one spring that melted the snow and caused all the rivers to flood. My father took my brother and me up over the hill behind our house and from there we could look down on the town. The larger valley along Laurel Hill

Creek was completely under water, like a huge lake, except I remember the water was moving very fast. I was scared, and I told my daddy that I thought the whole town of Confluence was going to be washed away."

"And what did you father say?"

"He said the new dam that had been built on the Youghiogheny would certainly help a lot, but the people had still better pray the rain stopped."

"There was only a light drizzle falling as we stood there, and by the time we got back to the house, the rain had completely stopped. An hour later the sun came out and for the next couple of days we had beautiful spring-like weather. I was glad, because a few days later, the warm weather brought the Johnny-jump-ups and the Buttercups into bloom."

"So the town of Confluence was spared?" Wesley asked his mother.

"I think the streets did flood and there was some real damage to a few businesses that sat directly by the rivers, but they survived. I remember my father said it was not nearly as bad as the flood of 1924. The strangest thing about that memory is that it never crossed my mind until many years later."

"Oh!"

"I remember one time shortly after you came back to Youngstown, you gave a sermon about prayers, answered and unanswered. I remember very vividly you said that often God answers prayers that He knows we have in our heart, but that we may not express in words."

"I don't recall it, but I keep the notes from all my sermons on the computer. I will have to try and locate that one, but why did it remind you of that time in your life?"

"Well, you know your grandfather Nelson was not a church going man until very late in his life. At that time, I don't ever remember him having gone to Church. Sometimes Mrs. Hannah would come by and take my older sister Kathryn and I to the Methodist Church in Harnedsville, and that was perfectly okay with him, but he and my mom never went. I asked mom one time why she didn't go, and she said it was because she didn't have any good clothes to wear. Anyway, that is not what I started to say. It was when you delivered that sermon; I recalled that on that day he had mentioned the people had better pray for the rain to stop. I am sure that a lot, if not most of the people of the town did just that, but later I thought my father might have prayed for the same thing."

"Probably so." Wesley paused for a moment and then went on, "Did you continue to go to the Methodist church until you moved?"

"No. After my mother told me why she didn't go, I realized that I also didn't have church going clothes. Most of what we had were hand me downs from other people in the town. It was hard enough going to school and sitting by some boy and him saying, 'that is my sister's old dress.' I didn't need to hear it in church."

"And your sister?" Wesley asked.

"I guess she was a duck and I was a chicken; that type of rain just rolled off her back. Of course there were a few other families just as poor as us, but that didn't help me any back then."

"I understand Mother," Wesley said.

"Yes you probably do, Son, because you work with many who are in the same situation, but a lot of people who say they understand really don't."

"That is the sad part Mother, you are completely right. They say they do, but they don't, and that is some of what makes my job so difficult." Wesley now realized their conversation had taken a turn toward the depressing side so he decided to change the subject.

They had now passed the Donegal Interchange on the Turnpike and started up the Laurel Ridge Mountain range. The Laurel Ridge was not that high; in fact the highest point in Pennsylvania was in Somerset County at Mt Davis, with an elevation of just over 3,200 feet, but these hills rose abruptly with a lot of rocky cliffs and were covered with hardwood trees of red and white oak, maple, ash, hickory, locust, wild cherry and others. Because of the varieties, the first frosts of autumn had caused them to each take on their own unique signatures that resulted in a mind-boggling array of colors. "A palette that only God could assemble," Wesley reasoned.

"This is really beautiful, isn't it," Wesley said.

"Yes, it truly is," his mother said in response.

For the next ten minutes they rode in silence. When they topped the summit of Laurel Ridge and the road leveled out on the approach to Somerset, he saw first a sign for Seven Springs Ski Resort, and less than a quarter mile later, one for Hidden Valley. He remembered seeing the same signs just before they reached the Donegal exit. "I guess this is ski country and the season must be fast approaching," Wesley said.

"I guess," Was his mother's reply, "although I am not sure I would want to drive in these hills in the winter.

"This old turnpike is a main east-west artery, so I am sure they are equipped to keep it open. I imagine that even on the smaller roads they hit them quickly with the snowplows and salt trucks just like they do in Youngstown.

His mother said nothing.

When Wesley saw the sign that said Somerset Exit, 2 Miles, he looked at his watch; it was 12:05 PM.

"We can check into the Days Inn and freshen up, and still have plenty of time to get to Confluence before the 2:00 PM viewing," Wesley said.

"Yes, but I do want to get there early enough so I can talk to the funeral director. I also want to be in the funeral chapel before it opens to the public."

"That should not be a problem, Mother. Would you like me to call Cousin Thelma and see what time she is going to be there, or see if perhaps she could meet us there at a given time?"

"That won't be necessary. I already talked to her and told her we would be there before the 2:00 PM viewing. She seemed a bit cold on the phone so I don't want to bother her again."

"Okay then, that seems to be taken care of. As for seeming a bit cold, she might just be distraught over the loss of her mother."

"Yes, maybe so."

At 1:15 Wesley and his mother reached the small town of Ursina. "Interesting name, I wonder if it is from the Latin, 'ursinus' meaning 'bear'," Wesley mused to himself.

"Up there where that car is turning, we want to turn," his mother said.

"I thought this road went right into Confluence," Wesley said.

"It does, but I want to go through Harnedsville and down. It will only take a minute longer. It goes by where we lived."

"Okay," Wesley said and turned on his left blinker. If she wanted to go by the old homestead, he assumed there must have been a few good memories. Of course, as poor as families may be, they usually make their own good memories.

The road crossed Laurel Hill Creek and then up a very steep grade. About one third of the way up was a railroad track. At this point the road got even steeper. "Is this the way you came when you moved?" Wesley asked.

"No, I wanted to because then we would not have to go through Confluence, but my dad was afraid that the brakes on the old wagon might not be enough and the horse wouldn't be able to hold it back."

"That makes good sense," Wesley said.

"This hill is called Hogback," his mother said.

"Why Hogback?"

"I don't know, ask your cousin Thelma when you see her. She can probably tell you."

Wesley noted a bit of 'iciness' in his mother's voice, but he let it slide.

At the top of Hogback, there was a beautiful panorama of the valley below, now decked out in its finest autumn colors.

"Beautiful," was all Wesley could say.

Down over the hill to his left, in the open field, was a well-maintained old cemetery. Wesley made the sign of the cross. He was glad to see that some one had enough respect for those who had gone before them to maintain this burial ground. In his travels, he saw so many that were completely ignored. He assumed that at one time, there must have been a church at this location.

As he crossed the bottom of the valley and neared the small village of Harnedsville, the road crossed a bicycle trail, part of a rails-to-trails project he assumed. He would have to remember this and check it out.

A short distance later, he came to a stop sign.

"Turn right," his mother said, and Wesley obeyed.

About a mile down the road, and just outside of Confluence, his mother instructed him to stop. He did as she asked.

"Look way over there against the hill, below where that house sits. See those four large pine trees," she said more than asked.

"Yes," Wesley replied.

"That is about where our old house sat. The barn and the main farmhouse sat further to the right. A man who worked at the Listonburg sawmill, where dad worked part time and where he broke his leg, gave them to him. My brother Harold and I planted them just about two weeks before we had to move. This is the first I have seen them since that time. The last time Kathryn was in Ohio to see me; she said they were the tallest pine trees in the area. You can go on now," his mother said.

"They grew well; a nice tribute to you and Uncle Harold. But I am beginning to suspect that you should have come back to visit at some time in your life."

Again his mother said nothing.

Chapter 2

Wesley parked the car in the lot in back of the funeral home, and then he and his mother walked to the front door. A young lady greeted them and Wesley let his mother respond.

She told the lady that she was the sister of the deceased and this was her son. She didn't fail to mention that Wesley was a priest. The young lady looked at Wesley knowingly, and gave him a courteous smile.

"Your niece and nephew, the children of the deceased, are here. They told me that you would probably be here shortly. Let me show you in."

She led the way to the entrance of the funeral home chapel. Seated down front, Wesley and his mother saw Thelma and Thomas, Kathryn's children. She stopped and Wesley and his mother proceeded on their own.

As soon as Thelma and Thomas saw whom it was that approached, they rose to greet them. Both greeted Wesley's mother first.

"Hello Aunt Karin," Thelma said as she gave her a loose hug.

Then Thomas repeated the procedure with a very warm hug.

When that was ended, Thelma gave her cousin Wesley a very warm embrace. Thomas then shook his hand and also embraced him.

"I would like to talk to you later about the service tomorrow, Wesley, if you don't mind," Thelma said.

"Of course, whenever it is convenient for you," Wesley said. He noticed that it was Thelma, and not Thomas, who was the "take charge type person."

His mother now looked at her niece and said, "Let me pay respects to my sister, and then I wonder if you and I could talk in private."

"Why sure," Thelma said, and Wesley and Thomas just looked at each other.

Wesley joined his mother as the two of them approached the open coffin. Wesley made the sign of the cross, and his mother followed suit. Both stood for a minute peering into the coffin, and it was only then that Wesley realized how much Kathryn resembled his grandmother, and how much his mother resembled his grandfather. He had earlier guessed that their personalities were different, and now he realized that their physical features were also different. He wasn't a scholar on genetics, but for just a moment he contemplated the present scenario: Was Thelma also like her grandfather, thus like her aunt. Wesley dismissed it from his mind and knelt before the coffin. When he arose, both he and his mother returned to the chapel seats.

Thelma met them and said, "I talked to the assistant funeral director, and she said we could use the office."

Wesley looked at his mother and she twitched her mouth as if to say, "Don't worry, it will be okay."

When the two women left, Wesley and Thomas sat down to talk. Wesley wanted to ask if he knew what the deal was between his mother and Thomas's sister, but he didn't. Since Thomas didn't live around here, he probably knew no more about this situation than he did.

Wesley started the conversation. He knew that Thomas was a pilot in the Navy, so he started the conversation on that track. "So where and what are you doing in the Navy these days?" Wesley asked.

"I just came back from assignment in North Island, California, and am taking over as a CAG in Norfolk," Thomas said.

"I am sorry," Wesley said, "I am not very good on military acronyms, what is a CAG?

"My fault," Thomas said, "you get used to speaking in military lingo to military personnel, and you forget to compensate for civilians. CAG stands for Commander Air Group, and it is always followed by a number to indicate a specific group."

"Commander," Wesley said, "I thought my mother said you made Captain."

Thomas laughed, "It is a bit confusing to civilians, I did make Captain, and in the Navy when you are head of a command, you are addressed as Captain, regardless of your rank. There are some exceptions in case you are an Admiral, but that is the general rule. However, I will be in charge of an air group that will be stationed aboard a carrier, which will have its own Captain. Like kitchens, ships only have enough room for one Captain, so I will be Commander of the Air Group as a Captain, and he will be Captain of the ship, also as a Captain.

"Clear as mud," Wesley said, and the two cousins laughed. "However, I am impressed Cousin, you have done very well, a real source of pride for this small town.

"Not such a great accomplishment. Throughout my career I have come across a lot of pretty successful men and women, officer and enlisted, who hail from very small towns similar to this one. I think it has to do with them coming to the realization that you can make it in the military if you are dedicated, and work hard, and if not, you may wind up coming back here with nothing to do. I love this area, but there is no future here for these young people."

"I work with a lot of young people, most of them from poor families, so I know exactly what you are saying. On a different subject, since you grew up in this area, there are a few questions I would like to ask you."

"Fire away, but if they are too involved, I may have to refer you to my sister. She is the one who knows the historical and genealogical aspects of this part of the County."

The assistant funeral director showed Thelma and her aunt Karin to the office and closed the door. In the office there was a desk with an executive type chair, and two other regular office chairs. Neither lady chose to sit in the chair behind the desk.

When they were both seated, Thelma started the conversation. "What did you want to talk to me about, Aunt Karin," she asked?

"It is a bit difficult for me to say, because perhaps I am over reacting."

Thelma said nothing, but let her aunt continue.

"Well from the tone of your voice in our phone conversations, and the greeting just a few minutes ago, I feel that I have offended you in some way. Please tell me what I have done wrong; I will be more that glad to apologize for my actions."

"You haven't committed any offense against me, so no apology is needed. If it seems that I have been less that enthusiastic in my greetings to you, you are probably reading it correctly. That is your sister in there; it is she whom you offended."

Karin sat stunned for a moment and then answered, "Thelma, I loved my sister; it is a great loss that I now endure. I know the loss is not nearly as great as your loss, but it is a great loss for me, nevertheless."

"You are correct Aunt Karin, we both have suffered a great loss, but I know how much I have lost. The sad thing is you don't know how much you lost."

"But I do, Thelma."

"No you don't," Thelma interjected quite forcefully. "There is no way you could. I don't hold it against you, but that is mostly because my mother, your sister, would chastise me for such actions, but I must say what is on my mind. After that, you can speak your mind, and we will put the matter to rest, as families should. Fair enough?"

"Of course."

"I know how hard it was on the family after grandpa broke his leg. I know it was very hard even before that, but eventually when the family moved to Ohio, you were able to rise above the poverty. I know that your getting pregnant with Wesley at such a young age must have also been very difficult for you. Your keeping him and still finishing high school was admirable. The fact that you met a man who accepted Wesley as his own was a wonderful thing. At least your life finally started to take a turn for the better. Certainly no one would find fault in that, especially your sister. She was your staunchest supporter. I have the letters mom received from Grandma Nelson that proves she, my mother, was truly concerned about your welfare. I also have the letters that you wrote to mom when the two of you exchanged letters. I only have one side of that exchange, but I know that what you describe of your life in Youngstown was nothing like my mother was going through here."

"I know this is starting to sound like sour grapes on my part, and that is not how I want it to sound. My mother was happy for you. I am also very happy that things worked out for you the way they did. I don't know that I can say this in the way I want to. Maybe it would be better if

I sat down some time and wrote it all out, that way I can make sure that no animosity creeps into what I am trying to say. I just want to know…," and Thelma had to stop as she fought to hold back sobs. After a bit she continued, "Why didn't you ever come to visit her? She went to visit you several times, and you could certainly more afford to make the trip than she could."

Karin nodded her head knowingly, but said nothing. She knew this was not yet the time. She would let her niece continue.

"Did my mother ever tell you how hard things were for her after the rest of the family moved to Ohio?"

Finally her aunt spoke, "No she didn't. You know your mother; she just wouldn't do that sort of thing."

"That sounds like her. She never complained. She just kept plugging on. Let me tell you how it was. I was born in the spring after you all left. I am from April to September older than Wesley. Dad worked in the coal mines at Listonburg at that time, but not long after that, the mine shut down. When Thomas was born, Dad was working on a sawmill close to Route 40. He had an old car, but it was broke down half of the time and he never had enough money to get it fixed, so often he had to walk the three miles to the mill. When I was five he got a job at the clay mines up close to Fort Hill, but that only lasted about two years when they ceased operations. After that he could only find part time work, and driving school bus during the term, so mom had to get a job. She helped clean house for several ladies and she also did some sewing. I suppose she was a pretty good seamstress. Finally, when they opened the new school she got a job working in the cafeteria.

"To me she always seemed tired, but she never complained. However, the thing I remember the most was that she was always on Thomas and me to do our school work. She would often tell us that she did not want us to have to work for so little like she and Dad did. And the only way we were going to get around that was to go to college. There was no money for us to go, but there were ways, she would always say. Study hard, make good grades and get a scholarship. Thomas was very good in sports, especially football, but Turkeyfoot High School was so small, that it was difficult to get college scouts out here to look around. In her mind, scholastic achievement was the only way, and it worked for me. I got a partial scholarship to Indiana University here in Pennsylvania that covered my tuition and books, and the counselors were successful it getting me a part time job.

"Just before Thomas started his senior year, I was home and I remember him saying at the supper table, that maybe he would joint the Navy. Mom looked at him for a long time and he said nothing, then she told him that if he wanted to go in the Navy, it was okay. We all looked at her in surprise and then she said, 'But not until you graduate from college.'

"The next day, she started to check out how you could get into the Naval Academy. She wrote letters, she talked to people and by the time his graduation neared, he had a congressional appointment.

"You know, during all that time, mom never had a store bought dress. She would get cheap remnants and make her some, but what little money she had, she spent on us. During my senior year in college, I got a pretty good job so I saved up money and bought her a nice three-piece suit for my graduation. She was like a five-year old child in her first Easter dress.

"After dad died, I was married and both Jeff and I had good jobs. Thomas was a young Lieutenant Commander then, so we tried to convince her to move from the old house in the woods above Dumas. She wouldn't hear of it, so we decided we would just take action on our own. We bought three acres above where the old house was that Grandma and Grandpap lived in before his accident. We had a small house built with a big lower porch. She always liked a big porch. It was just a few hundred feet above the pine trees that you and Uncle Harold planted before you moved. From that porch you can look down on this whole valley and the town.

"When it was finished, Thomas came home from Jacksonville with his wife Dora, and Jeff and I came in from Pittsburgh. We all drove up to the old house and picked her up with the pretense of going for breakfast. Actually we were taking her for breakfast, just not at a restaurant.

"She was a bit confused when we drove up to the new house, and even more so when we told her to get out. When she opened the door, her good friend from childhood, Stella Tressler, was standing there. Stella had a complete breakfast table set. Mom looked at her and said, 'what a surprise Stella, is this your new house?' 'Not mine,' Stella said, 'it is yours,' and she handed mom a ring of bright shiny brass keys. It took a long time to convince her that it really was hers, but when she walked out on that porch and sat down on the swing, she was just overcome. She cried for a long time, but she was hooked.

"Later that day, we took her back to the old house so she could supervise the movers packing up her meager belongings to transport them to the new house. Jeff and I had planned to spend the night with her that first day. Thomas and Dora had rented a motel room in Somerset. After Jeff had gone to bed, mom and I sat out on the porch, drank coffee, and listened to the night birds sing. She was still in shock, but there is one thing that she said to me that I will never forget." Thelma paused and large tears rolled down her cheek. She took a paper tissue from a box on the desk and dried her eyes. Then she continued, "She said, 'Maybe Karin will come and visit me now; she will really be surprised to see how big the pine trees have grown that she and Harold planted.'"

"That was seven years ago Aunt Karin. You never came." For the first time, animosity did show in Thelma's eyes. "Just two weeks ago when she took a turn for the worse, I drove up on Friday evening to spend the weekend with her. Again we sat out on the porch and she said almost the exact same thing. I didn't know what to say, so I changed the subject. Then I went into the bathroom and I almost called you to tell you get your butt in here. Your sister is dying, it is your last chance to see her, but I didn't call because I knew she would not want that."

Thelma paused for a long time, but her aunt knew it was still not time to talk.

Thelma continued, "I am sorry Aunt Karin, I didn't mean this as a guilt trip to be placed on your shoulders. It is just that I had to say what was on my mind, or I could never move beyond it. I know mom would not have liked me saying what I did, but now I have had my say so it is your turn."

Karin sat for a long time, almost as if in disbelief of what she had just heard, then with a trembling voice she began, "Thelma, you poor child. What you have gone through. How could I have been so foolish, so naïve? I was afraid to return, that is why I never did, but I never realized that I was hurting someone so much, especially my dear sister. And the pain you had for bearing it in your mind all this time. I was so wrong. I should have come. You have every right to be upset. I am sorry, so very sorry. What shall I ever do?"

Both sat in silence for a short period of time; finally Thelma got up from her chair and walked over to where her aunt sat. She placed her hand on her shoulder. "Mom always said you and I were a lot alike. She said we

17

took after Grandpap. We had to have our say, but when we said it, it was over. So, can I still be your niece?"

The tears flowed freely from Karin's eyes as she gave her niece a long hard hug.

Both ladies stayed in the office for a few minutes while they dried their eyes and gained their composure, and then they reentered the funeral chapel with Thelma holding on to her aunt's arm.

Wesley and Thomas gave their previous skepticism no more thought.

Thelma came first to talk to Wesley, while his mother went to talk to her nephew. Thelma wanted to know if Wesley would be part of the service. She knew that her mother would like that very much.

Wesley assured her he would be most happy to serve however she wished. She told him that the Methodist minister where her mother attended church would naturally be doing the service. She asked Wesley if he and her aunt would be at the 7:00 PM viewing, and Wesley said they would. Thelma told him that Reverend Stanton would also be there and she would introduce the two of them to each other, then they could work out the details. Wesley said that would be fine.

Then Wesley decided to venture out on a limb using his best professional approach. "I seemed to sense a high pressure system earlier," he said with a smile toward his cousin. "Did you and my mother work that out?"

"I don't know what on earth you are talking about, Cousin Wesley," was all Thelma said. She smiled and squeezed his hand. "Come let me introduce you to some of the other people. You know you could have made this simpler by wearing your Collar, that way I wouldn't have to say each time, 'he is a priest.'"

"You don't have to say that Thelma."

"Oh yes I do. First, I think it is interesting that a Methodist girl has a Priest for a cousin, but more importantly, since you don't wear a wedding band, I don't want any of the unattached ladies laying claim to my handsome cousin."

"Thanks Thelma, for looking out for my celibacy vows. I will wear the collar when we come this evening."

At 3:30 PM, the young female assist made an announcement. "Ladies and Gentlemen, we will be closing the chapel until 7:00 PM. The children of the deceased, Thelma and Thomas, have asked us to inform you that they will be returning to their mother's home until the evening viewing. They extend an invitation to all to join them there if you are so inclined."

Wesley quickly found his mother and whispered something to her.

"We will take that ride when we leave tomorrow after the funeral and everything else is taken care of," his mother whispered back. "We will now join the rest of the family at my sister's house."

"Good idea, Mother," Wesley said and she looked at him a bit askance.

Kathryn Leslie was laid to rest at 11:20 AM on the following day. The place of interment was the Methodist cemetery across the Casselman River. The ladies of the church prepared a wonderful meal for all of the mourners. By 1:15 PM, all farewells had been said and all departed for their respective homes, for some, many miles away. For Wesley's mother, there was one more trip to make, but she was now more at peace with herself than she had ever been in her entire life. Thelma had told her of a few things that her mother knew. She remembered a letter she had written a long time ago. She looked at her son, the priest, and was satisfied.

Wesley and his mother got in her car, and started to pull out of the church parking lot. Thelma and Jeff, and Thomas and Dora, stood by their respective vehicles and waved as they departed. They headed north back toward Somerset.

Chapter 3

esley and his mother left Confluence by the most direct route on 281 and crossed Laurel Hill Creek just outside of town. A mile north was the town of Ursina, and Thelma had confirmed his musing about the town's name. She also gave him a brief history of the New Jersey families who arrived here in 1770 as the first settlers. Even today they are simply known as the Jersey settlers and one valley is named in their honor, the Jersey Hollow.

Just north of Ursina they crossed Laurel Hill Creek again, and about a fourth of a mile further, Route 281 made a sharp curve to the right. As you started into the curve there was a small road tangent to the main road.

"Take the small road Wesley," his mother said.

"Okay, I assume you know where we are going?"

"Of course. Don't worry; it will eventually bring you back out on the main road at Kingwood."

"I really wasn't worried."

"You just believe that after so many years, I might have forgotten where we are," she said with a slight laugh in chiding her son.

Wesley was glad to see that her spirits were beginning to rise, so he said, "Believe me mother, for someone who remembers everything I said when I was three or four years old and most of what I say in my sermons, I have no doubt that you know exactly where we are." Then a large two story stone house caught his eye and he exclaimed, "Beautiful old stone house."

His mother didn't answer him on either comment, but as they rounded the first slight curve the road made to the right, she said, "Oh thank God, it is still there."

"What is still there?" Wesley asked?

"The old covered bridge. Look way out there to your left. See that red building, it is a covered bridge."

"Oh yeah, I do see it."

"We will stop there for a minute or so," his mother said.

"You won't have to twist my arm mother; I love those old covered bridges. There are still quite a few in Ohio, but they are going fast."

His mother didn't say another word. When he pulled off of the road to the right, directly in front of the old covered bridge, his mother opened her door before he had turned the key to shut off the engine. She opened her door and got out. "You stay there Wesley, I want a moment by myself," she said.

"No problem Mother, I'll just dig my camera out and get some pictures of this beautiful monument to a time long past."

By the time Wesley opened his door; his mother had crossed the road and walked down toward the river. It had been fairly dry in the late summer and early fall, so the river was quite low. He watched as his mother walked toward the river and then along the side to the entrance abutment. Wesley popped the trunk on his mother's car and retrieved his camera from a side pouch in the trunk. He walked to the front entrance of the bridge and looked directly down the throat. He read the sign above the entrance where it read" Lower Humber Bridge 1891. A sign to the left said, "Gross Weight Limit - 3 tons." He took several pictures from the front, some zoomed in, and some zoomed out. He moved up the road a few hundred feet and took several shots from the side. Then he walked back down the road and took some from the other side. He walked into the bridge and took several of the arched type support structure. He had visited a lot of the bridges in Ohio, and knew that this was known as the Burr arch type construction. As he neared the end of the bridge, he saw a very large dog approaching him and barking. He was about to turn around, he didn't want to run, but he wanted to let the dog know he was leaving his territory, then he heard a women's voice, "Don't worry, he won't bite, we didn't change his name to 'Coward' for no reason." Wesley stopped, but the dog kept right on coming. He sure hoped the lady was right, and he soon found out she was. The dog bounded up to him, put his front paws on Wesley's chest and lapped his face with a very wet tongue.

Humbert Covered Bridge. Built about 1876, the name is a misnomer. The town of Humbert did not come into existence until 1901 and was gone by 1935.

"Coward," the lady yelled in a harsh voice, and the dog immediately put his paws back on the ground and turned toward the voice. "He is such a pest," the lady said, "but we love him."

"Well, I also love animals, I just wasn't sure that he would love me."

The lady just laughed.

"I also love your bridge," Wesley said.

"Yeah, a lot of people do. It isn't really our bridge, but we like to think it is. My husband is a descendant of some of the early Kings in this area. He isn't exactly sure how he is related, but Christopher King once owned the land where our house there is located. His son David once operated a gristmill on the other side just about where your car is parked. I understand that Christopher once owned about the entire valley, and his son John C. built the large stone house you passed about a mile back."

The two talked for a few minutes and then Wesley decided he had better check on his mother. He came back out of the bridge toward the car and turned to walk toward the river. He saw his mother standing by the water with a few small pebbles in her hand. He said nothing, but watched as she tossed them into the water, one by one. When she had tossed the last one, she turned toward him and said, "You know Wesley, it is so ironic, the last time I sat under this bridge, I was walking behind a horse drawn wagon, now here I am so many years later riding in a Cadillac sedan. I was so embarrassed then, but I am so ashamed now."

"Why are you ashamed mother?"

"When we had to move after your grandfather broke his leg, we loaded as much of our belongings as we could onto an old horse drawn wagon. My mother drove, actually she walked along side and led the horse, and my brother and I followed behind, but we stopped here at about noontime to eat some sandwiches which mother had made. She also wanted the horse to rest and she gave him a little oats and some water. I remember she had made some tomato sandwiches and some cucumber sandwiches. I took a tomato sandwich and went down to the river here and sat underneath the bridge, right there," she said as she pointed to a large rock close to the bridge abutment. "I stayed there until she was ready to move on, and the reason I stayed there was because I didn't want any of my friends from school passing and seeing us with a horse drawn wagon loaded with old furniture. I told my mother that at the time, but she didn't say anything. Right now, I know it must have hurt her very badly, but she didn't want me to see her hurt, so she said nothing. I am sure she was just as embarrassed as I was, but she was doing for us what she had to do."

"Don't beat yourself up because of it Mother. I know Grandma probably didn't remember it an hour later, so there is no reason for you to dwell upon it almost sixty years later."

"I am not really dwelling upon it Son, but just coming here has given me some peace. I know you cannot understand that, but it has. Learning some things about my sister that I never knew has helped me, but some of that has also made me feel ashamed.

"I am sure I do not understand it to the same extent that you now feel it, but I do understand how important it is for you today, and how difficult it was for you back then. I hear it very often from a lot of the impoverished children I work with. It is one of the things I like to do with them, get them talking about it, that way it doesn't become something they lock up in their memories to haunt them years later.

The recent conversations of the last two days caused a thought to flash through Karin's mind, "You really are so much like your father," but she did not vocalize it, she simply said, "I guess it is time to continue."

When they were again in the car and Wesley started to pull back on to the road, his mother said, "Drive slow Wesley, I want to look around."

"Don't worry Mother, on this road I don't think you can drive very fast."

Less than a mile from the bridge, there was a sharp left turn in the road and it went up the side of the hill for about five hundred feet and then made a blind turn to the right. There was a dirt road that veered off at the bottom of the hill. Wesley read the street sign: Chickenbone Hollow. He laughed to himself. At the top of the hill, the road continued out along the side of the hill. It was a two-lane road, but just barely. The side toward the hill was a sheer cliff where the dirt had been cut away to form the roadbed. There were guardrails on the lower side and a very steep drop to the river below. The entire hill was covered with a nice stand of tall timber. Across the valley and the river, were some cleared fields and two houses.

Wesley was driving very slowly, perhaps slower than his mother had intended, but it was because he wanted to observe the scenery, and the road could be a bit treacherous. He was sure that the locals probably drove the road faster than what was advisable, and he did not want to be wondering into the oncoming lane, a fact that required very little wandering.

At the end of the hillside, the road went into a dip and then up again and around a slight curve to the right. To his left, Wesley noted a rustic looking old house with a beautifully patina metal roof. It had an upper porch the entire length of the house. The roof of the house and the porch was one continuous slope. It was obvious that the house had not been occupied for a long time. Wesley wandered what stories the old house could tell.

They crossed a short plain and then went down another small hill. His mother said, "There used to be a town here by the name of Humbert."

"Yes, when I turned onto this road I saw it was named the 'HUMBERT RD.' Can you remember it?" Wesley asked.

"No, it was long gone by the time I came by."

At the foot of the hill, there was a dirt road to the right; the sign said "COKE OVEN RD." A few yards later they crossed a little river and the road made a wide right turn. As they came out of the turn, Wesley saw an old log house on the right. There was a pickup truck parked on the well-manicured lawn, and a man was splitting wood by a small shed at the very base of the hill. Wesley had slowed to almost a crawl and he beeped his horn. The man splitting wood raised his hand and waved. Wesley waived back.

The road now started up a long grade, and for a while he could see another small river that paralleled the road. Eventually he lost sight of it, but knew it was still there, because there was absolutely no flat surface in this valley. The road had been cut in the less steep of the two hills that formed the valley. About a mile from the log house, they passed another house on the right. It was actually a double wide. A new car and a pickup sat in a gravel driveway.

From there, they rounded a curve to the left and the road leveled out for a few hundred feet. It again crossed the small river and then there was a very steep climb.

"You mean to tell me mother, that your poor horse hauled a wagon load of furniture all the way from your old house up this steep road?"

"That he did, and we are still over a mile from our destination. You will see worse."

After they topped the hill there was another dirt road that led off to the right. Wesley assumed that some one probably lived back there somewhere because the road sign said, KREGAR RD. A short distance later, he saw an old white house on the bank to the right of the road. It looked a bit strange. It had an old tin roof and it looked like one or two of the sheets had been replaced within the past couple of years. There was a porch running the width of the front, with two small windows above the porch roof. There were five windows on the lower side, four evenly spaced, but the fourth and fifth windows were right next to each other with no space in between, and the last one was wider and a few inches lower.

Rhodes one room school, Closed in 1954, it was converted into a private home.

Wesley's mother noticed that he had again slowed to a crawl and was observing the house. "That was a one-room schoolhouse a long time ago. It was still being used when we moved up here, but I was in tenth grade so I never went there. I don't know when it closed, or who converted it in to a home."

"Well that may account for the slightly unconventional use of windows," Wesley said.

They were again starting up a very slight grade and when they got to the next curve, his mother said, "Stop here for a minute."

Wesley pulled the car off to the left at the entrance of a driveway that went down over the bank to another doublewide.

"You want to get out mother?" Wesley asked.

"No, I just want to look. By the time we got this far, the horse was dead tired. Your grandmother, uncle and I were just about as tired. We had to get the horse some water and my mother gave him a little more of the oats. The lady that lived down there, but it was a different house then, she came up to talk to mother while I went to get a bucket of water and your uncle pulled some grass for the horse.

She had a son who I guessed was about my age, we looked at each other but neither of us spoke.

The lady talked for a long time, and she told my mother that she had better let the horse have a good rest because just before we got to our destination there was a long and very steep hill, longer than any that we had encountered so far. She even invited us to come down to the house for a while and have a bowl of fresh 'all around the garden' vegetable soup, but mother said she didn't want to leave the horse alone. But before we started on, she gave us a loaf of fresh baked bread, a jar of homemade strawberry preserves, a half-pound of white oleomargarine, and a quart of her vegetable soup. She said she would come visit us the next day and see if there was anything we needed. When we left and were around that curve that you see up front, my brother and I wanted to tear into that bread, but my mother said we could have it when our day was done. I remember she said, 'your day ends when old Spooky gets to shed his harness.' You can drive on now."

"So did the lady come to visit you the next day?"

"Yes she did. She brought another loaf of bread, some peach preserves, and half a dozen brown eggs. She often came to visit, and she and mother became good friends. She was an excellent seamstress and helped my mother sew some dresses for me. Mom had taught Kathryn to sew but I never had any interest in it. Probably accounts for the fact that I couldn't even hem your dad's trousers many years later," she said with a sigh. "Anyway, her husband was also responsible for a local farmer here doing us a very good deed. He never told us it was of his doing, but the farmer did. Remind me some time I will tell you."

"You mean you are not going to tell me now?" Wesley asked.

"It would take too long, and it needs telling with..."

"With what?"

"I don't know. Later. Remember, patience is a virtue."

"So they say," Wesley added, and as he started the car to drive on, he saw a definite tear in his mother's eyes.

For the next half mile the road was fairly flat, but as they rounded the last curve, Wesley saw the hill she was talking about. It was longer than any of the others between Confluence and here, and at the top he could see that the grade was very steep.

"You are telling me that the horse made it up this hill?"

"Yes, he made it. It was slow and every hundred feet or so, Harold and I would put a large rock behind the back wheels and mother would let the horse rest. Old Spooky was like the little engine that could. He huffed and he puffed, and with mother, my brother and I all helping to push, we some how made it to the top. I think God whispered in Spooky's ear and said, 'make this one and the rest is all down hill,' and it was."

When they got to the top of the hill, his mother told him to pull off the road and stop. The road was flat and on their left was a large field that during the previous season had been planted in corn. A farmer was working the field using a large John Deere tractor with a rotor type tiller to tear up the corn stubble and prepare it for planting. Perhaps winter wheat, Wesley thought, but his knowledge of farming was not that great.

His mother got out of the car and started to walk forward. He followed but stayed a few steps behind and observed. Behind them was a dirt road that went along the top of the hill. Below where they were parked, the land was covered in trees, and it sloped down into a deep valley. Maybe three hundred yards ahead, almost where his mother now stood, the land seemed level and the growth of trees were taller. Wesley quickened his pace to catch up with his mother. She was standing still and looking down over the hill.

"It is too grown up now to see anything."

"And this place I assume would be...?"

"This is where the old house was that we moved into when we left Confluence, and before we moved to Ohio. Of course the house sat more over there," she said, gesturing with her right hand. The old barn sat down below here. The road went in back there where that dirt road is and then down over the hill to below the house and out to the barn. Your Uncle Harold and I cut a hopper path from just below this fence, past the barn and clear down to the bottom of the hill.

"Pray tell, what is a hopper path, Mother?"

"Yeah, that is right you are a flat land kid. A hopper was a thing they built here to ride on during the winter. Some people call it a jack jumper, but we called it a hopper. I don't think you could buy them in a store, but there was a man, I think his name was Ed Trimpey, that lived down over that other hill who built a lot of them. Dad built one for Harold, but he and I use to fight over it. I think I could ride it better than he could."

"So what did it look like?" Wesley asked.

"It looked like a very short ski, maybe three feet long with an A frame on the back that was maybe eighteen inches high and a board for a seat on top of that. You sat on the board with the front of the runner between your legs and balanced yourself as you rode down the hill."

"Sounds like fun."

"It was. Lots of fun."

The farmer had finished his tilling for the day and was starting down the road toward them. When he got along side, he pulled the tractor off to the opposite side of the road and throttled it down. "Can I help you?" he asked.

Wesley's mother spoke up first. "When I was a young girl, a long time ago, there was an old house and barn down in there. Can you tell me if there is anything left of it?"

"Nothing left of the old barn, and all that remains of the house are the stonewalls that formed the foundation and the cellar."

"There was a spring house on the upper side. What about it?"

"Just like the house, only the stonewalls remain. However, it still produces a good flow of water."

"What about the black walnut trees and apple trees?"

"No apple trees, but there are three old walnut trees that still bear fruit."

"Really," she said and Wesley saw his mother smile. "I don't suppose there is any way I can get down there?"

"The road is completely washed out and grown over with brush. The only way in there now is to go through my pasture field, but it is very steep. I don't want to insult you, but I don't think you could make it."

"I am sure you are right, and I don't think I would be fool enough to try, but thanks for the information.

"You are welcome, but if I may ask, how do you know about it?"

"My family lived there for about four months when I was fifteen. We then moved to Ohio."

"Very interesting," the man on the tractor said.

"Do you own this land?" Wesley asked.

"Not that below the road where the lady was talking about. This land over here and from the beginning of that dirt road on back a ways is part of our farm. That below the road there belongs to Kregar. It has been in that family for a long time. That hill out there is named for the man who I think was the original owner."

"Barney, is that right?" Wesley heard his mother ask.

"Yes maam, old Barney Kregar, but I have no idea how far back he goes."

Wesley looked at his mother with amazement, but said nothing.

"Well, again we thank you for the information, Sir, and we need to be moving on," Wesley's mother said.

"You are welcome, and it has been my pleasure," the man on the tractor said as he put it in gear and drove away.

A short distance up the road, Wesley saw a road sign by yet another dirt road, it read: HEXIE. "Hexie, strange name for a road," Wesley said.

"Oh I didn't tell you, that is what this area is called. I guess it is really called Hexebarger, but everyone just shortened it to Hexie.

"Why is it called that, do you know?"

"No, I don't know why."

Just then Wesley looked to his left and viewed one of the most beautiful valleys he had ever seen. He pulled the car off to the side and stared at what lay before him. He realized then that he was not looking at one valley, but a series of hills that formed one valley after another. On the most distant ridges he could see 10 large wind turbines used to generate electricity. They marred the other wise beautiful landscape, but he accepted the fact that from an ecological viewpoint, they were a preferable alternative. He thought about getting his camera, but he had not brought a zoom lens or wide-angle lens, and his regular lens would not do it justice. "Isn't that magnificent," he finally said to his mother.

"It is very beautiful," she said in reply, but without a lot of zeal.

"I will have to come back here some time in the winter when the leaves are off the trees and there is snow on the ground. That way I can determine just how many hills and valleys one can actually see from this point. It would be great to hire a pilot and have him fly me over this entire region."

"You really love it, do you son?"

"I really do."

Wesley started the car and proceeded the short distance into Kingwood. He stopped at the crossroads and turned left back onto Route 281.

"See, I told you I knew where I was taking you."

"I never had any doubts about that, but I was impressed that you remembered the name Barney Kreger."

"Barney Kreger, Hexebarger, names from my youth, it is the things I learned yesterday that I can't remember," she said.

"You still have a great memory, Mother, now if you could just remember what Hexebarger meant," he said with a laugh then continued to reason out loud. "Okay, perhaps I should look at it etymologically. Hex is German meaning witch. Are you sure it is Hexebarger and not Hexeburger with a u, or with an e?"

"I never saw it written down, but I know the older people said Hexebarger, and the younger ones just said Hexie. Why?"

"Well, *b u r g* or *b e r g* could be German or English meaning small town, thus witch town, but there is no town. My guess would be that it was a German word that was Anglicized."

"You are not going to mull on that all the way back to Youngstown, are you Wesley?"

"I certainly hope to resolve it long before that," he said.

"Wait a minute, if it was German, the German e is a short sound, i is their long ee sound."

"The point of all that is?" his mother asked.

The German e could come out as a short a to an English man, so it may have been berg, in which, no pun intended, we have witch hill, or if plural, berge, we have witch hills. I still don't know how it came about, but I will bet that is what it means."

"Priests shouldn't bet."

"Just a figure of speech, Mother."

"So now that you have that figured out, and we still have lots of time before we get to Youngstown, perhaps you would like to tell me about this sabbatical you are planning to take."

Wesley looked at his mother in shock. "Who told you I was taking a sabbatical?"

"Father Broderick let it slip when I went in to see him the day I got the news that my sister had died."

"And what else did he say?"

"Whoops!"

"That is what he said, whoops?"

"Yes."

"Mother, believe me, at this point I am not planning a sabbatical. In fact, I never said the word, sabbatical; it was Father Broderick himself who mentioned it. We were discussing my projects, and I complained that I was not getting much assistance or encouragement from the diocese. With all my other duties, it seemed like I was asking Deacon Sullivan to do the homily every Sunday, although heaven knows he does a better job than I do. I said, maybe we should try and convince the Bishop to see if they could send in a young priest. Father Broderick said it wasn't going to happen, as there were not enough priests to fill active parishes, and ours wasn't large enough to warrant another man. So I said to him, what do I do, and he said just the one word, 'sabbatical.' I had never considered it, and I thought he was just musing, but maybe he was serious, and let it slip to you, knowing that you would bring up the subject. He is a sly old man, that Irishman."

His mother said nothing more, and it was now Wesley who sat in silence and pondered the future as he drove toward the Ohio border.

Chapter 4

In the latter part of the following April after her sister had died, Wesley's mother informed him that she was going back to plant some flowers on her sister's grave. Wesley asked her if she wanted him to drive with her, and she replied that she would prefer to go by herself. He knew not to insist.

"When do you plan to leave and how long are you going to stay?"

"I am going to leave very early tomorrow morning, and should be back by late tomorrow evening. Don't worry, I will call you when I get there and when I get back."

"Okay Mother, I won't worry, but I wish you would not push yourself like that. At least spend the night and come back the next day."

"I have no reason to spend the night. Don't worry about me, I will be fine." Thelma is going to meet me there. We will have lunch together before I return."

"At least I am glad to see that you and your niece have settled your differences and are enjoying a good relationship," Wesley said.

"We settled our differences that day in the funeral home office," she said, and then continued in jest, "For a Priest, you are not always very observant Wesley."

"Maybe so, but you always taught me to not stick my nose in other peoples' affairs."

His mother just smiled.

She checked her watch when she passed through the exit booth of the Turnpike at Somerset: it was 8:45. She had plenty of time for breakfast. She took the turnpike access road to Center Avenue and turned right. A half block away she saw a sign for the Summit Diner and decided that is where she would have breakfast.

She liked the atmosphere inside the diner, friendly and unpretentious. There were quite a few people having breakfast, and she could tell that many of them were regulars, as they talked and joked with each other at the counter and across table boundaries. She took a small booth at the extreme right side of the diner. Across from her by the window sat a couple that was about her age; she guessed that like her, they were travelers. The lady was a blond and fairly attractive for her age. Her husband was a baldheaded man with a white beard. She nodded her head to them in a gesture of good morning. They both responded with a verbal good morning. They had already finished their breakfast, and departed shortly after she sat down. Their booth was already being bussed and quickly filled by a young couple with two young children.

Before she left Youngstown, she had printed out a map of the area that included most of the secondary roads. She did want to go through Rockwood just to see if she would recognize anything from her days as a high school sophomore there, although she had only gone there for a little over three months.

Somerset was not a large town and she had no difficulty in finding South Edgewood Avenue. Outside of town and until it reached Rockwood, it was known as the Water Level Road because it ran parallel to Coxes Creek. She wasn't aware of the significance of the name, but it was named in honor of one of the earliest settlers in the area, Isaac Cox. He was a friend of the Old Quaker, Harmon Husband, who had built a house here and was later arrested during the Whiskey Rebellion.

When she got to Rockwood and drove up over the hill to where the old school stood, she was not surprised to see it had been torn down. As she remembered, it was a very old building back then. What did surprise her was that the building across the street was still standing. It had contained a classroom and a wood shop in the basement, an auditorium and music room on the ground level, and two classrooms and the home economics department on the top floor. The building was now the town's city hall.

By the time she arrived in Confluence, it was still an hour before she had told Thelma she would meet her at the cemetery. She was not a person who could just sit still so she remembered to bring a book with her to read. She parked the car by the little park in the center of town. There she could find a bench and sit down to read, but before that, she would take a short walk along the flood control dike by the Casselman River. When she returned, she found a bench and started to read. Within fifteen minutes her cell phone beeped. She assumed it would be Wesley, although she had promised she would call him, and it was not late enough where he would start to worry. When she answered, it was her niece Thelma. She said she was at Ursina and would be there in a few minutes. She placed the bookmark back in the book and waited.

Thelma parked her car next to that of her aunt. They greeted each other, and then each retrieved a small potted flower from their cars. After that they walked to the pedestrian bridge that crossed the Casselman River to where the church and cemetery was located. Karin remembered that as a young girl, this was a one-lane bridge for cars. Apparently some years ago it had been replaced, and although the new bridge was wide enough for emergency vehicles, a post was placed in the center that precluded its use for normal traffic.

Thelma and Thomas had placed a beautiful marker at the gravesite years before when their father had died. The stonecutter had just recently entered the date of Kathryn's death. The two ladies stood in silence for a brief period, and then Thelma pulled a small garden trowel from her large bag and they planted their flowers, one on each side of the marker.

From there, they walked to the Yough Café where they asked to be seated on the porch, and then enjoyed a light lunch and reminisced. They talked for about an hour when her cell phone beeped. This time it was Wesley; she had forgotten to call. She apologized to her son, and told him that she would be starting back within an hour. When she terminated the call, she told Thelma that she had better say her goodbyes. There were one or two places where she wanted to stop before she returned to Youngstown.

When they started to walk back to where their cars were parked, Thelma broke what was a short silence. "Perhaps I shouldn't ask this Aunt Karin, and if you don't want to answer, just tell me to butt out, but have you ever wondered what happened to him?"

"Yes, but I never dwelt upon it. He helped me at a very uncertain time in my life and gave me some self-assuredness. I only hoped that things turned out well for him," she said.

"Maybe I shouldn't say this, but I just can't keep it a secret from you. You would be pleased to know that he is doing well," Thelma said. "Thomas met him once. Thomas knew who he was, but he did not know who Thomas was. He said they talked about this area for twenty minutes or more."

Her aunt nodded her head but said nothing more.

When they got to their cars, they said their goodbyes, and each left for the trip home. Karin knew that she had at least one stop to make. North of Ursina, she again took the road less traveled. When she got to the little white house that had once been a one-room schoolhouse, she turned left. A mile later she pulled into a church parking lot. There were two cars in the lot. She saw a sign that pointed to the church office. She walked to it and rang the bell. A young lady greeted her and they conversed for a moment, then she invited her inside. After several minutes she came out of the church office, walked across the road and then to the back corner of the cemetery.

When she was finished, she returned to her car and started back to Youngstown.

Two weeks later, she informed Wesley that she was going to fly down to Mobile, Alabama, to see her brother Harold. She had talked to him after returning from Confluence, and he wasn't doing too well. He had been unable to make the trip when their sister had died. He was a diabetic and did very little in the way of diet and exercise to help his own cause.

She made reservations for the following Thursday and flew down. Saturday started out as a beautiful day, so she asked her brother if he would like to take a drive. He asked if she wanted to go to New Orleans, but cautioned that it was still rebuilding from the effects of Hurricane Katrina. She said no she wanted to go to Pensacola. She mentioned to him that Thelma had said Thomas was stationed there several years ago as a pilot instructor. Harold said he knew that because Thomas had come to visit him and Clarissa a couple of times. He also thought a trip to Pensacola might be nice. As long as he had lived in Mobile, he had never gone to Pensacola to see the Aviation Museum. Perhaps they could spend an hour or two there, although he knew it was a first rate museum, and to do it justice, one had to spend the better part of a day, or even two.

After about two hours walking about the impressive display of aircraft in the Museum, Harold apologized and said that was about as much as he could do. His sister said that was okay, and when they got back to the car, she told Harold she would drive and he could relax for a little. That was okay with him.

They had entered the Naval Air Station by the back entrance off of Blue Angel Parkway, which was what the Navy publicized for those planning to visit the museum. She had memorized her map and knew that she wanted to depart by the front entrance onto Navy Boulevard. The gentleman at the information counter had told her how she wanted to go as she departed the parking lot. He said that as soon as she passed Barrancas National Cemetery on her right, she should get in the left turn lane. That would take her to the front gate and Navy Boulevard.

She knew there was a shorter route to where she wanted to go, but it involved residential streets. She didn't want to get lost so she took Navy Boulevard to Highway 98. From there she went west until she found the housing subdivision she was looking for. Harold looked at her when she turned into the subdivision, but he said nothing. She followed the entrance until she came to the first street with a cul-de-sac at the end. She turned in and drove to the end. In front of the house at the very end she saw a woman trimming azalea bushes with electric clippers. In the driveway, a man with a white beard was washing his truck. She stopped in front of the driveway and pressed the button to roll down the passenger side window. The man washing his truck stopped what he was doing and walked toward the car. Then he asked, "Can I help you?"

"Yes," the driver said, "Can you tell me how I get back to I-10 for Mobile?"

"Certainly," he said and gave the direction to Blue Angel Parkway, and then I-10.

She took one last look at the man, thanked him and they started back toward Mobile.

"What was that all about," her brother asked her when they pulled back onto the main street, but he thought he knew.

"Just a hunch," she said.

"Just a hunch, huh?"

She didn't know if he knew or not. She would not ask him.

Four months after she had made the trip to see her brother in Mobile, and just one month after the first anniversary of her sister's death, Wesley's mother passed away. She hadn't been sick, and seemed in good spirits. She just went to bed as usual and never woke up.

A week after his mother was buried, Wesley went into tell Father Broderick that he was requesting a sabbatical. The elderly priest put his arm on Wesley's shoulder and said, "Come on Son, let's take a walk over to the school. The sixth grade children are practicing a skit for the Thanksgiving Day Mass. I understand they are using one of your new programs about helping the poor."

Part II

Coincidence or Destiny

Chapter 5

It had not been a severe winter and March had been like the proverbial lamb throughout, thus permitting the builder to get the house framed earlier than expected. It was now the first week in April and Wesley had brought along a sandwich and a large thermos filled with coffee. He sat on his stone bench and poured some coffee into a china cup and watched the roofers start to apply the bottom row of shingles.

He could see the beginning of buds on a few brave trees, but being a city boy and not much of a botanist, he didn't know the species. He told himself that by next year he would know them all. Easter lilies were blooming where some one had planted them many years before, and the Forsythia were at their peak. He knew these flowers very well because they were in abundance around his former church in Youngstown, Ohio.

It was the beginning of a beautiful day. He saw a robin flit by, circle and then return to perch on a low branch close by. "Good morning to you too," he said half amused, and then the robin flew off. He sipped his coffee and marveled at the rebirth the continually warming days of spring would bring, and he just let his mind go blank. A "thank you" to his creator might have been in order, but at this time he didn't offer it.

Momentarily, the beautiful solitude was broken when he heard the approach of a vehicle coming down the road. It would only be a short interruption as the vehicle passed. It was something that he tried to ignore, although for a small country road it had a fair amount of traffic and it wasn't always easy to ignore the noise. In this case the car went by, and then, although he couldn't see it from his bench, he could tell it slowed down and came to a stop just before the crest of the hill.

He now stood up so he could see the vehicle. The driver put the car in reverse and slowly backed up along the shoulder of the road until he was directly adjacent to where the house was being built. He turned off the engine, opened the door and got out. He walked toward the front of his car still staring at the house that was taking shape. The driver did not see Wesley standing by the stone bench, so he spoke.

"Good morning."

The driver of the car, somewhat startled, turned toward the voice, and now spotting him, replied, "Good morning, I didn't see you standing there."

"Yes, I gathered as much. I assume you were more fascinated by the house?"

"You are correct in that assumption. Is it your house they are building?"

"It is," he replied. "All the locals know of it, so my second assumption would be that you are not from this immediate area."

"Well, in regard to your second assumption, would you care to qualify it time wise?" the driver asked.

"What do you mean?"

"I mean I was from this immediate area a long time ago. I was born and raised about a mile down the road. What caused me to stop was that I remember the old house that once stood just about exactly where you are building. There is still a spark of nostalgia in my heart for it. In fact, I remember the last family that lived there. Then there was an old man who lived there after the family moved. I can't remember his name. Now let me ask, are you from around here?"

Wesley heard what the man had said and he felt a jolt, as if he had been hit in the stomach. He could not speak for what seemed like a minute but was perhaps just a few seconds, but he did sense that he had to gain some time to recompose his inner self, so he said, "Wait, let me crawl through the brush and over the fence."

"Okay," the man on the road said, "I would help you but you look like a much younger man than I and quite capable of doing it without assistance."

As if by remote, he answered and said, "Oh yeah, no problem," but his mind was reprocessing a conversation he had with his mother a little more than a year before, just before she passed away. It was if she had known this day would come, the first time he told her he would love to buy some land here and build a log house on it.

He pressed down on the second strand of the barbed wire with his hand and placed his right foot through to the other side. Then for a few milliseconds his body froze in place and in his mind he heard again his mother's voice as clear as he heard the voice of the stranger just a few feet away.

"*Promise me you will not do anything to interfere with the lives of others.*"

"*Mother, I don't know what you are talking about, but as a Priest, I give you my promise.*"

Then he heard the stranger on the road ask, "Sure you don't need my help?"

"No, just thought I felt a cramp coming into my leg." He lied, which was something that he never did, and it flashed through his mind faster than the data bits in his computer, why had he lied?

When he got to the road he extended his hand to the stranger and said, "Hi, my name is Wesley Donaldson."

"My name is Jacob Grant, and it is a pleasure to make your acquaintance."

"Likewise I am sure. You say you were from here a long time ago, where do you live now?'

"Florida."

"Miami, Tampa, Orlando, where?"

"No, we, well now I mean I, my wife left me about six months ago, live in what the locals call the land that Florida forgot, the Panhandle."

"Oh, I am so sorry to hear your wife left you," Wesley said, a little embarrassed.

"Rude of me to confuse you like that," Jacob quickly answered. What I meant was, she left me alone because the Good Lord saw fit to take her first.

"Okay, now I understand, and I am sorry to hear of your wife's passing," Wesley said.

"Thank you for caring, but I guess death isn't something to be sorry about," Jacob replied.

"Yes, that is exactly right."

"Actually that is why I am here. I came up to put some spring flowers on her grave. I plan to plant an Easter Lilly for her, and some later blooming flowers. She loved flowers. In that respect she was much like my father, he also loved flowers. Spent the better part of his days under ground in the mines, but during the spring and summer, tired as he may have been, he would spend countless hours tending his flowers. She would do the same thing. Every morning she was out before the sun got too hot and watered her flowers. We used to have little spats about it, because she would lose all track of time and never make it into the shop on time. I would get on my high horse and complain when she did come in, and she would promise me she wouldn't do it again, but she would always relapse. Her working in the yard with the flowers was fine with me. I was born and raised out here in the country and worked for my cousin on the farm, but I had no desire to work in the yard. Don't get me wrong, I too love flowers, but I feel that Mother Nature does a much better job than I could. The other thing we disagreed about was she liked to cut some flowers and put them in vases in the house, whereas I always thought you should leave them uncut for the bees and the birds."

Wesley immediately detected that the man loved to talk. Maybe it was because he was now alone and had no one to talk to. Anyway, that was great, he thought. Maybe he could steer the conversation.

"If you are interested in digging up an Easter lily, there are a lot of them further down, some close to the house I am building. Also a lot by the old stone fence that goes down over the hill."

"I brought one with me, but perhaps another time. I would venture to say that the ones you have here were planted a long time ago. I am not sure who first owned this land below the road, could have been Struckoffs, Leighliters, even Garrison Smith might have got this far up that valley, but I think it was Kregers, or early Krugers. There were Younkins here too, but they were on the opposite ridge, and further down the hollow. Well, enough of that, I am probably boring you."

"Quite the contrary, I am intrigued. How do you know so much about the early inhabitants? To these country folk I am definitely an outsider, so I would like to get to know as much as possible about them and the area."

46

"I know what I know because I was born and raised here. Of course over the years, I have researched some of the people who were here long before me, and I try and keep up with current happenings. So it is a long story, are you sure you want to be bored by it?"

"Most definitely. Listen, I have a thermos of coffee down there on my bench, maybe you would like to share a cup with me?"

"Thanks, but I am not sure I can crawl through that fence and the brambles."

"That won't be necessary, I cut a path in off of my driveway so we can just walk that way. Beside, you can tell me more of this amazing history as we walk."

"Well, okay I will accept your hospitality and have a small coffee."

They walked the short distance to the driveway that ran perpendicular to another Township road that branched off to the right. It was still a dirt road, but under the 911 system of identifying all roads, it was known as the Lemmon Road. Although it appeared on topographic maps, and Google Earth as going the entire length of the valley, it was no longer passable for vehicles after about a mile.

"I assume Dwight Lanning still lives back that road," he said.

"He still lives in the old house by the barn. He said that his barn burned down not too long ago, but with the help of the Amish, they were back in business in a short period of time. He is pretty old, but both he and his wife still get around quite well. One of their sons built a new house close by, and the other one lives in the house below the road after you leave Kingwood. He told me the farm on which that house sets once belonged to George Romesburg. Both sons help to run the farm."

"I think the sons have run it for quite awhile now," Jacob replied. "The old man is a real success story when you consider he was a city boy from Pittsburgh. His parents used to have a little cottage further back the road on what was the Harry Nicklow farm. The farm was really run down from years of neglect when he bought it. The fields across the road were not part of the original farm. They were part of the George Romesburg farm that he now owns.

How did you convince him to sell you these few acres? From a farming standpoint they are worthless, but a lot of these old farmers take stock in the number of acres they own."

He almost said that he had pleaded a special situation, but knew that would draw inquiries he didn't want to answer, so instead he picked up on what Jacob had just said and answered, "I guess it could have been one city boy to another, except you see it belongs to the old Kregar farm and not the one that Lanning owns."

"By golly, that is right. One more of my many senior moments, I guess," Jacob said. Then without pausing, he continued, "How did you get the Kregars to sell you the land? Theirs is more than a century farm."

They didn't sell it to me, but I was able to convince them to give me a fifty-year lease.

"Never thought of that, but a very interesting concept," Jacob said, but suppose you outlive your lease, then what?'

Wesley laughed and then said, "That would make me a very old man and I doubt they would evict me."

"Yeah, just joking, I know most of these Kregars and they are good people. But you still haven't told me where you are from. From what you said previously, I assume a city somewhere."

By now they had reached the stone bench. Wesley dug into his bag and pulled out a Styrofoam cup, opened the thermos and poured some still steaming coffee for Jacob. His own cup was still sitting there, but by now it was cold so he tossed it out and poured himself some more.

"I apologize for having to offer you the coffee in a Styrofoam cup, I hate them myself, but always keep a few in case of situations just like this. I suppose you could say it is hospitality with a second-class nuance. I also apologize for not having any creamer with me, but I never use it."

"No apology necessary. As for the container, this is how I get it from 'Macky D's,' and I stopped using milk in my coffee back when I was a young Navy man stationed in Germany. We didn't have powdered creamer then and the cans of condensed milk we used would often look so disgusting, that I decided to quit using it. However, if my wife were living and here, she might ask you to give up your china cup; she might even send you to get her a saucer. She would definitely ask for milk, and perhaps a bit of hot water. She hated strong coffee. As for myself, I always used a mug, but she used a cup and saucer, part of her German upbringing, she always said. I use to tell her that was pretty pretentious for a Fraulein from a Kuhdorf, and her stock reply was, 'that compared to where I was from, her Kuhdorf was a city.'"

"She must have been a very interesting lady," Wesley said.

"Yeah, that she was," Jacob replied, his words trailing off.

"Okay," Wesley said, " Back to your question, where am I from? I was raised in Youngstown, Ohio, and lived there until just a few months ago." I am currently renting a small apartment in Somerset until the house is finished.

"You look a bit young to be retired, but I suppose it is possible. How did you wind up in this part of Pennsylvania and how did you find out about this place?"

"I think I will save the last part of that question for another time, but I am not really retired. My father worked in the steel mills of Youngstown, and although he was a bit frugal, he also knew how to invest his money so he left my mother very well situated financially. Being the only child, when my mother died, I inherited it all. She did leave a substantial sum to a couple of her favorite charities. As for my personal background, I am a Roman Catholic Priest without a charge or congregation. I am on an indefinite sabbatical. And to save you the question you might ponder but probably not ask, I did not denounce my faith, and I was not asked to leave. As a matter of fact, I had a wonderful flock who still write me and ask when I am going to return."

"And the answer to that is?" Jacob asked.

"As their parish priest, probably never. As their friend, as often as I can."

A sly smile formed on old Jacob's lips and he said, "Roman Catholic, with a name like Wesley Donaldson, I would have assumed a Methodist."

Wesley also smiled and he said, "Well, the Catholics do sing a lot of hymns written by the Wesley brothers, and to be perfectly truthful, my mother did name me for those famous men of God."

"Yeah, Charles was quite a prolific song writer," Jacob said. "Maybe sometime I will have a chance to tell you a story that is related to the Christmas Carol we sing, called, 'Hark the Herald Angels Sing.' It does have a small relevance to a legend of this area."

"I would love to hear it now."

"I don't think so, I am always a bit verbose when telling stories, and so if I started it, we might be sitting here until nightfall."

"Well promise me you will tell me at another time."

"Yeah, the Good Lord willing," Jacob replied. "But back to your name, you are Catholic so why did your mother name you after a Methodist?"

"When I was born, my mother was a Methodist, as was my Grandmother. My Grandfather never went to church until very late in his life. My mother converted to Catholicism after she married my father when I was about three years old. I was born out of wedlock, a bastard as the old saying goes, but my father adopted me immediately after they were married.

For some unexplained reason, Wesley felt compelled to say more about his father so he continued, "I could not have asked for a greater father. He was a good bit older than my mother, but he taught me all the things a boy should know. He attended every sporting event I was ever in, and all my school activities. He would take me for long walks, and each time he would explain a small fact of life to me. He only had an eighth grade education, having to quit school to help support the family. He also served most honorably in World War II and received several battle stars, but he never talked much about that. He was a self-taught man. On those walks, he would often recite lines from some of the great poets, or expound on philosophical subjects that he thought might help me at a later date. He was fairly faithful to his Catholic upbringing, but it was my Aunt Leona, his oldest sister that got me interested in the priesthood. My biggest disappointment was that he died about a month before my ordination. He never got to hear me say Mass as an Ordained Priest."

"What about your mother, since she wasn't born as a Catholic, what did she think about your decision to become a priest?" Jacob asked.

"Surprisingly, she was very much for it. Later, she would often drop it in her conversation, 'my son is a priest you know.'"

"That account is very interesting, Wesley, but leaving your flock can be quite traumatic for some of them, you know. There is always an old widow who was sure you would say a wonderful Mass at her funeral, or some youngsters who looked forward to receiving their first communion from you."

"Are you trying to lay a guilt trip on me?"

"Perhaps a little bit, but just for your own benefit. I just wanted to make sure you had considered that."

"I suppose I should thank you for your concern, and in fact I do. And yes, I did think of that. It gave me many restless nights when I was considering it, and I had several conversations with the Bishop about it. In the end, we both concluded it was okay, but I still pray about it. I should add that the choice was made somewhat easier because the senior priest, and my mentor, Father Broderick gave me his blessing. He even encouraged it somewhat. Maybe I will get a chance to tell you all of that at a later time."

"Interesting," Jacob said, "that would be nice. Without getting too nosey, I presume you have other plans, or other races to run."

"Yes I do."

"Well, I remember an old saying," Jacob continued. "It goes something like this: '…let us run with perseverance the race marked out for us.' Probably by some philosopher, or maybe even in the Bible."

"I thank you for reminding me of that, it may help me later when I have a tinge of guilt for leaving. And it is from the Bible, an outstanding excerpt from the book of Hebrews. I believe it is close to the end of the book."

There was a moment of awkward silence as both considered what had been said, then Wesley continued, "I would offer you some more coffee but I think the thermos is empty."

"That is perfectly okay, and I am sure my kidneys are thankful for that."

"Would you like to walk down and see the house?" Wesley asked.

"I would love to, but I really should be going."

"Oh, come on, it won't take long."

"Okay, give me the two dollar tour," Jacob replied.

"I'll just take my bag and the thermos along and throw them in my car."

They started to walk down the path toward the driveway in silence.

"I see there are still some Sumac growing here where they can still catch the sun between the taller trees. When I was a kid, my dad always had us cut Sumac for kindling. When dry and split very thin, you can start a fire without using paper or kerosene.

"So I have been told. I had a large stone fireplace put in the great room of the house, so I guess I will find out. Up at the road, you said you were taking flowers to plant on your wife's grave, where is she buried?"

"If you go out there to the top of old Barney's hill, look across the valley to the little country church, well it was a little country church in my day, now it is a pretty elaborate country church, but that is where she is buried. My parents are also buried there; three of my brothers are buried there. My maternal Grandparents and great Grandparents are buried there, along with aunts, uncles, cousins and lots of friends.

"I suppose it is safe to say, that when your time comes, you will also be buried there."

"Yes, that is the way it is planned at this time as I have given my daughters a sealed letter with specific instructions. Part of that is also a story, and I am going to tell it to you unsolicited as we look at the house, and then go do what I came to do, and let you get back to what you were doing before I so rudely interrupted."

"I wasn't doing anything but daydreaming when you came, and so far, the interruption has been most interesting."

As they started to walk down the driveway to the house, Jacob began. "Let's hope it stays interesting. Anyway, here goes. I am a retired Navy man and could be buried in any national cemetery that has space. There is a large one close to our home in Florida that just expanded its size by quite a few acres, but getting buried here was a small compromise I accepted from my wife several years ago."

"You see when I was born in that old house that once stood about a mile further down the hollow, my mother once planted my feet on the ground above the porch. As the Indians of this area might have said, the spirit of the ground flowed up through my feet and reached my brain. If you want to put it into today's technological vernacular, it became an imbedded property on the hard drive of my brain. At least that is what I tell myself, and tried telling Monika to give her a guilt trip. I guess you can see the latter part of that didn't work, but I did convince myself. When I was sixteen, I left here and went to college in Ohio, where, believe it or not, I started to study for the ministry. After about two years I think I had a dream where the Good Lord said, 'Jacob, why don't you think this over, maybe there are other things you would rather do,' or maybe I was just tired of going to school and 'wanderlust' over came me. I was working four to midnight at a Kodak color processing lab and going to school during the day. I was carrying fifteen semester hours, and one morning after working three overtime hours, I slept in and missed a physics exam. I decided that was enough, I quit college, joined the Navy and traveled all over the world for the next twenty years, but always this land, these hills, went with me."

" My first assignment was in Germany, and just before my tour of duty was up, a coworker had an emergency need for a stand in groomsman and I reluctantly agreed. Being a naïve country boy, I succumbed to the beauty of this German city girl by the name of Monika. She was a bridesmaid in the wedding. We fell in love. I guess it was love at first sight as the saying goes. Anyway, I cancelled my rotation back to the states, married her and she bore me two wonderful daughters. For the next sixteen years we moved about the world and finally came to rest in a place called Pensacola, Florida. Nice town, nice people, beautiful beaches, but the most boring countryside you can imagine. Not a single hill for over three hundred miles. Then after a few years the boredom of the surroundings kept getting the best of me and I kept hinting that maybe we should move back to Pennsylvania. My wife would smile and basically ignore me. I persevered, assuming that when our daughters got married and moved away, empty nest syndrome would kick in and she would be most happy to relocate. After all, she really did like the green hills of Pennsylvania. What she later let me know was, she did not like the white hills of Pennsylvania."

"Now I am the type of person who does most things on impulse, and I tend to vacillate. My wife on the other hand, thought things through and always remained quite focused. While I was dreaming of a house or cabin in the hills, similar to what you are building, she was adding to our modest, middle income home, until it was fit for the pages of Southern Living. She would buy this for the house and that for the house, and I would rant and rave about her sending me to the poor house, but when my tantrums subsided, I would acknowledge to myself, that it looked great.

"It was a similar story with the yard. Our house was built on a sand pile about five feet above the water table. Unlike here in Pennsylvania, where grass just grows, there you have to beg and plead and fertilize. You need one of two things, a degree in Florida horticulture or a good lawn service. I told my wife we could not afford a lawn service, and she said we might just as well sell the lawn mower because we were never going to have any grass to cut. She had already turned down my idea about artificial turf. I called her bluff and said we could sell the lawnmower and she could keep the money. Then she said what she really meant, and we got a lawn care service just to add all the fertilizer and chemicals in the right amounts, and at the right times. Everything else was up to us, and I use that word, us, inappropriately, because I played no part in the beautiful yard that came about. It too could have been a spread in Better Homes and Gardens.

"I was still bellyaching about moving back to the hills, when she told me to find a place at least as nice as what we had, and she would go back in the summer. There was no way she was going to spend her winters there.

"Of course there was no way we could afford two places, so finally, one day in desperation, I thought I would play on her sympathy and I said in an exasperated tone, 'well I guess the only way I am going to get back to the hills is if I buy about an eight foot square plot in the cemetery.' She thought that was a good idea, so here I am planting flowers whether I like it or not."

Wesley smiled and then said, "See, that wasn't a bit boring. Besides, I sort of like working in the yard myself, so in your absence, I wouldn't mind being your gardener."

"Ah! I didn't mean to imply that."

"I know you didn't, but I am very serious. I would consider it a privilege and honor."

"Okay, you are on. I'll give you my address, just send me a bill."

"Call me a friend, and friends don't charge."

"Okay friend, but that is a pretty big step you are taking, seeing as we just met," Jacob said.

"Perhaps, but then I have always been a pretty good judge of character."

"For your sake, I hope so."

"So what do you think of the house?" Wesley asked.

"Well, Exodus 20:17 comes to mind.

"I am impressed, book, chapter and verse."

"But are you sure that I am correct?" Jacob asked. "I often misquote."

"I assume you are referring to, 'Thou shalt not covet thy neighbor's house, etc., etc.'"

"That is the one."

"Then you quoted correctly."

"Yeah, well I guess I learned a few things in what was that little country church across the valley."

"I don't doubt that, but my guess is that you have kept up with it a bit more over the years. I have researched a little bit about that church and it's previous denominational affiliation. I can probably guess where you went to college.

"Touché, Father."

The word father again sort of sucked the air from his lungs, but he recovered to say, "I know the denomination is not in Florida so what denomination do you belong to?"

"Ah, you err in your reasoning Father."

"Wesley, please."

"Right, Wesley, but you err in your reasoning in assuming that I belong to a denomination. Let me explain further. My wife, being from northern Germany, was Evangelisch-Lutherisch, that is to say she was Lutheran. Both of our daughters were baptized and confirmed as Lutherans, although both ended up marrying Catholics and converting. I have absolutely no problem with that. For a long time we attended a Missouri Synod Lutheran church. Missouri Synod is the very conservative branch of the Lutherans. I completed a course of instruction in the precepts of the church and the liturgy, and with that, and a reasonable contribution each Sunday, they permitted me to partake of the sacraments of Holy Communion, but I never felt compelled to say I am a Lutheran. Of course they never approved of my Catholic grandchildren taking communion by my side, the same as their Priest wouldn't invite me to share the communion table with them. I mean, we sing this old Negro spiritual, 'Let us Break Bread Together on Our Knees' and preface it with, 'provided you are of the same faith.' I just think denominations put to many restrictions on open communication between God and me. Mostly, I guess I was a thorn in the flesh of that Missouri Synod minister, because several years ago we had a parting of the ways."

"Oh, how was that?"

"It is also a long story, and I won't go into it here, but basically it resolved around the fact that because I wasn't a member, I wasn't allowed to teach an adult study group."

"But you said you were baptized there and attended a course of instructions. Wasn't that sufficient to make you a member?"

"But I never signed the book saying I was a member," Jacob continued.

"Technically, I suppose one could argue for that, but it seems a moot point to me," Wesley replied.

"That is the way I saw it, but I had no desire to cause a disruption within the congregation, so my wife and I went to another Lutheran Church within the ELCA. It was difficult for we had a lot of very good friends at the previous church."

"I can imagine it was very difficult, but you were probably correct in the course you chose to follow."

"We never questioned our decision, but I can argue, let me retract that and say, I can advance some good points for my beliefs."

"Jacob, I fully believe that you can, but until I get to know you better, I am not going down that road."

With a slight laugh, Jacob said, "But you said you were a friend."

"Precisely, and that is why I will refrain. I have my own struggles with my faith, but it can keep until later."

"I was only joking, Padre."

"Wesley."

"Right! Wesley. Well, let's change the subject, and you tell me why you didn't have them cut down that old black walnut tree there at the end of the house?"

Wesley didn't want to answer the question directly because he didn't want to hedge on the truth so he changed the subject just slightly. "This from a man who tells me he doesn't believe in cutting flowers to put in a vase."

"Oh, I think it is great that you didn't have the tree cut, it is just that later it could be a threat to the house."

He had dodged the bullet as the saying goes.

"You sound like my builder now, but in all truthfulness, I don't see it as much of a threat. I did the geometry on it and find that even if it falls directly toward the house, the highest branches would just graze the siding. If it starts to die, I will have it cut, in the meantime, let it bear fruit."

"It is an old tree, I remember picking nuts off the ground there more than fifty years ago, and it was a mature tree then."

"Really, you picked nuts that had fallen from that tree?"

"Twice actually, once back in the 1980s. My wife and daughters bought me a nice 12-guage, pump shotgun for my birthday and I came back here to do a little hunting for small game. Cost me sixty dollars for a non-resident license and I used it one day and had nothing to show for it. This hillside was the last place I hunted before calling it a day. I did jump a rabbit out there, but because of the high grass I did not get off a shot. I continued walking in the direction that the rabbit ran. I came to that clearing out there where the old barn used to sit. Not twenty yards away, just about where the old hopper trail was, there sat my rabbit, his ears raised and tweaking to catch the slightest sound. Easy shot, but I think to myself, 'what am I going to do with one rabbit?' There was no hesitation for an answer; I raised the shotgun perpendicular to the ground and fired once into the air. The rabbit scurried off again into the tall grass and I heard myself say, 'I hope you survive to die of old age.' I pumped the gun twice to unload it, and never went hunting again."

"You're an old softie, aren't you?"

"Whatever, but I did fill my hunting jacket pockets with black walnuts."

"And the second time?" Wesley asked.

"Oh yeah, the second time. Kinda got lost in my great hunting adventure. The second time was actually the first time. It was back in 1952, the autumn after the Nelsons moved into the old house."

If there had been a previous doubt in Wesley's mind, this now confirmed it. This man had known his mother's family and without a doubt he had also known his mother. His mind was numb; he wanted so much to just evaporate into thin air. He wanted to be sitting back on the stone bench as he was before this man ever drove by, to be alone in his own daydreams and solitude. Somehow it suddenly seemed so long ago, but he knew it had been less than an hour, but in that time, so much had crossed his mind, and so much had been revealed. And now he knew much more was to come, but could he listen to this and conceal his inner feeling as he had promised his mother. He could say nothing, nor ask anything that would impact upon the lives of other innocent people. For perhaps the first time in his life, he silently asked for God's help and was afraid it might not be there. But in his heart he knew he had to hear what this man was going to tell him, and now he thought he knew who this man was.

Chapter 6

This man Jacob, whom he had just met, continued, "It was some sort of a custom back here in the hills, that when you butchered your hogs in the fall, you would take a mess of fresh sausage to a friend or relative, or two. Like most people here about, we normally didn't butcher until the end of November. We didn't have a freezer, and so the weather had to be cold enough so that the meat didn't spoil until it was canned or smoked. However, in this case, one of our hogs got out of the pen and try as we might, we couldn't get it back in. It finally crossed the little run below our house and got into a gully that was filled with large stones. Because it was scared, it tried to run across this stone filled gully. All it succeeded in doing was break a front leg, so Dad finally wound up shooting it and we had to butcher it. It was toward the end of October.

"The Nelsons had moved into the old house at the end of August. That September, my father was helping our neighbor, who was also my mother's first cousin, pick his potatoes. A discourse followed between the two men as they worked, and so the farmer left two short rows of potatoes unpicked. He told the Nelson's that if they dug them, they could have them. Naturally they did, and I remember there was another discussion that took place outside of the church when some of the people objected that the Nelsons were digging the potatoes on a Sunday. Some time I will have to tell you more about my father, but he was pretty quick at quoting

59

scripture and would often point his finger for emphasis. He came up with an applicable scripture reference and the discussion ended.

"Anyway, back to the butchering. Mom knew the Nelsons did not have any hogs to butcher so the next evening she told Dad she was going to take Cary Nelson a mess of sausage. She also took her a small can of fresh lard that had been rendered. I went with her because Karin and I had become friends. Karin was a year older than I, but because I had skipped the fifth grade, we were both sophomores in high school. She was then fifteen and I was fourteen.

"The old house that stood here had an upper and a lower porch. We came in on the upper porch where the springhouse was located. There was a wash bucket of black walnuts sitting on the porch, and somewhere in the conversation between my mother and Mrs. Nelson, it was decided that Mom could have some of the walnuts that still littered the ground. She liked to use them when she baked Christmas cookies. So guess who got to pick them up? If you said to yourself, Karin and me, you are correct.

"Mrs. Nelson gave us another old bucket to put the nuts in. We had just started to pick the nuts when I noticed that Karin would pick them up rather daintily with her thumb and index finger. I watched her for a moment until she saw I was watching her and not picking up any nuts. Finally she said, 'why are you watching me?' I told her that I was just amused at the way she picked up the nuts so gently with her thumb and index finger and asked her why. She told me that the outer husk really stains your fingers, which I knew was true, and she said she didn't want old Gina Lepley, who rode the bus with us, making fun of her. I laughed and told her I though she let Gina play too much of a part in her life. She just flipped her head back and inhaled through her nose, but said nothing."

"Who was this Gina?"

"She was a girl that lived out close to New Lexington. They owned a small farm and her mother used to bring printed feed sack for my mother to sew clothes for herself and for Gina. Sometimes Gina would come with her mother and we would goof around as kid do. She seemed okay to me.

"If Karin liked you, maybe she was jealous of Gina, or vice versa," Wesley said.

"I never gave that any thought. I will tell you this, the Nelsons were very poor, even poorer that we were. However, being poor has nothing to do with a person's character or worth. As a Priest, I am sure you have ministered to many poor people, so I do not have to tell you this fact. But, even by the worst standards, the Nelson's children had some pretty shabby clothes. It was the best that their parents could do under the circumstances, but one day when I got on the bus at school to come home, I noticed that Karin had been crying. Since we normally sat on the same seat, I asked what was wrong. At first she did not want to tell me, but finally I coaxed it out of her. She said that person, and tilted her head in Gina's direction, just called her 'Raggedy Ann.' I said to her, 'so what,' and sat down just as the bus started to depart. Karin didn't say anything more, and I would have let it go at that, had it not been that about half way to New Lexington, where Gina got off the bus, she turned around to me and said, 'I think you're in love with 'Raggedy Ann.' Karin and I were friends so to hear this girl call her a name that within context sounded derogatory, made me angry and I answered in rebuttal. As I said, my mother was the neighborhood seamstress in order to supplement Dad's wages from the mine, and so I said to Gina, 'what makes you so high and mighty. My mother used to make your underwear out of feed sacks.' The girl was aghast. There was of course nothing wrong with this; it was during the war and times were hard. Feed sack dresses and underpinnings were quite common, but she was also fifteen years old and for someone, especially a boy, to mention her, once less than glamorous underwear in front of everyone on the bus was a big embarrassment. She turned back around toward the front of the bus and to my knowledge she never bothered Karin again, but they never became friends. Of course, it wasn't long there after that the Nelsons moved to Ohio."

"What part of Ohio did they move to?"

"They moved to Warren. A lot of people from around here moved to that area to get work in the industrial mills. Another girl from my class, her parents moved out there. Some years later, one of my sisters and her husband also moved there."

"Did you see her before they moved?" Wesley asked.

"I did, but they left so fast that I didn't get to say goodbye."

"How is that?"

"Well, it was a Friday and she was in school. We were released about an hour early because it was the start of the Christmas vacation and it was also starting to snow quite heavily. Before she got off the bus above her house, she asked if I wanted to come up later on; we could go hopper riding. Do you know what a hopper is?" Jacob asked.

There was a slight pause and then Wesley said, "Yes I do. Why do you ask?"

"Well, the terrain around Youngstown is pretty flat. I thought maybe a flatland city kid might never of heard of them."

"Of course I never rode one, but I have heard of them. They are a short ski with an A frame toward the back and a seat."

"Yes, good classical description," Jacob said.

He paused, but Wesley didn't contribute anything further, so Jacob continued. "After supper, and after I had taken care of my chores, I told Mom I was going up to the Nelsons to go hopper riding. She told me it was okay, but I was supposed to be home by 9:30. I assured her I would.

"I was just starting up the Barney Kreger hill, when I saw someone approaching from the top. It was dark, but there was a three quarter moon and I could tell it was Karin. When we were about ten paces apart, we both said 'Hi' almost simultaneously. I was carrying my hopper under my left arm, and Karin came along side and hooked her left arm under my right arm. She didn't say anything at first, but then I could hear her suppressing a sniffle. Karin was a rather sensitive person; she cried very easily.

"I said, 'are you crying?' She said, 'no.'

"I didn't press the point and we walked a while in silence, and finally completely out of the blue she said, 'we are moving to Ohio.'

"I asked her when, and she just shrugged and said 'soon.'

"The hopper and sled riding path was just beyond the barn so we walked there to get her brother's hopper. The upper door of the barn was open and we went inside. She said, 'Come on, let's sit down and talk.' And we did. Much later when I left, I told her I would see her tomorrow. She gave me a kiss and a very long hug, but said nothing.

"I was a bit late in getting home and my mother was waiting up for me, which was usual, and of course I had to listen to her reprimand.

"On Saturday, my brother and I had to help our dad haul dead limbs from the forest belonging to our neighbors and cut them up for firewood. That normally took until noon time, then we had to hand carry it to the wood shed and some to the lower porch where Mom could get it as she needed it. When we were finished we would take a bath and walk over to where my grandparents lived. My uncle had a girlfriend in Confluence so my brother and I, and another cousin, would ride with him to town and go to the movie. Then we would just hang around, generally by this little restaurant, until he was ready to come back. Sometimes it was midnight.

"On this Saturday, I told my brother I didn't think I would go to Confluence, as I wasn't feeling well. Of course my mother wanted to know what was wrong and I told her it was nothing.

"Later, after my brother had left and we had eaten supper, I told my mother, I thought I would go up to the Nelsons. Then I told her what Karin had told me the night before about them moving to Ohio. Mom told me she knew of it because my dad's boss at the clay mine had told him that his brother was moving to Warren to work at Copper Weld, and he thought Mr. Nelson's oldest son had also gotten Mr. Nelson a job at the same place.

"My mother said to me, 'I know you like Karin, but you be home on time.' Defensively, I said, 'Karin and I are just friends, but I will be home by eleven, the same as if I went to Confluence.'" She looked at me a bit disapprovingly, but didn't say anything.

"When I got to the Nelson's house, I went in on the upper porch and knocked on the door. I was expecting Karin to open the door, but instead, it was her younger brother Harold. He invited me in and then hollered to his mother, 'it is Jacob Grant.' Mrs. Nelson came into the kitchen from a bedroom."

"Karin said you might come by," Mrs. Nelson said.

"Is she here?" I asked.

"Didn't she tell you?" Mrs. Nelson asked again.

"Tell me what?"

"That we are moving to Ohio."

"Yes she did tell me, but she didn't tell me when."

"Then Mrs. Nelson said to me, 'I am so sorry Jacob, but she left this morning with her father. Her brother Carl drove in with his pickup and took her, her father, and some of our things out to Warren. He is coming in again tomorrow for the rest of our stuff and will take Harold and me along with him. Carl got Lester a good job at the steel mill, and they want him to start on Monday. I wanted to see your mother before we left because she was so good to us, but I won't get the chance so you be sure to tell her thanks for all she has done.'"

63

"I said I would, but I was a bit dumfounded. Finally, I said, I guessed I would go."

"Then Mrs. Nelson told me to wait. She went into what was Karin's room and came back and handed me a letter."

"Karin said I was to give you this," Mrs. Nelson said.

"I took the letter and said thank you, but I really didn't know what else to say, so I just said I guess I would go, and I did."

Wesley wanted to ask what was in the letter, but he knew that was too personal so instead he asked, "Did you stay in touch with Karin?"

"About two weeks after they moved, I received a letter from her. I answered her letter, and in about another week I again received a reply. I immediately answered this letter, but didn't receive a reply. A couple of weeks later, I wrote again, but again, I did not receive a reply. At that time my feelings were a bit hurt, and I assumed she had met someone else. With some difficulty, I told myself that at least that was okay if she had met someone to sort of look after her."

Wesley decided he would push the matter slightly to see what the outcome would be, although he knew it might take him to an area to which he did not want to go at this time, but he said, "You say that like you and she were more than just friends?"

"In time we might have been, but at that time we were kids; we were just good friends with some unanswered questions and groping for answers. I was always a bit of a loner, and at the time, Karin was a bit of an outsider, so I suppose we gave each other solace. When she didn't write, I assumed she had found a friend, male or female, and although I wasn't happy about it, I could accept it if she was happy."

Wesley was silent for a minute and then he said, "Well, come on Jacob, let's start the nickel tour, or two dollar tour as you said. Inflation is a terrible thing."

The stairs leading to the lower porch were wide and included a middle railing in addition to one on each side. Jacob ascended about half way and paused to stare out across the valley, and then he turned his gaze toward where the old barn once stood. There was an almost imperceptible nod of his head and he climbed the rest of the way to the porch landing.

Touring the house took no more than about ten minutes, then Jacob said, "Well Wesley, this is truly magnificent. You have solitude with a great view. There are the Whippoorwills to sing you to sleep in the summer, and the howling winds that sweep across the upper flatland in the winter. In the autumn you can hear the crack of rifles and shotguns from the hunters in the valley below. There are sounds for spring also, but that is a time for visual perception more so than audio. There is only one thing that I see missing."

"And what might that be?" Wesley asked.

"An outhouse. You definitely need an outhouse to give it authenticity."

"I think I will forgo that authenticity Jacob, besides, it would just cause the EPA people to descend on me."

"You sound like my granddaughter Eliana. Quite a few years ago, Monika and I brought our two oldest grandkids up here for their first visit. Their great-Grandmother was in a home and not in good health and we wanted them to meet each other. Down at Beckley, West Virginia, we would get off the Interstate, which was also the West Virginia Turnpike, and take old route 19 for about sixty miles to where it connected with I-79. Just past Summerville you go up a long hill and then down the other side. At the foot of the hill is Birch Creek and a small town. To the left, across an open field and at the very base of a hill, someone had built a rustic looking two-story house. It was sided with rough sawed lumber, and I thought it was a great idea. About a hundred yards away was a small building that looked most definitely like an outhouse. I pointed it out to the grandchildren and jokingly told them that perhaps their Oma and I would buy the house.

"Then I said, 'I think the outhouse is just for show.'

To which my granddaughter Eliana said, 'Pappap, I should certainly hope it is just for show.'

"And I guess you are right about building one here. You would never get it approved by the EPA people. Well, Wesley, I really must go now."

They walked back to where Wesley's car was parked at the end of the driveway.

"It is a pretty steep driveway, would you like me to drive you up to your car?"

"No thank you Wesley," Jacob said with a bit of sarcasm. "When I can't climb the hills, I will stop coming to the hills. I may be huffing and puffing when I get to the top, but I will make it."

"So when are you going to head back to Florida?" Wesley asked.

"I plan to go in and see my sisters for a little this evening and will head back tomorrow."

"Oh, I thought you might be staying for a couple of days. I was hoping you could fill me in a bit more on the area."

"Well, I usually come up here in July for a couple of family reunions, so if you get moved in by that time, I could swap you some stories for a couple of grilled burgers out on the lower porch."

"That is a deal. Let me give you my telephone number and you can give me a call before you come."

"I noticed you had a laptop in your car, just give me your e-mail address."

"Better still, let me give you my card, it has all that information on it."

"So how long does it take you to get back to Florida?" Wesley continued.

"About eighteen hours. Used to take me about sixteen, but my kidneys demand more pit stops and now my leg joints are in collusion with them."

"You don't drive straight through do you?"

"Normally I do, but it depends on when I leave here."

"You have got to be kidding me."

"No. I like to leave very early, drive a couple of hours and stop for breakfast down around Clarksburg, West Virginia. I generally bring along a couple of audio books to break the boredom, and like I said, about every hundred or hundred and fifty miles I stop to use the restroom and stretch my legs. On the trip up, I usually take two days because I go via Louisville to see my daughter, son-in-law and grandkids."

"Well, Jacob, I will let you go, but I want you to know that I have enjoyed this visit so much. You can't imagine how glad I am that you spotted the house and decided to stop. I am already looking forward to your return in July."

"I have enjoyed it too Wesley. Anytime I can bend someone's ear to listen, I enjoy it. That is some of what I miss most about my wife being gone. Sometimes at the house, I will go outside by the pool, or walk around the yard and talk to her still. Sometimes I think I hear her answer me, mostly she is saying, 'don't forget to water the flowers.' But it is not as much fun now, because it is done in a low key. Before she left me, we would holler at each other about a lot of things, but it was not with malice, it was with many years of love and understanding.

" Okay, don't let me get melancholy. So, do you want me to tell you what you should do?"

"If I said no, would you still tell me?"

"Probably not, but then you would be missing some good advice."

"In that case, tell me."

"First, get to know the people in these valleys. I think you are going to have to make the first step, but I am sure you will be surprised at the way they receive you. Second, take some time and drive the back roads. Park your car along the side sometimes and walk the trails. I might add that many of the farmers have posted "No Trespassing" signs for good reasons, observe them but you will still find a lot of places you can explore. You will love it. However, your being a city boy, you might want to get a few pointers from an experienced woodsman."

"You mean so I don't get lost?"

"Well yeah, that too, but with your GPS unit, that shouldn't happen. I was thinking more about your knowing where you might come across rattlesnakes, and momma black bears out teaching their 'youngins' how to survive on their own."

"Oh, now you make me feel like I really want to get out there and jeopardize my life."

"Ah! It isn't as bad as I make it sound; besides they would probably not mess with a man of God."

"At this point, God might not consider me one of his men."

"That brings me to my third point. I feel confident that God won't mind if you go on a Sunday morning or a Wednesday evening and study his word with the people who attend that church across the valley. Stay away from 'man interpreted doctrine' and stick to Bible basics and you should learn some things from them, and I am sure you can pass on some wisdom."

"By Bible basics, you mean fundamentalism?"

"Yes, as defined by Mr. Webster, not the television 'send me your money so you can go to heaven' type. As a courtesy, and so your Catholicism doesn't cause them to put up an infidel shield, you might want to talk to them first, but I can almost guarantee you, they will welcome you and what you can offer. Of course if they don't, they are missing a chance to convert you. Just kidding on that. If you want, you may mention my name. Some of them still remember me. The former pastor and I were related, and although I have only talked to Reverend Pritts, the present pastor, a few times, I found him to be a person fairly easy to communicate with. So, that all having been said, I take my leave and start the huffy-puffy climb up your driveway."

They shook hands and Jacob started walking up the driveway. As he neared the curve in the drive close to the top of the hill, which would take him out of view, he turned and yelled, "You do know the name of this area, don't you?"

"Hexabarger or Hexie, I have been told," was Wesley's answer.

With that, Jacob raised his right hand slightly, turned, and waved with an upturned index finger. He nodded his head and rounded the bend and was out of sight.

Chapter 7

Jacob was in fact, huffing and puffing when he reached the road. As he stopped to catch his breath he also looked around. And he thought to himself, the man he had just met must think he was a blabbering fool, going on about anything and everything like that. But he did seem very interested in what Jacob had to say, and since Monika had passed away, he didn't have many people he could talk to, actually no one that was interested in hearing about this place.

Years earlier, he had written a lot of articles about this area. Some were published in the Historical Society's quarterly publication, but many were just a pack of papers in folders in his file cabinets. He had always included the disk on which they were stored, but he knew the technology would change and these would eventually be useless just like old 45 and 33 music recordings, and VHS tapes. His only solace was that, perhaps after his passing, his grandchildren would take them and his great grandchildren might read them, but if not, so be it. There were many more significant moments in history that have been lost forever. He loved the ones he knew here, and for now, that was enough.

Jacob walked to where his car was parked on the shoulder of the road and hit the remote to unlock the doors.

At the bottom of the Barney Kreger hill, he went straight instead of taking the shorter route to the church and cemetery. Just past the intersection he saw a lady in the yard. It was his Aunt Jean so he beeped the horn. She turned and waved, but probably did not know who it was. He didn't have time to stop and talk now, but he always had a great deal of respect for his Aunt Jean.

He was now in his favorite part of this valley, perhaps his favorite spot in the whole world. He slowed the car down to about twenty-five miles per hour. The road was curvy, but that wasn't the reason he was going so slow. He just wanted to take it all in one more time, the same as he did every time he returned here over the past fifty years.

When he rounded the first turn he approached the old Lyman and Minnie Nicola Trimpey farm. The barn had been torn down a long time ago, but to Jacob, it was just as visible as ever. The house had been remodeled, but again, in his minds eye view, it was also just as before. Past the house was a garage, and it hadn't changed much. Lyman and his brother William "Willy" had built it in 1948 to house the brand new Ford pickup that Lyman had bought.

Having driven an old Model T Ford car that he bought new in the late twenties, this new pickup was difficult for him to get use to and within two months he had crunched both front fenders in two separate accidents. Nothing serious, and he wasn't hurt. At church it was a bit of a joke and he laughed with everyone else. Only his wife Minnie, who was a bit frugal and didn't want him to buy the truck in the first place, didn't think it was a laughing matter.

Just past the garage was a very small field on the right. It was hedged in by the road on one side and the upper reaches of Redd Run on the other. The road paralleled Redd Run for its entire distance from where it rose from a spring halfway up the Barney Kreger hill, until it emptied into Laurel Hill Creek at what was once the coal mine town of Humbert. The field did not go all the way to the banks of Redd Run; there was a space of perhaps fifty feet in width that was very swampy. There were a few willows and other trees in this divide.

When Jacob was a young boy, they owned some ducks and Redd Run was their domain. It was usually his job, or that of his brother to round up the ducks and bring them home to be cooped up for the evening. One evening in the fall of the year he saw a small tree that caught his eye at just this place. It was a young chestnut tree and it had some nut pods on its branches, although the nuts had not matured. He was very excited when he told his father about this, and he remembers his father telling him not to be too optimistic. After the blight had wiped out the majestic nut tree around 1909, people often reported seeing young trees, but like the roots that produced them, they too soon met the same fate. Two years later, his chestnut tree was dead.

At this point, the road made a slight turn to the right and for the next quarter of a mile it was level. From here he could look down the valley and see where the old house in which he was born had once stood. A bit closer was another reminder of a former time. It was the place where his great grandparents, Mahala and Isaac Firestone once lived, and where his grandmother Martha Ann was born. It was a log house, having been built by Garrison Smith, and like his own home it burned down, but that was long before Jacob's time.

Garrison Smith had built the house on the side of the hill, just a few feet above what would have been the flood plane of Redd Run during an exceptionally bad rain. Part of the hill had been cut out to form a cellar under the house, and that was still clearly visible, including some large stones that formed part of the sidewalls. There was a large bush on one side of the house planted by one of the early occupants. Jacob never knew the correct botanical name; they just called it the fire bush. So named because it produced bright red flowers in early spring, and then it would receive its new coat of leaves. On the other side of where the house stood, there was a lilac bush. It was there when Jacob was a young boy, but now it was dead.

A short distance from the house was a spring, and at one time, again, before Jacob's time, there was a springhouse.

Jacob remembered a very interesting story about the springhouse told to him by his grandfather, although his grandmother denied it. His grandfather was a great storyteller and so Jacob always held on to this one, but he knew that his grandmother was not likely to tell a lie, so maybe it didn't happen just as his grandfather had said.

According to his grandfather it went something like this: Colonel John Miller owned the house just a few hundred yards down the river. It was a one-story house so in the fall of 1903, Colonel Miller contracted Harrison King to add a second story. Harrison had his younger brother Samuel assist him with the project. From the roof of the house you could readily see the Firestone house and the path to the springhouse, and vice versa.

71

He, Samuel, saw a young girl go to the springhouse for a bucket of water. He hollered, 'Hello' and waved. The young girl looked but did not return his wave. Later, she returned for a second bucket of water and the procedure was repeated with the same result. According to him, the young girl made at least five trips for a bucket of water.

Jacob considered this might have been why his grandmother said the story was untrue, and thus he was justified in believing most of his grandfather's story.

As the story continued, after he and his brother Harrison had finished for the day, he decided he would call on the Firestones. He reasoned that if the young girl had carried in that much water, it must be very good water and he would say he was thirsty. When he rapped on the door, the young lady, Martha Ann answered the door and the rest was history.

On December 12, 1903, Samuel George Newton King took Martha Ann Firestone as his wife. Martha Ann, later known only as Mattie, was fifteen years old. They would later have fourteen children.

Thirty-two years later, their daughter Alice, Jacob's mother, would move into the house he and his brother had worked on and live there until it burned down in 1978.

As Jacob approached that point in the road, just above where the old homestead stood, he parked his car on the upper side of the road and got out. He hadn't planned to do this. He hadn't done it for over twenty-five years, but something just pulled at him. He had to stop.

He walked back a few paces to where there were two mailboxes. They were at the same place their own mailbox had been as far back as he could remember, almost seventy years by now.

The people who had bought the property after the house burned down had built a one-story house at about the same location. The property was a bit less than two acres. Closer to the road, someone had placed a singlewide trailer home.

At the trailer home, a dog was chained to a clothesline that provided it with a long path of controlled freedom. As Jacob approached, it started to bark very loudly. A lady opened the door to the trailer and came out on the small, uncovered upper porch.

"Can I help you?" she asked.

"Hello, my name is Jacob Grant. A long time ago, I used to live in the old house that burned where that house now sits. I was just in the area and was reminiscing. Was wondering if you mind if I crossed your property to the other side of the run?"

"Don't mind at all," was her answer.

Jacob thanked her and started to walk down over the hill toward Redd Run.

Back when he was just a very young boy, this entire field that he was now crossing was covered with large sugar maple trees. His mother's first cousin, who owned the land, tapped them every spring, collected the sugar water and made maple syrup.

When Harry Nicklow's barn burned down, Joe Rugg moved a sawmill in to cut lumber so he could rebuild the barn. Most of that lumber came from Harry's own land, but Mr. Rugg had convinced Chester to sell him the large maple trees. When the sawmill was moved, only two huge trees remained, and that was because they had rotted from the inside; they were hollow shells.

As Redd Run meandered down through the valley, there were several places the land was very swampy. You did not walk across these areas unless it had not rained for a long time. It was not that it would suck you down like quicksand, but the muck was so thick and sticky that once you went in over your shoe tops, you had a difficult time getting back out.

There was one of these swampy areas on this side of the run at the foot of the hill Jacob was descending. It was not caused by the river, but rather by an underground source of water that instead of coming out at one point like a spring, it seeped out of a bank over a distance of about two hundred feet. On each side of this bank, the land was dry. Jacob was now standing in one of those spots. As a boy, he stood here more times than he could contemplate; it was the place his father had built a sawhorse to cut firewood.

If they were cutting slabs, his father and brother manned a short crosscut saw, and his job was to set on the slab to keep it from moving. He didn't mind it too much in the summer, but in the winter, the slabs were often covered with snow and ice and within half an hour his butt was wet and freezing.

He once mentioned to his father that they should build a fire to keep warm while they worked.

"You want to cut more wood just so you can have a fire here?" his father had asked.

When he thought about that it made sense, and he never broached the subject again.

After the wood had been cut, it had to be split and carried into the coal/woodshed. A bit more than a one day's supply was always stacked on the lower porch. In the winter this was quite a bit as the kitchen stove was used for both heating and cooking. There was a register in the ceiling above the stove so that the heat would also go up and warm the bedroom directly above. It wasn't the most efficient system, but it helped some.

The house had three bedrooms upstairs. There was no hallway; one room just led into the next. The stairs went from the kitchen up to the first bedroom, which was where his mother and father slept. There was a door between the first and the middle room, but only a curtain covered the doorway between the middle and the back bedroom. The middle bedroom was directly above the heating stove in the living room, and it also had a register and vent through the ceiling and floor above. This was the best room in the winter. The coldest bedroom was the back one, and that was the one he and his older brother shared. His younger sister and two younger brothers shared the middle bedroom.

Close to the wood cutting area, his father had laid two logs across the run and nailed slab boards to them to form a rough bridge. In the summer time when there hadn't been any rain for a long time their well would go dry and then they had to carry drinking water from a spring a little ways up the run. When his father saw that the water level was getting low in the well, he would have him and his brother build a small dam across the run and carry water for everything except cooking.

On Monday, that meant washday, and when the well was low, he remembers carrying a lot of water, a job he thoroughly hated. One thing about his mother, she believed in cleanliness. They didn't have a lot of clothes, but they were always clean, and her whites were always white, no gray. Washing clothes was an all day job. A large copper boiler was placed on the kitchen stove to heat water for the washing tub that was set up on the lower porch. Next to the washtub sat two other tubs, one for a first rinse and one for a second rinse.

Normally it required filling the washing tub four times, twice for the white or light colored clothes and twice for the dark clothes. Rinse tubs were also changed at least once.

When he was twelve years old, they finally got electricity in the house, and his mother got an electric washing machine. It saved her a lot of backbreaking work bending over a scrub board, but it still meant carrying as much water.

The house was old and rustic, but it was always clean. Of course, as he and his older brother had to help their father with the outside chores, his three older sisters, likewise, had to help their mother.

If Monday was washday, Tuesday was ironing day, and she ironed everything, or when they were old enough, probably about the age of six, his sisters ironed everything. He never forgot the first time he mentioned this fact to Monika. She too was as neat and particular as her mother-in-law, except there were a few items she deemed did not need to be ironed. He once said to her, "My mother always ironed my t-shirts and skivvies."

Her answer was the time worn retort, "I am not your mother."

That subject was also never broached again.

Standing here now looking down at the small stream that was Redd Run, he remembered it all with such clarity. And then another memory flashed into his mind, the subject of which he had just discussed with Wesley; it was the first time he met Karin. And although it had happened at this very spot, he didn't want to think about it, or anything else here. He wanted to ascend the other side of the hill to what was once his favorite spot.

The hill was somewhat semi-circular, sharing one half with two separate valleys. The half to his right as he stood facing it, the side that faced the road he had just traveled, had been cleared many years ago. During the time of horse drawn plows, it had been cultivated almost to the very bottom, but even when Jacob was a boy, the lower half had not been cultivated and was used as a pasture. There was a barbed wire fence that separated the pasture area from the tilled area.

The left side of the hill was still a forested region, the trees being mostly beech, a wild cherry here and there, and a few locust and butternut trees at the very top. From that very top, one was afforded a wonderful view of the valley surrounding this hill for about two hundred and seventy degrees. From here you could also look across the portion of the hill that was still covered with trees and get a great view of the "knob" on top of the opposite hill. But the opposite hill was much different than the one Jacob stood facing. Whereas the one in front of him had a peak, the one with the "knob" was a plateau. Everybody hereabout knew what you were talking of when you said the "knob," but Jacob had never ever heard anyone give it any consideration for what it might have been. It was the highest point on that plateau and rose above the relatively flat surrounding area by about one hundred feet in height. It was rectangular and perfectly flat on the top. The "knob" and the area surrounding it had been tilled for many years so it was impossible to say just what the original shape had been.

About three miles away as the crow flies, there is another flat-topped hill. It is know as Fort Hill, although that may be a misnomer. Several archaeological digs have shown this site to have been occupied by early Indian tribes, some going back at least nine hundred years. Jacob always considered the "knob" might have had a similar history. His father had found several nice arrowheads when in the process of hoeing his garden.

Jacob was now ready to start his assault on the hill. It was very steep and his spot was almost two thirds of the way up. He knew he would probably regret it later, but he also knew he may never have the chance to do it again. He crossed the run, and then across the flat land where the sawmill once was. It was also here where he, along with his older brother, and other boys in the area, played baseball, or a modified version of the game.

Although the area was pretty flat, it still left a lot to be desired for a baseball field. Redd Run paralleled the first base line and shortly past that it went to the left and made for a very short right field. Anything across the run was a ground rule double, and of course if it went across on the fly, it landed in the swampy area and was sometimes not retrievable. More than one game ended when the last of the two or three balls they might have ended up in the swamp. They tried to make left-handed batters become switch hitters, and if they refused, they would often receive an intentional walk, especially if they were down to the last ball in their possession. Center field was no problem except for one old tree stump and a large rock that projected out of the ground. Left field was flat for about two hundred feet and then it met the base of the hill. The hill rose abruptly, and had its slope been smooth, the ball would have rolled back down. Needless to say, it was not smooth so three lines were laid out, the first was a ground rule double; the second a ground rule triple; and the third, a cow path fairly far up, was a home run. He never remembered anyone getting a home run.

He had now crossed the flat area, and Jacob decided that the best plan to get to his favorite place was to follow the old cow paths. In his youth, he went straight up over, normally keeping just inside the tree line. Following the cow paths back and forth now would take longer, but time was what he now had most of. Beside, if he attacked the hill directly on, he might never make it.

After about ten minutes of zigzagging back and forth, he was about half way to his destination. How he wished he had thought to bring a bottle of water with him, but he had not. A cane or walking stick would also be some help. He decided he could obtain this. After he had rested for a couple of minutes he started again, going diagonally toward the tree line.

At one time there had been a barbed wire fence here, and the remains, one low strand of rusted wire and a few rotted posts was all that gave a clue to the past. Jacob stepped across the wire and looked for an old tree limb that he could use for a cane. He found one with little difficulty and also a path that paralleled the old fence line toward the top.

Old Homestead. The author's old home place. The original house burned in 1978 and the property was sold.

When he finally reached the top, he went back out into the open field, walked about thirty yards and sat down. From here he could survey the old homestead, and the path of Redd Run until it disappeared a long way down the valley. He thought to himself, he should have brought his camera, but quickly reasoned, "why?" He had climbed to this point several times and taken pictures. Somewhere in the vast pile of unsorted and undocumented pictures, he had more than several from this vantage point. At this point in his life, why did he need another one? Few people, if any, would be interested in seeing it, and for him, the view was so imbedded in his mind that he could never forget it even if he tried.

He stood and decided it was time to go. It had taken him nearly thirty minutes to climb to this point, and now after sitting for no more than two minutes, he was ready to leave. What had been the point? He stood, and then smiled to himself as he remembered his granddaughter Eliana many years before when she was less than two years old.

He had been sitting in what was now his office, but what was earlier, Eliana's mother's bedroom. It was furnished with a drafting table, a hutch with a television, an over-stuffed chair and a hickory limb rocker that Monika had bought from the Amish in Pennsylvania a couple of years earlier.

He had his video camera out because he loved to catch Eliana and David in normal childhood activity. Great things to show them years later, or their children, if he lived that long.

Eliana decided that she wanted to sit in the rocking chair, and so she made the effort to climb in. The chair would rock forward and thwart her effort. She tried again; same result, Then again, and again. Finally she stomped her feet, whined and turned as if to leave, and Jacob almost stopped the camera to help her but decided against it. She turned and made one more assault. This time she was successful in getting her right knee on to the edge of the seat, and grasped the cushion that was tied to the back of the chair. After a bit more groaning, she succeeded and seated herself perfectly in the chair. Her small legs dangled off the front and she rested her small hands on the arms of the chair. She rocked back and forth twice or thrice, and then climbed down. She had accomplished what she had attempted, victory was sweet, but there were many more mountains to climb. She is still conquering them with finesse, but in this moment, living a form of déjà vu, Jacob wondered how many more of them he would witness.

It was time to go back down the mountain and finish what he had come to do. Talk to Monika and give her some flowers.

Jacob kneeled by the grave and planted the flowers he had brought from their yard in Florida. When he had finished, he sat by the side of the stone that also contained his name, lacking only two numbers to be chiseled in. His lips didn't move, but he talked to Monika. As he sat there, he again started feeling the pain in his lower abdomen that had plagued him on the entire trip up.

When he stood up, he did verbalize in a low tone. "I don't think I will spend the night Monika, I am going to start back and maybe go see Dr. Cantrell tomorrow. If you get a chance, say a couple of good words on my behalf to the Master as I probably need them."

Chapter 8

There was still about three hours of listening on the audio book CD that Jacob had started on the way up. He wouldn't start it until he hit the interstate at Bruceton Mills, West Virginia, and it should keep his mind occupied until he got to Wytheville, Virginia. There he would probably stop for the night.

As he left the Old Bethel Church parking lot and started his descent out of Hexie, he couldn't help but reflect on what all had happened this day. Meeting Wesley Donaldson had been such an unexpected event; it was almost surreal. He almost literally did have to pinch himself to make sure it wasn't a dream. There was something about the meeting and the ease of their conversation that was also a bit unsettling. Jacob couldn't put his finger on it, but then he let it go. Maybe he would think about it later.

Chapter 9

Shortly after Jacob had departed, Wesley decided it was time to head back to his apartment in Somerset. He had some work to do and a couple of e-mails to write but wasn't sure he was in the mood to work. He too had a strange feeling about this meeting with Jacob Grant; it was almost like destiny.

The next morning, Wesley decided he would take Jacob's advice and try to meet some of the local people, but the question was, how best to do it? He reasoned that probably the best way was to start with the last thing the man had recommended: attend some of the church services.

He realized that with him being the outsider, most of the people probably knew a lot more about him already than he knew about any of them. He would go see Reverend Pritts, pastor of Old Bethel Church, but instead of going by the pastor's house, he would call and see if he could meet him at his office in the church.

When Reverend Pritts answered the phone, Wesley was a bit taken back because he expected the secretary to answer, but he explained who he was, and did in fact tell him that he had talked to Jacob Grant. Reverend Pritts just said, "Oh, yeah, Jacob Grant, an interesting personality," then he said he would enjoy meeting him personally, and they set a time of 10:00 a.m. the next day.

The meeting went exceptionally well, and the two of them hit it off immediately, even though some of their religious beliefs were probably a good deal apart. Reverend Pritts came up with a great idea; he suggested that at this Sunday's service, he would announce that they were going to have a surprise speaker at the Wednesday night service. He would not say whom it was going to be, but he was sure they would find him interesting, and if the congregation wanted to know, they would have to attend that service. The Wednesday night service attendance was only mediocre and he thought this might serve to bring out a large gathering.

Wesley agreed with the suggestion.

The church secretary may have leaked her suspicions since she was the one that had actually showed Wesley to Reverend Pritts's office, but if so, it worked. On this Wednesday evening, the church was nearly as full as it was for the normal Sunday service.

The Reverend Pritts was a dynamic speaker with a good sense of humor and before he started the service, he made some announcements. Then he said, "I am really pleased to see such a large crowd here this evening. It is too bad that we don't have some building project in progress that we could ask for donations. We could probably pay it all off with the offering tonight."

The congregation laughed.

He continued, "I would like to meet with the Elders immediately after the service to discuss giving tonight's offering to missions. I have also asked our guest speaker to stay in my study and review some of our doctrinal videos until time for tonight's lesson."

Again there was some laughter among those congregants who apparently did know who the speaker was going to be.

The Wednesday evening service used an abbreviated format so more time could be spent on the lesson. Normally it began with prayers, a hymn and scripture reading related to the lesson.

After the hymn had been sung, Reverend Pritts addressed the congregation and said, "The scripture for tonight was to be taken from the book of Daniel in our ongoing study of that portion of God's word, but instead, I want to read a couple of verses from Romans, chapter 10, beginning with verse 10 wherein it is written: 'For with the heart man believeth unto righteousness; and with the mouth confession is made unto salvation. For the scripture saith, Whosoever believeth on him shall not be ashamed. For there is no difference between the Jew and the Greek: for the same Lord over all is rich unto all that call upon him. For whosoever shall call upon the name of the Lord shall be saved.'

"Now I chose these verses for a very good reason, Reverend Pritts continued. Paul is making a point. The people to whom he was speaking were sure to be taken back by this statement. They knew there was considerable difference between the Jews and the Greeks of that day.

"The way they lived their everyday life, the food they ate, just about everything you could think of with reference to these two groups was different. Paul is reminding them that in the eyes of the Lord there are no differences. If Paul were talking to us this evening, he would perhaps paraphrase what he had said and state it in this manner, 'there is no difference between Baptist and Presbyterian, between Lutheran and Methodist, between you here this evening and Catholics, for if any of you call upon the name of the Lord you shall be saved.'

"I would like to just share a short story with you and then we will hear from our guest speaker. This is his cue to turn off the indoctrination videos and come on down."

Again there was laughter from the congregation.

"Several months ago I read a story about one of the founders of a protestant denomination, and it recalled a dream he had. In the dream, he is outside the gates of heaven and is speaking to the keeper of the keys, and he asks if there are any Methodists in there and the answer is no. He asks if there are any Episcopalians there, and again the answer is no. And he continues, Baptist? No. Catholics? No. Lutherans? No. This goes on for a while and finally he asks, who is in there, and the answer comes back, only Believers.

"I see that our guest has arrived at the back portals of out sanctuary, so I am going to relinquish this spot to him. I could introduce him, but I feel he can accomplish that better, so let me just say, "welcome to Old Bethel Church, Reverend Father Donaldson."

Father Wesley Donaldson walked down the center aisle, but did not enter the chancel area. Reverend Pritts met him there. The two men of God shook hands and then Reverend Pritts sat down in the first pew. Father Donaldson had previously been given a lapel microphone that he now switched on.

He was looking at the small device clipped to his lapel to find the on-off switch and without looking at the group of people in front of him, he said, "As you know, Roman Catholic Priests do not have wives, so a lot of times when I am by myself, I like to talk out loud. While I was sitting upstairs in the Pastor's study, I was just praying that Reverend Pritts hadn't given me a device with the on-off switch reversed."

The congregants laughed, and he now raised his head, looked at them, smiled and said, "Ah! Thank God he did not." Again there was laughter.

"Thank you Reverend Pritts, and I am truly thankful to you all for permitting me to come here this evening. I understand that this Wednesday evening service is normally conducted in one of the larger classrooms, but Reverend Pritts was so confident of a large turnout that he asked me if I would be comfortable doing it in the main chapel. I told him I didn't mind, but since I don't know the protocol observed in the chancel area, I would like to do it from this point.

"First, let me go through the formal introduction of myself, although I am sure that a lot of you know about me. There are a few of you that I recognize, but I am still hesitant to call you by your name, lest I have you confused with someone else.

"My name is Wesley Donaldson and I am a Catholic Priest. Sometimes people will say I am a former Priest, or ex-Priest, and that doesn't bother me. Although within the church, it is generally considered once a Priest, always a Priest. There are rare exceptions of course, but I am not one of them. Technically, I am a Priest without a church and without a flock. I chose to take an extended sabbatical for personal reasons, but I still do a lot of church related work, mostly writing for my former diocese, which is in Youngstown, Ohio. As most of you probably know, I am the guy who is building the log house, ah, let me rephrase that, I am the guy who is having the log house built down over the bank at the top of the Barney Kreger Hill. Until it is ready for occupancy, which the builder guarantees me will be by the 10th of May, I am living in a small furnished apartment in Somerset. My household furnishings are in storage in Youngstown, Ohio.

"Now, for the reason I am here this evening. I recently men a man who was born and raised in this area and he told me I needed to meet and get to know my neighbors. He is a man whom some of you know, and who I just met less than two weeks ago. He was born in Hexabarger. See, I know a little about the area already. My German is fairly good, so I did figure out what the name means, although I don't know how it came about.

The man I am referring to told me he would enlighten me on the subject the next time we met. Anyway, as I was saying, he was born here, went to school here and according to him, attended church here when it was a small wooden structure across the road. He has a lot of family buried in the cemetery across the road over there. He doesn't live here now, hasn't for a long time, but last fall his wife passed away and she too is buried across the way. He told me he still has a lot of relatives living in the area and a lot of old friends. By now, of course, some of you probably know I am talking about Jacob Grant.

"Our meeting happened like this. I was sitting on my stone bench just below the road, and above from where the house I am having built is located. Some of you may have noticed it. I was watching the men put the roofing shingles on when Jacob drove by. He saw the construction and stopped to take a better look. We met and got to talking, and over the course of the next hour we discussed a myriad of subjects. It was, without a doubt, one of the most informative and interesting first encounters I have ever had. Unfortunately, he had very little time; he came up to plant some flowers on his wife's grave and was returning to Florida the next morning. However, I heard from him when he got back and he told me he started back the same day. He spent the night in Wytheville, Virginia before continuing the next morning. Anyway, before we parted he gave me some unsolicited advice, and I emphasize, *unsolicited*. He told me to get to know the people and the area. He knew that much of our getting to know each other would center around this church and this congregation. He also knew that because of my being Catholic, of which I am probably the only one in the valley, there was the possibility for misunderstandings or suspicions that should not be. Having only talked with him for a little over an hour, I am not sure how religious of a man he is, but I felt very comfortable with him and accepted his advice. Well, not all of it, because he also told me to walk some of the backwoods trails, then he cautioned me about rattlesnakes and momma black bears with young cubs, so I haven't worked up my courage to do much of that yet."

Again there was some laughter.

"Just before he left, he said to me that he didn't think God would hold it against either of us if we got together to discuss his word. He had smiled when he told me we should stick with the basics and not discuss doctrinal matters. That is why when I was waiting upstairs I put on the video of the children's Christmas program, and not the doctrinal videos that Reverend Pritts spoke about."

"Oh! I love it," Reverend Pritts said with a laugh and the congregation agreed.

"As I mentioned, I am not sure of Jacob's religious beliefs, but I think he is fairly devout without being a denominationalist. In other words, I don't think he wanted me to try to convert this congregation, and vice versa."

Again there was slight laughter.

"He felt we could study God's word together, and I would enjoy that if you see it in your hearts to accept me without feeling uncomfortable. And to put you a bit at ease, let me say this, I know that Protestants often feel uncomfortable calling a Priest 'Father,' and I prefer if you don't. I prefer to be called by the name that my mother gave me, Wesley, which Jacob told me made him think I was a Methodist. Or if the younger people wish to defer to my age, then it is Mr. Donaldson.

" You do not need to give me your answer on that, but I make my case in good 'Paulinian' fashion. Reverend Pritts used Paul's writings to the Romans. I would like to quote from 1st Corinthians, 12:4-6: 'There are different kinds of gifts, but the same Spirit. There are different kinds of service, but the same Lord. There are different kinds of working, but the same God works all of them in all men.'"

"Praise the Lord on that," Reverend Pritts added.

An offering was taken, two verses of another hymn were sung and the Benediction said. The congregation waited until Wesley and Reverend Pritts had walked down the isle and stood by the doors to the chancel, and then everyone filed out.

By the handshakes and comments, Wesley thought that it had gone quite well. He knew there would be some who had doubts, or at least were a bit apprehensive, but he would try very hard to do his part. He would continue to attend Mass in Somerset, and figured the Wednesday service was a good place to start here.

Chapter 10

By the middle of May the house was complete and ready for occupancy. So Wesley drove out to Youngstown and rented a U-Haul truck to bring his belongings back to the new house.

As he had mentioned to the people at the church, as a Priest he did not have a lot of his own personal furnishings, but he had inherited his mother's things. Some of it he had given to the St. Vincent De Paul Society, but some, mostly her personal things and a few pieces of her favorite furniture, he could not depart with. It would now come in handy, as the new house was much larger than his previous apartment had been.

He had mentioned to Reverend Pritts that he planned to leave for Youngstown on Friday evening. Some people from his old Parish had volunteered to help load the furniture and his belongs on the truck. He would stay for Sunday Mass, as Father Broderick had insisted when they spoke earlier in the week, and he could visit with some old friends and then drive back Monday afternoon.

After Wesley had left, Reverend Pritts placed a call to Youngstown, Ohio. He called just to ask if someone would be so kind as to let them know on Monday when Wesley left to return to Pennsylvania. He got in touch with the church secretary, and after he mentioned briefly to her what he wanted, she let him speak with the parish Priest, Father Broderick. He wound up talking to the Priest on the other end of the line for at least twenty minutes.

Father Broderick told him that Wesley was dearly missed by many of the people in the congregation, especially some of the young people who felt they could talk to him with such ease. Even though he was now fifty years old, many of the young people still saw him as a peer, or close to it.

Reverend Pritts told him about the meeting in his church and how it came about. That he had already attended one more regular Wednesday night service and they all seemed quite at ease with each other.

Father Broderick on the other end said that did not surprise him, and they should make use of his talents, as he is a very intelligent man. He knew of no one else whose knowledge of the Bible came even close to matching his. Then he added somewhat reluctantly, "He is also a very sensitive individual, and very dedicated to his cause. I suppose that is why he asked for an indefinite sabbatical after the death of his mother. Some of the older, or more conservative priests, and even a few Bishops, consider him a bit of a renegade, but he isn't. He is very true to his calling and his vows. He wanted to see the church grow and he knew that some things had to change if that was to happen. He wanted the young people to be more involved, and if you looked at all the churches in this diocese and surrounding dioceses, you could see that the programs he had set in motion in this parish were bearing fruit. But the church hierarchy didn't necessarily see it that way, and I guess he felt it better to step aside for a while. I have talked to our Bishop about him and he too was sad to see him go, but he himself had felt pressure from a higher source. I know that Father Donaldson left with a heavy burden on his heart, so that is why I am so glad to see that he is fitting in there and seems to be handling it well. I worried about that, but now I will just say that our parish loss is your community's gain. I also hope that the church where he attends Mass will recognize what they have."

At one thirty on Monday afternoon, the church secretary in Youngstown called Reverend Pritts to say that Father Donaldson and Father Broderick had just finished lunch and he was now on his way. Reverend Pritts estimated that should put him back here at a little after 4 p.m.

When Wesley arrived back at the house and came down his driveway, he was surprised to see five cars and about fifteen people waiting for him. He recognized all of them from the church. Some of the ladies had spread a tablecloth on the picnic table he had set up under the old black walnut tree and it was covered with dishes of food. His new neighbors had arrived about a half hour before he had, and they were there to help him unload the truck.

"Wow, this is so great to see you all here, but how did you know when I would get back?"

Sheldon Kemp, who was a long distance truck driver was the first to speak. He said, "We put a GlobalTrax in your car, knew exactly where you were every minute you were gone."

"Did you really?"

"Don't believe him," Ginny Kemp said. "However, I put a secret one in his truck to make sure he doesn't stop at unauthorized 'girlie' truck stops, and he hasn't found it yet."

Everyone laughed.

"Truth of the matter is," Ginny continued, "Reverend Pritts just made a phone call to your old church and they let us know when you left."

His new neighbors had rolled up the back door of the U-Haul and were now starting to help unload the truck. Wesley stood by the door directing them with their load to the respective rooms where the furniture and boxes were to go. Later, he could take his time to arrange one room at a time.

After everything was off of the truck and in the house, Helen King called for attention. She said, "It is time to eat, but before we do, our own singing lark, Bethany Larkins, has asked to sing a song. After that, Jake Grayson will say grace and then we can eat.

"Bethany."

"Mr. Donaldson, we are very pleased to welcome you to this area. We are sure ours will be a great and lasting friendship. The song I want to sing is titled, 'Oh, Blest the House,'" Bethany said, "and it is very special to me, because my mother sang it when I was a young girl of eight. Friends had given us a house warming party shortly after we moved into our new house and she sang this song. I have paraphrased a couple of places; I hope you don't mind Mr. Donaldson."

"I am sure I won't young lady," he replied.

In a pure soprano voice, without accompaniment, and what must be angelic tones, Bethany began.

Oh, blest the house, what e'er befall,
Where Jesus Christ is All in All!
For if he were not dwelling there,

How dark and poor and void it were!
Oh, blest that house were faith is found,
And all in charity abound
To trust their God and serve him still
And do in all, his holy will!
Oh! Blest that house; it prospers well!
In peace and joy, therein I dwell,
And in my heart's desire is shown
How richly God can bless his own.
Then here will I with you today
A solemn covenant make and say:
Though all the world forsake his Word,
My house and I will serve the Lord.

There was complete silence when Bethany finished the song. Wesley, somewhat astounded, simply nodded his head.

Finally Jake Grayson spoke, "After something as beautiful as that, do you think God will hear my humble words?" he asked. And then he said, "Let us pray."

When Jake had finished his prayer, all responded with the appropriate, "Amen." Then Helen said, "Okay, everybody, help yourself. There is plenty of pop in the cooler over by the stairs and iced tea in the pitchers on the third step. Sorry, no coffee."

"Oh, listen," Wesley said, "I am a big coffee drinker, and would be more that glad to put on a pot for anyone who would like some."

"Well, I see that Helen did bring some of her famous carrot cake," Jim Trent replied, and I think I would prefer coffee with mine instead of iced tea, so if you don't mind, Wesley."

"No problem, and I think you are right on that score, coffee will go better than iced tea or soda with that cake."

"Do you need any help Mr. Donaldson?" Bethany asked.

"Not in making the coffee, but if you would be so kind, you can help with a tray to bring cups, sugar and creamer."

Inside the kitchen, Wesley gave Bethany a tray and showed her were the sugar and creamer was. "Since my good cups are still some where in a box, I wonder if we can make do with styrofoam?" he asked.

"I am sure the folks will understand," Bethany answered.

Wesley was within inches of her now and he couldn't help notice a very bad bruise on her left cheek, although she had apparently tried to hide it with makeup. He almost asked her what happened, but then reconsidered.

While Wesley was making the Coffee, he said, "Bethany, you have a beautiful voice, and the way you sang that song, it was almost angelic. I was truly awe-struck."

"Thank you Mr. Donaldson. I am glad you liked it."

"I don't think I have ever heard it before. Where did you get it, and do you have the words for it printed down that I might have a copy?"

"Sure, I can get you a copy of the words and the music. My parents are Lutheran and it is in the hymnal they use in their church. I sang in the choir there before Carl and I moved back here. The choir director gave me a soft leather bound copy as a going away present."

"So you are not from around here?'

"My home is Independence, Missouri. Carl is from here. He teaches history and is also the coach for the wrestling team at Rockwood. We met while we were both attending college.

"I have an uncle named Carl. Is your husband Carl here this evening?"

"No."

"I don't suppose I have to ask if you sing in the choir at Old Bethel Church," Wesley said.

"Yes, I do. music is one of my great loves," she said.

"I certainly can understand that, and you do it so well.

"Thank you. I hope some day to get my masters degree and teach music, but that seems such a long way off right now," Bethany said.

Then before Wesley could say anything, she changed the subject. "I wanted to ask you, is there anything else I can call you? I can't call you Father, but Wesley is too informal, and Mr. Donaldson sound so cold. Is it proper to call a Priest, Reverend? I know it means a member of the clergy, it is not a denominational term, and technically you are still a member of the clergy, am I right?"

"You are right, and if you so desire, you may address me as Reverend, but what about Reverend Pritts?"

"I generally just call him 'Pastor.'"

"Okay, sounds like there is no conflict. It looks like the coffee is ready, so, shall we go?"

"Okay, and maybe we can talk some more some time soon," she said, and they started down the steps.

"Yes, Bethany, I would enjoy talking to you some more."

At the bottom of the stairs, Jake Grayson stood talking to Reverend Pritts about nothing in particular. "If I might interrupt," Wesley said, "Jake, I am sure God heard those humble words. You have the voice and the delivery that some of the tele-evangelists would probably die for, as the saying goes."

"He certainly can make you say a few 'Amens' can't he," Reverend Pritts replied.

"My mother says I got it from my grandfather Mitchell," Jake said. "The way I see it, if that is so, it must have been a talent God gave Grandpa, and then let him pass it on."

Then Wesley said with out thinking, and regretted it immediately, "Has Reverend Pritts ever told you that maybe you should study for the ministry?"

"Yes, he has, but I don't think that is in the scheme of things," was Jakes reply.

Wesley knew he had spoken out of turn and quickly changed the subject. "Is Jake your given name or is it short for Jacob?"

"No sir, Jake is my given name. I was named for my Grandfather whose name was Jacob Mitchell, but everyone just knew him as Jake. So when I was born, my mother was going to name me Jacob, but she reasoned that everyone would call me Jake anyway, so she might just as well name me Jake. Until Granddad died, everyone called me 'little Jake,' even though I was two inches taller than he when he died."

Jake said he would have to leave soon to go to work so he was going to have some cake and a cup of coffee, and then excused himself from their company.

Jake was the first to leave, but he did come by and shook Wesley's hand and again officially welcomed him to the area. The rest of the people took a cue from Jake and one by one they left, but they all came by and shook Wesley's hand and like Jake, officially welcomed him to the area. Several of the ladies offered their help in getting the house in order, but Wesley declined saying he would take his time and it would help him keep busy when he wasn't writing, or trying to learn all the back roads.

Reverend and Mrs. Pritts were the last to leave. They stood and talked for a few minutes and Wesley said, "You have some remarkable talent in your congregation, Reverend Pritts."

"Yes, the Lord has bestowed some good talent upon us, but he has also given us some challenges. Now is not the time to discuss that, but I am sure we will talk many times hence."

"I am sure we will and I certainly look forward to it."

"Don't want to commit you to anything, but we would like to see you at the Wednesday evening service if you can make it."

"Thanks for the invitation, I will try and make it."

When the Reverend and Mrs. Pritts had left, Wesley pulled his car into the garage, and then instead of going into the house from the garage, he pressed the button to close the garage door and walked outside. The evening had a bit of a chill to it and he wished he had a sweater, but if he went to get one, he knew this moment, what ever it was, would fade away. It had been a wonderful evening, but there were a couple of things that made him uneasy, and he couldn't quite put his finger on what it was. Especially with Reverend Pritts's last comment. It was almost like he wanted to say something more, but then decided against it.

He walked below the house and across the yard toward where, according to Jacob, the old barn had stood, and it was here where he said the hopper path passed by.

It was the night of the full moon, and he could just now see the yellow orb climbing above the trees across the valley. The light it provided was sufficient for him to see a rabbit sitting on the path just a few paces ahead so he stopped. He knew that even if Jacob's rabbit, the one he could not shoot, didn't get caught by a less compassionate hunter, it was certainly dead by now, but perhaps this was one of it's descendants, so he turned and walked back to the house. The momentary feeling of uneasiness that he had experienced had now left him.

He climbed the stairs to the lower porch, turned and leaned against the post by the banister. He looked out across the rest of the valley now bathed in silvery moonlight. He stood for a moment in reverent silence, then turned and went into the house.

He closed and locked the latch on the screen door, but left the interior door open to let in the cool spring breezes. He then went into the room he decided would be his temporary office until everything in the basement was finished. The men had put his desk in here but it was covered with boxes of papers, files, and books. His desktop computers were also here, but he would have to do a lot of organizing before he set them up. He decided, though, that this is where he would begin in getting the house organized. Well, maybe the kitchen, and then here. But at the moment he wanted to send an e-mail so he went back to his car, retrieved his briefcase and laptop, took it to the kitchen counter and opened it up.

Since Jacob had returned to Florida, they had exchanged a couple of short e-mails. Jacob had sent a brief one liner saying he had arrived back safely at 10:00 p.m. Then he had sent one to Jacob telling him that Reverend Pritts had invited him to a Wednesday night service as a get acquainted time, and did he have any advice. He didn't receive an answer until after that Wednesday evening service was past, but then he remembered that Jacob had said he didn't always check his e-mail every day.

When he did receive a reply it said, "Whoops! Sorry, this being Thursday, I guess I am too late to give you advice. I am sure you did fine without it. Let me know. Also, how is the house coming along?" Jacob.

He had sent an answer saying that the house was ready for occupancy, and that he was planning to go to Ohio next weekend to get all his household goods and other belongings. Was he still planning to come up in July?

He had not received an answer to this and he was a little worried since it had been ten days. He thought to himself that maybe the letter he was about to compose would be futile, since he would need, well not necessarily need, but like to have an answer before Wednesday. He decided he would write anyway.

From: wesdon31@aol.com
To: jbgrant@gulfcoast.com
Subj: Advice

Jacob,
I haven't received an answer to my last e-mail, but am sending this in hopes that you read it before Wednesday. But first let me say, I went to Ohio and picked up all my earthly belongings and brought them back here

A Place Called Hexie

today. When I arrived there was a group from the Old Bethel Church here to help me unload the truck. The ladies brought some really delicious food and when the truck was unloaded, we had some good fellowship.

Now for my dilemma. Reverend Pritts asked me if I planned to attend the Wednesday evening service. I did not give him a specific answer because I know they are studying the book of Daniel, and I also know that many churches have a different view of apocalyptic writings than the Catholics have. Would you have any idea of what their stand is, and can you give me any advice?

Here is hoping all is well on your end.

Your friend,
Wesley

97

Chapter 11

The previous day had been a long one, what with the drive from Youngstown and the events of last evening, so he slept late the next morning. Rising at about 8:30, he put on a pot of coffee, dug through a box for the toaster, got two slices of bread from the bag the ladies had left from the previous evening, and turned on the computer. He clicked on to his internet provider and checked his mail. Much to his surprise, but pleasantly so, there was an answer from Jacob to his letter of the previous evening.

> From: jbgrant@gulfcoast.com
> To: wesdon31@aol.com
> Subj: Advice:

Wesley,

My brother once told me it was bad manners not to answer your e-mail promptly. Just so you know that our parents didn't raise any of their eight children to have bad manners, I thought I had better tell you; I was out of town for the past two weeks. Went first to Annapolis, Maryland to see my granddaughter Eliana. She is a second year midshipman at the Naval Academy and they are getting ready to take their first cruise. Didn't get to spend as much time with her as I would have liked, because they keep them pretty busy. From there, I went down to Gainesville, Florida, where my grandson David is a third year law student at the University of Florida. He had just finished exams, so he had a bit more time to spare than his sister. He is planning to stay there this summer to take some summer classes and he got a part time job in a law office. He realizes he will be a "gopher," but it will give him a little bit of a view of what he is getting into. They both are such intelligent young adults. Get it from their grandfather I assume. Ha! Ha! From there I went to see my brother and his wife for a day, and then headed home. Decided to take the scenic route along the coast, and spent the night in Perry. Got up late, spent about two hours in Apalachicola for lunch; had some of their famous oysters on the half shell. Stopped in Destin and walked the beach for a bit and had a sandwich. Got home at about 10:30 p.m., checked my e-mail and found a couple of messages from you.

Glad that you got moved in to the house, and was not surprised to hear that you had some unexpected help. As for the food, if my memory serves me correctly, and I know it does, there are some pretty good cooks around there and they don't do the "lite" bit. You eat too much of that food and you won't be able to walk up your driveway any better than I did.

Now, as for advice; you are asking someone who has attended a Lutheran church for the past thirty years to tell you something about a church that he hasn't attended except once every couple of years over the past fifty years. And what's more, I don't know your position on apocalyptic and pseudonymous writings, so I can only assume that the Catholic views are somewhat similar to those of the Lutherans.

I have found that many of the people in religious study groups are somewhat ignorant of the historical facts as related to the time and people they are studying. Or maybe they just choose to ignore them. Some of this, I suppose, is the fault of the Church leadership, in that they believe, if you put it in to its true historical context, it will diminish the religious significance. Nothing could be further from the truth; however, many still refuse to cross that bridge. But that is a story for another soapbox dissertation at another time.

My advice, for what it is worth, would be to play it by ear, as the old cliché goes. Remember, you will see the accounts in Daniel 1-6 and understand them within the history of what is outlined in 1 Maccabees. The people at New Old Bethel do not have that book in their Bible and may know very little about the oppression brought upon the Jews by Antiochus IV Epiphanes. However, I think a little knowledge of that time is necessary if they are to understand what the writer of Daniel is saying. Conceding that fact, I would still walk there cautiously. If you have a copy of the works of Josephus, and I am quite sure you must, I would take that along as a reference guide and use it instead of your Catholic Bible. I am sure you get my gist.

On a different note, I wasn't planning to come to PA again until the family reunions in July, but I had an e-mail from my nephew in Ohio, and he said his mother, my sister Vadna, is not doing too well. I plan to go up some time next week to see her. I will probably leave here early Monday morning. She lives in Warren, Ohio, so I will go through Kentucky and see my grandkids, Sarah and Nathan. Of course I will see their parents also. That is my daughter Sylvie and son-in-law Kevin. Anyway, I thought I would just make a big loop and swing through Somerset on my return. Say hello to my other sisters, see how they are, and let them know how Vadna is doing. Will call you from the motel and invite myself down for breakfast. That will most likely be on Saturday. If you have something else planned, let me know by priority e-mail. Maybe you will have an hour or so to spare and we can ride around some of the back roads. I will give you a brief lesson in "who, where, what and when."

Til later, your friend and advisor Ha! Ha!
Jacob

From:	wesdon31@aol.com
To:	jbgrant@gulfcoast.com
Subj:	Gratitude

Thanks for the advice as requested, and will be honored to have you come for breakfast. No schedule problem with me. Look forward to touring the hills under your guidance.

Your friend,
Wesley

PS. When you have time, could you give me a little of the history of the Church?

Wesley cleaned off the table in the kitchen and put the dishes in the dishwasher. Receiving the e-mails from his new friend Jacob had left him in a relaxed mood. He decided that he would work a few hours putting the furniture and his belongings in a more orderly fashion. He would start at the front bedroom and work his way back. He planned to put most of his mother's furniture in this room, and he would designate it as the guest bedroom. He would work until about noon, make a sandwich, grab a bottle of water, and perhaps take a walk on one of the trails that Jacob had suggested. He would also get some advice so he didn't get lost and didn't stumble into any of the snares Jacob had cautioned him about.

The men from the church, who had helped unload the truck, had placed all his mother's bedroom furniture in this front room. All he really needed to do was place the dresser, the chest of drawers and the night stand where he wanted them and then set up his mother's old four-poster bed.

After he had everything positioned where he wanted it, he started to carry in the few boxes that contained most of her very personal belongings. He didn't plan on unpacking them at this time, perhaps not until some cold winter evening when he had nothing else to do. He carried in one large cardboard box that looked quite old. The lettering on the side showed it was from a moving and storage company, but the lettering had faded over the years, and the flaps were curled up at the corners. He had removed it from the closet in his mother's bedroom with out opening it and planned to put it in the closet until later. He did know it contained some of his mother's photo albums and other memorabilia, much of it no doubt about him. He wasn't so vain that he had to peruse it at this time. He started to set it on top of the dresser to get a better grip, and then put it on the shelf in the closet, but when he did so, the old tape across the bottom flaps gave way and all the contents spilled onto the floor.

He went to his temporary office and searched through the boxes stacked all around searching for some wide cellophane tape to repair the box. Finding it without too much problem, he went back to the bedroom, turned the box upside down and re-taped the flaps. He then started to put the things back into the box, and as he knew, it had held a lot of photo albums, and other pictures, and cards. When the contents spilled out they also spread out on the floor. He picked up one large album and under it he found a Bible. It was not the Bible that his mother normally used; he had already placed that one on the nightstand that was on the side of the bed where she always slept, and where she kept it.

He picked up the Bible and noticed the gold lettering on the front; it read, "Holy Bible," and in smaller letters, "King James Version." This took him back a bit, because he knew his mother had converted to Catholicism shortly after she married. It seemed to him in that instant that it had never been used. He opened the cover and the first inside page. There on the right hand page he read, "The Holy Bible," under that was a scroll works and then the words:

CONTAINING THE
OLD and NEW TESTAMENTS
IN THE

KING JAMES VERSION
RED LETTER EDITION
CRUSADE BIBLE PUBLISHERS, INC.
Nashville, Tennessee

He turned the next page and again on the right hand page were the words :

Presented to.

Below that it said:

To: *Karin Nelson*
By: *Reverend Stanley Whitmire, First Methodist Church,*
Date: *September 20, 1953*
For: *On the occasion of the birth of your son. May the Grace of our Lord and Savior, Jesus Christ be with the two of you forever and ever.*

He turned to the next page, which was for the marriage information. It was blank. Likewise, the next two pages, which were titled: Husband's Genealogy and Wife's Genealogy. On the next page it was titled: Our Children. There was one entry, dated September 20, 1953 for Wesley Nelson.

He fanned through the pages and it opened to Psalms 67 and 68 where a letter had been placed. Underlined in red was verse 5, Psalms 68. He read it: *A father of the fatherless, and a judge of the widows, is God in his holy habitation.*

Then he read the addresses on the envelope. The return address was from: *Karin Nelson, 384 West Hinton Street, Warren, Ohio.* It was addressed to: *Jacob Grant, RFD1, Markleton, Penna.*

He held the letter in his hands and stared at it for a long time. He began to shake. He could not think; he could not make his mind focus. What did it mean? Jacob had told him that he had written to Karin several times, but had only received one letter in return. Apparently she had answered a second letter, but for some reason she had decided not to send it. He wondered when it was placed there. Just a rapid fire of short thoughts raced through his mind as he tried to bring himself back to the reality of the moment. Almost without thinking at all, he rose and took the letter with him to his office. He sat down in the chair by his desk and searched for a letter opener. When he finally found one, he inserted the point into the slightly loose end of the flap at one corner. Then he discovered, that he could not force himself to open it. He did not know what he would find and he didn't know if he could accept it after he read it. Then again, maybe it was nothing. Perhaps it was just her telling Jacob that she had found someone who made her happy and she would not be writing anymore, but she would always remember him as a friend. Maybe it would answer some question he had occasionally wondered about but never asked. Things his mother never volunteered.

Then another thought possessed him, it was addressed to Jacob, so rightly it belonged to him, or did it? His mother had addressed it to Jacob, but she had never put a stamp on it, and for some reason she chose not to send it to him. Why?

From a legal point of few he imagined it belonged as much to him as to Jacob, or even more so, but the legality of it was not the important thing right now. The important thing was what to do about it, and the only thing he could resolve at this time was to put it back where he found it.

He went back to the bedroom and started to put the contents on the floor back into the repaired box. Although he had moved some of the contents, he reasoned that the Bible had been in the very bottom, so that is where he placed it. The unopened letter, he again placed between the pages containing Psalms 67 and 68. Everything else was neatly packed back in as though it had never been disturbed. When he finished, he folded the flaps so they were locked in place. He then placed the box on the top shelf of the closet and closed the door.

He decided he would start his walk earlier than he had planned. He didn't feel like making a sandwich. He just wanted to get started so he could clear his mind. However, his better judgment overruled him and he made a sandwich, took a small bag of dried fruit and nuts, and a bottle of water and threw them in a small backpack. At the last minute, he decided he would take his digital camera. He checked the battery, it was good, and he put it in the bag with the food and water, and slipped it onto his back. He walked out onto the lower porch, and then thought it might not be a bad idea to also take his cell phone just in case he got lost.

Chapter 12

$\mathcal{I}$t was only about 10:30 when Wesley walked up the driveway from his house that followed the fence that separated his property from that of Dwight Lanning. Inside the fence was a stand of trees for about fifty feet, and then it opened up on a cleared area. He looked across the very hilly pasture field where a large number of Holstein milk cows were grazing, having moved some distance from the barn where they had been released after the morning milking. He noticed a lot of large rocks jutting out of the side of the sloped field and reasoned that this field was probably never used for anything except pasture. When he reached the Y in the road, he took the dirt road that was designated Lemmon Road. It was just a short distance to the house and barn. Above the barn, he saw the elder Mr. Lanning parking a John Deere tractor by the shed across the road.

"Hi there," Wesley called.

"Hello," Dwight Lanning returned. "Did you get all moved in?" he asked. And without waiting for a reply he said, "Manda and I came back from town last eve and saw some of the people waiting for you to return. We assumed you had enough help, and at our age, we would just get in the way, but as I have said before, if there is anything we can help you with, don't be afraid to ask."

"Thank you for that offer, and I will certainly call on you if there is anything I need. Some of the people from Old Bethel Church were waiting for me and they helped get everything moved in and even fed me."

"Yeah, it is a pretty good bunch of people down in this hollow," Dwight replied. "One or two slightly off the smooth path, but all in all, a pretty good bunch."

"Tell me Dwight, if I continue down this road, where will I come out?"

"Well, if you stay strictly on the road, you are going to make a small loop and come back out on the Humbert road by Nolan Gant and Roger Knight. This is a Township road and they only maintain it for a little ways past where our son and his family live. Shortly after that you will cross the boundary between our farm and that of Roger Knight. There are no other houses back in there, and since Roger uses the main road, he has placed a gate across the road with a "Do Not Enter" sign. I suppose that is a good idea since it keeps people from driving back there at night and dumping their trash. You wouldn't believe what some people will dump along the side of the road if they think no one will see them."

"Actually, Dwight, I would believe it. It is the same thing in Youngstown. The city has to employ a full time inspector to get people to cleanup their own property."

"Yeah, I guess some people have no respect for their own property so they certainly aren't going to have any respect for other people's property. Any way Roger's parents bought the farm from Harry Nicklow's widow after his accidental death. They lived in the old house until they died and then Roger built a new house on the main road next to Nolan Gant. The old road comes out between their respective homes.

"A lot of people down in here owed a great deal to Roger's dad. The main road was pretty low on the priority list for being cleared of snow in the winter. Roger's dad had a snow plow built for the front of his John Deere tractor, and he always saw that the roads were made passable. I believe he did it all out of his own pocket.

" There used to be a trail that went down through the valley and came out on what is known as Smith Hollow, although most people now know it as Beaver Clevenger hollow. That trail is all grown over, but it did come out where the Kregar Road and the Coke Oven road meet. At that point, if you went up over the hill you would come out by the Scott Kregar farm. If you go straight, you come out at Humbert.

" I suppose you haven't been here long enough to know that there is no town of Humbert any more; hasn't been for over seventy years, but the locals still call it that. I don't know how ambitious you feel this morning, but clear to Humbert and back would be a pretty good walk."

"Well, I am getting a pretty early start, and I guess I will just play it by ear. I do know that Humbert hasn't been around for quite a few years. Let me ask you something else Dwight, are there any black bear down in that direction?"

Dwight gave a little laugh and then replied, "Personally, I haven't seen any for a long time, but there are some in the area. They roam around a good bit, and some people have had them raid their garbage cans, I wouldn't worry too much. If you stay on the road, I am sure you will not encounter any, and if you take the old trail, you would not be close to any of the rock ledges where they might have a den or resting place. You will eventually come to where Smith Run comes close to the trail, but there are no fish in it that far up so the only time any bears would go there would be for a drink and that would generally be in the evening. There are a lot of berries down in that region, but they are not ripe yet so they wouldn't be feeding there. So, like I said, I don't think there is anything to worry about."

"That is a bit reassuring," Wesley said. "I guess if I am going to make it down and back before dark, I had better get going, but I don't want to breach Roger Knight's no trespassing so will go a different route. Perhaps I will follow the path of the little stream below my house. Do you mind if I cut across your property a little farther out and go down over the hill to the run?"

"Be my guest, but let me warn you, that hill is very steep. Also, I am sure that Roger would not mind you crossing his property, but it is always better to check first," Dwight said. Then he continued, "following the little run may also be difficult, but at least you know for sure where you will come out."

"I certainly respect his privacy and security, and I will talk to him when I get a chance to meet him personally."

"Were you thinking about coming back the same way?" Dwight asked.

"I was thinking of going to Humbert, and then coming back via the road."

"That sounds like a good plan," Dwight said.

Wesley was just ready to depart when Manda Lanning came out on the front porch. "Good morning Wesley. Out for a walk are we?"

"Good morning Manda, and yes, I thought I would take a walk before I seriously got involved in getting the things in the house organized."

Manda left the porch and started up the path to where Wesley and her husband were standing talking.

"I can understand your postponing it a bit, but that is the problem with you being a Priest," she said.

"How is that, Manda?" Wesley asked with a smile. From the time he had first met Dwight and Manda, he had really liked the couple. Manda, was a bit outspoken, but had a great sense of humor, and he wondered how she maintained it living this far back in the quiet area of civilization.

"Well, if you weren't a Priest," she continued, "I know of a couple of ladies who might be at your house right now fighting to help you red it up," she replied.

"Red it up?" Wesley said with a look of puzzlement on his face.

"Careful now Wesley," Dwight cut in. "You are going to give yourself away as not being from here. 'Red up' is local dialect meaning to put everything in it's place. I probably know one of the ladies of whom my wife refers and she has a rather colorful country vocabulary. It probably bothers my wife more than anyone that you're are a Priest because she likes to play matchmaker."

"That is not true, Dwight Lanning," Manda replied.

Wesley figured this may be a good place to butt in so he said, "Okay, I will have to add 'red up' to my vocabulary." Then he replied to Manda, "You know what the other side of being a Priest is, don't you?"

"No, but I bet you are going to tell me."

"In seminary, they teach us to red up by ourselves."

"And do they teach you to cook?" Martha asked.

"Not really. I think they assume that your mother will take care of you until the ladies of the Parrish can bestow their cookbooks and favorite recipes upon you."

"So you can cook?"

"I am no gourmet cook, but I don't starve."

"It looks like you are on your way to check out the highways and the byways, mostly the latter, so I will tell you what, since Dwight and I didn't get a chance to help you move in last night, how about I make you a nice casserole for your supper this evening?"

"That would be very nice, but it certainly isn't necessary, Manda."

"I know. Say about six o'clock, provided a bear doesn't get you down there in the hollow," she said with a laugh.

"You had to say that didn't you, just after your husband was so reassuring that I would be okay, but six o'clock would be fine." He raised his right hand slightly, motioned with his index finger and started on his journey.

Then Dwight called after him, "Why don't you just come over here and eat with us and we can enjoy a little conversation?"

"Ah, let me take that on a little different tack, Manda can still make the casserole, but why don't the two of you come over to my place. We can eat out on the lower porch and then I can show you the house."

"I vote for that," Manda said. "That way you get to clean up the dishes."

"Okay, it is agreed," Wesley said, and this time he actually started to walk away.

Dwight and Manda had two sons.

Gordon the oldest, lived in the old George Romesburg house just outside of Kingwood. It had been completely remodeled some years earlier and sat just below the road overlooking a deep valley. There was a wraparound porch on the upper side and the north side, which faced Kingwood. The first time Wesley had seen it, he wondered why they hadn't continued the porch around to the lower side. From the lower side one could look out and see the long valley below and four distinct ranges of hills that represented four more valleys, or 'hollers' as he noticed some of the people here called them. He had stopped to view this spectacular series of hills and valleys the first time he was ever here. Once he got settled in, he planned to do seasonal shots using a wide-angle lens to capture the entire panorama. He knew that even with a wide-angle lens, he would have to take two or three shots and then combine them into one.

The youngest son, Curtis and his wife, had built a new house just around the first curve in the road from the original old house where his parents lived. It sat just above the road on a fairly steep bank and it overlooked the same valley as his house, but the elevation of theirs would be a couple hundred feet higher. It too had a porch that ran the entire length of the lower side. There was a huge, well-maintained yard surrounding the house, and flowers surrounded a lot of large rocks sticking out of the ground at various places. A significant number of trees were spared when the house was built, and to Wesley, the majority of them looked like Maples and some Ash.

As Wesley neared the house, he heard the unmistakable sound of a riding lawn mower. In driving around the area, he noticed that a lot of the country people had very large yards, this mostly made possible by the riding lawn mower.

As he approached the far end of the house, he saw the mower and the operator, Curtis's wife, as she started a swath down over the back end of the yard. She saw him and raised a gloved hand and waved. He waved back and continued on his walk.

The dirt road continued along the edge of the hill and at places there was no leeway between the edge of the road and a nearly vertical drop of several hundred feet. The road was level from left to right, not banked toward the hill, so he reasoned that in winter it could make for a dangerous situation if two cars had to pass.

Around the next curve sat another house on the right. It too was older construction, and although there was a mailbox out front, it didn't appear the house was continually occupied. Perhaps it was a weekend home or a hunting lodge.

There was another outbuilding associated with this last house, which might have served as a detached garage or some type of workshop and storage shed. It was in urgent need of repair. Beyond this building, the road curved right and moved away from the edge of the hill. It climbed slightly and was completely canopied by trees for about a thousand feet.

Before he got to that point he saw what looked like a good place to descend the hill. It was very steep, but there was not much underbrush so the descent was less difficult than he had expected. Coming back up would have been a completely different story.

When he finally got to the bottom of the ravine without too much trouble, he immediately came across the little run that started from a spring just below his house. He guessed he was now less than a half-mile down stream and the run was still not much more than a trickle, but he noticed now that the terrain was leveling out.

The location where he had built his house was Upper Turkeyfoot Township, and he knew that when he got to Humbert he would be in Lower Turkeyfoot Township, but he didn't know where the demarcation line was. When he had first heard these terms, Upper and Lower Turkeyfoot, he assumed it referred to a north-south relationship, but when he looked at a map, he saw that the two townships were east and west of each other. Then it dawned on him that it had to do with altitude, not geographical position. When you left Kingwood on the Humbert Road, you started a slow descent until you got to the position just above his house. Once you started down the Barney Kregar Hill, the descent was quite rapid for the next two miles until you hit the area known as Humbert. From there it was basically one long flat valley clear into Confluence.

As Dwight had mentioned, there was no longer a town of Humbert and hadn't been for many years, but he did not know the story. He supposed it was something Jacob would tell him, and if not, he would ask.

He had walked for approximately twenty minutes when he came upon a dead tree that had fallen across the run. He was just about to crawl over it when he detected the sound of rustling in the underbrush just ahead and to his right. A few yards back on the trail he had spotted some rock ledges further up on the slope. He had remembered that Dwight had said this might be where the black bear would have a den or resting place. His heart started to race for he just knew he was about to encounter a momma bear and her babies. He would try to keep his cool, but at the same time he would slowly turn and retreat the way he had come. The bear would see that he was no threat and would most likely not pursue him. As he started his retreat, he turned around, and sure enough, into the small clearing on the trail came a momma and babies, but it wasn't a bear, it was a doe and two fawns.

He couldn't detect any breeze, but he assumed he must be upwind because the big doe and her two offspring just stood looking down the trail. As quietly and as motionlessly as he could, he removed his backpack and retrieved his digital camera. He snapped several pictures before the trio started walking down along the run. Shortly they were out of sight, but since he had his backpack off he decided to eat a couple of handfuls of trail mix and take a sip from his water. He would give the deer time to get further away, and he assumed that at some point they would again go into the underbrush.

As he sat on the fallen tree eating the mixture of dried fruit and nuts, it suddenly dawned on him how quiet and peaceful it was. There was the occasionally 'tsk' sound of a squirrel, or a few notes from a songbird up in the trees, or a crow as it passed far over head going from one hill to the next. The air smelled cool and fresh.

He listened closely and could hear the sound of water flowing across the rocks. This he knew was the upper reach of Smith Run, It was making its way down the valley where it would meet with Laurel Hill Creek. Several miles down the valley at the small town of Confluence, Laurel Hill Creek and its larger sister, the Casselman, both would then join their still larger sister, the Youghiogheny. In its turn, the Youghiogheny would join the Monongahela at McKeesport. At Pittsburgh, the Mon, as most people who lived along the river called it, would be met by the Allegheny. The Allegheny formed in Potter County in the northern part of the state and flowed north into New York State. There it made a big loop and started south. In Warren County, Pennsylvania, there was a flood control dam, the Kinzua, that formed the Allegheny Reservoir. When the rivers met at Pittsburgh, they formed the Ohio. Other rivers would join the Ohio, but they would lose their identity at the point of juncture. But the Ohio too would lose its identity when at the small town of Cairo on the Kentucky and Missouri border, where it joined the mighty Mississippi. Eventually, this water that he could just barely hear crossing the rocks would flow past New Orleans, also known as the "Big Easy," but now remembered more for Hurricane Katrina that nearly wiped it out, and then out into the delta to become part of the Gulf of Mexico.

Close to here in this secluded spot, horse-drawn wagons had passed in earlier days, but none for many years; he savored the moment. There was no beeping of horns and rushing traffic, no smell of noxious fumes from cars and factories, no pushing and shoving by people, all in a hurry to get somewhere, but yet nowhere. He knew he would probably never miss Youngstown again as a place to live, some of his friends, yes, but the city living, never. Now for the first time he understood and appreciated why Jacob had said he always yearned to return.

Even wonderful moments must end, and when he thought of Jacob, he also remembered why he was here in the first place. He hadn't give the letter he had found in his mother's personal belongings any thought after he had started down the road towards where Dwight and Manda lived..

This walk, this new adventure had given him a feeling of euphoria. He had been at one with his world and his surroundings like never before in his life, but in a moment it was slightly dulled as he was brought back to reality.

He delved upon it in his mind for a few moments, and then resolved that he would not let it ruin the rest of his day. After all, it might be nothing, and regardless, there was no use worrying about it. He must remember his own lessons when he had counseled others; to worry was not a solution, it was only a wasteful expenditure of time and energy. Have faith in God and in your fellow man he would say.

He stuck the digital camera in the leg pocket of his pants so he could access it easily if a situation again presented itself. He then put the backpack over his shoulders and again started down the river trail.

Shortly after he had resumed his walk, he passed what looked like an old trail that ran perpendicular to the run. It was mostly overgrown, but he wondered where it went. If he had time when he got back to the house, he would call up terraserver.com or Google Earth on the web and see where it led. Undoubtedly this old abandoned trail ran past a farm on the other side of the hill, and then perhaps as far as Route 281.

He walked for about another five minutes and when he rounded the next bend in the trail he saw an open space just ahead. It was not cleared fields for farming, but he assumed that at one time, perhaps when the trail that came down this valley was still being used, these fields were also tilled.

He exited out of the underbrush by the run onto a passable dirt road. It was very narrow so that two cars would have a difficult time passing, but walking would, nevertheless, be easier. The trail had joined the road at a point where the road made a ninety-degree turn. To the right would take him up over the hill, which at a glance seemed very steep. One he would not like to undertake in the winter with his car. Today he would take the portion that continued on down the valley to Humbert, although he didn't know how far that was.

The road was level and it paralleled the river, or run as it was known here. The bed of the run was wider now and the water flowed on a solid rock bottom worn smooth over the ages. He wondered what the geological term for this stratum of rock was called.

For a moment he stood by the bank and leaned against a large old beech tree with its branches offering shade both on the road and over the water. He looked at the short thick trunk of the old tree and noticed it held the carving of many initials, most probably of lovers over the years. Beech trees were a favorite for this ritual because the bark was very smooth. The initials fairly far up the trunk were so distorted now by the growth of the tree over the years that they were undecipherable, but he noticed one set that was newer and still very readable. It was B.L. + C. L. inside a heart. He took his eyes away from the tree and again looked at the water rushing past him on its way to the Gulf of Mexico. He remembered a country and western song he had heard some years earlier. It was sung by Brad Paisley and had to do with two tear drops that joined on the river as it marched to the sea. One was a tear of happiness from a new bride, the other a tear of sadness from a previous suitor. In another verse, a young man sheds a tear of happiness upon receiving the word he has a new daughter, sitting close by an old man sheds a tear of sadness as he learns he has just lost his wife.

Wesley sat there and contemplated that for a moment. He wondered what tears had been shed in this valley over the past two hundred and some years. Then he enlarged his thought, how many and what tears had been shed in this valley ever since man first walked it. He knew that long before the earliest settlers came here, the Indians lived in these hills and valleys. Somewhere in a long lost grave, there is perhaps an Indian mother who shed tears of joy for a new baby, or tears of pain upon losing it to what ever. Perhaps she too sat by the rivers edge all alone and shed tears that fell into the rushing waters as they headed for their ultimate destination, the likes of which she could never imagine. Even for him, it was all too deep to contemplate at this time so Wesley brought his thoughts back to the present and continued down the road.

As he rounded a small bend in the road, he could see the roof of a house over the top of the high weeds and crab apple trees. It was just then that the quiet of the valley was shattered as he heard the voice of an angry man shouting invectives. He wasn't sure what to make of it so he paused for a second on the side of the road away from the river and out of view of the house. Momentarily, he heard a vehicle door slam, and then heard that vehicle spin up gravel as it backed out of the driveway onto the dirt road and head away from him. He moved back to the middle of the road just in time to see a red pickup truck crossing the small bridge over Smith Run a few hundred yards ahead. It went around a bend in the road and disappeared out of sight.

There were several more houses on the right hand side of the road but he didn't see any of the occupants. He continued walking and when he was almost opposite the house where the truck had just left, he saw a woman sitting on the top step of three that led onto the porch. She was bent over, her elbows resting on her legs and her face in her hands. He stayed on the road, but hollered to the lady, "Can I help you?"

She immediately raised her head and even from the distance he could see she had been crying, but moreover, he recognized her and she recognized him.

He asked, "Beth, are you alright?"

Her answer was immediate, but not what he had expected. She replied, "Please Reverend Donaldson, don't come up here."

"But Beth, what is wrong? Are you okay?"

"Yes, I am okay, it was just a misunderstanding between Carl and I, but please, as a friend, just go on. I will explain later."

"Okay," Wesley said, "I will honor your wish, but remember not long ago you asked if you could confide in me, and I said yes. So whenever you are ready, please don't be afraid. I will keep everything in strictest confidence."

"Thank you. I will," she said, and then got up and went into the house.

When she stood, Wesley could see that one sleeve of her dress was almost completely torn out. He knew this was more than just a misunderstanding. He got a flashback to when she helped him make the coffee at the house when he had brought his furniture and the people from the church were there to help. He remembered the bruise on her left cheek. He wanted so much to turn around and go back, but he had promised he would honor her wish. But if this situation was what he suspected it was, how could he live with it if something terrible happened to Bethany. He turned and started back, walked a few steps, then turned again and headed toward his original destination.

The serenity he had witnessed over the past hour and a half was now gone. He knew the rest of his walk would not be pleasurable. But it would provide a good way for him to sort through his thoughts. He thought that perhaps he should talk to Reverend Pritts, but then again he might not know anything. Perhaps that is why she had asked if she could talk to him. She knew he was a Priest, and as such, she could rely on him to keep her confidence, but most pastors in their role as counselors would do the same thing. If her husband was abusing her, she may be ashamed to talk about it to friends and acquaintances. Or maybe she was very much afraid of him finding out that she had mentioned it. He would have to be careful of what he said and how he approached the matter, but he knew for her sake that it had to be fast.

He picked up his pace to a fast walk like he did in Youngstown when he worked out and would walk a brisk five miles each morning before breakfast at six thirty. His mind and eyes were not attracted to much of the scenery the rest of the way down the valley, except for a large mound of gray clay that he assumed was the refuse from an old coal mine operation years earlier. Shortly after that he could see where this dirt road dead-ended into the Humbert-Kingwood road. Here at the end was where the town of Humbert once stood. It was all grown over and nothing marked its ever having been there.

He was almost to the end of the road of this hollow when he saw the red pickup coming down the paved road at a high rate of speed, brake sharply and turn onto the dirt road to go back the way it had previously come. He saw the driver look at him as he passed, and then heard the truck stop and back up until it was alongside him.

The man rolled down the window of the truck and stuck his head out looking directly at Wesley. "What are you doing nosing around down in here?" the man in the truck asked in a surly tone.

Normally Wesley would have tried to calm what might become an ugly situation by answering in a non-threatening tone, but what he had just seen and heard minutes earlier made him decide this might not be the time for pacification. He didn't think this adversary would accept it anyway, so he answered in kind. "I am just taking a walk, not that it is any of your business."

"I am making it my business, and I am telling you now to stay out of this hollow."

"According to what I know, this is public property upon which I tread so I will continue to walk it whenever I wish," Wesley answered in a slow and distinct manner.

"Yeah, and you may just get your ass stomped," the man in the truck replied.

"Listen, Mr. Larkins," and the man in the truck was a bit taken back when he heard Wesley call him by name, "You may be the bully in this hollow, but where I came from there were lots of bullies. Some who would eat you for lunch, so don't waste your breath spouting threats against me."

"How do you know my name?"

"Never mind," Wesley said, but the man was already opening the door of the pickup and getting out.

Wesley took a few steps backward, not out of fear, but allowing the man space to reconsider what he was about to do. He did not even remove the backpack from his shoulders, lest the other saw it as a sign of confrontation. He saw that Mr. Larkins was about his height, and he knew he was at least fifteen years his junior. Wesley also knew he taught physical education at the high school and was the wrestling coach. He was banking on him not knowing the martial arts as well as he. He had taught the martial arts for about fifteen years to young boys and girls in the neighborhoods surrounding his parish in Youngstown. He had given many demonstrations, but because his ability was legend in the Youngstown area, he never had to employ it in an actual case of self-defense. He realized that this might now be the time.

Mr. Larkins saw Wesley retreat a few steps and misread the meaning. He spread his arms and dropped them low as he went into a slight crouch and started to circle Wesley, in much the same manner that he probably taught his wrestling students to do. Wesley then realized this was going to be easy as he let the backpack slide off his shoulders. Mr. Larkins continued to circle and Wesley let him get close enough to where he would commit himself. He made his move to try and grab Wesley and pull him to the ground, but Wesley was way too quick. As his adversary made his move, Wesley sidestepped him, caught the man's right arm, twisted it and flipped him onto the ground, face down. Before the fallen Mr. Larkin could even move, Wesley had his right knee firmly planted in the man's back just above the waist and his right arm twisted behind his back. The right side of his face was firmly on the hard surface of the road. He must have known that Wesley could break his arm if he so desired, and there was no way he could break this hold.

"Say uncle, and promise to be good and I will let you up," Wesley said.

Mr. Larkins may have known he was beat, but he still insisted upon being defiant. "F… you, you son of a bitch," he said with some difficulty because Wesley now had his hand on the man's head and was pushing it harder onto the road surface."

"No," Wesley replied, "you don't understand how the game is played, those are not the words, the word is 'uncle.' Now you say it, 'uncle,' and he twisted the man's arm until he heard him yell in pain.

"Okay, uncle, you son …"

He did not finish the last invective because Wesley gave the arm another twist.

"The word is uncle, and only uncle, do you understand?"

Finally all Mr. Larkins said was, "uncle."

"Good, and now the second part," Wesley said.

"What second part?" the man on the ground asked.

"The part that says, 'I promise to be good.'"

Mr. Larkins now realized that his position was hopeless, and the man on top of him could do what he pleased so he relented and said what Wesley wanted to hear.

Wesley knew that later Mr. Larkins would probably not abide by his promise, but that was okay. He hoped he had learned a bit of a lesson, but again, he doubted it. Wesley did not see any reason to further humiliate the man who was probably proud in his own way, and must now reckon with his own defeat, but he did need to reiterate his previous statement. "Remember what I said, Mr. Larkin. I will walk this hollow any time I wish. I will not come to bother you, or anyone else in this hollow, but when I wish to walk this way, I will do so."

When Wesley let him get up, Mr. Larkin said nothing, but got in his truck and drove away at a reasonable speed.

Wesley had planned to return to his house via the paved road, but decided that now he must return from whence he came, but he would take the dirt road up over the hill as opposed to the trail he had come down. He knew this would eventually bring him back out on the Humbert-Kingwood Road.

He was now interested in getting back to his house. The time for leisure strolling had long since passed, and so he retraced his path walking at a fast pace. When he again passed the house where Bethany and her husband lived, he saw the truck parked in the driveway. He did not look directly at the house, but could see it as he rolled his eyes to the left. He saw Mr. Larkins standing by the edge of the garage working, or pretending to be working, on a riding lawn mower. And for a moment, he thought he saw the edge of a curtain drawn back in the front window of the house, but then again, he may have been mistaken.

The climb up the side of the hill toward the Scott Kregar farm caused him to slow his pace considerably. Several places along the road he saw where the recent heavy rains had washed deep gullies across the road, making it impassible to all but four-wheel drive vehicles. By the time he reached the top of the hill, he was breathing very heavily. He decided this was a good time to eat his sandwich.

As he sat by the gate of the fence that surrounded the field, he heard the sound of a large motor start up. The sound was too loud to be that of a tractor and it was being revved up to a high rpm. Shortly thereafter he heard the high-pitched whine and the unmistakable sound of a saw cutting into a large piece of wood. The sound of the motor changed and the high-pitched sound continued as the saw made its pass through the wood. Shortly the whine ceased and he could hear the motor rev back up as the resistance offered by the wood was removed. Apparently there was a sawmill just around the bend where the cleared field curved and sloped upward. Wesley was about to go check it out, but decided it could wait until another day. He finished his sandwich, took a big drink of water and started out the lane toward the Humbert-Kingwood road. He passed a house trailer on the right with a well tended yard, and about a half mile later he came to the paved road.

After he had hit the paved road, several cars stopped and offered him a ride, but he graciously declined.

By the time he got back to the house it was ten past three. He would take a shower, and then, as some of the locals said, he would red up the house some more. After that he would put some place settings on the table on the lower porch and wait for Manda and Dwight.

When he had finished everything, it was still just twenty-five minutes until six so he decided to turn on the computer and sign on to Google Earth and see if he could find out where the other trailhead he had passed this morning terminated.

Finding his house was easy because Humbert was a centered quadrangle and he just followed the Humbert Rd. north. He left the projection set on 8 meters until he got back to where he went down over the hill. Then he zoomed in to 4 meters and moved down the trail until he came to where the other trail started. He now zoomed out to 8 meters and then to 16 meters. The trail was so grown over that he could not track it through the trees, even though this projection was done during the time when the leaves where off the trees. He was able to see what looked like a farm road that ran from the edge of the tree line to Route 281. He was pretty sure this is where the other trail would come out.

Earlier, after he had finished his sandwich and started to walk out of the lane, he came to another trail just where the cleared field ended. This one was currently in use and he decided to see if it showed up on the projection. It did, but it was very faint, and would have gone undetected to the untrained eye, unless the person knew it was there. It was very visible when he passed, so he assumed it had been reopened. He tracked it the entire way through the trees and discovered it came out at the top of the ridge on Roger Knight's field. Had he taken it, he would have been home at least a half hour earlier, but it didn't matter.

Plotting these old trails was becoming very interesting, and he decided that walking them, as Jacob had suggested, would also be interesting and a challenge.

He was still zooming in and out on the surrounding territory when he heard Manda and Dwight pull up in the driveway. He left the Google earth window on the computer open and went to meet them.

Wesley waved from the porch and then went down the steps to meet them. Manda opened the door of the car on her side and started to get out a large casserole dish that was wrapped in a towel.

"Here, let me get that Manda," Wesley said.

"Okay, but be careful, it is still pretty hot. I just took it out of the oven," Manda said.

They went up the steps to the porch and Wesley sat the casserole dish on the table.

Wesley asked what they would like to drink, and both said water or unsweetened ice tea. He brought out a pitcher of each and a container of ice cubes and tongs.

"I took the privilege of making a cucumber salad. It was my mother's recipe. You slice the cucumbers very thin, then you add a bit of vinegar, oil and sugar. I also add a bit of lemon juice. If you don't like it, you will not offend me by not eating it."

"I am sure we will like it Wesley. We are not finicky eaters, but I will tell you the same thing about the casserole, if you don't like it, you won't hurt my feelings. However, I can blame it on our daughter-in-law as it is her recipe."

Wesley said a common catholic prayer: "Bless us O'Lord for these thy gifts which we are about to receive, from thy bounty, through Christ our Lord, in the name of the Father, and the Son and the Holy spirit, Amen," Both Dwight and Manda said the Amen at the end.

When they had started to eat, Manda asked how his walk had gone.

Wesley told them about his slight scare when he heard the doe and two fawns rustling in the bushes and thinking it might be a bear.

Manda found that amusing. Then he mentioned his unpleasant encounter with Mr. Larkin. He did not mention that he thought Mr. Larkin had beaten up on his wife before he roared out of the driveway in his truck.

Dwight hadn't done much talking, but then he said, "I told you this morning, there were a couple in the area who didn't always walk on the smooth path, and that is one of them. I suppose I should have warned you."

"No, Dwight, you did the right thing by not mentioning it. Had you said something, it might have prejudiced me against him unjustly. But his wife was with the group from the church last night, and she said her husband was a teacher and coach. It just seemed strange to me for a high school teacher to take such a position against me when I had done nothing to provoke him."

"They tell me, most of the time he seems like a very nice and likable guy," Dwight said. "It just seems that on occasions he goes off the deep end. He is on probation at school for supposedly roughing up a student. He might have lost his teaching position for that, had it not been for the fact that the student involved was considered a troublemaker, and several other teachers attested to that fact. There was another case earlier, where he supposedly threw a hammer at a student in one of the shop classes. It was just the student's word against his so nothing ever came of it. Since you subdued him rather easily, he might never bother you again, but if I were you, I would occasionally glance behind myself," Dwight finished.

"I will keep that in mind, but I don't anticipate any further confrontation," Wesley said. "Now let me change the subject. Do either of you remember a man who lived down the road here in his youth, by the name of Jacob Grant?"

"Oh, yeah," Manda said, "he was one of Albert Grant's sons. He was about three years behind me in high school, but we rode the same bus. He was very bashful, never said a word on the bus. I think he had skipped a grade in elementary school and was only about twelve years old when he started high school. He and Loraine Palmer, who used to live back this lane, both skipped the same grade and both started at that age. He had an older brother who was a year ahead of him, but a couple of years older. I remember he was a real good-looking guy that all the girls liked, but he too was pretty quiet. I think he was named for his father, because as I recall his name was Albert. It was a big family, seven or eight children. I think his father worked in the clay mine over at Fort Hill."

"Yes, he did" Dwight joined in. "He never owned a car so every day, morning and evening, summer and winter, he would walk from their house to the top of the Ed Kreger hill. There he would catch a ride to work with Ed Trimpey. Several times in the evening I picked him up and gave him a ride. I offered to take him the whole way home, but he would not have it. I remember one time he told me that farmers had longer workdays than most, no days off and no vacations with pay."

"Some years after he had retired, their house burned down and they moved into Somerset. I don't think I ever saw him after that."

Then Manda continued, "The last I heard about Jacob, he was going to college somewhere to be a minister. I don't know if he ever made it or not."

"No, that endeavor never came to fruition, but he tells a pretty interesting story about it," Wesley said.

"So you know him?" Martha asked.

"Actually, I just met him less than two months ago, but we have formed a strong friendship," Wesley said. And then he went on to tell Dwight and Manda about their first meeting, and their exchanging e-mail correspondence, and that he was expecting to see him Friday or Saturday.

He also told them that Jacob was going to show him around and tell him some of the history and legends of the area.

"That is so interesting. You please be sure to tell him that we said hello," Manda said.

"I certainly will," Wesley said.

"Wesley, I have been sitting here looking through your window at your computer. What do you have on it?" Martha asked.

"You are probably seeing my screen saver. I took a lot of pictures of the house as it was being built and then strung them together randomly as a screen saver. Before I heard the two of you drive up, I was looking at Google earth to get an idea of where I was today. Are you familiar with that web site?" Wesley asked.

"Dwight and I do not have a computer, but I am familiar with that site," Manda said. "I was over at Curtis's house some time ago and my grandson Eric came running out and said, 'Grandma, come and look at this.' So I went into his room and he had something on the screen and I asked him what it was. 'Don't you see Grandma, that is Roger Knight's field where he has all that old farm equipment. It is a photo taken from a satellite'. Needless to say, I was amazed," Manda said.

"It is a pretty good site. It has been around for a good while now, but they are always adding to and improving it.

Wesley offered to make some coffee, but both Dwight and Manda declined saying they never drank coffee after what they had for breakfast. Manda did say that she would like a tour of the house and Wesley obliged. After that, they excused themselves to go and thanked him for the hospitality and conversation.

Wesley said he was the one that owed the thanks for the wonderful casserole and really appreciated their being his first official visitors. He said he would put the leftover portion in a bowl and bring her casserole dish back to her tomorrow. He walked them to their car, came back and cleaned off the table and went to be bed early. Somewhere further up the ridge, he heard his first whippoorwill sing. The notes drifted in through the open window riding on the warm spring breeze that slowly wafted the thin curtains to and fro. In a few moments he was sound asleep. His sleep was deep and dreamless. The hills were an elixir all their own.

Chapter 13

Wesley rose early the next morning. He poured water into the well of the Krupp coffee maker, replaced the filter and added two heaping tablespoons of coffee. He then put two slices of Jewish rye bread with caraway seeds in the toaster. While the coffee was dripping, he poured himself a small glass of orange juice, took it, a pot of margarine and some cherry jelly out to the table on the porch. He heard the toaster pop the bread up and he went back into the kitchen to retrieve it and the pot of coffee. When he sat down and began to spread margarine on his toast, he thought there was one more thing that would make this just perfect, the morning paper. He knew that wasn't going to happen out here, although he did subscribe to the Somerset Daily American, which was delivered with the mail, and he found out that his mail didn't come until about one in the afternoon. Perhaps it was time to adapt to a new regime.

He ate his toast slowly and thought how quiet it was, when suddenly it dawned upon him that it was not so quiet after all. It was just that there were none of the sounds that he was accustomed to hearing at his apartment in Youngstown or even in Somerset. No traffic, although if he listened closely, he could hear when a car traversed the road above the house, but they were few and far between. There was no honking of horns, no people yelling, nothing like that, but there was a symphony of other sounds. Several different songbirds were belting out their melodic notes. He didn't know if they were for pleasure, or perhaps mating calls.

He heard other unidentifiable sounds, and then a solitary crow call from high above as it approached from across the valley. It swooped down and landed on a dead branch of a locust tree no more than a hundred yards from the house. He watched it as it sat there, moving its head from side to side. Then from the distance, somewhere beyond the road that ran above the house, he heard another crow call. His breakfast partner again tilted its head, answered the caw and took to flight. Why did he need a newspaper he mused to himself?"

When he had finished his second cup of coffee, he looked at his watch, and realized he had sat and enjoyed this new inspirational interlude for over an hour. All good things must end he thought, and so be it for this morning, but tomorrow was another beginning, and if the weather was good, he would be provided with a completely new nature symphony. As for now, he must get busy and "red up" the house. This newly learned colloquialism seemed almost natural to him already.

He knew that sometime today he would have to go to Giant Eagle in Somerset for some groceries and cleaning supplies, but he thought he would wait until early afternoon. That way, as he was putting everything in its proper place, he could see if there was anything else he would need. He already knew he would have to stop at a building supply place for some hardware items. Perhaps he could get them all at Wal-Mart, but he would wait and see.

By two o'clock he had just about everything in place, and all of the packing boxes emptied. Then he remembered, he had to return the rental truck by 5 p.m. and the return place was in Johnstown. He quickly placed his car on the tow dolly he had rented with the truck in Youngstown and headed to the Johnstown Regional Airport.

Chapter 14

On Friday evening Jacob sat down at his computer and sent Wesley an e-mail.

From: jbgrant@gulfcoast.com
To: wesdon@aol.com
Subj: Trip and this-n-that

Wesley,
Just a line to say that I will be leaving here on Monday morning.
You had previously asked me for some information about the Old Bethel Church. I apologize for being so remiss in getting it to you promptly, but I had to find some old files to give you the entire story. It is quite long so I am sending it as an attachment, that way you can save it on a disk and read it at your leisure.

Take care,
Your friend, Jacob Grant

On Saturday, Jacob called Jennifer Thornton to see if she would be able to check on the cat while he was gone. The cat was named Muchi. Monika had given her the name, and he knew it was a generic German name for a cat when one didn't know the cat's name. Like we would say 'Kitty, Kitty, Kitty,' they would say 'hier Muchi, Muchi, Muchi.' Of course, cats being what they are, they don't generally respond to their name anyway so it made no difference to him. But over the years he had learned that she did respond in her own way. She had a split personality, but it was only because he and Monika had each treated her differently from the beginning. Monika had wanted a loving cat, while he wanted a feisty cat. Although in the beginning, he didn't want a cat at all. He didn't want any more animals. It wasn't that he didn't like them; he actually thought they were great stress relievers, but because he and Monika were at a point in their life where they liked to travel, he didn't think it was fair to the animals.

Their last dog, a poodle named Leibe, also German for love, had died several years before and Monika had continued to press for another dog, but he was adamantly against it. Liebe had actually drowned in the swimming pool and he had been so thankful that it was he who found her and not Monika. She was about twelve years of age and nearly blind. During the day she would lay on one of the chaise lounge chairs by the pool. When it got hot, she would jump off and lay under the chair in the shade. On this day, the chaise lounge was close to the edge of the pool and he theorized that when she jumped off, she went into the pool. As a younger dog, she had no problem going to the ladder and climbing out, but by now her vision was so bad, and they surmised she could not locate the ladder and thus drowned. For some reason, he later reasoned it was providence, he had returned home before Monika on this day. He saw the dog lying on the bottom of the pool and knew what he had to do. An azalea bush now grows atop her grave.

Monika wanted to get a cat. Her thinking was that you can leave a cat for a day or two and they survive, whereas a dog tends to get pretty nervous, thinking it has been abandoned.

One day Monika comes into the shop and she was carrying a young cat. No longer a kitten, but probably less than one year old. She had picked it up at the plant nursery where the owner said he was overrun with cats because the lady who lived next to the nursery had a house full of them. His son would feed this one in his office and so it had adopted his place of business, although he didn't want to keep it on the premises. When she came into their shop and showed it to him, he said emphatically, "No."

Monika took it back, but when she returned to the shop he could see that she was upset. He figured she would get over it, but after several hours she still hadn't said a word to him. Finally he said, "Go get the cat."

She came over, gave him a big hug and a kiss, and with a thank you, she was out the door.

When she returned, cat in hand, he was sitting in front of the embroidery machine computer. Monika put the cat on the floor and it immediately jumped on his lap. He was hooked, although it would be some time before she would jump on his lap in the same fashion. She too may have been telling him thanks.

Over the years, it wasn't so much that Muchi developed a split personality, as she recognized the difference in the personalities of the people she owned.

He was rough with her, not mean, just rough, and she learned to behave accordingly. Her favorite time with him was in the morning just before he left for work. He would sit on the brick stoop in front of the fireplace to put on his socks and shoes. There was an overstuffed chair by the fireplace, and as soon as Muchi saw him sit down, she would jump on the chair ready to do battle. She had been de-clawed right after they took her home, which he later realized was a mean thing to do, and you had to make sure she did not get out to roam. This act had left her pretty much defenseless against other cats, but in their morning ritual, she was still often fast enough to get a bite on his arm and draw blood.

If he and Monika were sitting on the couch, she would come and lay between them, but as soon as he saw her eyes close, he would stroke her paws or hold her tail. This irritated her and she would strike at him with her clawless paws. After two or three times, she would get up and cross to the other side of Monika and lay down, but she never changed the pattern of the ritual.

She would often go and lay on Monika's lap, but almost never on his lap. The exception was if he was reading the newspaper or a book, then she would come and try to nose it out of his hands. She did not travel well. When she saw a suitcase she would go hide under their king size bed so that you could not reach her from either side. A broom had to be used to push her so one of them could reach her. Once in the car or truck she would give the most pitiful cries for at least the first thirty minutes. She would then tend to settle down on the console in between them. Once when Monika had gone to Germany and he went to Kentucky to visit their daughter Sylvie, he had made her a nice bed on the passenger side seat. He had put a box on the seat first so she would be able to see out of the window. He even used her blanket from the hickory rocker to cover the box, but she would have no part of it. She rode the entire six hundred miles perched on the seat behind his neck. It drew a lot of smiles from people that would pass him on the highway.

The grandchildren Sarah and Nathan were always glad when Muchi came to visit, but from Muchi's point of view, the feeling probably wasn't mutual. They wanted to hold her when she didn't want to be held. She would generally find a place to hide, and then get even with them in the middle of the night by walking on top of them.

For days after Monika's death, Muchi had roamed the house giving the same pitiful meows. She would often wake him up in the middle of the night with her sad cries. He even noticed that she changed. She would no longer jump on the chair when he put on his shoes, and she would now come and lay on his lap, always performing the perfunctory ritual of punching his stomach with her front paws as if kneading bread. When she finally positioned herself, half way on his stomach, halfway on his chest, and closed her eyes, he no longer pestered her. If he were reading a book, he would lay it down until she decided to move. They had worked out a new pattern of acceptance. Like him, she was now pretty old as cats went, but after so many years, she would still not drink water from her bowl if she were not alone. You had to turn on the water in the bathtub for a rapid drip and then she would drink.

Jennifer liked cats and Jacob had known her some years before when she was stationed here with the Blue Angels. She had since married and when her husband got stationed in Pensacola, she requested and also received similar orders. She had looked his name up in the telephone book and gave him a call. He had been very pleased to know that she remembered him, and he had always thought she was a very nice young lady. She was also from Pennsylvania, if his memory served him accurately. She had been a petty officer, second class, back then, but she was now a senior chief petty officer.

She agreed to look in on Muchi so he told her where he would leave the key to the front door, the temporary password, and the four-digit code for the security alarm system.

Chapter 15

On Sunday evening Jacob packed a few things for his trip and loaded them in his truck. He set the alarm for 3:00a.m. and went to bed at about 8:00. He would take a shower in the morning and be on the road by 3:30. If everything went well, no accidents or excessive roadwork delays, he hoped to be in Louisville by 3:00 in the afternoon. Louisville was slightly further west than Pensacola, but it was in the Eastern time zone while Pensacola was in the Central time zone, which meant he lost one hour.

He woke at about 2:30 with a need to go to the bathroom. He looked at his watch and decided he would just go ahead, brush his teeth, shower, get dressed and hit the road.

It was 3:05 when he backed out of the driveway. He would stop at the convenience store on the corner of Lillian highway and Blue Angel Parkway for a cup of coffee. That would hold him until he reached I-65 northwest of Flomaton, Alabama. There he would get a second cup of coffee and that would hold him until he stopped for breakfast somewhere north of Montgomery.

About three hours later he was just north of Montgomery at Prattville. There was a Waffle House here where he often stopped for breakfast, and a Cracker Barrel a few miles further on where he stopped when Monika was along. He looked at his watch and saw it was only 6:00 a.m., he had made good time with out breaking the speed law by no more than 5 mph, but it was too early to eat so he decided to continue on to just south of Birmingham where he knew there was another Cracker Barrel restaurant.

At about 1:00 p.m. he made a rest area stop just south of Elizabethtown, Kentucky. When he came back to his truck, he called his daughter Sylvie on his cell phone to tell her he would be there in about one hour.

She asked him what he would like for supper, and he said he thought he would just take them all out to eat. That would give them a bit more time to talk.

When she asked him how long he was going to stay, he said he was just going to borrow a bed for the night and hit the road early in the morning. She chastised him for this, but knew it wouldn't do any good.

He pulled into their driveway at 2:10. Sylvie met him and gave him a kiss and a big hug.

"So when do Sarah and Nathan get home from school?" Jacob asked.

"They get out at 2:55 and it takes them about five minutes to walk home," Sylvie said.

"I'll tell you what then, I was getting very drowsy when I hit the city limits so I think I will crash on your couch for a couple of minutes. When the kids get home, we will take a walk, if that is okay."

"That is fine with me Dad, but I worry about you pushing yourself like you do. Time is no longer a critical commodity for you and you are not getting any younger you know."

"You are right Sylvie. I'll tell you what I am going to do. I will come back this way on my return and spend a few days to spoil my grandkids. How is that?"

"I think you spoil them enough, but I know they would like that. So would I. By the way, Sarah and Nathan purchased a flower yesterday, they would like you to take it with you and plant it on their Oma's grave.

"Thanks, Sylvie, I am sure she will like that. Just put it in the back seat of the truck. I will thank them personally when they get home from school."

Jacob fell asleep almost immediately when he laid down on the couch and slept soundly, but when he heard the front door open, he awoke just as abruptly, and two young children came to give him a hug.

He asked the perfunctory questions of, "how have you been? and how is school going?" He received the same perfunctory answers of "fine."

"You know what?"

"What?" They both chimed in.

"Since your daddy won't be home for about two more hours, why don't we take your mother for a cup of coffee and we will all have some ice cream."

"Great," Nathan said. "Can we go to McDonalds?"

"No, Nathan," his mother replied, "Pappap is taking us out to eat later, so why don't we go to the new Graeters that just opened down the street."

"Yeah, let's do that," Sarah said rather enthusiastically, "it is the best ice cream. Did you know that the original Graeters came from Ohio?" Sarah asked.

"I did not know that, but I have tasted it before and I know it is very good.

It was about 8:30 in the evening when they got back from dinner. Sylvie reminded Sarah and Nathan that they had to do their homework.

Nathan said his Pappap could have his bed and he would sleep on the fold-out couch downstairs.

When Jacob went to bed, he left the bedroom door slightly ajar and when he saw the kitchen light come on in the morning, he knew that Sylvie was up making coffee. He got out of bed and headed to the bathroom to shower, brush his teeth and then get dressed. He and his daughter would have a few minutes to talk before Sarah and Nathan arose.

When he got dressed and came out of the bedroom, he sat his overnight case by the living room couch and his daughter greeted him with a cup of coffee.

Jacob waited until his son-in-law, Kevin, had left for work and Sarah and Nathan left for school before he told his daughter it was time for him to depart.

"So are you going directly to Warren to see Aunt Vadna?" Sylvie asked.

"No, for many years I have been trying to get to Somerset and New Lexington in Perry County, Ohio to do some research, but never made it. I thought this might be a good time to do that."

"Who do you know of that lived there?" Sylvie asked.

"As far as relatives, only a great-great uncle, Lewis Caton, who is buried at Shawnee in the southern part of the county. He was the great-grandson

135

of your better-known 5th great grandmother, Priscilla Rugg. But there are a lot of family connections between Somerset County, Pennsylvania and Perry County, Ohio. That is why you have the two towns of the same name, Somerset and New Lexington. Many Somerset County settlers moved west to Perry County in the early 1800s. Perry County is also mostly farming, but part of its history also had to do with coal mining and union problems, similar to that of southwestern Pennsylvania.

"I will probably stop first in Somerset, and then spend the night in New Lexington. As far as the populations of the two Ohio towns go, they are just the opposite of their Pennsylvania counterparts. In Ohio, New Lexington is the larger, and is also the county seat. Maybe in the morning I will drive down to Shawnee and get a picture of my great-great uncle's grave. He served in the Civil War with a regiment from Somerset County, Pennsylvania. He served at Fredericksburg, the same place where his stepfather, Peter Growall is buried. He was not killed in battle, but died from typhoid fever.

"Very interesting," Sylvie said.

"Yeah, that is your history lesson for the day. Not that I expect you to remember it," Jacob said with a smile as he embraced his daughter and gave her a kiss goodbye.

"I probably will remember it, because it is a bit of history I will pass on to your grandchildren."

"That would be nice," he said as he opened the door to his truck.

Chapter 16

There were dark rain clouds covering the area when Jacob checked into the motel in New Lexington on Monday night. When he looked out of his window the next morning, he saw a heavy rain was falling. It would not be a good day to visit a cemetery and he decided to continue on toward Warren.

He checked out with the motel clerk at the front counter, and then got a cup of coffee and a doughnut to take with him. In the truck, he put the coffee in the cup holder and placed the doughnut on the passenger side seat. He retrieved his Ohio map from the center console. He knew he would get back on I-70 at Zanesville, but he had to look at the small roads that would get him there. He always carried a legal pad in the truck and when he got into areas where he did not know the roads or streets in town, he would write specific instructions, that way he did not have to jeopardize his life and the lives of others by trying to look at a road map while driving. He had a GPS unit, but he found he still preferred the old way better. If he got lost or disoriented, then he would check the GPS unit.

He would take state road 13 east out of New Lexington, and six miles later he would turn north on state road 93 for about fifteen miles. At a little town called Moxahala Park, he would connect with US route 22. That would take him into Zanesville and then I-70 east.

The rain had let up some when he started out, but a light rain continued to fall until he got to Zanesville. It was just enough that he had to keep the wipers set on the intermittent position, and that always got on his nerves. A couple of exits east of Zanesville, he saw a sign for the Zane Grey Museum. It was one of those places where he always wanted to stop, but the time never seemed right. It was the same thing today. But by now, the sky had mostly cleared and the sun was shining. It looked like it might be a beautiful day after all.

His route would take him to the juncture of I-70 and I-77 going north and south. He would take I-77 north to Akron and then pick up I-76 and go east towards Warren, where his sister lived.

When he got to Cambridge where I-70 and I-77 intersect, he saw a sign for a Bob Evans restaurant. It was about 9:30 a.m. and his stomach was telling him it was past time for breakfast.

As he was eating his breakfast, the hostess seated a young lady at a table directly across from him. When the waitress brought her a glass of water and introduced herself, the young lady said she was ready to order. The waitress left and returned shortly with a pot of hot water and a cup with a tea bag and a handful of small creamers. The young lady poured the hot water into the cup and let the tea bag soak. She then removed a map from her purse and opened it up. He could see it was a Pennsylvania map. She partially opened it and then continued the ritual of fixing her tea. She put in two packets of a sugar substitute and the contents of three of the small creamers.

Curiosity got the best of Jacob and he spoke. "I hope you don't mind me asking, but where in Pennsylvania are you headed?"

"I don't mind at all. I am going to Connellsville to interview for an exchange teacher position."

"Exchange teacher," Jacob said rather quizzically.

"Yes, it is similar to the exchange student program, except you exchange teachers. It is getting a lot of attention now, both in my country and here."

"Judging by the accent, and the way you prepare your tea, I guess that your home country must be somewhere in the United Kingdom. I am not real good at discerning accents, so I guess it could be Irish, less likely Scottish, but my first inclination is English."

"You are perhaps better than you think. I am from a small town in northern England that I am sure you have never heard of."

"Oh, Northern England, maybe. Try me."

"Teesdale," she said.

"Sure, I know of Teesdale."

"You are kidding me of course," she said.

"Of course not," Jacob replied. "It is in Durham County close to some little towns like Darlington, Richmond, and Stockton on Tees. Do you want me to continue?"

"That won't be necessary. I believe you, but how?"

"Some of my family roots go back to that area so I have done a lot of research. My grandmother was born in Binchester. She came with her parents to the US in 1877 when she was just six months old."

"That is so interesting. Where did they settle?"

"This will also really amaze you, seeing as you are going to Connellsville. Coming from that part of England, my great-grandfather was a coal miner and so he wound up working in the coal fields surrounding Connelsville."

"That is so unreal," she said. "It was that common thread, the coal, that caused me to select Connelsville. My great grandfather was also a miner. He wrote several books on the subject."

"Sort of a male version of Catherine Cookson," Jacob said.

"Not really, his was more historical fact. He also wrote some text books concerning mine operations and safety. Ms. Cookson, as you know, wrote novels.

"Yes, I know, I was just kidding. She is one of the few older novelists from that area that I know by name. I have listened to several of her books, and thought I would just impress you with that."

"Well this entire conversation has impressed me," she said.

Just then the waitress brought the young lady's food, and while she was placing it on the table, Jacob took a folded napkin from the container and wrote down his e-mail address.

When the waitress had left, Jacob said to her, "I will let you eat in peace, but it has been very interesting talking to you. I hope you get the job, and if you have a chance, here is my e-mail address, drop me a line."

"I have certainly enjoyed our talk. It was so much better than just sitting here waiting for the food to arrive. I don't have a new e-mail address yet, but as soon as I get one, I will certainly write. I would like to hear more about your ancestors here and their connection to my home area. By the way, do you live around the Connellsville area?"

"I was born and raised close to there in Somerset County. Connellsville, I assume you know is in Fayette County."

"Yes, I do know that. Where do you live now, if I may ask?"

"I live in Florida now, have for many years, but I still have family in that area. I am going to Warren, Ohio, to see my sister, and then on to Somerset County to see other sisters and a friend. I now take my leave, but you have a good trip and I hope you get the job."

"Thanks. I will let you know either way."

Chapter 17

When Jacob traveled, he was always intrigued with the names of some of the small towns that he passed through or came close by. He liked to imagine how these names came about, but there were just too many to stop and read all the signs on the outskirts of the towns that often contained this information. And because of the interstate highway system, you seldom got into these towns anyway. Having just spent a day in Somerset and New Lexington, two towns with roots in Pennsylvania, he knew there was a connection between lots of these small towns, but when he crossed the county line into Tuscarawas County and saw a sign for Newcomerstown, he assumed some of the early settlers didn't want to name their town after the place they just left.

The name made him curious, so he exited to gas up and see if he could find out how the town got its name. To his surprise, in reading the marker outside of town, he found that it was named for an Indian Chief. He was of the Delaware Indian Nation and his name was Netawatwes, but he was also known as Chief Newcomer, probably because a lot of the early settlers couldn't pronounce his name. When he paid for his bottle of water, he engaged the lady at the cash register in conversation. She knew a lot of the history of the area, and told him about two of their most famous native sons, the great baseball pitcher, Cy Young, and one of the greatest college football coaches of all times, Woody Hayes. She told him enough about the area that Jacob decided to use an hour of his time and go to the public library.

What he discovered was that Tuscarawas County had been home to a lot of early German settlers, and was reflected in names such as Gnadenhutten and Schoenbrunn. He discovered that John Knisley and some of his friends from Bedford County, Pennsylvania, settled the areas around Gnadenhutten and New Philadelphia.

Jacob spent a little over an hour in the Newcomerstown library, but when he left, he felt it was time well spent. He still had plenty of time to make it into Warren by his own appointed schedule.

South of Akron, he saw exits for Greensburg and then Uniontown, two more towns with possible connections to southwestern Pennsylvania. In Pennsylvania they were in Westmoreland and Fayette counties respectively, and in Medina and Stark counties here in Ohio.

He got on I-76 at Akron and headed east. About fifteen miles later at Rootstown he exited the interstate and got onto Ohio Route 5. This would take him into Warren.

When he made his exit from the interstate, he called his sister Vadna and told her he would be in Warren in less than an hour. He asked for the name of a motel close to her house, and also think of a good restaurant they would like to go to. His treat. She said he should spend the night with them, but he never felt comfortable putting that burden on her; he preferred to stay in a motel where his schedule didn't interfere with others. She told him, in that case, he should take the bypass and get off on the East side of Warren. There were several motels at that location.

He had a good visit with his sister and brother-in-law. They went to dinner at about seven in the evening and stayed talking until about ten. At no time was the restaurant full, so they were not holding a table required for others.

He had planned to leave Warren early the next morning and go through Youngstown. He wanted to check out Catholic Churches and cemeteries, but when he woke, he saw that the weather he had left behind yesterday in Perry County had caught up with him this morning. He would just have a leisure breakfast with his sister and her husband and leave by ten or eleven. Maybe the bad weather would pass by then.

By 11:30 a.m. the rain was still coming down at a good pace so he told his sister he would continue on to Pennsylvania. She did convince him to have a sandwich and some coffee before he left. Any time he visited with Vadna, he always drank too much coffee. She loved her coffee and had a bottomless pot.

He finally got on the road by 2:00 p.m.

Chapter 18

On Thursday evening, at about six o'clock, Jacob called Wesley from the parking lot of the Summit Diner in Somerset. He was using his cell phone and he still considered it rude to call from inside the restaurant, although most people now did it without giving it any thought.

"Hello Wesley, Jacob here. How are you doing?"

"I am doing fine, Jacob. When did you get in?"

"Oh, just about thirty minutes ago. I registered at the Days Inn, threw my bag in the room and decided to walk over to the Summit Diner for a bite to eat. I really needed to stretch my legs."

"Are you still planning to come down here in the morning?"

"Actually, Wesley, I won't make it down until Saturday morning. Before I left Warren this afternoon, I called and talked to my youngest sister Beth. She said our sisters, Janice and Florence, were not doing too well either, so I plan to spend most of tomorrow visiting with them."

"I can certainly understand that," Wesley said, "and I pray that you find them better than you anticipate."

"Thank you, and perhaps if they are feeling up to it, you might enjoy meeting them. I have mentioned you to them and I am sure they would enjoy meeting you. As a matter of fact, when I talked to Beth, she said she had gone down to the cemetery to put fresh flowers on our parent's grave, and found fresh ones of the same type on their graves and Monika's grave. She thought maybe you had done it."

145

"Yes, I did, just a couple of days ago. I didn't want you to come back and see that I had not fulfilled my promise. Back to you first statement, it would be my great pleasure to meet you sisters whenever it is convenient for them. Now, I will let you go so you can get your bite to eat, but tell me, what would you like for breakfast? Your having lived for so long in the south, I though maybe sausage, eggs, grits, biscuits and a side of hash browns," Wesley said with a laugh.

"Well, if you are trying to impress me with your culinary skills, let me say: When I come up here, I prefer ham and eggs, some buckwheat cakes with real maple syrup, scrapple and a side of home fries. Besides, I have eaten Northerner's biscuits, and I hate to admit it, but the Southerner's do them much better. Truthfully, my doctor says I am supposed to go easy on those big breakfasts, so after eating in the Cracker Barrel, and Bob Evans on the way up, and tomorrow at my sister's, I had better go with fruit and cereal."

"I know what you are saying Jacob, so if you give me a rough, estimated time of arrival, I will have the coffee on and then we can decide what to have for breakfast."

"Well, I am a pretty early riser, and I am terrible at sitting around trying to kill time, so how is eight o'clock?"

"Eight o'clock is fine. If you get around earlier than that, give me a call when you hit the road and I will have a cup waiting for you."

"Okay Wesley, see you bright and early Saturday morning. Oh, and I almost forgot, I wanted to thank you for sending me the history of the church. I plan to read it this evening so that if I have any questions, I can ask you while you are here.

On Saturday morning, Jacob was a bit surprised when he looked at the clock on the stand beside the bed and noticed it was already seven o'clock. His body, of course, was still on central time so in essence it was only six o'clock, and besides, the past three days of traveling had probably made him more tired than normal. Also, he had sat and talked with his sisters until about eleven. Besides, what was he worrying about, he had an hour to take a shower and get dressed. He should still make it to Kingwood by eight.

He sat up on the edge of the bed and turned on the light. For being a strange bed, he reasoned he had slept quite well. He walked to the window and pulled the drapes back to catch a glimpse of the type of day it was going to be. He was delighted to see the sun already shining brightly from a cloudless sky. Maybe the rain that had fallen on Warren had gone north of Somerset, at least he hoped so.

Next to his truck, a man was loading luggage in to the trunk of a Lincoln while a boy and girl of about eight years of age, perhaps twins, harassed each other. Across the road at the entrance to the turnpike, a tractor-trailer truck with the lettering, Palm Mattress Company, Pensacola, Florida, on the side, was slowing to a halt so the driver could pluck the toll ticket from the automated dispenser. A lady and a young girl of perhaps thirteen now joined the man who was loading the luggage into the car. Each dragged an overnight bag on wheels. It was just the third week of May and most schools had not let out for the summer, so for a moment he wondered where were they headed and why? Not really any of his business so he let the drapes fall back in place and headed for the bathroom area.

By seven-thirty five he was ready to go. He would spend the night here and leave early the next morning for Florida, so he just flipped the card on the bed that said, "Don't Change Linen," and went out to his truck. He punched the button on the remote to unlock the doors and retrieved his cell phone. He dialed Wesley's number and when he heard him say hello, he replied, "I am on my way."

At exactly 8:00 a.m., he pulled into the driveway at Wesley's house.

Wesley was standing at the top of the stairs that went from the porch down to the walk and to the driveway.

"Boy you are right on time," Wesley said.

"Actually, I was three minutes early so I sat up at the top of your drive and waited," Jacob said as he closed the door to his truck and started up the stairs.

"You didn't really, did you?"

"No, quite the contrary, I had to exceed Pennsylvania's speed limit once or twice to make it here on time."

"Well, I can't imagine anyone breaking the speed law, but it wasn't necessary. The coffee is ready, but I make it in a thermos pot so it will stay hot and fresh for at least an hour," Wesley replied as the two shook hands and embraced.

Wesley noticed that Jacob embraced him tightly and held it for a brief period of time.

When Jacob broke the embrace, he turned away from Wesley, looked down over the valley and said, "Well, I don't like to be late. My wife hated my predilection for timeliness, and my oldest daughter once told me I was blessed with a curse."

Jacob now turned and faced Wesley and continued. "I told her that was an oxymoron, and she said, 'no it wasn't, it was a blessing for those people waiting for me, and a curse to her and her sister, and their mother.'"

"And your answer was?"

"My answer was, 'whatever, just get your clothes on and let's go.'"

"You sound like a real curmudgeon, Jacob."

"So odd you should say that, that same daughter once gave me a book for Christmas entitled, 'The Lovable Curmudgeon.'"

"Isn't that also an oxymoron?"

"I am sure your knowledge of Webster and the American 'sprache' is better than mine Wesley, so I will go along with what ever you say."

Wesley let that slide for the moment and changed the conversation to the situation at hand. "It is still a little chilly, but I thought you might enjoy having breakfast out here on the porch."

"Oh, that would be great. It is such a beautiful view from here. I try hard not to be covetous, but sometimes I think I am losing the battle. You know it is funny, all the years that I pestered my wife to try and get her to move back here, I envisioned so many places where we could build a house, but I never thought about this place, even though I knew it well. Then you come back here as a complete stranger and spot it right away. Seems to me there must be some meaning in that somewhere, perhaps something foreordained. Oh well, I won't bore you with one of my melancholy moods," Jacob concluded.

"Oh, you have yet to bore me Jacob, and believe it or not, I think I fully understand what you were trying to say. As for the house, I'll tell you what, if I get tired of it in a year or so, I will make sure you have first right to purchase, okay?"

Jacob gave a slight laugh and said, "That is mighty nice of you, but I have a feeling you are not going to get tired of this place, in fact, I think you will learn to love the area the way I do. It will become a part of you and you a part of it. "Ashes to ashes and dust to dust, and all that," I guess this is where the good Lord got my dust," Jacob said and then continued, "and if it is his will, this is where it will be returned. Perhaps it is where yours will also go someday, Wesley."

"Perhaps so, and I can accept that," Wesley replied. "Now, why don't you have a seat and pour yourself a cup of coffee. Since you said you didn't think you wanted a heavy breakfast four days in a row, I took the liberty of opening a couple of boxes of cereal, a half gallon of lo-fat milk and I cut up a medley of fresh fruit."

"That sounds like it will work. I wonder if I might also trouble you for a glass of water or a glass of orange juice so I can take my blood pressure pills."

"Certainly, I have some of Florida's finest."

"Do you need some help?" Jacob asked.

"No, I have it under control."

"Good, I didn't really want to leave this spectacular view, and the old bones are getting more contrary every day. Too much sitting and driving I guess."

Wesley brought a serving cart out onto the porch, positioned it close to both of them and said, "Okay, help yourself."

Jacob already had a cup of coffee so Wesley poured some for himself, and said a proforma prayer. "Now back to what you were saying about my knowledge of Webster, etcetera. I am not so sure my knowledge is better than yours, but I think you were trying to test me with the 'sprache' bit. I should tell you, foreign languages are one of my loves. Ich kann ein bischen Deutsche sprechen. I can also speak a little French, Spanish, Italian, Russian, Greek, and Hebrew. The latter two I had to take while in the seminary, but can't say that I really mastered them. It may have had to do with learning a different alphabet, although the Greek and Russian alphabets are similar. Anyway, it was then that I became aware of my aptitude for learning foreign languages."

"And Latin?" Jacob queried.

"For a Priest, that used to be a given, but not anymore."

"I suppose that is because The Mass is no longer said in Latin?"

"Correction, it isn't normally said in Latin, but Latin is used on rare occasions for special services. I had an old gentleman in my Parrish who had specifically requested that his burial Mass be said in Latin."

"And did you do it?" Jacob asked.

"Oh, I could have struggled through it, but I called upon an old mentor of mine who was long retired, but lived close by, just south of Cleveland. He agreed and it was a beautiful Mass. That is the thing about it, even if you do not understand a word that is being said, it can still be a very uplifting experience."

"That is very interesting," Jacob replied. "I suppose it is like listening to a great opera in the language in which it was written. Something is lost when it is translated."

"Good analogy, but don't get me wrong, I think the church made the right decision by doing the Mass in the language of the people."

"So tell me Jacob, what do you have planned? You know I have been waiting with great anticipation for this."

"Glad that you asked. I am going to impart my lifetime of knowledge about this area to you in one short day, Wesley. So you will have to pay attention and don't blink."

"Believe me, I will definitely pay attention," Wesley said. I do have a question I would like to ask you. Like yourself, I like to write, and I envision that some time down the road, I might like to write my memories of this place. And a lot of it may have to do with things that will relate back to this very day, so I want to make sure that I have the facts correct. What I am trying to say, do you mind if I wire each of us with a mike and record our conversation?"

"I have no problem with that, except where it might involve persons still living. I don't want to be sued for libel or slander, or have my great name tarnished among these people," Jacob said with a bit of a laugh. "However, I planned ahead to make it a little easier on you, and also knowing I often experience senior moments and may get the facts wrong, I brought some crib sheets. I went through my entire disk collection and took excerpts from some of the stories that I have written, along with annotations about the places we are going to see. I placed them in a folder for you, but remember, if there is a difference between what I tell you today and what is in the notes, the notes rule."

"Thanks, that will be a big help, and with reference to people still living, I understand that perfectly well," Wesley replied. "I have given it some thought and came up with a simple solution. Anytime you want to mention something that you feel should not be recorded, just raise your right hand slightly and I will stop the recorder. This is a pretty sophisticated recorder and has voice recognition features that can be used to start and stop recording, but I have found that it isn't always one hundred percent accurate, especially with other voices."

"The raised hand should work fine," Jacob replied, "but I was only jesting. Most of what I have to tell you won't involve anyone living here now. It may have to do with some of their distant relatives, but that is history, and you can't be sued for history."

"As long as it is the truth", Wesley said.

"If it isn't the truth, then it is simply a fabrication and not history. And before you say it, I know a lot of what we call history, a lot of what a lot of people call history, is nothing but a distortion of the facts, or even pure fabrication, but that has no bearing on us."

"I never really thought about it like that, but you are exactly right," Wesley said.

"You said a minute ago that you like to write, and I was sort of counting on you doing that Wesley. I have a proposal to make to you, but I will tell you about it after we return.

"As I was saying earlier, there is something about this area that grows on you, becomes a part of you. Perhaps not for everybody, but at least it has been that way with me, and somehow I feel it will affect you in the same way. I am not much of a believer in the lingering spirits of those who have gone before me, but I have walked these hills, driven the back roads of these hills, written about the times and people of these hills until sometimes I feel I know all of them personally. I haven't lived here for over fifty years so I don't know too much about the present inhabitants. Although, my sister Beth and I made a quick run through yesterday so she could refresh my memory. All the old timers I knew when I was young have long since gone to their great reward, but every time I come back here, it is like returning home as if I had never left."

"Monika used to growl at me when we would come back. She would say, 'the closer you get to this place, the faster you drive.' I don't think that was the case, I think she was just not used to driving in the hills on winding road. Of course, it could have been a little of both.

"If you have that recorder handy, Wesley, you can go ahead and start it while we eat. I will give you a little introduction, or preface," Jacob said.

"I have it right inside on my desk. Let me go get it."

Wesley returned with the small recorder, sat it on the table along with a small mike, and said, "It is rolling, anytime you are ready."

Jacob began. "As I mentioned to you before, the area is known as Hexabarger. There are a lot of variations on the spelling, and for the past fifty or sixty years, or as long as I can remember, a lot of folks just call it Hexie. The early German settlers originally applied the moniker so the correct form should be Hexe Berge, or witch hills."

Wesley smiled to himself, but he said nothing to Jacob. He had figured it out correctly the first time his mother told him the name of the area.

"An interesting fact is that most of the more colorful people of the area were women. Not all were considered witches, of course.

"Hexabarger is quite well known in Somerset County. It has been mentioned several times in the Laurel Messenger, the quarterly publication of the Somerset Historical Society. So although many people may have heard about it, very few people can tell you exactly where it is. In fact, if you ask ten locals for the boundaries, you will probably get ten slightly different answers.

"Back fifteen years ago, a guy by the name of Clyde Miller started to publish a quarterly newsletter called, 'The Hexie Gazette'. It was well received, but he only lived long enough to publish four volumes before he succumbed to the effects of leukemia.

"I knew him, so before he published the first issue, we swapped a lot of e-mails and telephone calls on the very subject of the boundaries of Hexie. We considered how the name originally came about and the roads and trails of the time. The time being 1790 give or take a few years. We also considered what our contemporaries called the Hexie area. Most agreed that it terminated at Humbert, but we reasoned that it terminated there only after Humbert came into existence around 1901 and became a much more recognizable entity. When you consider how the name came about, the people who gave it the name and the person for whom it was named, then you have to increase the range down the valley from Humbert for at least another mile.

"As to the northern terminus, most people will say that when you leave Kingwood, you are entering Hexie, but we never really considered that to be correct. You are entering Hexie when you go down the Ed Kreger Hill further up the road, or down the Barney Kreger Hill on this road or back the lane past the Lannings.

"If you look at a topographic map, or one of various satellite photo web sites such as Google Earth, you will see there are four distinct valleys, each with a small river that forms the upper area of Hexie. Three of these come together at Humbert and flow into Laurel Hill Creek. The fourth also flows into Laurel Hill Creek, but about a mile further up river.

"The first one, Smith Run, which has also been referred to as Brown's Run, begins down below your house. The second one, Redd Run, begins off to the right as you go down the Barney Kreger Hill. Next over is May Run. It is the shortest of the four. All of these first three flow into Laurel Hill Creek at what was the town of Humbert. At that point, they are just a few hundred yards apart. The fourth one is known as Moses King Run, but it too has been known as Mudd Lick Run. The ridge that is part of May Hollow, prevents Moses King Run from continuing its southern flow so it makes a bend back north at Schweibensville, then turns west to flow into Laurel Hill Creek about a mile north of Humbert.

"Interesting thing about Schweibensville, there is no town there, never was a town there, but nevertheless, it still shows up on some maps a in the Somerset County Platt book. Go online to 'Map Quest' and you will find it.

"Back in the latter part of the 1800s, Max Schweibenz, a partner by the name of Heiner, and perhaps a Mr. Leisenring came to the area around Confluence and Draketown to start a lumber operation. They ran a narrow gauge railroad up to their operation at what is now Cranberry Lake on the west side of Laurel Hill Creek. Apparently, they had planned to cross the river at this point and cut timber in the Hexie valleys, but it never materialized. By 1895 their operation ceased. Some one hundred ten years later, the site of the town that never was, still exists. Mr. Leisenring was a bit more successful in getting his town built, but his venture had to do with coal in Fayette County. My grandfather and father worked in some of his mines in the early part of the 1900s. My father was actually born in West Leisenring."

By now, both Jacob and Wesley had finished eating breakfast.

"Let me help you clear the table and we can get started if you are ready," Jacob said.

"I am ready," Wesley replied. "If you clear the table, I will get the gear I want to take along.

Jacob took the few dishes from the table, rinsed them in the kitchen sink and loaded them into the dishwasher. Wesley took the food items and put them in the refrigerator. He took out two large bottles of water, got some crackers, dried fruit and other snacks and put them in a small cooler. They were ready to start.

"We will take my truck," Jacob said.

Wesley put the small cooler in the back seat area, got in on the passenger side and handed Jacob a small wireless mike that he clipped to his left side shirt pocket. "The tape is rolling, or to be more correct, the disc is activated, Jacob. From here until we return it is all your show. I won't say anything, unless it is absolutely necessary," Wesley said.

"The folders I mentioned to you just a few minutes ago are all here in these hanging files on the floor rack between our seats. They contain a lot of photographs that I have taken over the years, but I am sure you will want to take some of your own. Anytime you want me to stop, or wish to ask me something, just speak up."

"Don't worry, I will."

*Hexie Rd. The wrong name for this road. It is
known locally as the Ed Kregar Hill.*

As they exited the driveway at the top of the hill, Jacob turned right toward Kingwood. He drove for about three tenths of a mile until he came to a dirt road that went down over the hill to the left. There was a green road sign that read: HEXIE RD.

"See that sign?" Jacob said. "It identifies the wrong road. We are on what should be called the Hexie road, or the main street of Hexie, if you will. I know of at least two others in the area that identify the wrong roads. The WYNO Road is also misspelled as WINE-O. I wrote to the 'powers to be' to see if I could get it corrected, but they said it was too late, the roads have already been programmed into the emergency system. So because of a bureaucratic screw up, history will forever be incorrect. It would take some programmer about two minutes to correct it in the system, and a work crew about one hour to changes the three signs. It still galls me, but I have relented. Might be a good undertaking for you some day, Wesley. Tell them, some old man tried in vain."

They now started down the steep hill where the road was completely canopied in hardwood trees of the area.

"This, as you may already know, is often referred to as the Ed Kreger Hill, as distinguished from the Barney Kreger Hill that starts just above your house. I know some of the history of old Barnhardt, or Barney, but I do not know who this Ed Kreger was. It is very surprising to me that this road has never been paved, but personally, I hope it never is."

About one third of the way down the hill, the road turned sharply left, and on the lower side you could see an open area that had once been a tilled field. Small trees and scrub brush now dominated, and within another fifty years it would again be a wooded area. At about the two-thirds point, the road made a sharp right turn and started to level out as it crossed a small run and then went back up a small knoll for a short distance. Jacob stopped the truck over the large culvert pipe that channeled the water under the road.

"This is the first of the runs in Hexie. It is known as Moses King Run. It has occasionally been referred to as Mudd Run. The name, Moses King Run, comes from the first early settler to farm this valley back in the late 1700s. It was originally warranted to his father Christopher, who we will talk about later. When Christopher died in 1811, he willed this farm to his son Moses, and another tract further down to his grandson, Christopher. Later on, Moses willed it to his son, Moses King Jr. In 1834, Moses King Jr. had to file a petition for insolvent debtor, or in today's vernacular, bankruptcy. According to his petition, he only owed a total of about seventy-five dollars, not a great deal, but apparently more than he could come up with.

"I mentioned that the run was sometimes called Mudd Run, and it is interesting to see that one of the persons who held a judgment against Moses for $7.00 was A. Mudd. Garrison Smith also held a judgment for $9.00. I'll tell you more about Garrison Smith when we get to the other hollows. Joseph Cramer was assigned to settle with the creditors. The Cramers and Kings were closely entwined. As a matter of fact, the next time you go to Somerset and pass through New Centerville, look out into the field to your right and you will see the Cramer/King cemetery. My third great-grandparents, John 'Tanner' King and Rebecca are buried there, they were first cousins. I guess back then, that was not all that uncommon."

Jacob started to drive again, and went to the top of the small knoll where the road made another left turn. He stopped and pointed to his right.

"If you go up over the bank there and proceed for about three hundred yards, you will come across a small family cemetery. It is known as the Williams cemetery. Buried there in are Curtis and Annabelle Firestone; their son Warren; Annabelle's parents, George and Rebecca Williams; and I believe her grandparents. Also buried there are a husband and wife by the name of George and Elizabeth Briggs. I can't recall their connection at this time. Curtis Firestone was my great-uncle, a pretty hard man as I have been told. He was also the great-great-grandson of the woman for whom Hexie received the moniker. At one time, this was Curtis Firestone's farm."

Jacob drove on for about a quarter mile until they came to three houses on the left. The first and third were fairly new single story houses, and the one in the center was an older two story house. Jacob spoke, "When I was a young boy, a Trimpey family lived in the older house. His name was Ed, and if my recollect is correct, he was probably a fourth generation Trimpey in this area. I think the name was initially spelled Trimpe, (German of course). It was the site of Curtis Firestone's house, which was a log house. If I am not mistaken, Ed and his father tore it down and built the structure that still stands. They used lumber from the old houses in Humbert that were torn down starting about 1935. I would have preferred the preservation of the log house, but I am sure, Ed's wife, Rosie, probably would have disagreed with me. "

At the first house, a car was parked in the dirt driveway and a young man was taking a couple bags of groceries out of the trunk.

"Stop a minute, Jacob," Wesley said. "I know that young man."

Jacob stopped the car, and the young man set the bags back into the trunk and turned to look in their direction. Wesley opened the truck door, stood outside and looked over the roof. "Hello Jake," Wesley called.

"Hello Mr. Donaldson. What are you doing down in here?" Jake asked as he started to walk toward the truck.

"My friend Jacob is giving me a complete guided tour of Hexie," Wesley said.

"That should be most interesting," the young man said with a laugh.

Jacob put the truck in park and opened his door and got out as Jake approached.

"You remember the first night at the church, I mentioned I had met a man who used to live in this area. Well, this is him," Wesley said.

"I do remember. I don't think we have ever met, but I mentioned it to my mother and she said she remembers of him."

At this point Jake was close to the car and extended his had to Jacob.

"Hi, I am Jake Grayson."

"Jacob Grant here. Glad to make your acquaintance Jake. Now tell me, who might your mother be?"

"Gladys Mitchell, she was the daughter of Jacob Mitchell."

"Oh my gosh," Jacob replied. "I do not think I remember your mother other than as a very young and bashful girl, but I knew you grandfather and grandmother very well. I assume that Rosalie Conn was your grandmother?"

"Yes, she was. I don't remember her because she died before I was born, but I have heard good things about her."

"Rightfully so, she was a beautiful young lady. I always considered your grandfather to be a very lucky man to capture the prettiest girl in Addison," Jacob said with a smile and raised eyebrows. "I dated her once, but that scoundrel of a grandfather of yours beat my time. I am just kidding you about that Jake, your grandfather was also a wonderful person.

"Most people here say my mother looks just like her mother, and from photographs we have, I guess I agree, although others perhaps see it more than I do."

"How long have you lived here in Hexie?" Jacob asked.

"We moved here from Mill Run about two years ago," Jake replied.

Jacob just nodded his head and at this point he said, "We have to get going if I am to complete this tour of Hexie for Wesley, but please tell your mother I send my regards in memory of her parents. Perhaps the next time I am back here for a longer period of time, I can stop down and visit for a few minutes," Jacob said.

"I will tell her you said that," Jake said. "I am sure she will be pleased that you remembered her, or at least her parents, and I am sure she would like to see you whenever you have the time."

Then Jake went around to shake hands with Wesley.

Jacob looked across the hood of the car and said, "By the hat you are wearing, I would say that you are a Penguin fan."

"Yeah, big time," Jake said. "Do you like hockey Mr. Grant?"

"Love it. It is my favorite sport and the Penguins are also my favorite team. The Lightning are probably second."

"Do you ever get to see them play?" Jake asked.

"Occasionally, when they play in Atlanta, but even Atlanta is over a three hundred mile drive. How about you?"

"Not a lot, but I know Hank Armour personally so if I get a chance to go, he always gets me tickets." Jake pulled off his hat and handed it to Jacob so he could see the autograph on the visor. It was signed, 'To my good friend Jake, I will always owe you one'. Hank Armour #65.

"Very impressive, you must have done him a great service," Jacob said.

"It wasn't that much," Jake said. "Mr. Donaldson can tell you if he wishes."

Jacob handed the hat back, and then Jake turned to Wesley and said, "I really enjoyed your comments at the Wednesday night Bible study. It was very enlightening. I suppose you saw I took a lot of notes. Perhaps I can borrow your copy of the history of the Jews by Josephus sometime," he said.

"Any time you wish, Jake," Wesley said. "Remember, I just live up over and down over the hill."

As they started to drive, Wesley saw Jacob raise his right hand and index finger. He immediately stopped the recorder. Then Jacob asked him, "Do you know how Jake's mother is doing?"

"You put me on the spot, Jacob. I am not sure I know what you are talking about.

I have yet to meet her, because she never came to the church any of the times I was there, but I never asked any questions about that. What is her problem?"

"Okay," Jacob said with a sigh, "perhaps I said something that I should not have, but since I did, I might as well try and explain.

"I don't know all of the details myself, basically just what my sister told me. I will tell you what I know of it after we complete our tour and get back to the house. You can also turn the recorder back on now," Jacob said.

"Okay, it's on. Please continue," Wesley said.

"Well, that old house we just passed on the right was once owned by another Jacob, Jacob Gary, some spelled it Geary, and his wife Minnie who was a Minerd, which is also now most often spelled Miner or Minor. Their daughter, Rosie, was married to the Ed Trimpey I mentioned back there.

"Jacob was a fine man and a great friend of my grandfather, although the two did not exactly walk the same path. Jacob was a devoted churchgoer who in his deep bass voice could say a prayer that you just knew God used to train his angels." Wesley rolled his eyes but let that pass. Jacob continued, "My grandfather on the other hand, never went to church, but he was still a very moral and ethical man. The two of them often worked together in the woods cutting timber, or working on the township roads. It was always Sam and Jake.

"Anyway, you will discover that there were a lot of Jacobs and Minnies in the area. I hope you get them all straight."

"I'll just listen and try to get them sorted out later," Wesley said, "But there is one thing I would like to ask of you."

"What might that be?"

"When you get back to Florida, how about checking your e-mail a bit more often as I know I am going to have a lot of questions."

"Okay, I'll try," Jacob said. He then stopped the car just past a small house that sat on the bank to the right of the road.

"I never checked the courthouse records to see how Moses King's farm was divided up, but some of this upper portion was later owned by Freeman Nicola. I believe his father was Jacob and his mother was an Ansel. Anyway, he married Phoebe Vough and they had one son, William. Phoebe died not too long after William was born, and Freeman then married Nellie Firestone. They had a son named Bruce and a daughter named Minnie. Bruce married Susan Romesburg, and Minnie married Lyman Trimpey. All stayed in Hexie, and I will point out their farms when we pass them. Also, up to this point, all names mentioned are German or the Anglicized form thereof.

"Freeman's oldest son, William, who later went by the form Nicklow, married Minne Stairs, and they had five children, three sons and a set of twin daughters.

"All three sons stayed in Hexie and owned farms, which I will also identify as we pass them."

"When I was a young lad, William and Minnie lived in the small house just back of where we are parked. A descendant of another long time resident of this valley now lives in the house. The house down over the bank to my left was the farm of William's son Clarence. Clarence's first wife was Lillie Faidley, and after she died he married Mary Warrick. Lillie's family lived further down the valley, and Mary's family I believe was from down around Ursina."

"Many of William and Minnie's grandchildren were my contemporaries, give or take a few years.

"I am not sure when Clarence's descendants got rid of the farm, and I am not sure who lives there now; however there is a rather gruesome bit of history related to the son of a family that did live there.

"Back around 1998, their son killed his wife. I think they were separated and she lived in a trailer house somewhere on the other side of Somerset. After he killed her, he cut her body in pieces and brought them down here."

Jacob drove down the hill and near the bottom he stopped.

You see that strange structure there to your right. He built that house, if you can call it that. He put his wife's body parts in a large barrel that he used to burn refuse, put wood in the barrel, doused it all with gasoline and lit it. He is now serving life in prison. There have been a few strange things that have happened here in Hexie, but to my knowledge, that is the only truly gruesome happening."

Jacob started to drive and the road passed over Moses King Run again and then the road turned sharp right. Jacob stopped the car just briefly and pointed to the entrance of a road that once was there, but now the vegetation was starting to take it back.

"I suppose you know that at the top of this hill is the Old Bethel Church. This was the second church hill. The first one also started here, but went almost directly up over. It was a bugger in the winter for cars to get up, especially since there was a sharp left turn close to the top and the grade increased. The fact that as kids, we would often use it for sled-riding probably didn't help. Then they cut this second road with two switchbacks, but again the last two hundred yards at the top were quite steep. It was still a good sled-riding road, not as fast, but longer. Finally, a few years ago, someone got smart and decided to straighten it out and follow the more gradual slope. It is still pretty steep, but at least now you can get a run for it."

About a hundred yards down the road, Jacob again stopped and pointed to an indefinite spot on the side of the hill. "Back in the early 1940s, a man by the name of Heil had a little shack right in there. He was German, and although he spoke English, he had a heavy German accent. He was a harmless old man, but some people saw all Germans as Nazis. One night a couple of local thugs took it upon themselves to show Mr. Heil their twisted version of patriotism. They beat him most severely, but he did survive. For many months my grandmother tended to him and his wounds. The perpetrators of this cruel act were never discovered."

They moved further down the road to where the new church hill started its ascent.

"I suppose the reason they didn't cut the road this way before was because my grandparent's home sat right there, and their property rights went further back. My great- grandfather, Harmon King, obtained the approximately eight acres when he received a five-hundred dollar bonus for Civil War service. He fought at Gettysburg, one of the lucky ones who returned. His younger brother Harrison was not so lucky. Hermon later named his first son Harrison. Hermon was married to Mary Cramer and in addition to Harrison, they had a daughter Sarah who died in infancy, Rebecca, and of course my grandfather, Samuel George Newton King.

"My grandmother was Martha Ann Firestone, but everyone just called her Mattie and that is how she is remembered on her gravestone up there at the top of the hill. I mentioned Curtis Firestone when we stopped at the foot of the Ed Kreger Hill; well, they were brother and sister. There were ten in the family, but I won't bother you with all the names.

"The house my grandparents lived in was a rustic, rough lumber, four rooms and a "path." Kitchen and living room downstairs, two bedrooms upstairs. Here they raised twelve children. They had fourteen, but two died young.

"The strange thing about the house was that Grandpap was a pretty good saw and hammer man, and his brother Harrison was excellent. Harrison built several of the finer houses here in Hexie and a lot of barns, and Grandpap often helped, but neither of them lived in any luxury. I suppose it kept them busy feeding their families and they could never accumulate enough cash to purchase the necessary building materials for their own places of abode.

"Great Uncle Harrison was a very religious man, an eloquent speaker and writer. His brother, on the other hand, that is to say my grandfather was not a church going man, but from what I understand, he did believe in God.

"Some years ago I stopped in Durham, North Carolina, for an hour to visit with my uncle and his wife. My uncle told me this story about his father. It seems that a man by the name of Archie Faidley, who lived on a farm just down the road and around the bend, asked my grandfather to trim some fencerows for him. I am sure he probably paid him in kind, but that is neither here nor there. It was a hot day and sometime in the early afternoon, Archie's wife Mable told their daughter to take a jug of water down to where he was working. As she approached, she saw my grandfather leaning against the trunk of a tree, his head down and his hat in his right hand by his side. He always wore one of those pinstriped hats that railroad workers seemed to prefer. She thought he was dead, but as she got closer, she could hear him talking. He was talking to the Lord. She knew he did not go to church, and so if he knew she had heard him, he might be embarrassed. Quietly, she retraced her steps for a little ways, and then again approached, this time lowly singing some song. When she got close to him this time, he had placed his hat back on his head and greeted her in his normal jovial fashion.

"So I suppose he saw God in his own way. Most Christian Churches will say that is not enough, but perhaps he had faith in the words that God spoke to Moses, 'I will have mercy on whom I will have mercy, and I will have compassion on whom I will have compassion.'"

"You know that Paul quotes that passage in Romans and continues on it when he added, 'it does not therefore, depend on man's desire or effort, but on God's mercy.'" Wesley said.

"Yes, I did know that Paul used it, but I wasn't sure just where it could be found.

"I could sit here and tell you stories all day about my grandfather, but we need to keep moving," Jacob said.

About a quarter of a mile down the road, Jacob pointed out a house on the bank to the right. "That was once a one-room schoolhouse. It was known as the King School, and it was there that my mother got her 'learnin'. She was the third in line, born in 1910, and the school was not new then so I suppose it goes back to at least 1900. It was her sister Freda and her husband, Jim Matheney who purchased it many years later and converted it into a home. My sister told me who lives in those other houses and the one you see to the left across the run, but I don't know the people. Those were all built long after I left. I suppose if I lived back here now, I would be a little bit like Dan'l Boone, too many neighbors, too close."

Less than a half a mile further, they came to a branch in the road. The main road they were on went to the right, but from this point on it was no longer considered Hexie Road, but Faidley Road. There was a dirt road to the left called May Road. "This is roughly where Schweibinzville is located," Jacob said. "If you take the road to the right, it will eventually bring you back out beyond Kingwood, or if you take a left before you get to the main road, it will take you to Whipkey's Dam. We never considered anything past this point to the right as being Hexie so we will take the road less traveled to the left.

"When I was a kid, there was only one house back in here. It was the Charlie May farm. The Mays also inhabited this area going back to the early 1800s when old Daniel May received a warrant for over 100 acres. But more important to us when I was growing up, it was the way to the old swimming hole in Laurel Hill Creek. There was a road to your right there, although even back when I was a kid, it was not passable for a horse and wagon. At the bottom of the hill there is a narrow flat area bordering Laurel Hill Creek and there was a swinging bridge across the river. The lumber company that moved into Humbert around 1909 may have built it, but Mr. Schweibinz and his partners could also have built it. The lumber company at Humbert came in several years after the coal company had moved out. They built a narrow gauge railroad up along the west bank of the river to carry their logs down to the mill. It extended up as far as Barronvale. They may have built the swinging bridge so the timber men who lived in these valleys could cross and get to work. By the time I was first back in here around 1948 most of the footboards were missing. To cross on the bridge, there were several places you had to hold onto the top cable and slide your feet along one of the bottom cables. There were several large flat rocks and a deep hole under the bridge. In later years it always amazed me that no one ever fell off onto the rocks. We would walk out over the deep hole and then drop in. The water flowed pretty fast and it was always cold, but as kids, who cared? When we surfaced, we would swim toward the large rocks where the white water started and it would take us about fifty yards down stream. We would climb out and go back up and start over.

"Back then, the old swimming hole served another function. It was where the local church held baptisms. I suppose you know that the Old Bethel Church denomination does not do infant baptisms, although they now do dedications. They adhere to the belief of 'age of accountability' and a personal confession of your sins and request for forgiveness. This can take place at any time, but is usually during a time of revival, and for young people, generally when they are about twelve years of age. The new church building has a baptistery, but in my day, the old wooden church, had no such thing. So, at some date after the revival services had concluded, a date was set, usually a Sunday afternoon, when the entire congregation would meet at this point where we now sit and then everyone would walk down the trail to the deep hole by the swinging bridge. If revival was held in the late fall, the baptisms would normally be postponed until early spring. Sometime in May, and I can vouch for the fact that in May, the water in Laurel Hill Creek is still very cold.

"The pastor didn't go out and put a few drops of water on your head, you went out to where the water was waist deep, and then he took you by the head and dunked you under and said, '(your name) I baptize you in the name of the Father,' he brought you up and then dunked you a second time and said, 'the Son,' and brought you up again and dunked you a final time saying, 'and the Holy Ghost.'

"I don't want to diminish the baptismal ritual of your faith Wesley, or that of the Lutherans, or any other denomination that practices infant baptism and sprinkling, because I believe the amount of water and the way it is applied is immaterial, but every time I hear a sermon about John the Baptist, and the baptism of Jesus, I feel I can relate to it better than many of those sitting around me."

"You know Jacob, many Catholic churches have baptisteries and perform immersion baptisms," Wesley said.

"Yes. I do know that. Both my daughters married men of the Catholic faith and converted to Catholicism. I attended the Confirmation rite when my oldest daughter crossed over. There were several in her group who were baptized at the same time, and it was by immersion, but it was not in a cold mountain stream."

"I would like to witness that sometime," Wesley said. "In fact, I would like to perform such a baptism. Maybe I will ask Father Kirkpatrick in Somerset if he would be receptive to that. I think it would be a wonderful experience."

"I am sure it would, but just be careful, you might start a trend."

"Well that couldn't be a bad thing," Wesley continued.

"I guess, but it may be a moot point, because you may have to look a long time before you find a mother agreeable to bringing her two week old baby back in this wilderness to be baptized."

"That is probably also true," Wesley said.

"Well, back to when it was also a swimming hole," Jacob said. "That was the most fun when we were ten to thirteen, after that the hormones started to kick in and you spent more time laying on a blanket with your sweetie, or taking a short walk down the various paths to steal a kiss. Of course, you still might drop off the swinging bridge to impress the current love of you life, but you knew things were changing. We were putting childish ways behind us then, and eventually they became but dim reflections in the mirror of our mind. I suppose a priest knows those words are not an original thought," Jacob said.

"Yes, a paraphrase from one of Paul's most well known commentaries about love to the early Corinthians, but from what I am hearing, your reflections in the mirror of your mind are not so dim, Jacob."

"Maybe so, but sometimes when I get into those old remembrances, I wish that Monika could have been a part of them. Maybe then she would have realized how important they were to me because they would have been important to her too. Maybe then she would have moved back here.

Of course, we had some great times in Germany and we didn't go back there either, so I guess que sara, sara."

They started to drive again and the narrow dirt road now started up a fairly steep grade. About halfway up they met a pickup truck coming down the hill. There was not enough room to pass so Jacob stopped the truck and started to back up. He was following the unwritten rules of the road; vehicles coming down the hill had the right of way. In an earlier day this would have been more of a problem, but now the hillside was dotted with a lot of small summer homes or hunting cabins with driveways leading in off the road. As Jacob turned to back up, Wesley watched the approaching pickup, which was just a few feet in front of them. He recognized the vehicle. It belonged to Carl Larkins, and he could now distinguish the person behind the steering wheel as Carl. He was certain that Carl could also recognize him. Jacob backed up about one hundred yards and then pulled into the narrow driveway of one of the small cabins. About twenty feet in, there was a heavy chain stretched between two posts on opposite sides of the lane. It was padlocked and a large sign hung from the middle, it read: 'NO TRESPASSING.'"

As the pickup truck passed, Jacob looked up to wave at the driver, but the driver looked straight ahead.

"Right inhospitable cuss, isn't he," Jacob said.

"Maybe he was thinking about other things," Wesley replied.

Jacob didn't answer. He drove to the top of the hill and parked the truck off of the road close to a barbed wire fence that surrounded an open farm field that hadn't been tilled in many years.

To their left was a cleared area of several acres. There were still a lot of trees in the clearing and a lot of tree stumps. A doublewide trailer sat about a hundred yards from where they were parked. There was a tree bark covered driveway just below the home and a parking area in the rear with a garage. The garage had an oversize door and was probably used to house a tractor-trailer truck. Quite a bit further back, at what seemed the edge of the cleared area, sat another doublewide. There was a white car sitting in front of the house. Two young children, a boy of about four or five years of age and a little girl, a bit younger, played in the yard.

To their right was a blacktop driveway leading to a large new house. It was by far the most impressive house in this outback. It also had a large detached garage that was just barley visible from their viewpoint. Apparently the owner of this house was also a truck driver.

"This is as far as we can drive, but why don't we get out and stretch our legs and walk down the old trail a ways," Jacob said.

"That sounds like a good idea. Let me get my backpack. Maybe we can find a place to sit down and relax for a minute; have some trail mix and some water," Wesley said.

The two men started walking toward the entrance of the trail. At one time, perhaps as far back as the late 1700s when old Daniel May received his land warrant, this trail was a passable road for horse and wagon. Now most of it was grown over and at places it was difficult to discern exactly where the old trail was. However, in recent years someone had cleared about two hundred yards of the old trail to a point where the lane branched off to what was later the Charlie May farm. As they approached the cut off for the lane, Jacob continued to relate the history.

"When I was a kid, this was the Charlie May farm. Charlie was probably the great-great-great nephew of the original owner, Daniel May, who obtained it through a land warrant back in the late 1700s. He had three sons, Daniel, Jacob and Charles; all are buried in an old abandoned and neglected cemetery on the second ridge over," Jacob said.

They had now entered a small clearing and it was evident that at one time this was the yard surrounding the house. To their left were the remains of a stone foundation that once supported the barn. Close by was a smaller stone foundation.

Jacob looked around and then continued, "That larger stone foundation was where the barn stood and here on this smaller foundation, where you see the water still flowing freely, was the springhouse. I don't know what a city boy knows about early farm buildings," Jacob said.

"Not much, but keep talking, I am all ears," Wesley replied.

"Well, the springhouse and its water source served several purposes. It provided your drinking water. It was also used to keep dairy products like milk, cream and butter cool and the overflow went outside to a trough that provided drinking water for the cows and horses; sheep and goats if you also had them."

"Okay, some of that I know from my builder, because he asked me if I wanted the old trough restored when he was doing the basement. I didn't know what he was talking about, so he explained it to me in much the same fashion as you just did," Wesley said.

"I haven't been in your basement, but did you have him do it?"

"I most certainly did."

"Great, I want to take a look at it when we return."

"I am sure you will approve. He even brought an Amish stone mason along to do the work."

"That is great he got one of the best. Now, back to this one. It doesn't take much of an archeologist to determine the layout of this springhouse. Because it was made of stone, you can still see the remains of the old inside trough. It had two depths; the deeper end was used to submerge the five-gallon 'cream cans' as they were called, and the shallow end, which in this case was less than twelve inches deep, was used to place crocks containing butter, or anything else you wanted to keep cool since this was all before electrification."

"If a farmer back then was milking ten to twelve cows, it was considered to be a fair sized herd. So what you did with the milk depended to a large part on the number of cows you milked. These small farms almost never sold milk in bulk. They might sell some to a neighbor who didn't own a cow, but normally they sold either butter or cream. Butter was generally sold directly to neighbors or to the small country stores. They would also sell their extra eggs in this fashion. If they sold cream, it was generally held in the five-gallon cans that were stored in the water trough and once a week was taken to the train station in Confluence. Here it was put on the train and taken to a creamery in a larger town or city.

"The springhouse was normally where the separator was located. The milk was carried from the barn in the milking pails and poured into the top portion of the separator. The person in the springhouse would then grip the handle and turn the large wheel on the separator creating a centrifuge. I am sure you are familiar with the process. The lighter cream is forced to the top and out through a spout to a receiving crock. The low-fat milk that remained would go to a crock at the lower portion of the separator.

"Let's walk over to that old apple tree above where the house once stood. We can sit down and have some of your trail mix and a drink of water. If you have some plastic cups, we can try some water from the old spring," Jacob said.

"That all sounds like a good idea Jacob, and if you don't mind, I will check my voice messages. My phone vibrated twice in the past five minutes so maybe it is urgent. I have my home phone programmed to follow my cell phone," Wesley said.

"Oh yeah, very difficult to get away from the ubiquitous clutches of civilization. I'll tell you what, give me two cups from your backpack and while you check your voice mail, I'll go back and get us some water from the spring," Jacob said.

"Okay," Wesley said and placed the backpack on the ground and pulled out two plastic cups. Jacob took them and started back toward the spring. Wesley took the cell phone from his shirt pocket and punched the button to retrieve his messages.

Jacob walked past the foundation of the old springhouse to a tree growing by the wall where the barn once stood. He desperately needed to empty his bladder. When he had finished, he went back to where the water pooled below the spring. He purposely did it so Wesley could see that he washed his hands after relieving himself, and before bringing him water. But Wesley was not looking in his direction.

When Jacob returned to where Wesley was now seated on the ground, he noticed he had a strange look on his face.

"Something the matter?" Jacob asked.

"No emergency," Wesley said. "The first message was from the secretary at the Holy Spirit Church in Somerset. Father Dunnen wants to talk to me tomorrow about subbing for him next week. But the second message was from Jake's mother. You need to listen to this."

Wesley handed the phone to Jacob. "Punch 4 and listen."

Jacob took the phone and did as Wesley had said.

The message started: "Hello Mr. Donaldson, this is Jake Grayson's mother. Jake told me that you and Jacob Grant had stopped by on the road. I didn't know that Jacob was in the area, but I wonder if you would do me a favor. I don't remember much about him, but my mother spoke so highly of him. I would like to talk to him while he is here, but for my own personal reasons, I do not want Jake to know. Would you ask him if he could stop by tomorrow between 9 and 12 o'clock? That is when Jake is in church. I would ask that you not call to confirm this or extend his regrets if he can't make it. I will just wait and see if he can. I do not want to obligate him, but I am desperate and very worried, so please tell him he would be doing me a great favor if he can come by. Jake speaks so well of you so I know I can put my faith and trust in you. I thank you so much." There was a click as the call ended.

When Jacob handed back the phone, Wesley said, "So what do you make of it?"

"I don't know. But obviously she sounds very serious and I certainly owe it to her mother to go talk to her."

"Listen Jacob, when we left their place you said there was something you would tell me, but after we got back to the house. Is there any possibility you could tell me now?"

"Considering the circumstances, that might be a good idea. What do you say we eat and drink up and then hit the road? I will tell you as we drive."

Wesley pulled two sandwiches out of his backpack and the two men started to eat in silence. Both were thinking, but in different directions. Finally Wesley broke the silence with a bit of levity in his voice, "I noticed you made an extra effort to let me know you washed your hands after relieving yourself and before drawing our water."

"You weren't even looking Wesley. Do you priests have eyes in the back of your head?"

"Just part of our omniferous training," Wesley replied with a laugh.

When they had finished their snack and started walking back to the truck, Jacob said, "I was planning on going up by New Old Bethel Church and take the road that goes down the valley that is before us, but I think that under the circumstances, we will go to the lower limits of Hexabarger where it all started. That will give me more time to tell you what I know about Jake's mother. I don't mind you recording this, but I would ask that you put it on another cassette so you can dispose of it later."

"Okay, I see what you are saying Jacob, but this is not a cassette recorder. It is a compact disc recorder, and because of its capacity, I did not bring a second disc. I will honor your wishes and not record if you say so, but I will be glad to promise you that I will transfer that portion to a separate disc as soon as we get back to the house."

"No need to promise Wesley, if you can't trust a priest, who can you trust?"

"Well, there are a few unscrupulous priests, as I am sure you are aware, but I hope I am not one of them."

When they got back to the truck, Wesley noted a young woman sitting on the front porch of the big new house he had seen for the first time when they arrived. There was no car or other vehicle around so earlier he had assumed that no one was home.

When they were belted in, Jacob turned the truck around and started back down the narrow dirt road.

"Okay, here is what I know," Jacob began. "This is how I got it from my sister. The Graysons were living on a small farm close to Mill Run. Apparently, Jake's father was a scoundrel. I guess he was a womanizer, but worse than that, he had a drinking problem and may have used or dealt in drugs. I never knew any of the Graysons, but from what I gather, he was also a very cruel son-of-a-bitch, pardon the term, who liked to beat his wife and that young man back there. He came home drunk or stoned one night and began to beat on Gladys, Jake's mother. He took a hunting knife and started to carve on her face. Young Jake was about thirteen or fourteen at the time and he came to his mother's defense and jumped on his father's back. The boy was, of course, no match for his father and he threw him off his back and sent him sprawling across the living room floor. He then proceeded to go after the boy, picked him up and hit him with his fist. Again the boy went reeling across the floor and landed against the stair rail by the back door.

"Gladys had gone through the beatings many times before, but of late, she saw that Delbert, that was her husband's name, was now very mean and rough to young Jake. I guess it was because he was now old enough to realize what was going on and took his mother's part and tried to defend her. She knew things were only going to get worse until something terrible happened, and she had prepared herself.

"Delbert had cut her several times lightly across the face, and if had not been for Jake jumping on his father's back, he might have continued until he killed her then and there. She had been lying on the floor when he went after Jake."

"Delbert was standing in the middle of the living room just ready to go after his son again, when he heard Gladys give a terrible scream. Jake would later testify that she did not scream a name or word, just a very loud piercing sound like that from a wounded animal. Delbert turned to look at her and took one round from a double barrel, 12-gage shotgun in the upper chest area. She lay down the gun, went to her son and became completely hysterical. He called the police and tried to comfort his mother."

"There was a trial, of course, but there were enough witnesses who told how Delbert had treated her, and she was found innocent. His family was also from the same general area and they naturally felt she wasn't justified in shooting him. How you figure that, I don't know, but according to my sister, they occasionally give her grief. That is probably why they moved to this area.

"Her mother and father were very religious and because of that upbringing, Gladys could not cope with having killed another human being even in light of the circumstance. I guess she underwent a lot of therapy, but, nevertheless, she has become somewhat of a recluse. Her face was disfigured from the cuts, and although she may still have slight scars, the plastic surgeons apparently did a remarkable job of rebuilding her face. I guess the problem is how you rebuild heart and mind."

They had just passed the Old Bethel Church when Wesley said in an exasperated tone, "Oh crap."

"Nice words from a priest," Jacob said.

"I know," Wesley said with a big sigh as he blew much of the air out of his lungs through slightly parted lips. "I know, I know, but we may have more trouble in Hexie, than you or I realize Jacob. Now there is something I must tell you. I wasn't going to mention it, but somehow I sense a correlation, and my senses are generally on track."

Wesley then told Jacob about his previous encounter with Carl Larkins.

"I really wasn't going to tell you about that scuffle, because I felt bad about using force against another individual, even in self-defense, but now it may be important.

"The night the people from the church helped move my furniture in, both Jake and Bethany were there. Bethany sang a beautiful song in blessing to the house, and Jake said grace before we ate. I got the impression that the two were good friends, although there was certainly nothing improper about their actions. But the fact that they go to church together, and Bible study together, most likely they know a bit about each other's life. And then there was a comment that Reverend Pritts made that evening before he and his wife left. They were the last to leave and I mentioned that he had some good talent in his flock, and he said, 'Yes, but we also have some challenges.'

"He didn't want to elaborate at that time, and I didn't want to press the issue, but now I am wondering if that is perhaps what he was referring to."

"Have you seen him since you had the encounter with this Larkins guy?" Jacob asked.

"Yes. I saw him on Wednesday immediately after the encounter, but I did not want to say anything then. I just didn't think it was the proper time or place. I did hear one or two people say they wondered why Bethany wasn't at the meeting, and now that I think about it, I noticed Jake was listening keenly but didn't say a word."

"And your thoughts now?"

"I don't know Jacob, I was trained as a priest, not a detective. Much of that training has to do with not judging, especially not, prejudging your fellow man."

"Yes, of course, but at the same time you can't shut your eyes to what may very well be a problem. Think back Wesley, is there anything else that was said that you recall that might give another clue?" Jacob asked.

"Yes, there was, and yet maybe it was nothing. Before we left the kitchen that evening with the coffee, Bethany put her hand on my arm and asked if she could call me Reverend. She also asked if she could talk to me some time. At the time, I thought it was just general conversation, but thinking back on it, the fact that she put her hand on my arm to stop me makes me think it was more significant."

"You may be right, Wesley, but at least you now have the advantage of being circumspect."

Both men sat in silence.

Jacob didn't mention the fact, but they were now passing the site where the old coke ovens had once been. Immediately after that they passed the old Growall log house and rounded the curve toward where the town of Humbert once stood. To their immediate right, buried under eighty years of fallen leaves and other vegetation, were the stone and cement remains of the old locomotive engine house. A few paces further, toward Laurel Hill Creek, were cement pillars, standing like cemetery markers. This was all that remained of the conveyer system that once brought the logs from the holding pond to the carriage of the old band sawmill.

Jacob was silent during all this time. His mind was split. He was thinking of the present, but it was being held in check by his thoughts of the past. A past, much further back, that even he didn't know first hand, but one that he had lived over and over through the memories of his grandparents, his mother, and others he had talked to over the years.

They rounded the curve in the road, and to their right they passed the entrance to a dirt road that led back to where the Upper Humbert covered bridge once stood. In earlier days, it was known as the Kuhlman Bridge. To their immediate left, and up on the side of the hill, stood the old Huff house. It was built as the house for the company superintendent of the coal patch town known as Humbert. An elegant structure in its day, and from its lower porch it provided an excellent view of the town. It is now the only structure that still stands from the Humbert era, but it is in great need of repair. "So sad," Jacob thought to himself.

When Wesley noticed that Jacob again seemed to be in a trance, he decided once more to break the silence. "Circumspect, good choice of words, Jacob."

"Boy, it sure took you a long time to come back with a reply," Jacob said.

"Well, there for a moment you looked like you were in a world of your own so I didn't want to interrupt you."

"I suppose I was. I always wanted to buy that old house back there and restore it to its former beauty, but I could never afford to do so. It has an absentee owner, so I don't know if he would even have wanted to sell it. I could never understand why he never bothered to fix it up. I am sure it would qualify for low interest, historical restoration funding. I always thought it would make a great Bed and Breakfast house. There would be so much fascinating information that you could talk to your guests about. It would certainly be more interesting than that stupid movie that came out about tens years ago called the Blair Witch Project. At least in this case the supposed witches were real and had colorful personalities."

They went up a small hill and out across a flat stretch of road along the side of the hill. "Down there behind those blue spruce trees is a restored log house. I don't know who lives there now, or who built it initially, but when I was a kid, some of my relatives by the names of Reeves lived there. And that house you see across the river was the old Goniak homestead. A Polish immigrant by the name of Kazimierz Goniak settled there around

1900 and built a modest two-room house. I belief the great grandson of 'Kaz' lives there now, a fellow by the name of Enos. He would have a slight connection to the person who used to live in this next house I am going to show you.

The road turned slightly left, went into a small dip and then came up close to a very old wooden house with a tin roof that hadn't been occupied for many years. Jacob pulled the car off to the right and stopped.

Sarah Jane Dodson House. A recluse, Sarah Jane was sometimes referred to as the "Goat Lady."

"This is another one of my favorite houses in Hexie. Everyone here knows it as the Sarah Jane Dodson house. Some people referred to her as the goat lady. I will tell you the story of her later. Suffice it now to say; quite a few years ago I took some pictures of it in the very early spring. The vegetation hadn't started to grow; in fact, the day I took the photos, there was a late spring snow. I was disappointed that there was no sunshine, but when I saw the photos, I realized the falling snow added to the mystique.

"A few months later, the art galleries in Pensacola were holding open house and had a 'meet the artists' night. Monika and I went and I saw the work of one artist who completely captured the essence of some old weathered houses and barns in the Deep South. I told Monika, 'I have to

175

meet this artist, I want so see if he will paint the old Dodson house from the photos I took a couple of months ago.'

"I talked to him and we set up an appointment to meet at his studio, which was an add-on to his home. He looked at the several photos I had taken from different angles and slowly nodded his head.

"The he spoke, 'Well, the house has great character, but I must tell you, I am a southern boy; I never learned to paint snow, white sand beaches yes, but snow, no.'

"The snow that had fallen was no more than an inch or two, but it covered the roof of the house.'Actually,' I said, 'I was hoping you could remove the snow from the roof. The old metal roof has such a beautiful patina, that I wanted to capture that aspect. That was one of the things that drew me to your paintings at the gallery the other evening.'

"He said, 'Removing the snow will be no problem. I suppose we need to talk about size and cost.'

"We agreed on those matters and I told him that when it was finished I would bring Monika along to help decide on the frame. She had a much better eye for that sort of thing than I did. At least I knew that if she picked the frame, she would be more apt to let me hang the painting. It really wasn't her idea of the type of art she wanted hanging on the walls in our house.

"That painting still hangs on the wall by our fireplace."

"So why didn't you try to buy this place?" Wesley asked.

"I did, but the owner is that lawyer who lives in that big house you see through the tree tops. He wouldn't sell. Damned doctors and lawyers from Pittsburgh come up here with their big bucks culled from others and buy up these properties. They build their fancy houses, and then don't do a thing to preserve what should be preserved."

"You sound a bit bitter, Jacob."

"No, I am not bitter about any of it, and I shouldn't have said what I just did. I have met the gentleman that lives down there and he seems to be a nice enough guy who does care about the environment. I would just like them to try and understand something about the area into which they move. Here in this small enclave we call Hexie, you can trace the history back to the earliest settlers and know exactly where their homesteads where. You can't do that in a lot of places. This was brought very clearly to my mind on one of my many trips up here. I was stuck in a typical, bumper-to-bumper traffic jam in Atlanta and I saw a sign that said, 'Cobb County.' Now, I know a little about the Cobbs that settled there, and if I can ever prove my Virginia relatives connection, then I am distantly related to the Cobbs, but that is not the point. The point is, the area is not one iota like it was when the first Cobb settlers went there. On the other hand, this area is still very much like it was when the first settler came in the 1760s. It is much like it was when the Indians controlled it all, perhaps thousands of years ago."

"Well, it isn't always possible to hold civilization in check, Jacob."

"To paraphrase a very old question by substituting a different word, what is 'civilization', Wesley?"

"Believe me, Jacob, I know what you are saying, I just don't have an answer for you, but when the snows come again and I have long evenings to myself, I will give it some thought."

Jacob then gave a slight laugh and said, "I can't ask for more than that, and I really believe you will. That having been said, I dismount from my soapbox and we continue the tour."

As Jacob started the drive, the road again made a slight left turn, went down into a deep dip, came up around to the right and followed a narrow winding grade on the side of the very steep hill. If you looked to the right, through the dense forest, you could see Laurel Hill Creek meandering far below.

"This road followed an old Indian trail, and was most likely the path that Priscilla took when the early German settlers tagged her as the witch of the hills. The road was more fun when I was a kid because, in addition to curving in and out to follow the side of the hill, there were also a lot of dips. If you drove real fast, you would get the feeling in your stomach a bit like riding on a roller coaster. That may have been the reason they eliminated the dips. Driving fast on a narrow road and around curves, it was a disaster just waiting to happen, although I don't know of any such occurrences."

At the end of the side of the hill, the road made a greater than ninety-degree turn to the left. Jacob beeped his horn before he entered it.

"You might remember to do that when you are driving this road, Wesley. It is a blind corner and sometimes people will tend to hug it going down and swing wide coming up, just the opposite of what you need to do. My grandkids call this Pappap's hill, because of something that happened to me when I was about fourteen or fifteen, and of which I have related to them, probably more than once."

They were now at the bottom of the short hill and the road made another much greater than ninety-degree turn in the opposite direction, but here visibility was good. There was a dirt road to the left that said CHICKEN BONE HOLLOW RD.

"So are you going to tell me the story?" Wesley asked.

"Patience, Wesley. Remember, Job had patience."

"Yes, but Job was only dealing with God, and God with the adversary."

"Are you saying I am worse than the adversary?"

Wesley raised his hands, palms up and fingers spread, "I am mute on that question," he said.

"Well, I am going to stop right here and tell you two stories at the same time. Maybe three," Jacob said.

Jacob pulled off to the right side of the road where the water from the river was no more than two feet below the road surface. They both got out and walked to the river's edge.

They leaned up against what was left of a large oak tree, then Jacob said, "I will tell you first about my hill back there.

"I never had a bicycle when I was a kid. That is a sad story in itself, but it is not the gist of this one. Our neighbor's son did have a bicycle, and one Sunday afternoon I talked him into the two of us riding to Draketown, a distance of about fifteen miles. I had a 'sort of' girlfriend there I wanted to see. I was older and bigger than he, so I would drive and he would sit sidesaddle, so to speak, which is between the handlebars and the seat. No problem until we hit the bottom of the Rose Hill back there. I didn't think I needed to use the brake; I would just lean into the curve, no problem. But there was a problem, my neighbor didn't lean when I did and we hit the gravel on the side of the road, the bicycle went out from under us and we crashed. My neighbor landed on his shoulder and the side of his face hit the gravel. I hit a fence post in the people's yard that owned the house, first with the side of my head and then my collarbone. I was knocked unconscious, but my neighbor wasn't, and he thought I was dead. So did the people who saw it all happen from their front porch.

"I remember when I gained consciousness, there was a lady wiping my face with a wet cloth. They wanted to take us to the hospital, but we were both very much against it, because we knew we would already be in a lot of trouble when we got back home. We convinced them that we were okay and started to walk home. The bicycle had sustained very little damage and we could have ridden it home, but we pushed it the complete three miles. When we were about halfway home, my neighbor asked me if I knew what the lady had used to wipe my face, and I said I suppose a washcloth. 'No,' he said, 'she grabbed a pair of underpants from the clothes line and dipped them in the small creek behind the house.' I said it was okay because if they were on the clothesline, they must have been clean. Years later when I told the story to two of my grandkids, my grandson thought that was pretty funny; gaining consciousness with a pair of lady's wet panties on my face."

"So did the two of you get in trouble?" Wesley asked.

"Not as bad as we had expected, but I got a bit of sympathy because my collarbone was broken."

"I assume you have driven this road once or twice?" Jacob asked.

"Yes I have."

"Well, then you know there is an old covered bridge just around the next bend."

"I do."

"Well, some years ago there was also a swinging bridge that crossed the river right at this point. If you look closely at the remains of this old oak tree, you can still see some of the cables that supported it. The tree had mostly grown around them over the years."

Looking up above his head, Wesley said, "By gosh, you are right."

"One afternoon back around 1938," Jacob began, "there was a torrential downpour that caused the river to rise to the point where the other end of the bridge was slightly under water. The bridge sloped down and was only a few feet above the water on the other side. A young boy by the name of Harry McCulley was on an errand for his mother that required him to cross the river to a neighbor's house. Perhaps the Goniaks, but of that I am not sure. Young McCulley did not want to go all the way down to the covered bridge so he decided he could still cross the swinging bridge. Perhaps he was showing off, being daring as young boys often are, or perhaps the swollen river had picked up a log that struck the bridge, thus causing it to lurch and make the boy lose his balance. He fell off the bridge and the swift current swept him downstream and he drowned. Several days later a man was fishing several miles downstream when he saw the sun glinting off of a shiny object. He went to investigate and found the body of the young lad; the sun was reflected off a silver buckle on his shoe.

"More recently, back in the middle 1990s, there was another situation involving Laurel Hill Creek as a raging river. It occurred just a few hundred yards further down the road, and there but for the grace of God, and a guardian angel, who in this case was the man that lived in that house up there, another tragic death might have occurred.

Car in the river. The female school teacher narrowly escaped drowning when the ice dam gave away and swept her car into the raging waters.

"If my memory serves me correctly, it occurred in early March of what had been a cold and severe winter with a lot of snow. The surface of the river had frozen solid, perhaps four or five inches thick, and the snow accumulation on the slopes of the hills was quite deep. The weather turned suddenly warm and in the early morning a steady rain started to fall. It rained most of the day and caused the snow to melt rather rapidly.

"Before I go further, let me explain, in case you have not already figured it out, that the reference to Upper and Lower Turkeyfoot Township has nothing to do with their geographical position to one another. As a matter of fact, they are pretty much east and west of each other. The reference has to do with elevation. The name Turkey foot came about as a result of an Indian scout drawing a map of the three rivers in the dirt for a young surveyor from Virginia by the name of George Washington."

Wesley had discovered the Upper and Lower naming himself, but he said nothing, not wanting to interrupt Jacob's story.

"This river is not very long. It starts in Jefferson Township, flows north for a short distance, makes a u-turn and starts a rather rapid descent through Middlecreek and Upper Turkeyfoot Township. The terrain is fairly rugged with a lot of valleys coming in from both sides. Each of these valleys naturally has a small river that empties in to this one. The flow isn't great so that during normal conditions there is no problem, but in case of a real downpour for any length of time, they produce a lot of run off. Again, as the river traverses the upper two Townships, there is little problem as the steep hills keep the river pretty much in check, but when it reaches this point, the left side gives away completely to this flat open valley. It is easy to see the potential for flooding.

"During most of the year it can be bad enough during bad rains, but in the winter with ice on the river, another dimension is added, and that is what happened in the situation I am talking about.

"That particular day, the water in the smaller tributaries was rising rapidly. The rain was causing the ice to break up along the length of the river and the rising water was bringing it downstream. At various bends in the river the ice would back up causing a dam effect. When the force from the backed up water became too great, the ice dams would break and send a wall of water further down stream. This effect became accumulative.

"If you look up the river there, you can see where it comes through the last pass between the hills, and you can see that there is a fairly sharp bend in the river. What happened that day back then, was that a huge ice jam formed at that bend in the river.

"In the early afternoon, a young female schoolteacher from the Turkeyfoot Valley High School was on her way home. Just about the time she passed the covered bridge further down the road, the rising water behind the ice dam caused it to give way. As she rounded the curve in the road right it front of us, she was met with a wall of water and ice. It spread out across the valley floor and started to wash away the roadbed. It pushed her car backwards and towards the river. At one point down there, the water gouged out part of the roadbed forming a small inlet that captured some of the ice. Her car was washed in against some trees and came to rest on ice floes lodged against other trees. Temporarily she was safe, but if the water caused this ice to break away, her car would be swept out into the raging water and she could possibly drown. She had to get out of her car, but without causing any disturbance, lest the ice upon which her car was resting, broke loose. She was successful in this endeavor, but she still wasn't safe because there was a lot of extremely cold, fast moving water between where the riverbank was and the safety of higher ground.

"Luckily for her, the man who lived in the house up there, and it may still be the same man, had watched the whole thing develop. He reacted quickly and his efforts were successful in rescuing a very scared, but thankful teacher."

"Wow," Wesley said. "I guess she really did have a guardian angel."

"Yeah, it seems that way. Too bad poor Harry McCulley didn't have one," Jacob said.

"Maybe he did, just that the circumstances were different."

"You could be right. I am getting too old to question the ways of the Lord," Jacob said, looking at Wesley with a slightly sideward glance to catch his reaction.

"Feathering your nest, so to speak, are you, Jacob?"

"Not really, if my nest isn't feathered by now, I suppose I am in a lot of trouble. I just don't want to knock it out of the tree," Jacob replied.

"It is never too late Jacob, but then you know that. Sometime I suspect you just try to ring my chimes."

"Ring your chimes, I like that. Something I would expect from a man of the cloth. When I was a kid, the saying was, 'you are trying to get my goat,' no pun intended there. I have never learned where that expression came from," Jacob said.

"So, shall we continue?"

"You are the leader, you go, I follow," Wesley said.

The two men got back in the truck. When they passed the Lower Humbert Covered Bridge, Jacob pointed to where David King, the early settler, had located his gristmill.

"There is an unanswered question that bugs me about David King, or David Kings. The four King brothers that moved into this area in the late 1700s were Philip, Michael, John and Christopher. They had an older brother, David, who supposedly never came west from York County.

Christopher settled this valley and he had a son David, and it was David who later had the gristmill. The problem comes in when you read the account of the Jersey settlers where it is said that David King went up the river, now known as Laurel Hill Creek, and built a gristmill. At the time of the Jersey settlers, David, the son of Christopher, would only have been four years old. I have never been able to resolve that discrepancy."

Just past the point of David's gristmill, the road made a ninety-degree left turn and crossed the flat valley. Corn had been planted in the fields on both sides of the road, and the new shoots were just starting to break the ground.

"The saying I always heard back here when I was a kid, was, if the corn is knee high by the fourth of July, your crop is okay. When I left Florida, most of it was about ready to tassel.

"You see that slightly elevated path that separates the two fields on both sides of the road," Jacob said, and continued without waiting for an answer. "That was the grade for the old North Fork Railroad. It was originally built about 1871 by the Pittsburgh and Baltimore, Coal, Coke, and Iron Company to reach their mines and coke ovens just north of where Humbert was later built. Their operation was known as Edna Mines, and they owned the mineral rights to over six thousand acres in this area. They only operated for about two years until 1873, when they closed their mine, pulled up their railroad tracks and left the area. Later the company, Edna Mines would open two operations in Westmoreland County. Twenty-eight years after the Edna Mines operation ceased, a company known as the Connellsville and Ursina Coal and Coke Company purchased these mineral rights to start their own coal operation. They put the rails back down and built the town of Humbert. If you are ever more interested in this, go to the Somerset Historical society and get a copy of the book, 'Stemwinders in the Laurel Highlands.'"

They had now crossed the valley and the road made another ninety degree turn, this time to the right. They traveled about a quarter of a mile until they came to a barn and an old, two-story stone house. Again, Jacob pulled the car off the road onto the shoulder, almost brushing against a barbed wire fence on the passenger's side, and shut off the engine.

"You want to take a little walk?" Jacob asked. "You may want to crawl out on my side."

"Yeah, that is a good plan," Wesley said.

"The walk or getting out on my side?"

"Both," Wesley answered, as he raised the truck's center console. "Let me grab another battery for my camera, just in case."

"I noticed you have been taking a lot of pictures. How many does that disk hold?"

"This is pretty recent technology and at best resolution, I can store thousands of photos and some video," Wesley answered.

"Wow," Jacob replied. "I still have my first digital camera, it is pretty obsolete by now. I think I can store about 512 pics before I have to download, or replace the memory card, but it still serves my purpose. I no longer see as many things that I want to record as a permanent record. Generally, I just enjoy things for the moment. My grandkids are perhaps the exception and as they get older, even that diminishes."

"So where are we going to walk to?" Wesley asked.

Jacob pointed to an area halfway up the slope of a distant hill where the trees were not as tall as those surrounding them.

"That is where the farm of Samuel Rugg and Priscilla, the supposed witch of the legend of Hexabarger, was located. They are buried somewhere up there by the main tree line, along with some of their offspring. The graves were only marked with fieldstones so it was impossible to later make any identification. I once searched for the graveyard, but was never able to find it. Anyway, before we proceed, I suppose it would be proper to go over to the house and get permission to cross the field."

"I will let you take care of that matter, Jacob, I want to get a few shots of the area," Wesley said.

"Okay," Jacob answered. Be sure to get one of the barn, my great-uncle Harrison King built it, with help from his brother, my grandfather, Samuel. I mentioned them to you earlier when we passed the place where my grandparent's old home stood."

Chapter 19

While Wesley was busily taking pictures, Jacob started toward the front door of the old stone house. A voice called to him from the front yard of the house across the street close to where he had parked the truck.

"There is no one home there right now. Can I help you with something?" the lady asked.

"Maybe," Jacob said and started to walk toward the lady who now stood by the side of the driveway where she had been planting flowers.

"You have a very beautiful yard, you must love working in it. I know from my wife that it requires a lot of work and loving care," Jacob said to the lady.

"Thank you, and yes, it is a lot of work, but I do love it. It is a little strange because my husband is the country boy, but he has no interest in it."

"I guess I lean more your husband's way, laziness is a terrible thing," Jacob said and laughed. "Anyway, my name is Jacob Grant and I was just going to show my new friend where the old Samuel and Priscilla Rugg homestead was located. I didn't want to cross the field without asking the owners. That used to be the Harneds, but I am not sure any of them still there."

"It is still owned by the Harneds, but none of them live there full time. They will often come for the weekend. The oldest daughter lives in Rockwood. I could give you her phone number, but I am sure she would not mind you crossing the field. But let me ask you, who is this Rugg couple you mentioned?"

"Long story," Jacob replied. "I was just about to relate it to my friend. You can tag along with us if you can pull yourself away from your gardening."

"No problem there, I need a little rest. I will tag along as you say because you make it sound , oh what should I say, 'interesting.' And by the way, my name is Janet Snyder.

Wesley took several pictures of the old stone house. He walked up the road to where he was perpendicular with the house and took some of the barn. He attached a wide angle lens and shot several pictures of the open valley. The he swapped that lens out for a telephoto lens so he could capture the covered bridge in the distance. He had previously take a lot of the photos from up close. When he had finished, he turned and saw Jacob waving for him to come over to where he and Janet were standing.

When Wesley arrived by their side, Jacob made the introductions.

"Janet, this is Wesley Donaldson, a recently acquired friend and the newest inhabitant of Hexie. I can't vouch for his character, but he says he is a Priest so I suppose he is okay, Jacob said with a smile on his face. Wesley, meet Janet Snyder.

The two shook hands and exchanged the usual "my pleasures."

"Janet is going to walk with us up to the old Rugg homestead, but let me tell you a little about this old stone house.

John C. King house. The oldest son of Christopher King, the original settler. The house was built in the early 1800s and was the first stone house in the area.

"It is currently owned by the Harned family, but the Harneds didn't build it. The original owner of this land was Christopher King who came to the area with his two brothers in the late 1700s. It was his son, John Christopher King who built the house. The Kings and the Harneds were contemporaries and this house contains some of the history of both. The earliest Harned came with the Jersey settlers also in the late 1700s. If you go into Ursina and take a left across Laurel Hill creek and up over what the Jersey settlers called, 'Hogback,' you will come to a little village called Harnedsville, named for Samuel Harned. Go on into Ursina and take a road to your right and you will be in the Jersey Hollow.

"Samuel Harned was the person who actually penned my great-great-great-great grandfather's will. Old Samuel could not read or write, but it is believed that Priscilla could do both.

"So if you two are ready, what do you say that we move out," Jacob stated.

As they started to cross the road, Janet said, "Jacob was telling me that you are the one that owns the new log house just below Kingwood. We have passed it quite often as it was being built. It is a beautiful house."

"Thank you," Wesley responded. "New approach to an old architecture style, but I hope they never change the concept used for the old stone house.

Then Wesley changed the subject and continued, "Excuse me Mrs. Snyder, but you mind if I recorded our conversation as we walk."

"Of course not, and if you don't mind me calling you Wesley, would you please call me Janet?"

"Thank you Janet, and would you mind clipping this small microphone to your blouse?"

"Like I said," Jacob interjected, "I think he is a nice guy, but you have to accept Wesley for what he is, 'a techno junkie.'"

"Really! Believe me; I know all about techno junkies, my husband Marshall is exactly the same."

Wesley handed her the microphone and the clip was bigger than the device.

"So who was this Samuel and Priscilla?" Janet asked.

"Living this close, I am a little surprised you have never heard of them, but then again, perhaps not. It is a very interesting legend and some say that the ghost of Priscilla still lingers in the area. It is too long and too complicated to give it justice here, but I will pass it onto Wesley and maybe sometime he can stop by and relate it to you."

"So after peaking my curiosity about this Priscilla ghost and legend, you are just going to leave me hanging to sometime in the future? I don't think so Jacob," Janet said. "What if I say I won't let you cross my neighbor's field until you tell," she said further and raised her eyebrows.

"Well, in that case, since I was going to relate some of the legend to Wesley as we walked, and since you are walking with us, I suppose I can expand it slightly from the condensed version. I still plan to send Wesley a copy of the article I did some years ago that goes it a lot of detail. Then you can ask him to let you borrow a copy if you are still interested. How is That?"

"Sounds like a good plan to me, now just let me change my shoes and grab my cell phone. I am expecting a call from my husband. He is an airline pilot and he calls me when he gets to Pittsburgh to tell me what route he is scheduled for," Janet said.

Jacob and Wesley waited outside.

"Did you get a picture of my great uncle's barn?" Jacob asked.

"Sure did. Actually I took several shots of it. Do you happen to know when it was built?"

"Interestingly enough, I do. My mother said that Grandpap was helping to work on it when her sister Ruth was born. My mother was born in 1910, and her sister Ruth in 1913. I have a copy of a record that contains most of the data about it. I know the entire contract was for $525.00, which included tearing the old barn down. Grandpap worked on in for about 250 hours and was paid twenty cents an hour."

Just then Janet returned and said, "So are we ready?"

"Did you get your cell phone?" Jacob asked.

"Yep, right here," she said as she held up her left wrist to display her watch. "Latest thing, Marshall got it about two months ago when he took a flight to Oslo. Noika technology. I think I saw an ad in a magazine recently where it is available here in the States. It is both a watch and cell phone. I told you my husband was also a techno nut."

"Real Dick Tracy stuff," Jacob said.

"Who is Dick Tracy?" Janet asked.

Wesley answered, "He was a comic strip detective before your time, almost before my time, but he had a two-way wrist radio long before it's time, probably back in the fifties. Is that about right, Jacob?"

"Yeah, probably about the fifties. Did you catch that Janet? He is trying to make me feel old."

"Well, Janet just called me a nut so I was trying to salvage my ego."

"Oh! I am so sorry, Wesley; I didn't mean it that way."

"Of course, I know that Janet," Wesley said.

"How long has your husband been flying for the airlines?" Jacob asked.

"About four years now. He was a Navy pilot and flew missions from the USS Roosevelt after that terrible terrorist attack back in 01. After that he flew two years with the Navy's Flight Demonstration Squadron, more commonly known as the Blue Angels.

"I know of those guys. See them practice all the time. I live about two miles from the end of their runway in Pensacola, Florida," Jacob said.

"Really! Small world isn't it," Janet said.

"Maybe smaller than you think," Jacob said. "I made their flight suits for twenty-five years, but I do not remember a Snyder, so he must have been a member of the team after I retired."

"When did you retire?" Janet asked.

"From the tailoring business in 04."

"Yeah, you just missed each other. He was part of the 05 and 06 teams. He got out of the Navy after that and started to fly for World Airways."

The three of them had now crossed the yard and entered the open field. The field was sloped, but not so steep as to cause extreme difficulty in walking. However, since Jacob knew he would also be doing most of the talking, he warned his two apt listeners that they might have to pause once in a while so he could catch his breath.

When they had entered the field, Jacob began. "Let me start at a more recent time and then slide back, it will make more sense.

"In the 1950s, The Rugg place was known as the Keck place, but I don't know when it was built. When Samuel Rugg's widow, Priscilla, who is the main character in the legend, died in 1837, the property was sold to Israel Rhoades. He lived there for quite a few years, but I don't know to whom, or when he sold the property. As I said, I don't know when the Kecks purchased it. But when I first visited the place in 1952, it contained

189

a large white, two-story wooden house. There was also a barn and a couple of other out buildings; I think a chicken coop and a corncrib. And if I remember correctly, there was a garage below and toward the back of the house. The house faced south and had a wide porch that extended along the entire lower side with steps going down to the road. It contained a basement, four rooms on the first floor and four rooms on the second floor. There was a very wide hallway in the middle of the house on both the bottom and the top floor. I don't believe the house was originally constructed as a duplex, but by the 1950s it was configured as such with separate kitchens and living rooms on each side of the hallway.

"My sister and brother-in-law moved there in September 1952 and lived there until August 1955. At the time, my brother-in-law's brother and his wife were already living in one side of the house. Both brothers worked for the Army Corp of Engineers on the flood control system of dams and locks on this side of Pittsburgh. This job often kept them away from home Monday through Friday.

"My own research into this legend showed that neither my sister nor her sister-in-law was aware of the legend of Priscilla, or Prissy as she is more affectionately referred to. And neither one knew they were living on the grounds where she once lived and supposedly mounted her great white horse. Also, they did not know that she, her husband Samuel, and some of their children were buried just a few hundred yards away.

"My sister never knew the house was haunted, or housed a ghost, while she lived there, but in retrospect, she can cite a couple of strange happenings. Her sister-in-law, however, always believed emphatically that the house was haunted and can recall numerous occasions when she and her husband would sit out on the lower porch steps at night and hear the bolt on the door being moved as if someone was arriving or leaving. The light switch would be thrown, but when they went to investigate, there was nothing.

"On one occasion when both ladies were there alone, they heard a noise in the basement. Together they went to investigate, but again found nothing; however, when they went to leave, my sister was in front and in her haste she closed the door with her sister-in-law still in the basement. Needless to say, she was a bit scared.

"The one situation that my sister recalls in retrospect also had to do with a door being open. Her brother-in-law and his wife moved before she and her husband did. Since the other side of the house was now empty, she would often let her two young sons play in the rooms on the first floor. She always made sure that the door to the outside was locked and bolted. One morning she got up to find the door to the other side of the house standing wide open, although she is positive it was closed when she brought the boys back to their side of the house the previous evening.

"I kidded her and told her my theory was that the ghost of Priscilla saw her as kin. She had left the door open to show that she had checked the other side of the house and found the intruders gone."

"Ah ha," Janet interjected, "there is a similarity already to what I have witnessed. Well, at least it has to do with a door."

"Go ahead and tell us," Jacob said." It will give me a rest from walking and talking."

Before Janet could say a word, there was a low chime that came from her wrist.

"Please excuse me a second, that is probably my hubby checking in."

She punched a small button on the side of the watch, held it close to her mouth and said in an accentuated tone, "Helllooo."

The answer sounded a bit tinny, but clear.

"Hi honey, just received my flight plan for Oslo. Should be back home tomorrow at about 7pm. So what you 'doin?'"

"Looking for ghosts."

"Say again."

"Never mind honey, I will explain it all to you tomorrow. Two things before you hang up, first, remember I am the only blue-eyed blond you are suppose to be ogling, and second, I met a man today who would like you to bring him back one of the wrist watch Nokia cell phones."

"You are telling me not to ogle any blue-eyed blonds, and then ask me to bring back a gift for a man you just met. What gives here?""It is not that way, but you can worry a little bit if you like," Janet said.

"Oh, I think I am safe, but I will do as I am told. Will see you tomorrow. I love you."

"Love you too, sweetie. Oh! Before you go, who made your flight suits when you were flying with the Blues?"

"Some company out in California. Why do you ask?"

"Did you ever hear of Jacob Grant who made their uniforms before you were on the team?"

"Yes, of course, but I never met him. One of my old CAGs, Denton McGill, who is now a three star, spoke quite highly of Jacob the Tailor. Again, why do you ask?"

"Because I just met him and he is here as we speak. Will tell you all about it when you return. Bye. Love you." Janet pushed the small button to end the call.

"I never heard so much romance in the middle of a cornfield," Jacob said.

"Just ignore him, he is too old to remember how it was," Wesley said.

"That from a Priest," Jacob said in retort.

"You two are good friends, I can tell," Janet said.

"Yes, just as long as he doesn't try to make me conform," Jacob said.

"That would probably be the biggest undertaking of my life," was Wesley's answer, and they all laughed.

The three started walking again, and Jacob picked up the story line.

"Okay, shall we continue with the account of Priscilla, the witch of these hills, or, *Hexe Berge* as the early German settlers called it."

Chapter 20

Jacob began. "What I am going to tell you is only a very cursory view. Over the years I have documented a lot of research looking for answers, and I have come up with more questions than answers. I once spent five days touring many parts of Virginia looking for answers. The problem with legends is you never know for sure what is truth and what is a figment of an over-active imagination. Each storyteller generally embellishes the legend, so you have to dig deep to try and come up with answers. And because this one has to do with a distant progenitor, the inability to find the link I am looking for has always given me grief. I have laid it aside for months, even years on end, only to come back to it hoping for a new angle, or lead. There is always that unanswerable question, exactly who was Priscilla and where was she from? Several great researchers have gone to their grave without knowing for certain the answer to those two simple questions.

"The legend has been passed down orally from one generation to the next, but the first person to put it into a written form was a lady from Ursina by the name of Nell Brach. Nell was a great researcher and storyteller. She wrote a lot of articles about local folklore for the newspapers, and such. She probably heard the story of Priscilla, or Prissy, from more than one source because there are a lot of Prissy's descendants in the local area. She could even have interviewed Priscilla's granddaughter, Elizabeth Rugg Growall. Elizabeth lived in the old log house just above Humbert until she died in 1902. That is also a story, but for another day.

"If Priscilla was a free spirit, then so was her granddaughter Elizabeth. Elizabeth's own granddaughter, Alice Firestone Tressler, told stories, some of which my sister can remember, about staying with her grandmother when she was a little girl, and how her grandmother would tell her all these great stories from her childhood about ghost and even the Indians. It must have been in the genes, because I can remember Great -Aunt Alice, and she was also a pretty feisty soul, but, on with the story.

"As told by Nell, when Samuel and Priscilla first came to the area, they brought with them a white horse that had been given to Priscilla by her father as a wedding gift. And here is the first problem. I don't know where they came from, but they did not come directly to Turkeyfoot Township from their place of birth or marriage. Records that I have found in the courthouse at Bedford show that prior to coming here, they lived in what is now Elk Lick Township.

"The court records show that in 1791 Samuel Rugg purchased two hundred acres from Joseph Francis. Two years later, in 1793, he sold the same property to Samuel Finley. By going back further to the 1790 census, there is a Samuel Ruck and his name appears next to that of Samuel Finley. In this census of Bedford County, the names were not alphabetized, but appear as the census marshals recorded them on their daily route. Samuel Ruck in this case was probably Samuel Rugg.

"This deed record also shows that the above-mentioned property was situated on the headwaters of Piney Run, on the Turkeyfoot Road. The Turkeyfoot Road is synonymous with Turkeyfoot Path, or the old Indian trail that goes from the present small town of Pocahontas to Salisbury. This is important to remember when reading my research records. It is not the same as the Turkeyfoot Road of Upper Turkeyfoot Township.

"Samuel Rugg first shows up in Turkeyfoot Township in the 1796 tax record, so it is fairly safe to surmise that they sold the property in Elk Lick Township in 1793 and moved to Turkeyfoot Township. However, there is one small piece of evidence to show that they arrived in Elk Lick Township as early as 1788. There is a baptismal record in the Berlin Lutheran Church that shows Mary Rugg was born on November 18, 1788. The parents were Samuel and Priscilla Rugg.

"By the time they got to Turkeyfoot Township, they probably had at least three children, and were certainly not newlyweds. But, of course, in her article, Nell never said they were newlyweds, she just states that the white horse had been given to Priscilla as a wedding gift.

"If you all don't mind, I think I would like to take a little breather here," Jacob said.

"You have been doing a lot of talking and we have only been listening, so I think you have earned it," Janet said.

"I agree," Wesley responded. "I have some water here in my backpack, would you like some?"

"Is that the same that we got up at the old May farm?" Jacob asked.

"The very same."

"Okay, I'll have a swig, but ladies first," Jacob said as he took the bottle from Wesley.

"No, you go first," Janet said. "I don't mind waiting."

"I insist," Jacob said.

"Go ahead, Janet, he is old school. Nothing wrong with that, but if you don't go first, none of us will get a drink," Wesley said.

Jacob gave Wesley a look across his left shoulder and handed the bottle to Janet.

After Janet had taken a drink, she handed the bottle back to Jacob.

Jacob took a deep swallow and then handed it to Wesley and said, "You all need to remember the protocol, it is ladies first, then deference to age."

"Did I just detect a bit of southern lingo in 'you all'?" Janet asked, directing her comment at Jacob.

"Yes, I also detected that," Wesley said.

"A lot 'y'al' know," Jacob said. "I said, 'you all,' two one syllable words. You're thinking I said 'y'al,'a one-syllable word. Besides, y'ore forgittin I grew up here, and I know there are a lot of linguistic nuances. Like, I betcha, Janet warshes her clothes, reds up the house, and drinks a pop now and then."

Janet laughed. "How right you are. And, of course if you want to be accepted as one of us, Wesley, you are going to have to learn some of this vernacular pronto."

"Well, Mrs. Lanning already taught me about reding up the house," Wesley said, "but I still think you dropped a couple of letters from that, 'you all,' Jacob."

"Okay," Jacob said,"If we have Pennsylvanian and Southern 101 out of the way, shall we continue?"

"One of the big unanswered questions is where did they come from, but one equally as big, if not bigger, is what was Priscilla's maiden name. There are two choices, Curtis or Rootes.

"There are proponents for both, and it is highly theorized that there was some illegitimacy, or out of wedlock activity, so it is possible that both names are involved. My own theory, and I have a lot of research to support it, is that Priscilla is a descendant of a rather well-founded Virginia family by the name of Rootes from King and Queen County.

"There was a Philip Rootes who was married to Mildred Reade, and the Reades have a good pedigree if you want to trace it back. Philip and Mildred had nine children, four boys and five girls. The boys were Philip, Thomas Reade, John and George. The girls were Mildred, Elizabeth, Priscilla, Mary and Lucy. As children, they had the best that wealth could provide. Philip Sr. had vast landholdings in several Virginia counties and a number of deeded plots in Fredericksburg. He was also deeply involved in the slave trade.

"The girls all married well, and the boys were successful in their own rights, at least initially. It proved to be a very fascinating family to research, but they didn't always leave good tracks; they were a bit elusive.

"I picked up on the family when I came across the name Priscilla Rootes, but she was one generation too old to be Priscilla Rugg. But it was this Priscilla Rootes and her brother George that showed a lot of promise.

"Priscilla Rootes married a much older man by the name of Benjamin Grymes. They lived in Spotsylvania County, and his best friend and wealthy neighbor was Rice Curtis. Rice had a son who was Priscilla Rootes' age, so there could have been some hanky-panky, but I have not been able to locate any record of it.

"George Rootes was a lawyer, dealing primarily in real estate. He lived first in Culpeper, and then Martinsburg, which is now in West Virginia. As a real estate lawyer, George did a lot of traveling, and often journeyed in to that part of western Pennsylvania that the Virginians said belonged to them. His route would have taken him through Fort Cumberland and then along the old Indian trails in what is known as the Turkeyfoot Path, starting at Wills Creek at Fort Cumberland and ending at the Turkeyfoot, or what we know today as Confluence. The interesting thing about this route is that it crossed Big Savage Mountain and entered into what is now Somerset County. This old Indian path passed close to Pochahontas, and crossed Big Piney Run in Elk Lick Township, exactly where Samuel Rugg later owned property. Coincidence? Maybe, but I am not sure."

The trio had now advanced to just below a trailer home that sat almost exactly where the old Keck house once stood.

"I suppose we should ask the inhabitants if they mind if we trespass," Jacob said.

"Don't worry," Janet said, "I know the lady that lives there. I am sure she won't mind, but if you wait here, I will go ask her."

When Janet left, Wesley turned to Jacob and asked, "I assume you have a lot more details about this family?"

"Lots," Jacob answered. "I have a folder with the basics in the truck. When I get back to Pensacola, I will e-mail my narrative to you, but that is still only part of the picture. I have many folders of supporting data. If my granddaughter doesn't want it, I will decree it to you when I pass from this earth," Jacob said with a smile.

"Thanks, I take that as a compliment, but I would be privileged if you aren't called to make that passage any time soon."

"One never knows. I remember a country western song with word that sort of told that story, it went something like, '...everybody want to go to heaven but nobody want to go right now,' but as for the material, you deserve it Wesley, you are a good protégée."

Jacob and Wesley saw Janet come around the corner of the trailer house and motion for them to come forward. She did not move toward them.

"Come here you guys, I want you to meet someone," Janet said.

As they came to the end of the trailer, they saw there was a fairly wide upper porch. An elderly lady sat in a wheelchair facing them. To her right was a low table and on the table was an artist's easel containing a canvas board. There was another table to her left containing a jar with brushes, some rags, and a palette containing dabs of paint. The old lady was an artist and had apparently been painting when Janet entered her domain.

As Jacob and Wesley entered the enclosed porch area, Janet started the introduction. "Gentlemen, this is my neighbor, Mrs. Colburn. Nellie, this is Jacob Grant and Wesley Donaldson."

"Nice to meet you gentlemen," Mrs. Colburn said.

"I am sure the pleasure is more ours," Jacob said.

"I told Nellie briefly what you are looking for," Janet said

"I don't think I can be of much help to you in finding the old graveyard, other than to say you are welcome to look about," Mrs. Colburn said. "Some years ago another gentleman and a lady stopped by asking about the same thing. I remember the lady said she had lived here once when it was the old Keck place. She knew of my family. The gentleman said he was doing some research on the original owners and that they were buried somewhere on the grounds, probably up by the main tree line."

Jacob smiled. "Mrs. Colburn that was probably me and my sister. I do remember your name. I didn't know you were an artist."

"Artist may be stretching the point some, I dabble. Started it about thirty years ago after my husband was killed. Had to have something to pass my time."

"Believe me," Janet cut in, "calling her an artist is not stretching the point. We have several great works of hers hanging in our house. I refuse to take anymore because she will not accept any payment for them."

"Janet is very proud and stubborn, you see. I have told her, I do not paint for money, I paint to pass time and for the love of it."

"May I ask what you are working on now?" Jacob asked.

"Haven't really decided on a name yet, but maybe, 'Goat Lady and Friends,'" she answered.

"Goat Lady!" Jacob exclaimed. I knew of a Goat Lady. May I see your painting?"

"But of course. Come here," Mrs. Colburn said.

Mrs. Colburn backed her wheelchair up to give Jacob enough room in front of the easel. Jacob moved forward and looked at the canvas board. He stared at the painting in disbelief. He shifted his gaze to the right and then to the left as if looking for something. Finally when he was able to speak, he said, "It is Sarah Jane, her house and her goats."

"And chickens," Mrs. Colburn added.

"Yes, how could I forget chickens," Jacob replied.

"So you also knew her?" Mrs. Colburn asked.

Jacob did not answer. His eyes remained transfixed on the painting. His mouth was tightly closed and from the slight movement of the lips, Wesley could see that he was in deep thought, but he didn't know why.

After a long moment of silence, Jacob regained his composure and then he said. "I knew her, but I didn't. As a young boy, I often walked by her house when I would come down to this very place to see my sister. Or when I walked to Confluence to see my young sweetie. If she were out side, I would say, 'Hello, Miss Dodson,' and she would say, 'hello,' but sometimes she would not even look toward me or raise her head. By then she was probably in her mid-fifties."

"I must tell you, Mrs. Colburn, some years ago I took a few snapshots of the old house. I had an artist in Pensacola view them and then capture them in a painting that hangs above my fireplace. He did an excellent job in interpreting the photos to a painting, but what you have here is unbelievable. Where is the picture you are working from?"

"There is no photo, Mr. Grant. All my paintings are from memory. Some people say I have a photographic memory, but I think most people have that when it comes to places you have known all your life. I guess God just blessed me with the ability to be able to put on a piece of canvas what I perceive in my mind's eye. One advantage of that is, no one knows if you make a mistake or misinterpretation," she said with a slight laugh.

"This is so truly amazing," Jacob said with a touch of awe. "I have seen this scene more than once, maybe fifty or more years ago. The goats on the roof of the porch and on the old shed, eating apples from the branches that over hang them. Seeing the chickens on the floor of the porch and wandering through the open door into the house. And Sarah Jane there working, head down, and weeding her garden. This is so unbelievable, how do you do it?"

"Well, I knew her too, Mr. Grant. I am guessing that I am a few years older than you, and perhaps I knew her better. She was a bit reclusive, always was after what happened to her when she was a young woman, but there were a few people she would talk to; I just happened to be one of them.

"This is so great Mrs. Colburn; could I impose on you and ask you to sometime jot down what you know of her?" Jacob asked.

"Mr. Grant, I paint, I do not write. I mean I do write, but you know what I mean. However, I will be more than glad to tell you what I know whenever you have the time to listen."

"Do you have the time to tell me now?" Jacob asked.

"Where am I going to go, or what am I going to do? Time is all I have, so to answer your question, yes, I do have time now. But before I start, you might want to get more comfortable, so won't you all please have a seat.

"I made some iced tea earlier if anyone would like a glass. I seldom drink coffee anymore and never drink pop, but you can also have some water if you please. Don't be afraid to say yes because I am in this chair. Actually, I can still walk with the aid of that contraption over there, but I get around better in the wheelchair, and I have it padded for comfort. Besides, I will impose on Janet, she knows the place well and I am sure she will get it for you, won't you dear?"

"Be glad to Nellie," Janet said.

"I would love a glass of iced tea," Jacob said.

"Me too," Wesley added.

"And what about you Nellie?" Janet asked.

"I suppose I will be sociable and have one with you. I also made some fresh peanut butter cookies this morning. They are on a tray by the microwave oven. Bring them with you Janet."

While Janet was in the kitchen, Mrs. Colburn continued, "My son normally stops in to check on me every evening, and peanut butter cookies are his favorite. He will eat any type. He likes chocolate chip and macadamia nut, but I can only make the latter when my great-grandson sends me some from Hawaii."

Janet returned with a tray containing four glasses of iced tea and a tray of cookies and some napkins. She set them on the table close to where Jacob and Wesley were seated. She started to take a glass to Mrs. Colburn, but she motioned her back saying, "I will join you there."

"These look and smell really delicious, Mrs. Colburn," Wesley said, "but I suppose we should exercise restraint, lest there be none left for your son."

"Don't worry about that, Mr. Donaldson. I put the ones for Curtis in a separate cookie tin. His wife Rosalie also likes them. She is also a great cook, but she says she will let me spoil my son, and then she laughs. He is only sixty-nine years of age, so I guess I still have time to spoil him," she said with a laugh.

"Since we are talking about age, and you brought it up earlier in reference to our mutual age, I am going be presumptuous and do what a gentleman should never do, and that is ask a lady her age, so, if you don't mind, how old are you Mrs.Colburn?" Jacob asked.

"Well, for taking that liberty, Mr. Grant, I will not let you off easy? How old do you think I am?"

"Ah! I knew I would firmly plant the hook in my mouth. Okay, let me see how smooth my logic is. I am seventy, and you said you are a few years older than I, which would make you about seventy-four and I could accept that, except you said your son, Curtis, was sixty-nine. I don't know if you have any other children, younger or older, but I am guessing not older. Also, assuming you were not a child bride, I put you at eighty-eight."

"Thanks Mr. Grant, I am sure you are trying to unseat the hook and flatter me, but you are wrong. Curtis is the youngest of my three children. I have a daughter who just turned seventy-one and another son who is seventy-three. It is his grandson who sends me the macadamia nuts from Hawaii. For your relief, I do not mind telling my age. I am ninety-three."

"It must be the mountain air of Somerset County. My father lived to be ninety- three and my mother was eighty-nine. I doubt if I will reach that longevity," Jacob said.

"Well, not if you have doubts, Mr. Grant."

"I know it is not polite to barge in on two senior citizens discussing their age, but when you get ready to tell us about Sarah Jane, do you mind if I record it"? Wesley asked.

"Obnoxious young whippersnapper, isn't he?" Mrs. Colburn said smiling at Jacob.

"Yeah, I don't know why. It isn't in his genes and I am sure it wasn't in his upbringing. May have something to do with his profession," Jacob said looking at Mrs. Colburn and raising his eyebrows.

"And what is your profession, Mr. Donaldson?" Mrs. Colburn asked.

"I am a Catholic Priest, but I am on an extended sabbatical," Wesley said. He too smiled and shook his head sideways at Jacob.

"Mr. Grant, you should be ashamed saying something like that about a man of the cloth," Mrs. Colburn replied. "And, yes, you may record what

I have to say. Are you going to give me one of those funny little bugs that Janet and Mr. Grant are wearing?"

"Yes, I am," Wesley said as he got up to pin the miniature microphone on the collar of her blouse. "And one other thing Mrs. Colburn, I know we just met, but would you mind just calling me Wesley? Janet brought this formality thing to our attention earlier this afternoon."

"That is fine with me," Mrs. Colburn said, "and as you have heard Janet say, my name is Nellie."

"So now that we are comfortable, had something to eat and drink, and are on a first name basis, let me tell you what I know about Sarah Jane. I caution you not to get too excited because it is not a lot."

Chapter 21

"Sarah Jane was born in 1896. The reason I can remember it is that we were born nineteen years and one day apart. Her birthday was April 30, 1896, and I was born on May 1st. She was the youngest of five children born to George and Elizabeth Dodson. Her grandparents were Thomas and Sarah Dodson. She was named after her grandmother. I am not sure how many children Thomas and Sarah had, but I think Sarah Jane mentioned two uncles, James and Benjamin. She never spoke much about her family, but her two sisters were Maudie and Anabelle. She had a brother, and I think one sibling who died as an infant.

"According to Sarah Jane, she was born in Draketown where her father and uncle worked for a farmer. When she was about sixteen, she met a young man from around Confluence by the name of Walton Enos. Walton was the son of Judson and Mary Enos.

"Now some people will tell you that Walton Enos got Sarah Jane pregnant and then married Mary Goniak. And then, being heartbroken, she became a recluse. But that is not exactly how it happened. She did get pregnant by Walton and had a son, but they never married. She would never tell me why they didn't get married. It may have been a family thing, but it was not because Walton married Mary Goniak. Walton did eventually marry Mary Goniak, that portion of the story is true, but Sarah Jane bore her son two days before her seventeenth birthday in 1913. At that time, Mary Goniak was only eight years old, too young to fit into the triangle.

"Whatever else happened in her young life, it made her a sad and somewhat dispirited person. I did not find her to be bitter; she just accepted her life as it was. That was the way it was intended to be. She was very reluctant to accept anything from anyone else, unless she could give him or her something in return. I once took her a cake when I went to visit, and she would not accept it until I promised to take some goat cheese she had made. It turned out to be some of the best Feta cheese I ever tasted. She had told me her grandmother taught her how to make it when she was just a very young girl. Her grandmother had learned it from a Greek lady that once lived close to them. She didn't know where that was.

"She said she liked her goats and chickens because they didn't ask for anything. They gave what they had; their milk and eggs, but they were no trouble. She said they were her friends, perhaps the only friends she ever knew. That may have been by her choosing, or her barrier so to speak, to keep from getting hurt. I tried to be her friend, and she accepted me, but I don't think I ever crossed further into the realm of her life. It was too bad, because she lived to be 82 years of age.

"She is buried in the Jersey Hollow cemetery, just one plot away from Walton and Mary, and that plot is reserved for their son. And that is about all I know of her," Nellie concluded.

Then Jacob said, "Two things you mentioned bring something to my recollection. I remember several years ago talking to a man from here. He and his wife, who is my first cousin, were in Pensacola to visit their daughter and son-in-law, who was in the Navy and stationed there. Monika and I invited them to our house one evening and he recognized the house from the painting I had commissioned. He told a story similar to the one you told about the cake, except he had taken her a load of firewood. She refused to take it because she said she could not pay for it. No matter how much he insisted that he did not want any payment, she still wouldn't let him unload the firewood. Finally he saw a pan with a bunch of black walnuts sitting on a table on the porch. He told her if she wanted to pay him, he would really like some walnuts. She consented and the deal was consummated.

"The other thing is something that I remember seeing when I was a young boy and walked by her place, especially in the summer. She left the door on the upper porch open, and more than once I went by and saw chickens and a goat or two in the house. I guess she really did consider them her friends. The only thing I regret is that I never stopped and tried to have a conversation with her. As I said earlier, if I saw her in her garden or about the shed, I would shout hello. She would say hello, and sometimes would and sometimes would not turn her head and nod, but I don't ever remember hearing her utter a word of greeting beyond hello.

"Nellie, on behalf of Janet and Wesley, I want to thank you for your hospitality and wonderful conversation, and filling us in a bit more about Sarah Jane."

Wesley stood and took Nellie's hand and said, "I want to reiterate what Jacob has already said. It has been a real joy in meeting you. You are indeed a remarkable lady, and I have one request before we leave."

"And what might that be?" Nellie asked.

"When you have finished with the paining, I would like to come and take a picture of it."

"Why would you want to do that? When I am finished with it, you may have it, if you wish. I will let Janet know."

"Oh! I couldn't do that Nellie," Wesley said.

"And why not?"

"I don't know. I just couldn't," Wesley continued.

"Wesley, you are a man of God. I imagine you have often given more than you received. Have you never stood in the pulpit and expounded on the greatest gift to mankind? Of course you have, and I would guess that much of your life has been about giving, so why would you deny someone else the joy of giving? Something probably happened to poor Sarah Jane that she could never know the joy of just receiving, but you can't plead that case."

It was now Nellie who was holding onto Wesley's hand.

Wesley glanced at Jacob and sensed a condescending look on his face. He put his other hand on top of Nellie's, bent and kissed her on the forehead, then said, "I most gratefully accept."

Then Nellie spoke again. "Jacob, I hope I didn't offend you by offering it to your friend."

"Nellie, you made the correct choice. Your painting captures the whole essence much better than the one I have, but mine represents a moment in my life that I will never forget. A cold, wet, and dreary spring day, snow falling and landing on the lens of my camera, and I, an aging man, standing there shivering, seeing the house and surroundings it as it was more than fifty years earlier on a bright sunny day. In one of the photos I took that day, there is a white haze over part of the roof, probably caused by a snowflake about to hit the lens of my camera, but to me it will always be the spirit of Sarah Jane finally looking at me and saying hello. I never showed that one to the artist," Jacob concluded.

"You know how to bring a tear to an old woman's eye, Jacob. Now get out of here, all of you," she said with a smile and a shooing motion of her hand. "I think I will rest a while before Curtis gets here."

When they were at the end of the porch, Janet turned around and said, "Give me a call if you need anything, Nellie."

"I will dear," was Nellie's reply.

Then as an afterthought, Janet turned and said, "Nellie, I have a huge pot of 'all around the garden soup' on the stove, would you like me to bring you some a little later on?"

"If it is not too much bother, I would like it very much," Nellie said.

"Consider it done," Janet replied.

Chapter 22

They walked across Nellie's yard in the direction from which they came. Finally Wesley spoke. "Are we going to look for the graves?"

"It would be futile at this time of the year," Jacob said. "There is too much vegetation now. The best time to look will be in the spring after the snow has melted and pasted everything flat."

Wesley walked in silence, and Jacob realized, that perhaps the day had been a bit too much for him to comprehend and neatly store in his mind. He knew that Wesley was a very organized person, but maybe everything that they saw and talked about, and most of all this last hour with Nellie, had caused Wesley's mind to overload. Perhaps it was time for some small talk.

"It is getting pretty late in the day, so I thought we would walk Janet back to her house and then retrace part of our path back up through Hexie. I would like to stop by the Old Bethel cemetery and say hello to Monika for a moment," Jacob said.

Janet didn't know who Monika was, but sensed it might be his wife. She did not ask.

Then Jacob continued, "I don't know if you remember, Wesley, but the first time we met, I chided you about being a Catholic when your name indicated you should be a Methodist."

"I remember," Wesley said. "You mentioned something about a song that Charles Wesley wrote and said it had something to do with this area."

"I didn't quite say it like that, or if I did, I gave the wrong impression. What I really meant to say was there is a story of this area with a relationship to the Christmas Carol, Hark the Herald Angels Sing."

"I think you are right, and I apologize for getting it wrong," Wesley said.

"Not to worry, my friend, we talked about so much that day, or at least I did, that I am amazed you remembered any of it."

Janet stopped walking and both men turned to see what the matter was.

Finally Jacob asked, "Is something wrong, Janet."

"Well yes, you two are being very impolite talking about something of which your newfound friend, namely me, knows nothing about," Janet said.

"I guess that is a bit rude of us, Janet," Jacob said. "Come, walk with us and I will try and catch you up. It goes along with the legend of Hexie and Priscilla that we were talking about on the way up.

"The first time I met Wesley and he told me he was a Catholic, I said it didn't seem right. With a name like Wesley Donaldson, he should be a Methodist. Do you know anything about the Wesley brothers?" Jacob asked of Janet.

"I realize that my ignorance is going to show here, but no, I know nothing of them," Janet said.

"Well, as Wesley is fond of saying, 'look it up, you will remember it better,' and I am sure you are very computer literate, so use the search word Methodist and you will get tons of articles about the religious denomination and about the Wesley brothers, John and Charles," Jacob said. "It is only marginally important to our story here."

"Very true," Wesley chimed in, "and that way Jacob won't be embarrassed if he gets his facts wrong."

"So that is why you use that, 'Look it up bit', Jacob said in retort.

"You bet you," Wesley said.

"Back to you, Janet. The Wesley brothers are considered to be the early founders of the Methodist denomination. Born in England in the early 1700s, John was considered the preacher, and Charles was the songwriter, although both did a bit of the other's specialty. It is reported that Charles wrote over five thousand songs in his lifetime. One that most people know is a Christmas carol titled: Hark! The Herald Angels Sing."

"Yeah, of course, I know that one," Janet said.

"Okay, keep that in the back of your mind. Let's get back to Priscilla and her hexing ways. According to the legend, Priscilla would often mount the white horse that her father had given her and take off riding the old Indian trails shouting to the top of her lungs. It was supposedly for this reason that the early German settlers tagged her as a witch.

"As Nell Brach retold the legend, she said, 'On catching the white horse she would take it to the riding stump where she would mount. Riding three times around the stump she would exclaim, 'When I die I'll come back and make this welkin ring.' According to Nell, the witch-sign of three was on Prissy.

"The first time I read Nell's account, I didn't put too much thought into this statement, because like most people, I didn't quite understand what she was saying. And there is the possibility that Nell was writing what someone else had told her and didn't fully understand either. It all hinges on the word welkin.

"I assumed that "welkin ring' was some sort of witchcraft lingo, especially in light of Nell saying that Prissy rode around the mounting stump three times, and also the witch-sign of three was on her. But when I looked it up in a dictionary, I found it means the vault of the sky, or vault of heaven as some would say.

"Look it up in the Oxford English Dictionary (OED) and you get a lot of examples and language derivations. Therein it is stated that after the sixteenth century, welkin was seldom used outside of literary (chiefly poetic) writings. So if Prissy had in fact made that statement, how did she know about it, or was it just something that Nell added to give her story more color?

"Nell had a great talent for adding color to her stories, but in defense of Prissy actually making the statement, there are some things that validate the possibility. One has to do with Charles Wesley's Christmas carol that I mentioned previously. The way we sing the first verse is: Hark! The herald angels sing, Glory to the newborn King, and the last two lines of the first verse are: With Angelic hosts proclaim, Christ is born in Bethlehem. But according to Bartlett's book of Famous Quotations, that is not how Charles wrote it. His original words were: Hark, how all the welkin rings, Glory to the King of Kings, and the last two lines are: Universal nature say, Christ the Lord is born today. Again, according to Bartlett's book, George

Whitefield substituted the words we now use not long after Charles wrote them. George Whitefield was a good friend of the Wesley brothers.

"Continuing, as that old radio personality, Paul Harvey, used to say, 'Now, for the rest of the story.'"

The trio was now at the yard by Janet's house and she interrupted Jacob to say, "I want to hear the rest of this intriguing story, so I would like to bribe you. How would you both like to sit out here by the picnic table and have a bowl of my delicious vegetable soup? That way Jacob can finish this part of the story." Janet said.

"Your call, you are driving," Wesley said.

"My mind was made up when Janet said soup," Jacob replied. "Monika won't mind if I am a couple of minutes late."

"Okay," Janet said. "Have a seat over there and I will get us each a bowl of soup. What would you like to drink? I have Pepsi, iced tea, or I can make coffee, and my husband Luke makes some good blackberry wine, but I don't think that goes with soup."

"I'll have iced tea," Jacob said.

"Same for me," Wesley said.

"Do you need any help?" Wesley continued.

"No. I'll be fine," Janet answered.

Jacob and Wesley walked to the picnic table that was positioned close to the trunk of a large maple tree. They sat down on the end of the benches opposite each other.

"Since you are going to stop and talk to Jake's mother in the morning, do you still plan to head back to Florida tomorrow?"

"I don't know," Jacob replied. "I guess I will just play it by ear."

"Why don't you go ahead and check out of your motel in the morning, and then if you decide to stay until Monday morning, you can just stay at my place," Wesley said.

"Yeah, that sounds like a good plan. Seeing as I will probably get to your house before you get back from church in Somerset, remember to turn off your outside security system. I don't want my face showing up on your surveillance cameras," Jacob said.

"Who said I had a surveillance system?" Wesley asked.

"Come on, Wesley, you are talking to an old cryptologic spy, you can't fool me. Besides, I would think it foolish if you didn't. It grieves me greatly that we can't trust our fellow man more, and not have to use such devices, but it is the time in which we live."

"You are right. I did have a system installed on the advice of the builder. I too, felt uncomfortable giving my consent, but seeing I am gone quite a bit, I agreed with his suggestion. I will turn it off and give you a key so you can get in," Wesley said.

"In truth, I don't worry about the system. I just wanted to yank your chain, but I don't want to take a key, because if I decide not to stay, I would just have to mail it back to you. Just leave a coffee pot ready to go on the lower porch, along with a cup. I will be fine," Jacob said.

"Okay, I can do that," Wesley said.

Janet appeared in the doorway carrying a large tray. "I will take a hand in helping with the second tray," Janet called.

Wesley immediately rushed to her aid.

When everything was positioned at the three place mats, Janet sat down. There was a moment of silence until Wesley realized the two of them were waiting for him to say grace. He did.

"Of course, you know it is bad manners to talk while you are eating," Jacob said, "and then after that, I have to go."

"In that case, finish with your story, and I will give you your soup after you are done," Janet said with a smile and raised eyebrows.

"You drive a hard bargain, Ms. Janet," Jacob said, as he took some crackers and broke them in to the bowl of steaming soup.

Jacob saw Wesley look at him and then said, "Yeah, yeah, I know, that is not proper etiquette, but when I was a kid back here in the hills that is the way we always did it. Janet, will just have to excuse my unrefined ways," Jacob said.

"Doesn't bother me. I am just glad you did it first. Now I won't feel bad about doing it," Janet said.

"Me too," Wesley replied and they all laughed.

"This really is great soup, Janet," Wesley said.

"Thanks," Janet replied. "Luke likes it better after it is a day old that is why I make it the day of one of his overnight flights."

"Vegetable soup, navy beans, and chicken and dumplin's all taste better as warm ups," Jacob said.

"And where is your husband from?" Jacob asked.

"Not too far from where you live in Florida. Do you know where Bayou La Batre, Alabama, is?" Janet asked.

"Sure do," Jacob replied.

"Why do you ask?"

"Because I noticed you included okra as one of the vegetables; northerners generally don't do that," Jacob answered.

"Of course, but Luke still says I don't make soup like his mother does," Janet said.

"You don't take offense with that, I hope," Jacob said. "No wife makes anything as good as their mother. It is part of the subliminal message that mothers start when the son is still in the womb. When they are all alone, they rub their expanding belly and whisper, '*Remember, no women will ever do things for you as good as your mother, remember, remember, rem....*'"

Janet laughed, and Wesley just sighed.

"Just wait until you are pregnant, Janet. You will see," Jacob said.

Jacob finished his soup before the other two and Janet offered him a refill but he refused.

"One of my few bad habits is I eat too fast," Jacob said. "But when you come from a large family that is also poor, you learn to eat fast or go hungry. That is more of an old cliché than a fact with my family. We were poor and although we did not have five course meals, I never remember of going hungry.

"You all continue and I will pick up with my story if I can remember where I was at," Jacob said.

"You had just finished telling how Charles Wesley's original words mentioning the welkin were changed," Wesley said.

"That's right," Jacob said. "The OED tells us that the word welkin was not in common use in the middle 1700s, and that may have been why George Whitefield changed them. But if Priscilla really did say what Nell attributes to her, then how did she know of the meaning?

"If she was who I think she was, the granddaughter of Philip Rootes of King and Queen County, Virginia, then history shows that she probably had the benefit of a good education and may have had private tutors. It is also conceivable that she could have seen a copy of Charles Wesley's original words."

"I think I am getting myself deeper into this story than I had intended," Jacob said.

"I am not going anywhere," Janet said.

"I have to go when you go, but I would like to hear the rest of the details," Wesley said.

"Okay, you asked for it," Jacob said. "The story of the Wesley brothers is pretty interesting, especially their short stay in the colonies. General James Oglethorpe was in what is now the state of Georgia at a settlement that we know as Savannah. Georgia was sort of a refuge for persecuted religious sects and so James Oglethorpe asked John and Charles Wesley to come help out. The year was around 1736. Charles stayed only a few months, apparently because he and Oglethorpe had some form of a disagreement. John stayed for almost two years, but his stay was troubled. It involved a woman named Sophia whom he apparently loved, an unscrupulous magistrate by the name of Causton who was also Sophia's uncle, and his devotion to his religion. Sophia felt that John had spurned her and she ran off with another man to be married. When she returned to the Savannah district, John refused to administer the Rites of Holy Communion at a public gathering without giving her a reason. This naturally upset her husband and her uncle, and they made life pretty rough for the good Reverend. John did write her a letter explaining why he justifiably denied her the Sacrament, but it was too late. Sophia's husband sued for defamation of her character, and John Wesley was brought to trial. It ended in a mistrial, but his troubles with Mr. Causton were not over. By this time John knew he was loosing credibility with the people and in 1737, or thereabouts, he returned to England.

"Sometime shortly after that, George Whitefield also migrated to Georgia, where he is best known for starting the Bethesda orphanage for boys which, I believe, still operates in old Savannah.

"Meanwhile back in England, a fairly wealthy young man by the name of John Thompson was getting ready to go to the colony of Virginia. Born in Ireland, and educated at Edinburgh in Scotland, he became first a Presbyterian minister. Later he joined the Church of England where in 1739 he was ordained as a priest in the Palace Royal of St. James of Westminster. In about 1740 he arrived in Virginia and shortly thereafter became rector of St. Marks Parrish close to what is now Culpeper.

"Reverend Thompson obtained a lot of land in the general area and in 1742 he married the widow of Governor Alexander Spotswood. Just east of Culpeper at the small town of Stevensburg on the old Fredericksburg road, he built for her a huge mansion, later called Salubria. It is reported that he had the finest library in the area, most were volumes he brought with him from England. He did cross paths with the Wesley brothers while in England.

"His first wife preceded him in death and in 1760 he married Elizabeth Rootes. Three of Elizabeth's sisters and her brother George lived close by. Now as I mentioned when we started out, I believe Priscilla was either the daughter of George Rootes, or the illegitimate daughter of Priscilla Rootes Grymes. In either case, she would have had access to John Thompson's library and his learning, although she would only have been between seven to ten years of age when he died in 1772.

"I realize this is a rather far out theory in connecting the word welkin, but when dealing with a legend, anything is possible and must be considered. There are other interesting bits of information that offer grounds for speculation in Priscilla's case. She could read and write. She owned a Bible, and that was a bit uncommon for this area in the late 1700s. She owned a sidesaddle, although if we are to believe Nell's account, she probably did not use it on her impromptu rides on the old trails. And she named her first daughter, Mary. Although it is a very common name, then and now, it was also the name of George and Priscilla's sister. Connected to this Mary is one last piece of reference material that I am hoping may solve the dilemma of who Priscilla actually was.

"Philip Rootes Sr. died in 1756, and he left a very specific will for the settlement of his estate. In 1790 a lawsuit was instituted, known as Thornton vs. Taliferro. It was instituted by Anthony Thornton to recover the legacy left to his wife, Mary Rootes who I just mentioned. By 1806 it was still working its way through the Virginia courts. It is important, because it contains the testimony of a lot of the descendants and names most of the extended family. I have read excerpts from this case, but not the entire record. It does exist in the old archives of the Library of Virginia in Richmond. You may obtain access to it, but you have to give the library advance notice so they can pull it. I have never done that, but suppose I should sometime before I die.

"And that is about all I know of the history of Priscilla, the supposed witch of this area," Jacob said. I did document my research down in Virginia and later put it into a paper I titled, In Defense of A Progenitor. I was going to submit it to the Somerset Historical society for publication, but I thought it was a bit too long for their quarterly publication."

"Really, that is quite a bit," Janet said.

"Yes, and very interesting," added Wesley.

"Do you think she was a witch?" Janet asked.

"If she did come from the Culpeper-Fredericksburg area of Virginia, I think here in the backwoods of Pennsylvania in the late 1700s she was just a very bored housewife," Jacob said. "You know, no cable TV, no cell phone, no shopping malls, life could get pretty boring."

"Okay, Wesley, lets help Janet take the dishes in the house and then hit the road," Jacob said.

"No need for that," Janet replied, "I can take care of them, no sweat. But let me ask you one question."

"Shoot," Jacob said.

"Who is Monika?"

"She is my deceased wife," Jacob said. "She is buried in the Old Bethel Cemetery."

"I figured as much, but wanted to be sure I wasn't keeping you from seeing someone who was going to yell at me later," Janet said. Then added, "My sister-in-law goes to that church."

"Who might your sister-in-law be?" Jacob asked.

"Bethany Larkin," Janet replied.

"I don't know her," Jacob said.

"I know her," Wesley said. "She has a beautiful singing voice."

"Yes, she does. She is a very sweet person. Too bad she has to be married to a scoundrel like my brother," Janet replied. "Sometimes he can be so nice, and then something just happens and he goes wild. I know he beats her, and I have told him if I ever see it, I will turn him in even if he is my brother. I also think he cheats on her with a woman that lives up the hollow. Her husband drives truck for Wal-Mart, but if he ever catches them, he will kill them both. Well, I had better shut up; I shouldn't be bothering you with family problems. Listen, I enjoyed it very much, and, Wesley, please stop down sometime when Marshall is home. The two of you can 'gadget and technoverse.' You too, Jacob, stop in the next time you get up this way."

Chapter 23

Jacob and Wesley drove in silence for several minutes, and then Jacob spoke. "Seems that you were right about this Larkin fellow. His sister didn't give him much of a glowing report, did she?"

"Yeah, you are right about that. At least she knows about it and that may be a start," Wesley said.

"True, but when push comes to shove, blood often runs thicker than water as the old saying goes," Jacob replied.

After that the two men were silent, each with his own thoughts until Jacob stopped his truck by the edge of the cemetery at the Old Bethel Church.

When he had turned off the engine, he turned to Wesley and asked, "So, how much do you know about this church and it's history?"

"I know it is independent and pretty fundamentalist," Wesley replied.

"Well, it has always been pretty fundamentalist, that is why the denomination was started in the first place. Ironically, the fairly recent move to independence and out of the Churches of God, General Conference, was for about the same reason that John Winebrenner started the denomination."

"That is very interesting," Wesley said.

"Yeah, it is a pretty interesting story, and if you are really interested in knowing more about it, simply go to one of your internet search engines and type in John Winebrenner. But in a nutshell, it goes something like this: John was a minister in several German Reformed Churches in and around Harrisburg. In the 1820s, his revivalist preaching and teachings were in conflict with those of the German Reformed Church, and then one Sunday he went to his church and found that the locks had been changed. So, somewhere around 1830, he broke from that denomination and along with some of his followers started his own denomination. A couple of years later they built their first church at Harrisburg and called it Union Old Bethel. The denomination was later known as The Churches of God of North America, and the hierarchy was the General Eldership.

About 1881 the young denomination was looking for a place to build a college. They settled on the small town of Findlay in northwestern Ohio. The town was also looking for an institute of higher learning so it was mutually advantageous. Findlay College was founded as a liberal arts institution and not as a Bible college. Later they did built a seminary; known as the Winebrenner Theological Seminary. It remained a very small college until sometime in the 1960s when there was a rebirth with a lot of new buildings and course offerings. The college eventually became a university and separated from the Seminary.

The first church built on this site, known as the Bethel Church and later as the Old Bethel Church, was dedicated about 1858. Actually an Elder, named William J. Davis, organized the congregation as a group about 1850. For most of those years prior to 1858, the congregation met in the old Methodist church further down the hollow that you see in front of you. That church ceased to exist before my time. Apparently there was a dispute and so it was determined that they would build their own house of worship. They acquired the land from a farmer by the name of Alexander Rhoads.

"I remember reading an excellent account by Harrison King, that the seed for the church was sown when an Elder by the name of John Hickernell came from Westmoreland County and preached some awe inspiring sermons. Some have said that Elder Hickernell was Elder John Winebrenner's right-hand man. I know he was a circuit preacher in several counties in this part of Pennsylvania, but his last specific charge was in Mt. Pleasant.

"Well, like I said, that is pretty much it in a nutshell, so now I take my leave and go do what I came here to do," Jacob concluded.

"I will just wait in the truck for you and review some of the photos I took," Wesley said. "Take your time."

Jacob just nodded his head, got out of the truck and started to walk to the far corner of the cemetery. He passed the graves of his great-grandparents, then the markers of a lot of names he recognized. Close to the back corner he passed his own parents graves and that of his brother and brother-in-law. One row further back was the marker that read, 'Monika Grant.' Jacob paused in front of it and lowered his head. He stood in silence for several minutes and then in a low voice he said, *"I still miss you very much. Contrary to what they say, it hasn't gotten easier. A couple of strange things have happened that I am not too sure about. Not bad things, you understand, just things I am not quite sure of. Maybe I will know more the next time I speak with you here. The girls and grandkids are all doing well. I will tell them hello for you when I get back. I love you."* He planted the flowers he had brought and then turned and started to walk back the way he came, but this time he paused briefly by some of the graves of family.

Wesley was still viewing some of the pictures he had taken earlier on a small monitor and printer that he carried with him. Before getting in the truck, Jacob noticed a truck coming from the same direction they had come. It looked like the same truck they had seen earlier in the day leaving the vicinity of the May place. Jacob started the truck, but didn't put it in gear. Instead, he said to Wesley, "Grab your camera but don't turn around; I think your adversary approaches."

The driver of the other truck recognized Jacob's truck sitting by the church and instead of proceeding further, he made a left turn on to the dirt road.

Jacob was watching in his rearview mirror as the truck made the turn. "Okay," he said to Wesley, "he wants to be evasive; perhaps we can give him déjà vu with a twist."

Jacob put his truck in gear and started down the hill at a slightly fast pace.

"So what is your plan?" Wesley asked.

"He is going to go up to the top of the hill there and park until he knows we have left and are out of the area. We are going to give him a surprise," Jacob said.

Jacob drove down the road until he came to the dirt road that went up to the May place where they had been this morning. He turned left on to this road and said to Wesley, "As soon as we get to the top of the hill, you jump out and watch for his truck. I will go, turn around and park so he can't see my truck. As soon as you see him turn onto this road, run to the truck, jump in and grab your camera."

"Are you sure he is coming here?" Wesley asked.

"Based on what Janet said earlier, I am pretty sure this is where he is headed."

When they were almost to the clearing where they had parked this morning, Jacob stopped and Wesley got out. Jacob drove forward, turned the truck around and waited. Within a minute or two he saw Wesley running toward the truck. Wesley jumped in, grabbed his camera and said, "Bingo. That is an old catholic term you know."

"Yeah," Jacob said as he started to move the truck slowly forward. He wanted to time this just right. He rounded the curve, bringing the hill into view. The other truck was about halfway up when Jacob started his descent. "Perfect," he said.

The other truck stopped and started to back up just as they had done this morning. The driver was turned around to see where he was backing and did not see Wesley record several digital photos.

The other truck pulled into the same driveway they had used this morning, and as they came abreast of the other truck, Jacob rolled down his window, extended his arm and waved. The other driver did not return the greeting. "Well, he is still an inhospitable cuss," Jacob said.

Jacob drove slow as the other truck backed out and continued up the hill, but not before Wesley had obtained several photos with telltale evidence, including a good close up of the truck's license plate.

At the end of May Road, before turning onto Faidley Road, Jacob stopped the truck momentarily and read a for sale sign posted by Coldwell Banker: It read: For sale, 167 acres more or less. There was a number and a name to call.

Then Jacob said, "They must have just put that sign up after we were here this morning. I was going to tell you I saw one back by the field and road going to the old homestead we visited earlier this morning."

Wesley acknowledged, "I think you are right," and then continued with, "Somehow I get the feeling that Mr. Larkins and I are destined to meet again," he said with a sigh.

"Probably so," Jacob answered, " but in retrospect, I am not sure what we just did, was a smart move. Actually it was my idea and it was a bit childish. Even if he is a scoundrel as his sister says, I am not sure I have the right to harass him and implicate you at the same time. I want to see you become a respected member of this community and spying on someone is not the way to do it. What would you say if I asked you to delete those pictures you just took of Mr. Larkin?" Jacob asked.

"I would say, you are right and I will do that right now," Wesley answered.

When they got to the top of the Barney Kreger Hill, Wesley asked, "Are you coming down to the house for a minute?"

"No, I'll just drop you off and head on back to the motel," Jacob answered.

"In that case, just let me off here, I'll check my mail and walk down over the hill," Wesley said.

"Okay," Jacob replied. "Incidentally, I assume that was Jake's car we saw him unloading this morning?"

"I suppose so, but he generally drives a small Ford pickup truck. It is a deep burgundy color. Why do you ask?"

"Apparently his mother does not want him to know she has asked to talk to me, so I thought I would make sure his vehicle is parked by the church before I satisfy her request."

"Good thinking Jacob, and I hope I see you sometime tomorrow."

Chapter 24

$\mathcal{J}$acob woke at about 6:30 the next morning. By 7:15 he had taken a shower, dressed and placed all his belonging into his truck. He went back into the motel room to make sure he hadn't left anything; he laid a ten-dollar bill on the nightstand for the motel housekeepers and placed the sign on the bed that said, "change bedding."

After he walked to the front desk, turned in the key card, and signed the card receipt for his room, he drove again to the Summit Diner. He wasn't sure when he would get back up this way again, and he wanted some good Amish scrapple with his eggs and toast.

The Summit Diner is a well-recognized eatery by all who live in the surrounding area, but in 2001 and again in 2002, it became very well known by much of the world. On September 11, 2001, United Airlines Flight 93 crashed about eight miles east of Somerset at the small town of Shanksville. All passengers, the crew and the al-Qaeda terrorist hijackers were killed. Slightly more than ten months later, about two miles west of Somerset, or ten miles from Shanksville, another tragedy struck. This time, nine coal miners from the Quecreek Number 1 mine were trapped deep below ground when the area in which they were working was flooded by water from an old abandoned mine. About 72 hours later, in an effort than can only be called miraculous, and thanks to a lot of modern day technology, all nine miners were safely extracted. They were brought up one by one in a 22" diameter cage lowered down through a 240-foot shaft that was only 26" wide.

In both cases, the Summit Diner and the McDonalds just down the street were the rallying points for the media and a lot of people involved in the investigation of Flight 93, and the rescue of the Quecreek Nine as they have come to be known.

Jacob thought about that as he approached "the" Diner. On his way in he put $1.50 into the machine and retrieved a copy of the Johnstown Tribune. He normally bought the Somerset American, but he liked the Sunday edition of the Johnstown paper better.

Immediately inside the door was the cashier's stand and the young lady behind the counter told him to sit where he pleased. The counter stools were mostly filled. Normally, the regular locals occupied these spaces. Several booths were filled, with travelers he guessed, having breakfast before hitting the roads to wherever this day would lead them. He took a booth in the corner by a window so he could look out on the street and watch traffic pass. Because it was so close to the turnpike entrance, this street, known as Center Avenue, was always busy.

He sat down and looked at the headlines. They had to do with the city council and problems with the waste treatment facility. In a way, Jacob viewed this as good news. It meant there were no new major problems affecting the world this day. A lady of perhaps forty, greeted him with a cheerful "Good morning, my name is Colleen and I will be your waitress." She handed him a menu and asked if he would like a cup of coffee to begin with.

"Coffee up front would be nice, and I really don't need a menu," Jacob said. "I would like two eggs over medium, an order of scrapple fried crisp, rye toast, and, of course, the coffee. Oh yeah, bring me a glass of tomato or V8 juice so I can take my pills."

"Which will it be, tomato or V8?" the waitress asked.

"If you have both, make it V8," Jacob said.

"Okey dokey," she said, "I like a man who knows what he wants. I'll bring your coffee and juice right up."

When she left, Jacob, now knowing there were no new major world problems, decided he would read the sports section first. The headlines read, "Bucs trounce Braves 10-1. Windber's own Jason Hawks hurls a one hitter." Reading further, he saw that Hawks had given up a home run to the leadoff batter for Atlanta, and then proceeded to retire the next twenty-seven batters in a row. A remarkable one hitter to say the least, but he remembered a guy from his youth who pitched for these same Pittsburgh Pirates. His name was Harvey "the Hat" Haddix, he pitched thirteen hitless innings only to wind up loosing the game.

Jacob didn't follow sports very close for the past few years. He felt most of the players were overpaid spoiled brats with huge egos. He did read enough to know that the Pirates were finally having a fairly decent year; they were in first place with a three and half game lead over the Cubs. He also saw that they would be opening a three game series in St. Louis on Tuesday. The Cardinals were just one game behind the Cubs so it would be a further test of their skills.. He probably watched hockey more than any other sport. Not that the players were any less demanding for their overrated worth, but because the game did require speed, agility and dexterity. It was rough, but graceful at the same time. He could watch it without caring too much who won or lost, as long as the players showed finesse and not fists. He did like Jake Grayson's friend, Hank Armour, #65 for the Pens, but because of the great season he had just completed, he assumed a big raise would be in his next contract negotiation and it might spoil him. For Jake's sake, he hoped that would not happen.

The waitress brought his coffee and V8 juice, set it on the table and said his breakfast would be ready in a minute.

Jacob thanked her and when she left, he reached in his shirt pocket to retrieve the three pills he took once a day for high blood pressure. He had been taking them for a very long time. His condition had never changed much from the first time a doctor had told him he needed to go on the medication, although the specific pills prescribed changed many times over the years. He always accused his doctor, in jest of course, of being in cahoots with the pharmaceutical companies. He didn't want to start the medication in the first place, because he reasoned that like mechanical pumps, some hearts worked with greater pressure than others. He mentioned this to the Navy doctor that had first examined him and she remained very calm. She did not debate with him, she just said, "Okay, Mr. Grant, you sign a paper for me saying that if you have a heart attack or stroke, you will die. You will not become an invalid and hence a burden on your family."

There was no arguing with that logic, so he told her to write the prescription.

His original analogy of mechanical pumps and the heart had never changed. He did know that he had outlived the doctor who originally prescribed the medication and he was older than she by twenty years, but he certainly did not take satisfaction in that.

The waitress brought his breakfast and set it in front of him.

"Would you like syrup for your scrapple?" she asked.

"Genuine maple?" Jacob asked.

"Somerset County's finest," she said. "And how about a coffee refill?"

"Yes, thanks," Jacob said.

When the waitress brought the syrup and the coffee, Jacob said, "I have a slight glucose problem so I shouldn't be eating this, but I have a couple of cousins who use to make this stuff, maybe still do, so I'll help their cause."

"So you are from here?" she asked.

"Oh, some fifty years ago," Jacob said.

"And who might your cousins be?" the waitress asked.

"Kings and Trimpeys," Jacob said.

"Well, I know some of both," she said.

"And your last name?" Jacob asked.

"My maiden name was Brubaker, my husband is a Miller."

"Lot of the latter around here," Jacob said.

"You got that right. If I can get you anything else, just wave. I will keep an eye on you," she said.

"I will, and thanks," Jacob said.

Jacob had nearly finished his breakfast when the waitress came by and asked if he needed another coffee refill. He declined, but said she could bring his bill anytime. She returned in a minute with his bill and placed it on the table. "It has been a pleasure to serve you. Come back and see us and have a nice day," she said.

"My pleasure, and thanks for the nice smile, it helps to start my day off on a nice note," was Jacob's reply.

She thanked him again and left.

Jacob put a more than adequate tip under the edge of his coffee cup. He left the newspaper on the table, picked up his bill and walked to the cashier to pay.

Jacob left the Diner's parking lot and headed up Center Avenue toward the courthouse. One block past this magnificent old structure, he turned right on Main Street, which was also route 31 and 281. They both followed the same route through town. Normally, he would have taken route 281 towards New Centerville, but when he looked at his watch, he saw he had plenty of time and decided to take route 31 towards Bakersville.

Just before Bakersville he turned left onto a road that would take him by an entrance to Laurel Hill State Park. He would take the drive through the park. The road twisted around following the contour of the hills, but always covered with a canopy provided by the old growth of hardwood trees. It was a beautiful drive, but with a lot of blind curves, it required the driver's full attention. He had often taken this road with Monika, and she had always reprimanded him for looking around and taking his eyes off the road. After a couple of miles the road comes out into a clearing. Higher up on the slope of the hill are buildings serving as dormitories for summer camp groups. He had served as a camp counselor here during the summer between his first and second year of college. One week for his church camp, and one week for problem teenagers from the Pittsburgh area. Interesting was how he remembered it.

Below the road was the lake formed by the Laurel Hill Dam. There were lots of picnic areas, walking trails and a swimming beach. He remembered the first time he and Monika had brought David and Eliana here. They were both good swimmers, but their total experience was in swimming pools and the salt water of the Gulf of New Mexico. The dive into the cold fresh water was a definite "waker-upper."

The road through the park terminated at the road leading from New Centerville past Seven Springs ski resort and across the Fayette County line into the small town of Champion. Jacob turned left toward New Centerville, but about a half mile later at a crossroad known as Copper Kettle, he turned right onto another narrow winding county road that would eventually bring him out past the Scottyland Campground at the foot of the Dickey Hill.

Halfway to that destination, on a sharp curve in the road, he saw the Barronvale Lutheran Church and cemetery. He had some old King relatives buried here. The side road by the cemetery would take him to Barronvale. He looked again at his watch and saw that he had enough time to make one more diversion.

227

Barronvale, named for an early settler, was also the site of one of three remaining covered bridges that spanned Laurel Hill Creek. This bridge was in good condition, but no longer used for vehicular traffic. It was a fine example of building techniques from an early time. The original road led directly onto the bridge, but it now made a sharp left turn. In the corner, where the road turned, sat the old mill house built in 1802.

Just past the old mill house the road divided, the left fork would wind back out to Scottyland, the other crossed the river and followed it closely for several miles.

Back in the early part of the 1900s, several lumber companies stripped the valleys along Laurel Hill Creek of their virgin growth of hardwood trees. A narrow gage railroad was built paralleling the river. Logs were dragged from the side of the hills to the railroad sidings, loaded on cars and transported to a sawmill further down stream. Likewise, the cut lumber would be loaded onto similar cars and hauled to Confluence or Ursina for transfer to Baltimore & Ohio railroad cars for transportation to lumber markets.

The road from Barronvale followed the river and crossed the road leading from New Lexington to Scullton where the old King covered bridge stood. Unlike its two sisters, Barronvale and Lower Humbert, this bridge was in poor condition. Jacob was pleased to see that some reconstruction was taking place. Large steel I-beams had been placed under the roadbed portion of the bridge. A sign posted on the I-beam facing the road stated that preservation was being accomplished through the efforts of the Rockwood Historical Society, but help was needed. Jacob was a member of that organization.

At this juncture in the road he could go one of two ways. Looking at his watch again, he decided to take the faster route on the paved road to the right of the river. Both roads would bring him out at Whipkey Dam.

The Whipkeys were here about the same time as the Barrons, Kings and others who helped settle along this portion of the river.

The road Jacob was on crossed Laurel Hill Creek just below the Whipkey Dam and traveled up over the hill toward Kingwood. At the top of the hill was a road to the right that he could have taken, but he went a hundred yards more to route 281 and turned right to go through Kingwood. He did not want to go directly to the Mitchell house, instead he would drive past the Old Bethel Church to make sure that Jake's car or truck was parked there.

As he approached alongside of the cemetery, he spotted the burgundy Ford truck parked close to the road on the left side of the church parking lot. He continued past and at the bottom of the hill he made the sharp right turn that would lead him to Jake and his mother's house.

Chapter 25

Jacob parked his truck in the driveway that was just two bare paths where the grass had been killed by constant vehicle usage. Grass grew in between the two bare paths. When he got out of the truck, he hit the lock button on the keypad and the horn sounded a short note. He locked the truck out of force of habit, but considered the short horn beep would alert Gladys of his arrival.

He was a bit apprehensive as he stood on the porch ready to ring the doorbell. When he did punch the button, the door was opened almost immediately. To his utter amazement, the woman standing in the door looked almost identical to a young woman he had known many years earlier.

The woman spoke first. "Mr. Grant, I assume."

"Yes, but please call me Jacob, and I do not need to ask who you are, you are definitely your mother's daughter," Jacob replied.

"So everyone says. Won't you please come in," Gladys said.

"I just made some fresh coffee, would you like some?" Gladys asked continuing.

She started toward the kitchen and Jacob followed. Pulling out a chair from the table, he sat down before Gladys had a chance to make the offer.

"Do you take cream and sugar?" Gladys asked.

"No, I drink it natural," Jacob said.

Gladys poured coffee into two mugs, and then said, "We could sit in the living room, and it might be more comfortable."

"Actually, I am quite comfortable sitting in kitchens, but I will follow your lead," was Jacob's reply.

"No, in that case this is fine. Jake and I normally sit here when we discuss things," Gladys said.

There was a pause in the conversation, neither person knowing for sure how to begin. Then Gladys broke the silence. "I am so glad you could stop by, especially under what must seem to you to be very strange circumstances. I assume you have very little time when you come home, and I feel guilty about imposing on you."

"Just hold it there for a second, Gladys," Jacob said. You are the daughter of two of my very good childhood friends. So let me put you at ease, there is no imposition. As a matter of fact, it is a pleasure to see you again. The last time I saw you; you were probably five or six years old. So for you to ask me to stop by, I consider it an honor. Now that we have that out of the way, please tell me how I can help you."

"Thanks, Jacob, now I know why my mother spoke so well of you. My father too, but you know my father never said much. Momma used to say that he was the best listener in the valley. Anyway, do you know of the incident with my husband?" Gladys asked and Jacob could see tears fill her eyes.

"Yes, I know most of it. My sister knew your parents and I were good friends so she sent me most of the newspaper clippings and filled me in on the blanks. My heart went out to you; you suffered a great deal. I even wrote a letter to you offering my condolences, but I never mailed it. I figured you would not remember who I was, and it might just add to your pain."

"Oh, I wish you had Jacob, but I can understand your reasoning. That all happened eight years ago, but I still can't deal with it very well. It has also been very hard on Jake, not only because he was a part of it, but also because I can't offer him the guidance that he needs and deserves. And now I know there is a potential situation where he needs guidance, but I don't know how to go about it. I can't bring myself to talk about some things, and I really don't know who to ask for help."

Gladys was now crying so Jacob felt he should interrupt her.

"Gladys, I will try to help you. I want you to know that I am not a very good psychologist or counselor, and unlike your father, I generally talk more than I listen, but I know when someone needs help. I know that you now need my help so you can help your son for whatever reason. I have talked with Wesley Donaldson, and he tells me that Jake is a fine young man. If you envision a future situation that might impact on Jake's life, then you certainly owe it to him to help, but you are not going to be able to provide that help if you don't go back and resolve the things affecting your own life. I hope you don't think I am being hard, Gladys, that is the last thing I want. Remember, I am your friend by inheritance; I owe you my time and shoulder. So you tell me what troubles you about the past, and what keeps you from helping you own son. You talk, I'll listen."

Gladys took a tissue and wiped her eyes and then used it to cover a snivel.

"I guess you are right, Jacob, I will try. One of the things I can't get over is that I killed another human being. He being the same one that I vowed to love and obey until death do us part. My parents gave me a good Christian upbringing, and I always considered it a sin to take another person's life, regardless of the circumstances. When I think back on that day, I can't help but think, maybe Delbert had realized what he had done and was going over to pick Jake up and comfort him. Perhaps I had created more of a monster in my mind than really existed; after all I had loaded the shotgun and put it in a place where I could easily reach it. During the trial, Delbert's family testified that because of the loaded shotgun, it was apparent that I intended to murder him. I am not a psychologist either, Jacob, but maybe there was in my subconscious, a desire to kill him. For what he did to me, I could endure, but when he started to be cruel to his own son, our son, it was unbearable and I broke. I should have been stronger and figured out another way, but I broke. I killed him, and now I am afraid I may have to pay for my sin because of what might happen with Jake."

"Gladys, why don't you to tell me about this perceived problem that might affect Jake, but first I would like to try and correct, or wipe away some of your misconceptions. From what I have read in my seventy some years, wife beaters seldom change their ways. And from what I read about the trial, there was no evidence submitted, not even by the family, to indicate that Delbert was going to change. As for him going back to Jake to comfort him, no way, the man was out of control. The court records show he was under the influence of alcohol and illegal drugs, so he did not suddenly become a rational being. Had you not done what you did at that exact time, the whole scene could have been much worse. Had he got back to Jake, you would not have been able to fire the shotgun, and he could have beaten Jake to death. Even if he didn't, he would have come back to you and perhaps killed you. Where would Jake have been then? His mother dead and he left with a ruthless father. Gladys, you did the only thing you could, and you did it out of love for your son, not malice towards your husband. I understand your Christian upbringing, and I know that the Old Bethel church follows a pretty fundamentalist doctrine, but that commandment of 'Thou shalt not kill' is not applicable in this situation. And even so, within your Christian doctrine, even killing under other circumstances is forgivable. Look at your religion, Gladys , it is one of forgiving and compassion; it is not one of vengeance. There is nothing that you should feel guilty about at this point, except not giving your son the guidance you feel he may need. That having been said, now tell me what you see as a problem that might affect Jake."

"I will think about what you have just said, and I know you are probably right. I will just have to work on it. I promise, for Jake's sake, I will really try. I must."

"I don't know exactly how to start this, and I am not sure of all the facts, but there is a young woman that goes to church at Old Bethel that Jake likes. I don't mean that he likes her as a girlfriend because she is married. I guess she is several years older than Jake, but that also wouldn't matter if it were a case of him having a crush on her, but he does not. Jake is very devout in his religion, just like his grandfather for whom he was named, so I know he wouldn't do that. The young woman's husband does not attend church and it is reported that he beats her just like Delbert did with me. I know Jake remembers what I went through, and he realizes what this young woman is going through. I am so afraid that sometime he may confront her husband and something tragic could happen."

Jacob was now caught in a dilemma. He did not want to alarm Gladys by telling her that just yesterday he became aware of this situation through Wesley. And, yes, it had the potential of turning into something unpleasant, perhaps tragic as she just said. That is what he had to prevent, but the question was, how?

"Have you ever spoken to Reverend Pritts about this?" Jacob asked.

"No I haven't," Gladys said.

"Any reason for that?"

"He is a nice man, but I do not feel comfortable talking to him. When I was in the hospital after the incident, he only came to see me once, and then he did not really offer me any consoling words or advice. He never came to talk to me before the trial, and say the community was praying for me. That is part of the reason I never felt comfortable returning to church there," Gladys said.

"Not all ministers are good at one-on -one counseling. Some actually feel very uncomfortable doing it, although we assume it is always otherwise. You could have gone to Kingwood and talked to Reverend Glessner," Jacob said.

"My parents always went to Old Bethel, my grandparents went there, and Jake went there from the time he was born until we moved away. I couldn't make him change.

"I see, but I do not I understand," Jacob said. Sometimes we have to do those things we don't like to do. It is often for our own good and for the good of others," Jacob said a bit accusingly.

Jacob could see that Gladys was about to cry again, so quickly he added. "Okay, be that as it may, let me ask you, what do you know of the new resident here in Hexie, Wesley Donaldson?"

"Just what Jake has told me. Jake likes him and says he is a wonderful person," Gladys replied.

"Yes, that he is. He is a priest who has spent most of his life helping people with problems of all types. From what I have found out about him, and I did my own research in his geographical area, that being a fact I ask you not convey to him, but he is a person who took his position very seriously. Not just in the pulpit area, any priest or minister can do that, but he went to the heart of problems. He went into the pain trenches where you, I, and others often find ourselves. He understands, he listens and he can help, so I am going to give you some advice. Please take it as advice from an old man who has been there, from a person who was a good friend of your wonderful parents, and now as a person who loves you as he does his own daughters. Go see this man and talk to him, or let him come here. I will see him later today, and if you give me the okay, I will have him give you a call, or you can call him. I would prefer the former. Gladys, please do this for yourself and for Jake. I will say this, he is aware of part of this problem you foresee."

Tears were now running from Gladys's eyes, but she stood and came over to where Jacob was sitting. She put her arms around his neck and hugged him, then backing away she said, "God really does answer our prayers sometimes."

Jacob didn't say a word.

Gladys continued, "Just yesterday morning Jake was telling me something he had heard about this woman Bethany and her husband. I could tell he was very upset. I prayed to God, 'Please help me out,' and then later that morning he came in and said he had talked to you and Mr. Donaldson. I just knew you were sent by God to help me. That is why I got Mr. Donaldson's number and called him."

Jacob now stood and embraced Gladys as she sobbed openly. Then he said, "Well, I'll be doggone, that is the first time I have ever heard that God used me for anything so good." He rolled his eyes upward and said, "Thanks, I owe you one."

After a minute, Jacob loosened his embrace on Gladys and backed away. "Then you will give Wesley a call?" he asked.

"I will. I promise I will."

"One other thing Gladys."

"What?"

"Tell Jake about our conversation. I think it will make his day. You think he is only worried about the welfare of Bethany; well, I bet he has been worried about his mother from that terrible day until now. That is a big load for a young man to bear."

"You are so right, Jacob, and I feel so guilty now."

"Oh, come on, Gladys, we just got you over one guilt trip, don't create another one."

Gladys laughed slightly and then said, "You are right, Jacob. You are so right. God Bless you."

"Thanks. At this juncture in my life, I can use all of those I can get."

"Would it help if I uttered the old cliché? 'this is the first day of the rest of my life.'"

"Perhaps one of the nicest things that anyone has ever said to me, so I had better leave before you see an old man cry."

Jacob headed to the door and Gladys followed him out onto the porch. They embraced tightly for a long period of time, and then Jacob grasped her by the shoulders and kissed her on the forehead.

"Bye"

"No, I'll see you the next time you come home," Gladys said.

Jacob walked to his truck, punched the keypad to unlock the door and then turned back to Gladys and said, "The next time you put flowers on your parents grave, tell them ole Jacob Grant says hello."

"I'll do that, Jacob."

Chapter 26

When Jacob got to the top of the Ed Kreger hill, he looked at his watch and saw it was only 10:45. He knew that Wesley would not get back from Somerset until close to 1:00 p.m. Fifteen minutes sooner and he could have made the late service at Old Bethel.

He thought about driving through the Clevenger hollow where the Larkins lived, but he figured that if Mr. Larkin was home, he would certainly recognize his truck and could say he was stalking him. That could prove to be troublesome in the future, so he decided he would just go to Wesley's house, take his book and go down by the pond and read. He would take the blanket he kept in the truck. If he got sleepy, he would take a little nap.

At 12:55 Wesley drove into his driveway. He saw Jacob's truck and went up on the porch to see if he had made coffee. Nothing had been touched. He decided he would walk down to the pond. He saw Jacob laying there, his book by his side and he in deep slumber. Wesley didn't wake him, but went by and picked up the book he had been reading: 'More than Friends' was the title. Wesley laid it back down where Jacob had placed it, then sat on one of the benches of the picnic table and waited for the older man to waken.

When Jacob finally stirred, Wesley said, "Have a good nap, did we?"

"Yes, thank you," Jacob replied.

"How did it go with Jake's mother?" Wesley asked.

"A bit sad, but otherwise good. And whether you like it or not, you are now involved."

"No problem, just tell me what I can do," Wesley said.

Jacob got up, walked to the picnic table and sat down. He told Wesley what had transpired.

When Jacob had finished, Wesley asked, "You don't know when she is going to call, do you?"

"No, but I would assume soon. Why?"

"Well, I received a letter last week from the Mayor of Youngstown. It seems that the city council has chosen me as one of their outstanding people of the year and want to know if I can be there on this coming Tuesday to receive the award at their regular Council meeting."

"That is great, Wesley. Congratulations."

"Thank you. I do consider it an honor, but I do not want to be gone if Jake's mother gives me a call."

"That is a good point, but I can take care of that. Before I leave in the morning, I will stop down and tell her of your good news. How long do you expect to be gone?"

"I was going to drive out tomorrow and come back on Wednesday," Wesley said.

"That shouldn't be any problem then. I will stop by in the morning. I told her to be sure and tell Jake of my visit, and she said she would, but just in case she doesn't do it today, do you know what time he goes to work?" Jacob asked.

"I think he leaves at about 6:30," Wesley said.

"Good, I will go by shortly after that," Jacob said.

As they started back toward the house Jacob asked, "So how do you want to kill the rest of the day?"

"Well, since we had some interruptions yesterday, I thought maybe we could continue the tour."

"You are a real glutton for punishment, aren't you, Wesley?"

"In all sincerity, I am enjoying it, hence it can't be punishment. Besides, for some reason, seeing how rapidly events are taking place, I feel I need to get this all as quickly as possible."

"Yeah, maybe so," Jacob said.

"Would you like to have a bite to eat before we go?" Wesley asked.

"I had an awfully big breakfast this morning so I am really not hungry, but I don't mind waiting for you to get yourself something," Jacob said.

"It is a bit early for me also, so just let me grab my gear and we can proceed."

"I'll tell you what we can do," Jacob started. "We will take the route I had previously planned for yesterday, that is, down the hollow past the Wyno place, the May girls' place, the Humbert coal mine area, the Edna Mines incline and come out by the old Growall log house. After that, we can drive down to Confluence where I will buy you supper at a nice restaurant located by the Yough River."

"I don't suppose you would let me buy, would you?" Wesley asked.

"No."

"I didn't think so."

As they started down the Barney Kreger Hill, Wesley asked, "Why did Jake's mother want to talk to you?"

"Well, she is worried for her son, and the possibility of a confrontation with your adversary. Apparently he and Bethany are good friends, and Gladys assured me it was only friends, but he is also aware that Bethany's husband beats her. She fears that Jake, having gone through that with her and his father, may decide to take action on his own. She was still laboring under a major guilt trip caused by that event some eight years earlier and has been unable to broach the subject with Jake."

Jacob signaled to make a right turn onto the dirt road at the bottom of the hill, but then changed his mind. "I think we will go the slightly longer way," Jacob said. Wesley didn't answer.

"Anyway, back to the subject at hand. I am sure I did not dispel all her guilt feelings in the short time we talked, but I did come away feeling that she is ready to confront her own feelings. Regardless of how much more time I could have spent with her, I don't think I could help her anymore. However, I am confident that there is a lot you can do for her and thus indirectly for Jake."

"That is a great vote of confidence, but it is also a very heavy burden. I only pray I can do as well as you suspect," Wesley said.

"You will. You have done it in the past."

"How would you know that?" Wesley asked.

"Well, Youngstown is honoring you as one of their people of the year, I doubt that you earned that by calling good bingo games," Jacob said jokingly.

"Perhaps you are right Jacob."

Again the rode in silence, until they reached the point where his old one room schoolhouse was located. It sat above the road and was now someone's home. Here Jacob did make a right turn.

"This is part of the William Trimpey farm, or 'Willie' as everyone here always called him. I believe one of his grand children or even a great grandchild lives in the double wide that you see over there. When I was a young boy there was a little white house that sat a bit closer to the road here. Willie's oldest son Ralph and his wife Ruth, my mother's sister, lived there until Ralph bought the farm from his father. The thing that I remember most about the house was that it had electricity when none of this area was yet wired for electricity. I don't know just how much education Willie had, but he was pretty handy in a lot of ways. He put a dam across that little river, erected a water wheel and used it to recharge a large bank of Delco batteries in the cellar that supplied electricity to light the house."

Jacob moved slowly on for about two hundred yards and stopped again. "Look down there to you right and you can see the remains of a stone wall and two large metal pans. It was a maple syrup, or what most referred to as a sugar camp. I have fond memories of that old sugar camp. Willie's son Ralph always ran it along with his oldest son, Ralph Junior. Sometimes my brother and I would help gather the sugar water, and then spend hours in there keeping the fire going as the water was slowly boiled into syrup. On a cold winter night you kept warm by the fire and smelled the sweet aroma of the maple steam as it rose from the evaporator tank. You had to be there. There are still a lot of people in Somerset County who make maple syrup, but the process is a bit more sophisticated now. If you get a chance, Wesley, you need to check one out."

"I will make a note of that."

Jacob drove on for about a half mile until he came to a two-story white house sitting on the bank on the left had side of the road. Okay, Willie also built this house, foundation and all. I believe, but don't quote me on this, he even sawed the lumber himself. He had a sawmill at least two different places that I know of. They were one or two man operations and because he did not have a lot of money, his equipment wasn't always the best. My father once bought some lumber from him to build a porch on the lower side of our house. I remember one Sunday after church he was talking to Willie and he said, 'You know, Willie, no two of your boards are the same thickness.' Willie just laughed. It wasn't that he didn't have the skill; it was just that his equipment left a lot to be desired. Of course my father was not much of a carpenter, so it probably made very little difference.

"The fact that he built the house himself, with the help of his sons I assume, is not what makes it unique. There is a natural spring just above the house so, similar to what your builder did, he built a large water trough in the cellar and routed the water into the trough. The runoff goes into a pipe and down under this road and into that little stream.

"Look ahead there and you see the remains of an old stone silo that he also built. His grandson tore the old barn down some years ago but he left the silo as a monument to his grandfather. I do not know of another one in all Somerset County, but there must be a few scattered about."

Jacob continued for about a half mile and soon came to the Old Bethel Church. Just before the church he turned left.

"Here we are, the road your adversary took yesterday to try and throw us off the scent. It used to be known as the May road, but now it is the WI NE-O RD, a misspelling of Wyno

WINE-O RD. It should be WYNO RD. The blur may be the spirit of Mary Wyno, the witch. The blur does not show up on a color photo taken at the same time, but then, Mary lived in white and black world.

At the top of the small hill, one was afforded a wonderful panoramic view of the valley that followed Moses King Run. The road they were on made a sharp left turn at the top of the hill and above the road was a fairly new house, but Jacob directed Wesley's attention to the log house that sat below the road.

"That old log house there was built around 1849 for Jacob Miner. The name was originally, or at least earlier, spelled Minerd. I may have told you that yesterday."

Wesley remembered that he had, but said nothing.

"Seeing as they were from Germany, it was probably Meinhard before that. If you are curious, the family is fairly well documented at the Somerset Historical Society library. Also, there is a fellow over in Fayette County by the name of Mark Minerd, who is an authority on the family. The only Miner I can recall hearing about was Ephriam, but he died long before I was born. I believe he was a nephew of the man who had this house built. He was married twice, and his second wife was Rosetta Harbaugh. She died in 1953 so I do remember her. Their home was pretty close to where Jake and his mother live. I remember their one daughter, she was about my grandmother's age and she was married to my grandpap's friend, Jacob Gary. I think I mentioned him to you yesterday.

"Up until about the middle 1970s, Alex Ohler and family lived in the house. At that time the outside of the house was covered with tarpaper shingles with a rock motif. This type of siding was very popular back then. I did not catch the name on the mailbox as to who lives here now, but sometime in the 1980s it was bought and restored. When I was a youngster back here, I never knew it was a log house.

"If you look across the valley, you can see the area we visited yesterday at the Charlie May farm."

Jacob started the truck moving again and said, "From here the road drops down into what I always knew as the May Hollow, but now it is called the Wyno Hollow. Another "Pittsburgher" built a weekend retreat further down the road, and apparently he liked the story of Mary Wyno, better than he did of the May girls. Mary was one of the other so-called witches of Hexie. The fact that it is now called the Wyno Hollow also galls me, but I think we had that conversation yesterday so I won't go there again.

"I do want you to make a mental note of this hill we are going down as it is an important factor in part of the Wyno saga."

Near the bottom of the hill, Jacob pointed to a gate across a small lane. "That was the entrance to the old Wyno homestead. I will park the truck down there where the road crosses May Run, and we will walk back up.

"Priscilla was the first witch of Hexie, but in my time and probably still, Mary Wyno is the best known.

"Beyond Nell Brach's account, not much is known of Priscilla's, or 'Prissy's,' actual bedevilment. She relates one episode where some children were picking berries on the old Rugg farm, and an apparition of Prissy on her white horse scared them off, but there are few other specifics. With Mary, there are a lot of stories, some probably true, or partially so, others being the product of a fruitful imagination. The thing with Mary was that she fit the description of most people's concept of a witch. She always wore black, including a black scarf covering her uncombed hair, and by a lot of accounts, she was very good at stealth. She came from a part of Europe where the type of behavior she exhibited was not uncommon. She may have believed in herself as a witch, and able to cast spell, but she may have used it as a form of defense, especially in the end when she was an old woman and all alone. If the latter was the case, it served her well.

"She and her husband Bolish, or Bolach, and son Andrew, always known as Andy, first appear in the 1910 census of Lower Turkeyfoot Township. You are at this moment in Upper Turkeyfoot Township, so I don't know where their first residence was, but probably Humbert.

"According to that census report, Bolish was 40 years of age, Mary was 37, and Andy was 5; however, if you look at their death certificates, which I included in the papers I brought for you, there are a lot of discrepancies. One discrepancy is that the name is spelled Whiner instead of Wyno."

"They spoke Slovenian, although both said they came from Austria. Bolish said he could read and write, Mary said no. Again there is a discrepancy, because her son Andy was killed in 1951, two years before Mary died, and she signed his death certificate. I believe that she could not read and write and someone else signed for her. On Andy's death certificate, Mary's maiden name is listed as Gills, but on her own death certificate, her father and mother's name are listed as unknown.

"The 1910 census report shows that Bolish immigrated to the U.S. in 1899 and Mary arrived one year later in 1900. Andy was their only child, or at least that is all the records show, and I say that because Mary once said to my grandmother, '*In old country, have baby, can not feed, Bolish take it to woods, kill it and bury it. Come to this country, have Andy no can do.*' According to my grandmother, those were her approximate words. Based on some other research, I have discovered that was not unheard of in that area of southeastern Europe, so who knows? Perhaps it was not quite as morbid as Jonathan Swift's, 'A Modest Proposal.'"

Wesley looked at him knowingly, but said nothing.

"Bolish was a coal miner and during the time of the Humbert coal operation, they lived in a company house. But very early on, the other locals started to look at Mary a bit askance. My great-Aunt Lottie and her husband also lived in company housing. One day Mary asked Lottie if she could borrow some money, to which my aunt said she didn't have any. Mary answered that she knew she did; it was in a sugar bowl in the cupboard.

"When the mine was working night shifts, the workers often reported seeing Mary roaming around at all hours of the night. Some tried to following her, but she would turn a corner or pass behind a tree and she would be gone. A man by the name of Stutzman, who had been hired by the company for security purposes, reported he once followed Mary down First Avenue, which ended by Laurel Hill Creek. To the right was the barn where the Company housed the mules and horses. He didn't see Mary at the end of the street so he assumed she went into the barn. The barn had electric lights and he was about to throw the switch on the outside by the doors, when a voice behind him said, 'You look for Mary, Mary find you. You go back, Mary not cause you trouble.' Mr. Stutzman turned to where he thought the voice was coming from, but he saw nothing. Not long after that, Mr. Stutzman resigned his position and took a job with a company over by Connellsville.

"When the Humbert mines basically closed in 1905, Bolish and Mary bought the farm where we are now. It contained about one hundred acres, but very little of it was cleared for farming. There was an old house and barn on the property, and I think another building, perhaps a pigpen or chicken house. I was pretty young and don't remember it too well.

"After the mines closed, and the lumbering operations started, Bolish worked helping to fell trees. He and Mary took on a boarder to help pay expenses. He was known as Andy Pushcart, although it was most likely

Pushkar. The 1920 census shows that an Andrew Pushkar was a boarder in the home of Kasimer Goniak. So I am not sure of the correct spelling, but that is unimportant to the rest of the story.

"The story is told that Bolish came home from work unexpectedly one day and caught Mary and the boarder in a very compromising situation. Mary apparently knew her husband's wrath and very quickly was out the window in a considerable state of undress. Bolish grabbed a large skinning knife from the kitchen and held the boarder by the head and threatened to cut his throat.

"Later Bolish would retell the story to just about anyone who cared to listen, and each time it was a bit different. As he told it, he made the border perform a rather undignified act upon his person. He also said that he made Mary stay out in the woods for three days. This part of the story may have been true because Mary confirmed it to some extent. She said at night she would sleep in a neighbor's barn, but she had to put a spell on the horses so they would not whinny, or neigh, as you might know it.

"Charlie May, whose farm we visited yesterday and is just up over the hill here, swore up and down that she could do this. He told the story about a lot of his smoked pork coming up missing. After he smoked his pork in the fall, he would move it from the smoke house to the granary in the barn. Not an uncommon practice because the granary was often more secure in keeping out the rats. The granary was on the upper level of the barn and the horses were in the bottom. He felt his pork larder was secure because if anyone went close to the barn, who the horses weren't familiar with, they would whinny quite loudly. However, to his surprise, he went out one morning to find that one smoked ham and a large side of bacon was gone. Charlie was sure that his midnight caller was Mary, but he was afraid to confront her.

"Several interesting stories about Mary were told by Nell Brach, the same lady who wrote much of the legend of Priscilla Rugg, which we have already talked about. They go something like this: It seems there was a man by the name of Webel who had a habit of peeping in her window. One night Mary caught him peeping on her and said, 'You no have two eyes in your head tomorrow night.' From then on, Webel had to be content with one eye. Nell doesn't say what caused him to lose one eye. A second story that I have heard in two slightly different versions has to do with her favorite goose. Nell tells the story that a neighbor shot the goose. The other version of the story is that the same neighbor was driving his horse and wagon by the Wyno place at a fast pace. The goose didn't get out of the road in time and he ran over it. Whichever the case, the result was the same, Mary gathered up her goose and yelled at the man, 'Now you walk like a goose.' A couple of days later, the man got hurt in the mine and thereafter always walked with a limp that caused his backside to move from side to side like a goose."

Then Wesley spoke, "Let me ask you this, Jacob. Apparently you did have personal contact with her, so do you think she was a witch?"

"Well, your question is time relevant. No I don't think she was a witch. If you ask, 'did I ever think she was a witch', the answer would be, 'yes.' Also you have to ask yourself, just what constitutes a witch? There were some who did believe she was a witch because she was refused burial at two different cemeteries.

"She died in early1953 and I guess the last time I saw her was probably a little more than a year earlier. It would have been sometime towards the last of November in 1952 when I was about fourteen. I was hunting over in the other hollow, that is to say, on the other side of this hill. I had a nice beagle hound by the name of King, in honor of my uncle who gave her to me. Just down the road, about where the May girls' house is, the beagle jumped a rabbit and chased it over in to the flat where those small trees are. At that time it was still tillable land or a grazing area for livestock. I followed him, but at some point he lost the scent and returned to my side. I continued walking in the general direction that I thought the rabbit had gone. I was in close proximity to the old Wyno barn, maybe three hundred yards away, when suddenly I saw a black blur jump out of the bushes and scurry off. I raised my shotgun, but didn't fire for two reasons, one, it was gone in a flash, and two, I knew it wasn't a rabbit. Also, my beagle did not give chase. When I gained my composure, I looked around and maybe fifty feet away, under an old crab apple tree, stood Mary. She was dressed all in black, including the scarf that covered her head. She was stooped and looked every inch like the witch as depicted in storybooks. She said, 'you no hunt here,' I said 'yes mam,' and quickly left the area. I didn't know it then, but years later when I read Nell's account; she said that Mary's sign was the black cat, which is true for most supposed witches. Had I known that then, I would probably have gone home looking for clean underwear.

"According to my grandmother, Mary was not an unattractive woman when she first came to this country. She would have been about twenty-seven years of age. However, history shows that the concept of the witch wasn't always the old hag. The Salem witch trials give evidence to that.

"I think that Mary may have believed in her own mind that she had witching powers, but since her husband died fourteen years before she did, in the end, it may have served as her security blanket.

"I will tell you what you can do if you want to really check it out. Some night when the moon is full and red, walk this valley from one end to the other."

"Did you ever do it, Jacob?"

"What! You think I am a fool?" Jacob said with a smile. "I have walked the Coke Oven Hollow, that is the next one over, many time, but this one, no way."

"Mary died in 1953, but her son Andy was killed under very suspicious circumstances two years earlier. On the death certificate and in the article that appeared in the Somerset newspaper, the coroner, A. M. Uphouse, said he died of a broken neck. That was true, but the circumstances surrounding his death make it suspect.

"Sometime around 1926, Andy left Humbert and went to Wilkes-Barre, Pennsylvania. In December of that year, he married a young girl by the name of Lillian Loretta Steele. She was seventeen years of age at the time. Together they had four children, two girls, one of whom died at birth, and two boys. Then sometime after 1932, Andy abandoned his family and returned home.

"I have corresponded with a man who was married to one of Andy's granddaughters in the Wilkes-Barre area. Apparently they did not know why he left, and from what I have been able to glean, nobody around here ever knew he was married.

"About two years after Andy made his exit, his wife was living with another man, but they could not have married even if they wanted to because she and Andy were not divorced. According to the person I corresponded with, Lillian died in 1949 from cancer.

"Later, Andy also had an illegitimate daughter here. Of course it was the same situation, since he and his wife were never divorced, he could not marry the girl's mother. I have the information in my records of her name and her mother's name, but won't mention it now because she may still be living.

"But, back to the 'accident' that killed Andy.

"I remember meeting Andy, but I can't recall much about him. From people I have interviewed, he was a very likeable person. Liked to talk and talked to anybody.

"On the Friday before his death, he sold a few head of cattle at the live stock auction in Accident, Maryland. On Saturday he went to Confluence, as was his custom, to have a few drinks, or perhaps more than a few when he had the money. On this Saturday night, he had money.

"Back in the fifties, Confluence was a pretty wide-open little town on a Saturday night. There were several bars in a two-block area. The most well-known was a place called Kelly's Bar located in an old hotel.

Several years prior to the time of this story, there was a disturbance at Kelly's bar between the constable, a man named Hoyt and two residents, a father and son by the name of Conway. The outcome was that the constable shot and killed both the father and son. The constable resigned and was exonerated in a court of law, but needless to say, he always watched his back. He may have moved from the area.

It was here that Andy went to drink on this fateful night. Several people reported that he was very free with his money, and bought a lot of drinks for other patrons. He left when the bar closed, probably at midnight, and his neighbor, who lived up at the top of this hill, caught a ride home with him.

"According to the neighbor, he dropped him off at his house and proceeded down the hill. Everything else is conjecture.

"When he never came home, his mother, Mary, went looking for him in the early morning. She saw him immediately as soon as she came out of the lane leading from their house to this road. The car, a Model T Ford, was about two hundred yards up the road and her son was caught between the fender of the car and the wheel. His neck was broken.

"The coroner stated that the car was on a steep grade and had apparently dragged him about two car lengths. He further included in his report that the car switch was turned on, but the car was not in gear. He said that Wyno (Andy) might have been cranking the car when it rolled over him. The crank was in the case.

"What cast suspicion on the case, was, if the car's engine died, all Andy had to do was kick it out of gear and coast down the hill and right into the lane leading to his house. Some people who had seen him at Kelly's Bar, said he was a bit inebriated, but even so, it is doubtful he would not have taken the easy way out and simply let the car drift down the rest of the hill. To me, the strangest thing has always been that the car engine died going down hill.

"There was no further investigation, but many people had their doubts and suspicions. There were several possibilities, and had he been anyone other than an old witch's son, there might have been an investigation, but there was none.

"Not too many years ago I did interview a nice old gentleman from these parts who was aware of most of the 'goings on.' He told me there was one person who steered wide of Mary's sight after Andy's death. He did not tell me the person's name, and I didn't press him for it.

"By this time, Mary herself was in very poor health and prior to her death; Smith Woods and his wife cared for her. Smith was the brother to the husband of one of my many aunts. His mother was Mamie Trimpey Woods. She was a sister to the William Trimpey we talked about earlier. I will show you where she lived out her life in a few minutes. She too lived as a widow for quite a few years, but was the subject of some questionable activity before her husband died.

"I don't know if Andy's illegitimate daughter had any children, but I kind of always hoped so, and further hoped they discovered who their grandfather was. Like my great-great-great-great Grandmother Priscilla Rugg, I think Mary Wyno with her strange ways was just misunderstood. Many of the stories told about her were just the result of a lack of understanding and vivid imaginations out of control.

"That is about all I know of the Wynos, so let's go around the bend to the May Girls' house."

Jacob next stopped the truck by a house whose sides were covered by brown imitation stone shingles. It sat very close to the road.

"This was the house of Cass and Sue May. Sisters of Charlie who lived on the farm we visited yesterday. The house is now owned by a group of men who keep it as a hunting lodge.

*May Girl's house. Cass and Sue, two hard working
spinster sisters. The house is now a hunting lodge.*

"If Mary Wyno was always viewed with a bit of apprehension, the May Girls were warmly received even though they had a few idiosyncrasies. Collectively, they were known as the May Girls, individually they were called Cass and Sue. Neither one was ever married. Sue's given name was Susan, but for Cass, I have seen it as both Cassandra and Catherine. I think it is Catherine on her tombstone, but I always liked Cassandra much better. I think one census report even has it as Cassa.

"When I was a young boy, eight or ten years of age, my mother's sister lived up the next valley. I suppose you would call it a sub-valley to the May Hollow. There were two old houses up in there at the time, one was known as the Hen, short for Henry, Trimpey place, and the other was the 'Wash' Younkin place. I do not know of a Wash Younkin, but at one time, much of the surrounding acreage was owned by Frederick Younkin. I never remember anyone living in the old Trimpey house, but I do remember it had a great spring house, and was a wonderful place to find morel mushrooms after the early spring rains."

Jacob saw Wesley jot down a note on his pad, but didn't ask what he had written.

"My aunt and her husband lived in the old Younkin log house just a few hundred yards down a path from the Trimpey house. My mother would visit her sister and then the two of them would come down to visit with the May Girls. They jokingly referred to them as Martha and Mary from the account of the two sisters referenced in the Gospel of Luke. Like Mary, Cass liked to talk and Sue had to do the work when they had company.

"The two girls worked very hard on their small farm and were quite frugal. They kept their monetary savings in a tin can hid under a board on the upper porch. According to my mother, when their brother Charlie went to buy the farm up the way, it was his sisters who gave him the money.

"My grandfather used to do odd jobs for them, repairing the barn and other out buildings. They never paid him in money, always in kind. But a couple of pounds of butter or a few dozen eggs, perhaps a quarter of a beef in the fall was always better than money to my grandfather anyway.

"If you look through the bushes there, you can see a house of new construction. A man from Pittsburgh built it as a weekend retreat. He is dead now and I don't know if his son still owns it or not. When the May girls were alive, that is where their barn was located.

"Cass and Sue weren't overly fond of their neighbor Mary; they accused her of raiding their chickens' egg nests, and milking their cows if they roamed on to her property. I imagine some of that was true."

As they continued down the narrow dirt road, Jacob pointed out a large pile of gray slag. "That is the refuse from the main coal mine that was opened when the town of Humbert was built in 1901. The company built their railroad line up to this point. Later the sawmill companies would extend it on to Barronvale."

They traveled out along the side of the hill on the road that was just wide enough for one vehicle and Wesley made a comment to that effect.

"If you meet an approaching vehicle, some one has to back up until a sufficiently wide enough space can be found for one vehicle to pull to the side and let the other one pass. That seldom happens."

When they were about a quarter of a mile from the end of this road, Jacob stopped the truck and pointed to a series of stone and cement abutments situated at regular intervals up over the hill.

Coke Ovens Incline. The incline was used to bring coal from the mouth of the mine to wagons that would transport it to the ovens on the other side of the hill. These were the first coke ovens in Somerset County.

"You see those old abutments," Jacob said. "They were built around 1872 when the Edna Mines Company came in here to dig coking coal. You can tell it has been some time since they were used because of the number and size of the trees now growing in their path. They were built to hold a chute, or incline that moved their coal from the mine entrance to wagons at this point.

"The mine opening was located up on top of the first slope. The coal was brought out and unloaded onto the mouth of the chute at the top of the incline. The coal was then systematically released down the incline supported by those abutments to mule-drawn wagons located about where we are now parked. The wagons then hauled the coal down around the point and back up the next valley to the coke ovens. When the coke was pulled, it was loaded onto rail cars parked on the track on the other side of where Redd Run traverses the gorge.

"Some years ago, probably ten or more, I was exploring up there on their refuse pile and I found a beautiful lump of coal, a geological specimen that I keep on the top shelf of my desk. I also took two bricks from their old coke ovens on the other side of this hill and had a friend build me two bookends.

"For reasons unknown, the company only remained in business for about one year, although they had the mineral rights to over six thousand acres. I can still find one of their old coke ovens, but if you are ever interested in it, my son-in-law used a GPS unit to fix the location and I included it in the papers I brought for you.

"I also wrote an article, "The Coke Ovens of Hexie" that was published in the Laurel Messenger, quarterly newsletter of the Somerset Historical Society. You can find it in their archives, but I have also included a copy in my files.

"Twenty-five years later, the Humbert Coal Company, correctly known as the Connellsville Coal and Coke Company purchased all the same acreage, and they built the town of Humbert. Their coal operations only ran for about three years."

Jacob then drove to where the narrow dirt road they were on connected to the Kingwood-Humbert road. There was a sharp curve to the left and the road made a quick drop down to the main road. Jacob again stopped the truck to give Wesley a good view of the old log house.

"We passed here yesterday, and I didn't say anything about this house, but I will give you a quick review now. It has a very interesting history that I have documented and is in the papers that I gave you yesterday. That article also appeared in the Laurel Messenger as, The Growall Log House. I need to go back and correct a portion of what I wrote in that article.

Growall Log House. More correctly the Samuel Jr. and Sally Rugg log house. Elizabeth Growall was their daughter and she moved in when her husband went to fight in the civil war.

I will only give you the highlights at this time. My cousin still lives there, and if you would like to talk to him sometime, drop my name and I am sure he would welcome you in. He is an easy going, slow talking, country boy with a lot of knowledge of this area. He can probably give you more information about the May girls and the Wynos, especially Mary.

"My great-great-great grandparents, Samuel Rugg Jr. and his wife Sally built the house. In my article I credited it to their daughter and son-in-law. Elizabeth Sarah Hunter was Sally's maiden name. They probably built the house sometime around 1838 to 1840 after he was forced to move from his birth home when it was sold upon the death of his mother, Priscilla Rugg.

"Samuel Rugg Jr. died in 1860 and his wife died shortly thereafter. Their daughter Elizabeth, also known as Betsy, and her husband Peter Growall then moved into the house, although I am not sure that Peter ever lived here. The 1860 census shows they still lived in Milford Township.

"Peter was the son of John Growall, and his grandfather was Anthony Growall, an immigrant from Portugal. At one time, the Growalls owned a sawmill or planning mill in Rockwood.

"Peter was in the Civil War and died from typhoid fever at Fredericksburg, Virginia. Elizabeth was left to raise her children, and later some grandchildren in this old log house.

"Elizabeth died in 1902 without leaving a will. That left the whole thing open for the County to settle. The powers to be in the Humbert coal operation had tried to purchase the place earlier because they wanted to open a mine on that hillside close to where the house stands. The house was in the way if they needed to build a coal tipple and a railroad siding. Elizabeth would not sell. Her four acres upon which the house sat was specifically exempted in the original acquisition by the Edna operation in 1872. The current company accepted those same conditions, so there was nothing they could do. However, when Elizabeth died without leaving a will, an opening for acquisition was made and the Company supervisor, Mr. I. T. Huff, immediately sought to acquire the property. He was eventually successful, but the estate wasn't settled until 1905, and by that time the coal company was finished. The old house received a reprieve.

"The house fell into disuse for a long period of time, but in the early 1950s, my aunt and her husband were in desperate need for a home. His mother now owned the old house so they took it over and sort of resurrected it. They built the addition you see to the left as a large kitchen. Just for the record, his mother was Mamie Trimpey and she was the daughter of the Henry Trimpey that I mentioned a few miles back. She was married to Fred Woods and I have an old photo of them with my grandparents as young couples. They were both very lovely looking young ladies.

"The article that I mentioned a minute ago that appeared in the Laurel Messenger was titled, 'The Growall Log House.'

"So now, what do you say we head for Confluence and get something to eat."

"That sounds like a good idea to me," Wesley said.

However, after they rounded the next curve in the road, Jacob asked, " How much did I tell you about the old Huff house that sits up there on the bank?"

"Not much, Wesley said.

"Well, lots to tell, but mostly for another day. Suffice it to say, 'that is where Mamie Woods lived out her life.' " She always kept a few cows for her own use. The couple that she milked, she kept fenced in, the rest she just let roam. If they got up as far as our place, Dad would always have my brother or I drive them back down to here.

257

Chapter 27

When Jacob and Wesley arrived at the Yough Café, the receptionist asked, "Inside or on the porch?"

"On the porch, of course," was Jacob's reply.

The young lady showed them to a table that afforded an excellent view of the Youghiogheny. She gave each of them a menu and said that their waitress would be Celeste.

The Yough Café sat about three fourths of a mile below the spillway of the Yough Dam. It was a good place for fishing and there were at least a half dozen fisherman in waders casting with lightweight fly rods. For a long time neither man spoke, then Jacob broke the silence, "There is a good German word for this, Wesley."

"And what might that be?"

"Gemutlich."

"I know that word, Jacob, and you are absolutely right. I was just thinking that it can't get much better than this, and that word just covers it perfectly."

Just then their waitress came by and introduced herself. "Good evening, my name is Celeste and I will be your waitress."

"Celeste, a beautiful name for an equally beautiful young lady," Jacob replied.

"Thank you. My father had a great interest in astronomy; he wanted to call me Cassiopeia, but my mother nixed that so he settled for Celeste."

"I think I like Celeste better," Wesley added. " However, you know that beside being a constellation, Cassiopeia was a queen, having been the wife of Ethiopian King Cepheus."

"Oh yes, my father told me that a long time ago."

"You all are too smart for me," Jacob chimed in, "I think I'll just order before my ignorance shows."

"So what can I get for you?" Celeste asked.

"You want to order first, Wesley?"

"No, you go ahead. Since you are buying, I want to see what you order, that way I know how much you are willing to pay," Wesley said, looking at Celeste with a smile.

"Hit him on the head for me, will you, Celeste?" was Jacob's retort. "I will have the country chicken salad, preceded by a cup of the homemade vegetable soup, and a large glass of unsweetened ice tea with lemon."

"Okay. And you sir?"

"I think I will have the hot turkey sandwich with mashed potatoes and gravy and green peas. I will also take a glass of unsweetened ice tea with lemon."

"Okay. I will bring your drinks and soup right out."

When Celeste returned with the drinks and Jacob's soup, she also brought a small loaf of hot bread and butter.

"Do you have any brothers or sisters?" Wesley asked.

"Yes, I have a brother who is fifteen months younger than I am. Would you like to know his name?" Celeste asked with an impish smile.

"I bet you are going to tell us," Jacob said, raising his brow and his glasses resting low on his nose.

"His name is Orion."

"And did your mother object to that?" Wesley asked.

"I guess she did a little, until Dad told her that if she had let him name me Cassiopeia, he could have called my brother Cepheus or Andromeda. I think my mother knew to leave well enough alone and went along with Orion."

"I don't get it," Jacob said, "but I will let Wesley explain it to me later."

"Your father sounds like a very interesting personality," Wesley said.

"Oh, he is a lot of fun. He can talk your leg off as my mother likes to say."

Celeste then left and talked to the couple at the next table that had just finished their meal. Apparently they ordered something else and Celeste picked up their empty plates. When she returned, she had two cups of coffee and two pieces of pie. On her way back to the kitchen, she swept by their table to say their order was coming right up.

A minute later Celeste came back with their order and placed it in front of them.

"So what does you father do?" Wesley asked.

"We own a small farm up the Jersey Hollow, but that doesn't pay the bills so both he and my mother teach school. My mother teaches third grade children, and my father teaches high school algebra in the classroom, and an honors class in advanced calculus via computer hookup."

"Very interesting," Wesley replied.

"And you," Jacob chimed in, "I put you at seventeen years of age. Are you still in school?"

"Actually I am eighteen, and I am still in school. I will be starting my second year at Pitt in just a few weeks."

"Second year! I am very impressed," Jacob said. Then continued, "I was originally from this area. What is your family name? I may know of them."

"My name is Rugg; my mother was a Tannehill."

Then Jacob threw up his hands, and said with exuberance, "No wonder you are so smart. We are probably related."

Wesley, either embarrassed, or feigning embarrassment, said, "You can just ignore him if you like. He gets like this sometimes."

"No, I learned a long time ago to never ignore something just because you might not immediately understand it. Why do you say we are related?"

"See, this young lady really is intelligent," Jacob said, looking at Wesley. Then looking back at Celeste he continued. "I have a connection to the Ruggs, six generations back."

"But there are a lot of Ruggs in this local area," Celeste answered.

"Ah, very true, but I believe they can all be traced back to the original settlers, Samuel and Priscilla who lived on a farm just north of Ursina."

"Really," Celeste said with amazement.

"I think he is telling the truth there," Wesley cut in.

"So then we must be some sort of cousins," Celeste said.

"Yeah, smart ones I would say, but if you are talking from a generational point of view, probably sixth or seventh with a 'removed' in there," was Jacob's answer.

Celeste was about to say something else when she saw the man from her other table motion that he wanted his bill. Very quickly she added, "Enjoy your dinner. I will check with you later."

She went to give the couple their bill. At the same time, the hostess was seating a family of four at another table in her section on the porch.

As Celeste took care of the preliminaries with the people at the other table, Jacob and Wesley started to eat. Then Jacob spoke. "She is a very personable young lady."

"Yes she is. I can see where the two of you might be related though."

"How is that?" Jacob asked.

"You both like to talk," Wesley replied.

"Touché! Now eat your supper, Wesley."

They ate in silence as the fog started to move in on the river, partially obscuring some of the fishermen and almost completely cutting off the view of the road on the opposite side of the river. Then Jacob spoke, "I have been here several times to eat at this time of the day and I have yet to see anyone catch a fish."

The words had no more than cleared his mouth, when the man fishing directly opposite them at about midstream, suddenly had a strike. The end of his light rod almost touched the water. Jacob and Wesley watched as the man pulled and reeled, pulled and reeled. Finally he had it close enough so that its tail was dancing on the water. The fisherman held his pole high with his left hand and took his net from his belt with his right. Very deftly, he placed the net under the fish and raised it out of the water. With the pole under his left arm, he took both hands and gently removed the hook from the mouth of his catch. He held it up by the gills, and it wiggled. It was a nice rainbow trout measuring at least twelve to thirteen inches in length. He then leaned over and gently placed it back in the water to swim away. It would possibly have a sore mouth, but it would perhaps live a few more days before another fisherman, who might not be so benevolent, caught it again.

Jacob and Wesley applauded lightly, but loud enough that the man in the river heard. He looked toward them, raised his right hand with the index finger extended, moved it slightly and nodded his head. He baited his hook and went back to fishing.

"As you were saying, Jacob," Wesley said with a slight tone of aloofness.

"God just let him catch that fish to embarrass me," Jacob said.

"I could perhaps buy into that, if I didn't know it may have been a way of God saying thanks to a guy who let a rabbit scurry off to die of old age."

"Maybe," Jacob said and they went back to eating in silence.

Celeste took the order of the people at the other table and turned it into the kitchen. After a few minutes she came back with their drinks. Each waitress had to bus their own table, so she then cleared the table of the couple that had dined when Jacob and Wesley had arrived. After that she came by to clear their dirty dishes and ask if they would like dessert.

"I saw on the chalk board by the front door that you have fresh strawberry shortcake," Jacob said.

"Yes, we do, and it is great."

"Okay then, I will have that and a cup of coffee." As an after thought he said, "Would you think I am strange if I asked for it in a bowl with milk on it?"

"Not at all, lots of people here about eat it like that," Celeste answered.

Wesley looked askance at the two of them, but didn't say a word.

"And you sir?" Celeste asked.

"I will also have the strawberry shortcake with coffee, but on a plate, sans milk," Wesley answered.

Jacob looked at Celeste and winked, then he said, "Wesley is still in the apprentice program learning how to become a country boy."

"He is pretty close to being correct on that matter," Wesley said with a smile and a slight tilt of his head toward Jacob.

"So, until you get past your apprenticeship, perhaps you would like a little ice cream or whipped cream with your shortcake," Celeste said to Wesley.

"A little whipped cream would be nice," Wesley answered.

"Okay, I will have that out in a jiffy," Celeste said as she left and went in the back door of the kitchen.

A moment later, Celeste and another waitress brought the food to the family at the table next to them.

The other waitress went back in the front door and Celeste came by their table to say she was now getting their dessert.

She returned with two cups of coffee, one serving of shortcake on a plate with whipped cream, and one serving in a bowl along with a small pitcher of milk. She set the items down in front of the appropriate person, and then, looking at Jacob she said, "Now, as I was about to say before I was so rudely interrupted by people wanting something to eat, '*joke, joke*' what is your family name?"

"It is Grant, and as I said earlier, I lived in this area when I was a kid. Left when I was about sixteen to go to college in Ohio and eventually joined the Navy for a career. After that, I only got back once in a while to visit family."

"So are you two related?" Celeste asked.

"There was a brief moment of silence, and then almost simultaneously, both said, "Just friend."

Wesley picked up the conversation. "Well, if the two of you are distant cousins, you have one thing in common, you both went to college pretty young. But with reference to the old gentleman sitting there, our friendship goes like this, I moved to the area only a few months ago. I built a house just below Kingwood on the Humbert road. Jacob now lives in Florida, but his wife is buried at the Old Bethel Cemetery in Hexie. He was on his way to put flowers on her grave when he saw that someone was ruining a past memory by building a house on it. To make a long story short, he stopped, we chatted and became friends. He then decided that since I was probably here to stay, he would have to indoctrinate me on the history and folklore of the area. It has been one very interesting history lesson. You are now privileged to know him as a distant cousin, and me as a friend," Wesley finally ended.

Celeste extended her hand to Jacob and said warmly, "I certainly am privileged to meet you cuz."

Jacob accepted the extended hand, and then said, "I am sure the greater pleasure is mine."

Celeste caught the man at the next table looking in her direction, excused herself and went to fulfill her duties.

When she returned to the porch with drink refills for the next table, Jacob and Wesley had finished their dessert. Jacob caught her eye and gave her a sign that they were also ready for the bill. She nodded back and went in to the cashier's stand to get the check.

When she returned she handed it to Jacob, and said, "I will take it when you are ready."

"I am ready now," Jacob said as he rapidly scanned the bill. He saw that sixty dollars would cover the bill and allow for a liberal, but not excessive tip. "Keep the change," he said to her.

Celeste saw that it was a nice tip and said, "Thank you very much. I enjoyed talking with the two of you."

"Likewise, I am sure," Wesley said. "Jacob is going back to Florida in the morning, but I am sure I will come here again to eat. I just hope that if you are back at Pitt continuing your studies, that my next waitress will be as nice as you."

"I doubt that," she said and then laughed. "Probably as nice but not as talkative," she continued.

"It is your cheerful conversation that helps to make you special," Wesley told her.

"Thank you very much," she said with a smile.

Jacob and Wesley then walked toward the front of the porch and the parking lot.

"Wait, Mr. Grant," Celeste called.

Jacob stopped and turned toward her. "It is Jacob to kin," he said.

"That is exactly right, Jacob. I guess we haven't known each other long enough to be 'kissin cuzzins,' but I would like to give you a hug for the family history lesson." With that she put her arms around him and embraced him.

Jacob also held her for a moment, and when he released his embrace, he softly kissed her on the forehead. There was a tear in his eyes when he said, "You really are a Celestial person."

When he and Wesley got to his truck, he turned back toward the porch. She was still standing there. He waved and she waved back, then she turned to go back to work. Jacob started the engine, backed out of his parking space and drove off in silence. Neither man spoke until they got to Wesley's house.

Chapter 28

It was nearly 7:00 p.m. when Wesley and Jacob got back to the house. Jacob pulled his truck into the driveway in front of the garage door. He opened the back door and retrieved his bag and a shirt and pair of trousers he had on a hanger. Walking up the steps to the lower porch, Jacob said, "Show me where I am bedding down and I will throw these things in there."

"First door on the right after the hallway bathroom."

"Okay."

The lights were motion activated, so Jacob just laid the bag and tomorrow's change of clothes on the bed and came back to the kitchen where Wesley was waiting.

"We can sit out on the lower porch and listen to the evening sounds if you wish," Wesley said.

"Yeah, that sounds like a good idea. I could take an hour or so of that preparatory to my trip back in the morning."

"Well, can I get you anything to drink then? Coffee, pop, or perhaps a glass of wine?"

"Maybe I will indulge in a glass of 'fruit of the vine,'" Jacob said.

"I only have a merlot and a chardonnay, so name your poison," Wesley said.

"The merlot will do just fine."

"Okay, go have a seat, I will pour and join you in a second."

Wesley came onto the porch carrying two glasses of the merlot wine. Jacob had seated himself on the swing that faced with a view out over the valley. He was sitting at the extreme left so he could set his glass on the porch railing. Wesley handed both glasses to Jacob so he could pull up a small stand to the right side of the swing to set his glass on. He sat down, removed his shoes and placed them by the side of the small stand.

When Wesley finally leaned back, Jacob handed him the other glass of wine and said, "So, a toast. Wesley, you have passed the test. I now bequeath all my written knowledge to you, and the Good Lord willing, the spirit of my memories of these hills to you upon my passing."

"I hope the latter isn't soon, and I hope I do not betray your confidence, but it is a pretty big load to accept. I will do my best."

Each took a sip of the wine, and then Jacob continued. "As we use to say in the Navy when I was a young man, 'No sweat,' I am sure you are capable. You are a good man, Wesley Donaldson."

"Thanks, Jacob. You know that the feeling is mutual."

"Okay, before we become slobbering idiots, let's move on to something else. I noticed that the spare bedroom has a bit of a feminine touch. I assume that is much of your mother's things."

"Actually, it is all of her things. I do have another spare bedroom, if you don't feel comfortable there," Wesley said.

"Ah, don't be ridiculous. I will be completely comfortable there. Beside, it is close to the bathroom."

"I guess you didn't look too closely; it has its own bathroom."

"No, I didn't notice," Jacob said, "but that is great seeing that I have to get up at least twice a night. Tonight will probably be worse since I had two glasses of ice tea at the restaurant, then coffee and now a glass of wine. It is shaping up to be an hourly night."

"Jacob, I was thinking about our waitress being a Rugg. I am sure you must have a genealogical outline of the Rugg tree. Would you mind giving it to me, and I will see if I can plug her family into it."

"Wesley, you are too young to have memory overloads. I just said a minute ago that I bequeath all my written knowledge to you, which includes all kinds of family trees. And I think talking to Celeste's parents would be a good idea. I have never documented the Tannehills, but they are also among the early settlers and have a colorful history. When I get back, I will seriously start cataloging, and boxing all that I have concerning this area. I will also talk to my granddaughter. If there is anything she wants, I will make duplicates."

"Okay, I really appreciate that Jacob."

Just then, further down the hollow, a whippoorwill began its call.

"See that," Jacob said, "the Good Lord embarrassed me down by the river; now he is appeasing me by letting the whippoorwill sing."

"Jacob, are you sure your name is not Israel?"

"Why?" Jacob asked with a laugh, knowing full well what Wesley was getting at.

"I have never before met a man who has had so many personal confrontations with God."

"I take it you have never read Joseph Heller?"

"Well, if you are talking about his book, 'God Knows,' I am familiar with it, but I haven't read it."

"I have, but I don't take as many liberties as he does. Of course, he is Jewish, I am not. Does it bother you, Wesley?"

"No, somehow I seem to think that the Good Lord expects that from you. Maybe I think like our Muslim brothers and concede that God made you for that purpose."

"Does that mean that I get the seventy-two vestal virgins when I die?'

"Well, according to Islamic belief, I think you have to be a martyr to get them."

"Yes, you are correct. Besides, Monika would never understand, but how did we ever get on this tangent anyway?" Jacob asked.

"Beats me. Let me ask you something in all seriousness. The first time we met you mentioned something about you and Karin Nelson, the young girl that once lived here. The way I understood it, you were slightly closer than just friends. When she didn't write to you after the first time, or answer your second letter, what were your thoughts about her?"

"Hmmm! That was a long time ago. I was a boy, probably too young to be called a young man, but there were things that happened between us that I could not forget. Eventually I resolved it to the fact that we were just impressionable young teenagers, and she was a girl going through a difficult time. Later on in the school year, I met another young lady and some of the hurt went away. You are a priest so I don't know if you have ever had these feelings, but some of it never goes away, at least as far as the memories. From my point of view, the hardest thing for me to come to grips with now is that not long after that, I dropped several young ladies that liked me in a similar manner."

"Do you think it is related to the situation with Karin?"

"No. I just think that very often, young love, or sometimes hormones, just block out common sense. Some people don't care that they hurt other people. I do, but it still didn't always keep me from doing just that. In retrospect, I always knew that Karin never intended to hurt me. Something happened, and I always hoped it was something that made her happy."

"You said just a minute ago, Jacob, that because I am a priest, you didn't know if I ever had those feelings. I am now going to tell you something, some of which I have never told another person, not even my mother. I don't want you to jump to conclusions; I never physically broke my priestly vows, but I do know of young love and the pain it can cause. There were two cases in my life before I took those vows. And like you inferred, you move beyond them, but you never forget them."

"Really," Jacob said. "Do you mind telling me about it?"

"Not at all, but if you get bored, just tell me and I will stop."

"Fair enough. Go ahead."

"The first, and most memorable situation started when I was sixteen. It was between my junior and senior year in high school. My very best friend at the time was a guy by the name of Dale Mason. The two of us were also very good friends with a young lady by the name of Violet Turney. We both liked her a lot but neither one of us asked her to go on a date or to a movie because we didn't want to jeopardize our friendship. Violet had a girlfriend by the name of Katie Bearman, and so the four of us would go to the movies and do fun things, but we never paired off, so to speak. Actually, Katie had a boy friend but his parents had moved out to Niles so she didn't get to see him much, but they still considered themselves an item, as young people say today.

"When school was out that spring, Father McGinnis of our parish asked me if I would like to help out at a summer camp that the diocese was going to operate for underprivileged children. It would be for four weeks, but the groups of children would change each week. The camp was up on Lake Erie close to Ashtabula. I said I would love to, but I would have to ask my parents. He told me to let him know as soon as possible. My parents thought it was a great idea, so I immediately called Father McGinnis and said I could go. I asked him when we were to leave and he said we had to be there Friday eve because the groups always arrived on Sunday evening. We would need Saturday to get everything organized.

"Many of the Catholic Churches in the Diocese were involved in it and all sent youth representatives to be part of the staff. There were two other people from our congregation, Tanner Knowles and his twin sister Tamara. I knew them from church, but they both went to a different high school. Dale and Violet were both protestants, but of different denominations. At that time I believe Dale was Presbyterian, and Violet was Baptist.

"Father McGinnis, or Father Mac as everyone called him, was one of a kind. In my opinion, he was the priesthood, personified. He was not a great preacher, that is, he did not deliver eloquent sermons. They were simple and basic, but you could ask just about anybody two days later what Father Mac's sermon was about on Sunday and they could tell you. He had a way about him that when he spoke, you just listened.

"He was born and raised in a very poor section of Cleveland, and did not have a good childhood, but he remembered his pain as a child and kept it with him until he died. Not as resentment, but as a reminder to help him in his mission in helping others. He knew that you could not eliminate poverty, drunkenness, cruelty and people's pain, especially that of young children, but you must try and offer hope. That was the story of his life. It was his idea to start the summer camp. He said it would be a Catholic Chautauqua. I didn't know what he meant, but on the drive up he explained it to us. Lake Chautauqua is about as equidistance east of Erie, Pennsylvania, as Ashtabula is west.

"Are you familiar with the Lake Chautauqua, New York movement?" Wesley asked.

"Yes, I am," Jacob replied. "As a matter of fact, I may know something about it that you don't know."

"That is certainly quite possible, but please tell me what it is?" Wesley inquired.

"Well, about nine years after they formed in New York, they went looking for a winter home. That brought them to a place in the Florida panhandle known as De Funiak Springs. There is an almost perfectly round lake in that little town and on its banks they built their assembly hall," Jacob said.

"Sorry to disappointment you, Jacob, but I do know about the De Funiak Springs site."

"Dang, Wesley, sometime I am going to mention something that you don't know a thing about, even if I have to make it up from scratch."

"I guess I will just have to be on the lookout for that so I don't make myself out to be a liar, or even worse, a fool. But the reason I know about it, is one of the attending Priests at that first camp I attended was from the Lake Chautauqua area. He gave a brief history of the Institution, the founders, Lewis Miller and John Vincent, and the Florida extension."

"Seems reasonable," Jacob said, "but I just diverted you from your story. Please continue."

"Well, the events during those four weeks, a long time ago, were very interesting and educational, but that is a story for another telling. My story continues when I got back home.

"We got back home at about 7:00 p.m. and after telling my mother and father a little bit about the camp and the wonderful experience it had been, I said I thought I would go see Dale.

"Before I left, my mother said, 'Incidentally, Katie Bearman called for you twice today. She said to give her a call as soon as you got in.'

"I said that was okay as I would probably see her.

"When I rang the Masons' doorbell, Dale's mother answered and she seemed a bit surprised to see me. She asked when I got back and I told her. Then I asked if Dale was home. She seemed to pause for a long time, and then she said, 'No, he and Violet went to the movie.' I asked if Katie went with them, and she said she wasn't sure.

"Later my mother told me that I had not been gone more than five minutes when Katie called for the third time. When my mother told her I was on my way to Dale's house she heard her say, 'Oh, no,' and hung up the phone.

"There was an Islay's ice cream shop about a block from the theater where we would meet and socialize with a lot of the other kids before going to the movie. I assumed Dale, Violet and Katie were there so I started to walk the four blocks. I had only gone one block when I saw Katie crossing the street toward me.

"I stopped and waited for her to reach me. When she was a few steps away from me, I said 'hi.'

"She said, 'Hi,' and then continued, 'Wesley, there is something I need to tell you.'"

"What?" I asked.

"Well, ah," and she trailed off.

"What is it Katie?" I asked again and then to keep from stammering, she just blurted it out.

"Dale and Violet are going with each other."

"What do you mean, 'going with each other?'" I inquired.

"You know, Wesley, like girlfriend, boyfriend."

"I just stood there for a very long moment waiting for it to sink in. Suddenly I felt hurt and very betrayed. In retrospect, I shouldn't have been surprised, but I was. Finally I asked Katie if she was sure, and she said she was. They had both talked to her because they did not know how to tell me.

"Then I asked Katie, if they had asked her to tell me. She said that they didn't, she just took it on her own to tell me before I saw them together. She thought it would be easier.

"I didn't say anything else. I just started to continue walking the way I was going when Katie stopped me.

"She called after me, 'Where are you going, Wesley?'

"'To Islays,' was my answer.

"'I wouldn't, if I were you,' she continued.

"I ignored her comment, but I did ask if she wanted to come along, and she said that she was going home.

"When I entered Islays, several kids who knew me called my name and asked when I got back. I immediately spotted Dale and Violet in a one of the booths, and when they heard my name they both looked up. I stood frozen for a moment; apparently the hurt was showing on my face, because when I turned to leave, no one said a word. I am not sure what I felt, but I left Islays and went across the street to a small park that extended for two blocks in the direction of the movie theater. I hadn't gone very far until I heard Violet call my name. I did not stop walking. Violet started running and eventually caught up with me. When she did, she placed her hand on my shoulder and said, 'Please Wesley, let me talk to you.'"

"I shrugged my shoulder from under her touch and kept walking. Then I heard her say again, 'Please, Wesley' and I could hear the deep emotion in her voice. This was a girl who had just hurt me very deeply, but I couldn't stand to hurt her back. I stopped and turned to face her.

"She was crying, and this time she took my hand. Again I wanted to shake it free, but I let her hold on. I saw Dale cross the street and enter the park. He did not come toward us, but sat on a park bench a short distance away.

"Then Violet told me how it had happened. The first week after I left for the camp, Katie's boyfriend who had just graduated from high school, got a job back in Youngstown. He was planning to go to college there in the fall so they went their own way. That was okay, but it left her and Dale together, and things just happened in the normal course of things.

"It has been a long time, but I can tell you almost exactly her final words to me that evening.

"She said, 'Wesley, Dale and I both knew it was going to hurt you, and if there was any way to relieve you of that hurt, we would do it. Believe me, we talked a lot about it, but we couldn't come up with a solution. We were expecting you home on Sunday and hoped to know what to do by then. Wesley, we have always been good friends, and I would hope that it could always remain so, but I will understand if you think otherwise. I know that regardless of what you think of me after this, you will still always be my best friend.'

"She let go of my hand, but stood there waiting for me to say something, anything. I picked up both of her hands and there were tears in my eyes when I said, 'You will always be my friend, Violet.'"

"I dropped her hands and backed up one step and suppressed the urge to hug her one last time.

"She backed up one step also and then just said, 'Thanks, Wesley.'

"When she turned to walk to where Dale was sitting, I called her name. She turned and said, 'Yes, Wesley.'

"Tell Dale, he is still my friend," I said. She nodded in approval and smiled.

"I knew it would still be difficult for Dale to face me, so on Sunday afternoon I went over to his house and as best as I could, I talked like nothing had ever happened.

"So, did you remain friends?" Jacob asked.

"Yes, we did, but there is a good bit more to the story. I assume you would like to get to bed early since you are leaving in the morning. The rest of the story gets pretty long so I will tell you another time."

"Hey, don't worry about me, I will make it in the morning. I want to hear the rest of this story and then about the second girlfriend."

"Well, the second girlfriend story is less complicated, and wasn't quite as traumatic. But since you insist, I will continue. Before I do though, remember as a priest, I believe in temperance in all things. That having been said, I also don't want to be a bad host, so would you care for another glass of wine?"

"I shouldn't," Jacob said, "but yes, I will."

Wesley poured one more glass of wine for each of them.

"I told you that when Violet and I talked in the park, I backed up to suppress the urge to hug her one last time. The truth of the mater is, that as friends I hugged her many times, mostly in times of joy, but twice in times when she needed a lot of consoling.

"When we graduated from high school the following year, I left almost immediately for South Bend, Indiana. I wanted to get a part-time job. I had a partial scholastic scholarship, and my parents were prepared to cover the rest of my expenses. Of course my dad's sister, who was the first to encourage me to become a priest and to try for Notre Dame, wouldn't hear of that, and she certainly had the resources to pay the balance. She and her husband were never able to have any children, so she naturally gravitated to her nieces and nephews. She could be a bit dominating, but it came from a heart of gold. There were a lot of poor kids in our parish going to different colleges who would occasionally receive anonymous gifts of money just when they seemed to need it most. She never said a word, but I know a lot of times it was from my aunt.

"Okay, I am getting away from my story. I went away to college and Dale and Violet wanted to get married. Both of their father's were blue-collar workers, and although they made a good wage, they also came from families where there were other siblings, so there wasn't a lot of extra money. They both had above average grades, but not good enough to be offered scholarships. Dale was a pretty good baseball player, but again, not good enough to get a scholarship, so he joined the Army. When he came home from boot camp in late August, he and Violet were married. Dale was assigned to Fort Benning for further training and became part of a ranger outfit. I think it was a Green Beret outfit. From there he went to Korea. Violet was later able to join him. We kept in loose communications and I had a letter when their first child was born, a son, whom they named Jonas Edward Mason, after his father and her father.

"About a year and one half later they had another child, this time a little girl they named April Violet.

"In the summer of 1974 they returned from Korea and Dale could have been discharged, but since Violet was pregnant with their third child, he decided to extend his enlistment for two years. I remember I had a letter from them when they told me the news. I wrote back, saying that with their concept of birth control, they would make good Catholics."

"After Korea, Dale was again assigned to Fort Benning, this time as an instructor.

"I graduated from Notre Dame and started my seminary studies in the fall of 1974.

"Their third child, a little girl, was stillborn. Violet took it very hard, because about a month later I had a telephone call from Dale. He told me that Violet could not stop grieving; for some reason she blamed herself. Her mother went down and spent a week with them to help take care of the two children and give her daughter some moral support. Being in a combat training unit, Dale's military duties kept him very busy. Sometimes they would be in the field two or three days at a time, and he worried about Violet's welfare. He asked if I could write her a regular letter, but not to mention that he had contacted me. It was my first real attempt at counseling, and apparently in my own stumbling way, I succeeded. A couple of days later, I received another telephone call from Dale thanking me. He said that when he got home in the evening after the letter had arrived, Violet greeted him with a hug that lasted for minutes. Then she read the letter to him. He told me I had said all the right things."

"What did you say to her?" Jacob asked.

"To tell you the truth, I can't recall anything specific that I said. I was just thankful that the Lord gave me the right words at a bad time in her live, but later there was to be a much worse time.

"Between my second and third year at the seminary, I went home for several weeks because my father was very ill. While I was there, Dale and Violet and the children also returned from Georgia. Prior to his discharge,

Dale submitted his application to the police academy at Youngstown. He was accepted and began his training in August of 1976.

"Just before the Christmas break that year, my father became gravely ill. He would not let my mother tell me how sick he was because he did not want me missing my studies. I arrived home for the Christmas break on the 18th of December. He died the next day. I wanted to take him to the hospital, but he refused. He said he knew his time was near and he was ready, he wanted me to sit by his bed and tell him what I had learned. I started to tell him about one of my papers being accepted for publication. He closed his eyes as if listening, and then passed into eternal sleep. He would not see me ordained."

"Dale and Violet attended the funeral for my father and they asked if I would stop and visit for a few hours before I went back to the seminary. I said I would. Classes weren't scheduled to start until the second week in January, a fact for which I was glad. My mother never did very well on her own volition, and of course that was partly my father's fault because if he sensed her wish, he made it happen. Not that my mother was demanding, she was not. I talked to my aunt about this matter and she assured me, she would pay close attention to my mother. I knew for sure, she would do just that.

"Two days before I was to return to my studies, I called Dale and Violet and they invited me over. They gave me the good news that Violet was again pregnant with the baby due by the end of May.

"Everything went fine this time, it was another little girl and they named her Rose May. I sent a card of congratulation and chided Violet for having a thing about flowers and the months of the year in naming her daughters."

"Dale had graduated from the police academy and was immediately hired by the Youngstown Police Department. While he was in the Army, he had completed most of the requirements for his baccalaureate degree. He would be able to complete his degree at Youngstown University in the fall.

"Two days after the birth of their daughter, I graduated from the seminary. My mother, and of course my aunt, attended the ceremony. I did not go back to Youngstown with them, but went straight to my first parish assignment in Dyersburg, Tennessee.

"It was a wonderful learning experience there, but my aunt, who knew the 'ins and outs' of Catholic politics, so to speak, got me assigned back to a parish in Youngstown.

"I later learned that Father McGinnis had a major hand in it. The Catholic High School was undergoing a major expansion, in which he was very much involved, and as he later told me himself, he wanted a subservient assistant he could rely on. I interpreted his 'rely on' to mean 'do with out questioning.'

"As soon as I got back and settled in, Dale and Violet told me they were expecting another addition. About two months later, Dale called me from the hospital. He was very excited. 'It is a boy,' he said. 'Violet and I would like to know if you would mind if we named him Zechariah Wesley?'

"I told him I would be honored, and if visiting hours were still on, I would rush over and wish the parents well, and meet my new namesake. And that is what I did.

"Dale and Violet attended the Baptist Church and so they didn't believe in infant baptism, but they did have a service where they dedicated the child to God. They invited me to attend and naturally, I did. It was held on a Wednesday evening and it was a beautiful service for family and friends. After the service there was a get together in the social hall of the church with coffee and cake. After about twenty minutes, most of the people had extended their congratulations and left. I was just about to leave myself, when I saw Dale take a call on his cell phone. He went out into the hall to answer the call and very quickly returned. He was breathing heavily when he came to me and said, 'Wesley, would you mind taking Violet and the baby home? There is a policeman down about two blocks from here. I have to go.'

"He went quickly to Violet's side and whispered to her. I saw her tense up, and then say, 'Oh please God, keep him safe.'

"When Dale had left, I went to her side and she stood and now with tears coming to her eyes, she hugged my neck. 'Please, Wesley, pray for his safety,' was all she said.

"'I have already started that prayer, and have held it open,' I responded.

"Our prayers in this case were for naught. When Dale arrived at the scene, there was a three-way shootout going on between two gangs of drug dealers and the police. Dale had just gotten out of his car and was in the process of putting on his bulletproof vest when a round caught him in the middle of the back. He died on the spot.

"Needless to say, it was very traumatic for Violet and the children, but it was also very difficult for me. I lost a good childhood friend, and had to try and offer counsel to another. Thankfully, Father McGinnis came to the rescue for me and I was able to help Violet as a friend. Her pastor naturally gave her the religious counsel she needed.

"Several years later I was again able to offer her some help. This time her oldest son got involved with the 'wrong crowd,' as the saying goes and got it some trouble. That time I was able to get him into the summer camp that Father McGinnis had set up the summer when I lost one good friend to another good friend. Of course, Father McGinnis had passed away a year previous to her son's trouble.

"I saw Violet quite often after Dale's death, but I was never able to be completely at ease with her. I just never knew exactly what to say. Does that seem strange to you, Jacob?"

"Not at all," Jacob said, "but I don't have an answer for you either. Wish I did."

"Oh, I wasn't looking for an answer. Well, in retrospect, an answer would be very welcome, but what I really should have said is, I wasn't expecting an answer."

"Yeah! Let me sleep on that Wesley," Jacob said as he stood and picked up his glass to carry it into the kitchen.

Wesley also stood up to follow Jacob. He picked up the wine bottle in his right hand and his glass in the left. Forgetting that he had removed his shoes and set them by the small table he earlier had moved to the end of the swing, he managed to trip over them. His fall wasn't hard but when he tried to break it with his left hand, the wine glass broke and a large shard from the bowl of the glass cut a deep gash into the meaty part of the palm at the base of the thumb. Wesley's only words were, "How clumsy of me."

Jacob couldn't see how severe the cut was, but he could see that it was bleeding quite profusely. "Stay right there and I will get some wet paper towels for you to put on the cut to stop the bleeding and then we can see what action needs to be taken." Jacob said this, as he was already under way with the task.

He came back with some wet paper towels and the remainder of the roll that was by the sink in the kitchen. He handed the wet ones to Wesley and he applied them to the cut, asserting pressure with the tips of his fingers.

"I assume that you have a first aid-kit?" Jacob asked.

"Yes, it is in the hallway bathroom."

Jacob followed Wesley down the hall and retrieved the first aid-kit from a drawer in the wash sink. He removed several gauze pads and told Wesley to remove the paper towels and hold the gauze pads in place with his right hand. This Wesley did, and Jacob saw that the profuse bleeding had stopped. He then took several more gauze pads and dowsed them liberally with hydrogen peroxide and wiped the blood from the rest of Wesley's hand. He threw the gauze into the wastebasket and took two sets of four gauze pads and laid them on the sink. He took two large band-aids from a container, removed the paper and laid them beside the gauze. "Okay," Jacob said, "remove that gauze and let me pour some hydrogen peroxide over the cut." He used four of the gauze pads to remove the excess hydrogen peroxide, applied a liberal amount of Neosporin, covered the cut with the remaining gauze and fixed it in place with the two band-aid strips.

"There, except for being a little sore in the morning, I think you will survive," Jacob said.

"You did that very professionally," Wesley said and nodded his head.

"Actually I didn't, or I would have used the latex gloves. Just don't report me for practicing medicine without a license."

"Why would I?" Wesley said with a smile. "You may have saved my life."

"Maybe, but it might get infected, gangrene will set in and they will have to amputate your hand."

When Wesley left, Jacob stowed the supplies back in the first-aid kit, then he put the paper from the band-aids and the soiled gauze in the trash basket, all except the gauze that Wesley had held on the cut. He put that into the lower right pocket of his cargo shorts.

"Does she still live in Youngstown?" Jacob asked when he entered the kitchen where Wesley was sitting at the table.

"Who?"

"Who? Who were you just talking about? Violet. Does she still live in Youngstown?"

"Oh! The great loss of blood must have made me woozy," Wesley said with a laugh. "Yes, she does. She and Dale bought his parent's house when they decided to get a smaller place outside of town. It is just two blocks over and down from where my home was. Our house numbers were just the opposite. Theirs was 325 Fenton, and ours was 523 Stafford."

"Do you think she will attend the presentation ceremony for you?"

"Maybe, if she hears about it. I have no idea how the city counsel plans to present the award to me. They just asked if I could be at city hall by 11:30 a.m.

"Based on what you have been telling me, I image she will have heard of it. And if she isn't there, will you be disappointed?" Jacob asked.

"Probably a little," was all Wesley said.

"Well neither one of us is going to feel like it in the morning, if we don't hit the sack. So I bid you a good night. See you in the morning"

"Good night Jacob," Wesley replied.

Chapter 29

Jacob started to remove some of the pillows from the bed, and yelled out to Wesley, "You are almost as bad as my wife with all these pillows on the bed."

"Well my mother liked a lot of pillows on the bed. My father always complained too, but she still put them on."

"I posthumously extend my sympathy to you father."

"I am sure he would appreciate that, Jacob."

Jacob closed the door and crawled in under the sheet. He had thrown the bedspread and the blanket to the other side of the bed. And although he was very tired, sleep did not come readily. A lot of thoughts played through his mind. He thought of the global positioning unit in his truck and it occurred to him that it would show that he was currently trying to sleep at the same spot on earth where Karin had slept the night before she went to Ohio. He was never one to believe much in spirits, but he suddenly felt a bit uneasy. There were some questions playing in his mind but he wasn't sure he wanted to search for answers.

After several times of turning from his right side to his left side and back and forth, sleep finally overcame him, but it was a restless sleep. He had a short dream that snapped him awake, and he realized he had to go to the bathroom. He looked at the digital clock by the side of the bed and saw that he had only been in bed for about two hours.

He went to the bathroom and sat on the commode to relieve his bladder. He hated to turn on the light, which tended to make him wide-awake, so for the obvious reason; he sat. When he finished, he did not flush so as to create noise through the pipes in the other bathroom; he would do that in the morning. But when he moved a few feet away, the toilet flushed automatically, and very quietly. He smiled to himself. Wesley's builder had thought of everything.

When he climbed back in bed, he felt a cool breeze brush over him and he reached across the bed and pulled the light blanket back on top of him. He reasoned that the air conditioner must have come on.

The next time he woke it was 3:15 and again he had to go to the bathroom. As he sat there, he looked back out into the bedroom and saw what looked like the shadow of a woman on the wall beside the bed. When he returned to bed, he realized that there was a full moon tonight, and it was causing shadows to appear on the wall.

At about 5:00, Jacob woke again feeling the need to go to the bathroom, but when he looked at the clock, he decided he would just hold it for another half hour and then get up and take a shower. He turned back to his right side and dozed off. This period of light sleep, or what researchers call REM, produced another dream for Jacob. Somewhere in the distance he heard a baby cry. It was not a wailing cry, but more like a cry when it was just waking, or about to go to sleep. Soon it faded and then he saw a woman sitting at a desk. He could not see the face, but it looked like she was writing a letter. At one point he saw her get up and go to the baby and give it a kiss. When he woke again, he saw it was now 5:40, and he sat up abruptly on the side of the bed. He tried to recall some of the dream vignettes that had plagued his sleep, but try as he might, he could only recall the last two of a few moments past, and they made no sense.

Chapter 30

Jacob had planned to drive straight through to Pensacola on Monday when he remembered he had promised his daughter and grandchildren he would spend a couple of days with them in Louisville. So before going to the bathroom to shower and brush his teeth, Jacob retrieved his cell phone and gave his daughter a call. He was surprised to hear Sarah answer the phone.

"Hello sweetheart, this is Pappap"

"As if I didn't know your voice, Pappap. So when are you coming by?"

"Well, that is why I called. Tell your mother I should be there by early afternoon. Now don't forget."

"I won't, but she is right here if you want to talk to her."

"Sure, but let me ask you, aren't you up a bit early?"

"Not really. I like to get up early so I have an hour of peace before my brother gets up."

"Hi, dad," Sylvie said as she came on the phone.

"Hi, hon. I just told Sarah that I should get there by early afternoon."

"Okay, we will be waiting for you."

"Sarah told me that she gets up early so she can have an hour of peace before Nathan gets up."

"Yeah, I heard that, but don't believe that for a moment. Nathan probably stays in bed an hour longer so he doesn't have to be bothered by her."

"Well, it is good to see such great sibling adoration. See you shortly, and I love you all."

"Love you too Dad. Take it easy and drive carefully."

Jacob knew that if he got to Louisville by this afternoon, it would give him plenty of time to visit and still be back in Pensacola by Thursday. He had an appointment with his Doctor for 2:00 p.m.

Before leaving for Pennsylvania last week, he had called and cancelled a previous appointment. His doctor was not too happy about that and had chastised him for his lack of consideration for his own good health. Jacob had never been a person who put too much stock in doctors and their advice, so he dismissed it without much thought.

By 6:15, he had completed his toiletry, dressed, packed his belonging in his bag and opened his bedroom door with the intent of making coffee. To his surprise, Wesley was sitting at the kitchen table with a cup of coffee and a piece of toast.

"I thought I would beat you up," Jacob said.

"I have been up for about an hour. Took a long walk, twice around the trails above and below the house. I like the early morning to do my thinking and plan my daily itinerary," Wesley said, and then added, "What can I get you to eat?"

"I already know where the cups are, the bread, butter and jam is on the counter, so I can take care of myself, but thanks for offering."

Jacob took two slices of the rye bread and put it in the toaster. He took a coffee cup and a small plate from the cupboard. He poured a cup of coffee and waited for the toast to come up. When it did, he put the toast on the plate, took it, the butter and the jelly to the table and sat down. Wesley looked at him, but didn't say a word.

"I don't like to butter my toast when it is hot. One of my little idiosyncrasies."

"To each his own," Wesley said.

Jacob placed his hand on the toast and decided it was cold enough that the butter wouldn't melt. As he started to apply the butter, he asked, "When do you plan to leave for Ohio?"

"Probably about noon or a little after, and you?"

Just as soon as I finish this coffee and toast, I will go by the cemetery, then stop and see Gladys for a minute and then I am Louisville bound. How does the thumb feel?"

"It feels fine. Throbbed a bit when I first went to bed, but no discomfort during the night. I will redress it before I leave. I suspect that a large band-aid might then suffice."

"Maybe so, but you might want to keep a larger dressing on it while you are driving," Jacob said.

"Okay, good point, well taken," Wesley answered

"I couldn't go to sleep immediately last night and I mulled over what you had said about not being able to converse freely with Violet. Let me ask you, have you ever taken Violet to lunch or dinner?"

"No, I haven't."

"May I ask why?"

"Well, I just don't think it would look right."

"Excuse me if I sound ignorant, but I am asking myself, why. What it looks like should have nothing to do with it. The Good Lord knows what is in your heart," Jacob said.

Wesley paused for a long moment and then he said, "Yes, the Good Lord and I know what is in my heart."

It was now Jacob who paused for something to say, and very quietly he said, "I see. I see, but I still think going to lunch might be a good thing. You said you couldn't converse freely with Violet; maybe you should let Violet lead the conversation. From the way you told the story, it was she who took charge when she saw your hurt after she and Dale became a couple. But from that time on, it has been you who has provided the counsel. To many people, a priest is omniscient. You and I know that is not true, but considering what has happened in Violet's life, and you always being there for her, I am not sure she wouldn't see it that way."

"I appreciate your advice, Jacob. I really do. And I will give it serious thought on my drive out this afternoon."

"Good," Jacob said. "Now one final thing, I don't want to pry into your personal decisions and affairs, but you said a minute ago that 'it wouldn't look right.' You never told me why you gave up the parish, and I really don't want to know, but you know what I mean."

Wesley laughed, "Yes, I know what you mean, and the answer is no. Next time you come up I will tell you why I gave it up. I think you will say I made the correct choice. But back to what I said earlier, that was just a poor choice of words. I am sure you remember a few years ago the priesthood and the entire catholic church took a lot of hits because of a few who lacked good judgment. Many of those have been weeded out, but it is taking time to heal the scars. And there are some, both inside the catholic faith and outside of it, who will always see the worst in any situation, therefore, many priests, myself included, believe that for the good of the religion, we must behave in the most upright manner to preclude unwarranted gossip."

"Yeah, I can see that but there has to be exceptions."

"Your are correct, Jacob. There must be exceptions, and we, meaning the clergy, must be brave enough to act on them. And by the way, thanks for enlightening me to the fact that I am not omniscient," Wesley said with a laugh.

"You are welcome," was all Jacob said.

When Jacob had finished his toast and his second cup of coffee, he rinsed his cup and put it in the dishwasher. "Well, my friend, it has been a very pleasant visit. Thanks for letting an old man bend your ear for so much of this local history and folklore. Hope I didn't bore you. It 'sorta' let me relive some of the old memories and remember some of the great people who lived here. They were simple people, but great people in my mind."

"It has certainly been my pleasure, Jacob. Don't forget to send me copies of your articles when you get home. Drive carefully, and have a good visit with your family in Louisville."

"I will, and you do likewise with your trip to Ohio. Congratulations again on receiving the civic award."

The two men embraced and Jacob departed. It was still five minutes before seven. He hoped Gladys was an early riser also. He was pretty sure she was, but he would give her a few extra minutes. He would go the long way and stop by the cemetery one last time to talk to Monika.

Chapter 31

The Monday edition of the Somerset paper carried a short story on the bottom of page one. The byline read: "Recent resident of Somerset County receives Youngstown 's People of the Year Award.' The story went on to give a brief history of Wesley. The last paragraph said that he would leave today to receive his award at the regular Tuesday meeting of the Youngstown City Council.

Chapter 32

It was 7:45 when Jacob left Gladys's house. He was feeling good about this final chat with her and gleefully headed for Somerset where he would get on the Pennsylvania Turnpike. He was glad that for once, the amount of construction on one of the oldest super highways was at a minimum.

He still had an audio book to complete, but decided he would wait until he got on the turnpike. He searched and found a good country and western station. It was when he started these long trips that he really missed Monika. A tear appeared in his eye as he thought about her, and he switched the radio station to easy listening; Monika was not too crazy about country and western music.

Jacob stopped at the gate entrance to the turnpike and pulled the ticket from the dispenser. He looked at the cost to go to New Stanton. Reached in his pocket and retrieved the correct amount and tossed in the cup holder of the center console. The access road said East, Harrisburg, West, Pittsburgh. He headed west.

He never did start the audiotape. Too many thoughts of the past week filled his mind, and as he passed the Donegal exit, he punched in the numbers for the information operator in Youngstown. When the operator answered, Jacob said, "Youngstown, for Violet Mason at 325 Fenton Street." He hoped she didn't have an unlisted number. When the operator came back with the number, Jacob hit the record button on his cell phone.

He thought maybe he could call her and ask her some questions, but decided he had better think about what he wanted to ask before doing so. He had a bad habit of jumping the gun and getting into situations where it was difficult to extricate himself. Just introducing himself without having to explain too much was going to be difficult. He doubted that she knew anything about him through Wesley, and so getting started would be difficult. He could explain that he preferred for certain undisclosed reason that she not mention him to Wesley, but that might put her in a position where she would have to lie, or betray his trust. He never asked anyone to put them self in that position. Finally he decided that calling was not an option, but by that time he had passed his exit at New Stanton. He would have to go to the Irwin exit and back track as there was no good route from Irwin back to I-70.

By the time he got to Irwin, he had formulated a different strategy; he would go to Youngstown and see if he could talk to Violet in person. It would certainly be easier to explain his intentions. Perhaps he could also duck into the courthouse and peruse a few public records. Then if he still had time, he could go to Warren and stop there at the

courthouse for a few minutes. That would be a little bit out of his way, and of course he would have to call his daughter to say he would be a little later than he had anticipated.

He got off the Ohio turnpike at the first exit and took I-680 toward Youngstown. His knowledge of the layout of the city was absolutely nil, so he decided to get off the interstate at the Route 224 exit. He needed gas anyway and could hopefully obtain a city map, although they were hard to find now that many people had global positioning and map quest systems in their vehicles. When he was in college, Route 224 was his way back to Somerset. That was of course before the Ohio turnpike was completed. At the end of the ramp, he saw the sign that pointed toward Boardman and Youngstown. He remembered Boardman and the next little town west, Canfield. He was returning to college late one Sunday evening when one of Ohio's finest stopped him in Canfield and gave him a speeding ticket. It would be forty-five years before he received another speeding ticket, this time in Summerville, West Virginia, by a city policeman.

He pulled into a BP station and filled the gas tank. He paid at the pump and then pulled into a parking spot next to the Subway sandwich shop that was part of the station complex. Inside, he asked one of the ladies behind the counter if they had city maps of Youngstown. She told him that they no longer stocked them, but if he knew how to use a computer, there were several terminals in the trucker's lounge. He thanked her and headed toward the lounge, stopping at the restroom on his way.

He had no problem obtaining the information he needed. The street addresses for Violet and Wesley's old homes were on the northeast side of town. The courthouse was not too far away. He jotted down a few notes of cross streets and route numbers just in case he made a wrong turn.

He was on Market Street and that would take him into the city. He crossed the Mahoning River to Wick Avenue and headed northeast. Within a few minutes he saw the street sign for Stafford. He turned right on it, and immediately discovered he was about three blocks away and going in the wrong direction for Wesley's home. He pulled into a driveway to turn around. This was strictly a residential area, and most of the houses along this street were of older construction, but certainly of what would have been considered middle class. The houses were well maintained with fairly large front lawns. The yards too were well manicured.

He pulled his truck into the curb at 523 Stafford and took a closer look at the house. It was a two-story house, as were most of the houses on this street. It was constructed of cut stone with a lot of detail around the windows and the front door. A driveway went in by the side of the house and presumably to the garage in back. A new Volvo sedan sat in the driveway toward the back of the house. Jacob shook his head in silent acknowledge of, 'okay, nice house.' He pulled away from the curb and stayed on Stafford into the three hundred block. He took the cross street for two blocks and found Fenton. He made a left turn onto Fenton and drove back toward the four hundred block. There was a small park on the right side of Fenton with swings, slides and other things for children to play on. There were benches close by and he saw several ladies, apparently the mothers of the children that were using the playground equipment.

He drove slowly and spotted 325 Fenton. Not quite as impressive as 523 Stafford, but still, a very nice home. He decided it was better to park on the next cross street. There was a convenience store on the far corner. After he parked the truck, he went in and purchased a pre-made sandwich from their deli counter and got a bottle of water from the cooler. He paid for the two items and made his way to the park to eat his sandwich and build his courage to go ring the doorbell of a complete stranger.

There were three benches close to the playground; two benches were occupied by three ladies who were watching their children play. Jacob approached the third bench and acknowledged the ladies with, "Good morning, do you mind if I intrude to eat my sandwich?"

"Please, be our guest," one lady said and the other two smiled in what he supposed was agreement.

Jacob looked at the young children running about, laughing and playing, and then still looking in their direction said, "Oh, to have such energy again."

One of the other ladies then said, "That is why we are here, to let them burn off some of that excess energy," and the other two 'yeahed' their agreement.

"I suppose that is true," Jacob said. "I will see two of my grandchildren later this evening, they are a bit older than these, but they still know how to tire me out."

"Where do your grandchildren live?" one lady asked.

"Louisville," Jacob answered.

"So, you still have a bit of a drive," the same lady said.

"Yeah, just thought I would give my old bones a short reprieve."

Just then, the first lady who had spoken to him said, "Here comes Violet with the twins."

From where he sat, Jacob could see the house where Violet lived. He saw her cross the street, hand in hand, with a young girl and a young boy of about four years of age. He unwrapped his sandwich and took the lid off the bottle of water.

From the way they greeted each other, Jacob could see that they all knew each other. The first lady who had spoken to Jacob now turned to him and said, "This is Violet, another of our morning group, but unlike the rest of us, these are her grandchildren so she gets rid of them by three in the afternoon." They all laughed. She then looked at Violet and said, "this is a passing stranger on his way to Louisville to see his grandchildren."

"Oh how nice," was Violet's reply.

"Thank you," Jacob said and then looked at his sandwich and water bottle as if to signal that they should get on with their own conversation.

He turned slightly away and began to eat his sandwich. He was nearly finished when he heard one of the ladies ask Violet, "When is Zack getting back?"

"Actually, he is coming in to Cleveland late this evening. He wasn't scheduled to be back until Wednesday but he wanted to make it back for the award ceremony at city hall tomorrow."

"Oh, that is right, you and Wesley were old friends."

"More than that, he is Zack's namesake."

"So are you going?" one of the ladies asked.

"I am sure I will," Violet said.

Just then, as Jacob took the last swig from his bottle of water, he heard a cell phone ring. He turned to see Violet take a small device from her blouse pocket. She answered with the customary hello, and then Jacob heard her say, "Wesley! What a wonderful surprise, we were just talking about you."

Jacob sensed that was his cue to leave. He picked up the wrapping from the sandwich he had eaten, took the empty water bottle and started toward where his truck was parked. Violet was in conversation with Wesley on the other end, so he raised the index finger of his right hand toward his brow and silently formed the words "good-bye" to the other ladies. They acknowledged, and even Violet raised her right hand and waved her fingers. Jacob thought she was a beautiful woman. He could now understand why Wesley had been so deeply infatuated by her. Perhaps he still was.

There was a trash container at the corner of the park by the street. Jacob deposited his trash and walked to his truck. Once he was seated and connected his seat belt, he punched the quick dial button on his phone to call his daughter. He told her he would be a little later than he had expected, but he should be in by three or three-thirty. He would not go to the courthouse today. He had formed a lot of questions in his mind, but at this point in his life, he wasn't sure he needed the answers.

He drove back towards the center of the city, picked up the I-680 bypass and started to leave Ohio for the last time.

Chapter 33

*L*ate on Monday evening a pickup truck pulled into the open area at the top of the Barney Kreger Hill and parked out of sight behind some trees. A lone person got out and stealthily crossed the open field to a point at the far edge of Wesley's property. The person looked for lights indicating an approaching vehicle. Spotting none, the individual hurriedly crossed the field toward the road, then crossed the road and entered Wesley's property through the barbed wire fence. Slowly the intruder walked toward the house. When the intruder was within two hundred yards of the house, the first sensor of the security system was activated. This put the computer, its communication system, and the cameras on standby.

Prior to departing on Monday morning, Wesley had activated the system for Away Mode. In a residential area, this would have meant that the audible alarms would have been set to activate at some point of intrusion, but here in the country, that was useless, so they were set to inactive.

The intruder continued until within the two hundred foot perimeter. The computer now came on and dialed two numbers. First, the office of the monitoring Company in Johnstown. Because of the location, no police force would be sent out, but audio and video monitoring from the site was possible. The second number dialed by the computer through a separate modem activated Wesley's cell phone. When his cell phone rang a fraction of a second later, Wesley checked his watch and saw it was 10:32 p.m. He quickly pressed the awake button on his notebook computer and activated the connection to the home computer. His screen showed the levels of the system that had been broached and the exact time. He waited.

At exactly 10:34:03, the intruder crossed the fifty-foot perimeter and eight small video cameras covering nearly ninety percent of the exterior area of the house and all doors and windows, were activated. Due to the darkness, the monitor screens showed only shadows. Due to cost, Wesley had opted not to use night vision cameras except for the ones covering the two doors that granted access to the house.

At 10:34:55 the intruder crossed the thirty-foot perimeter and night was turned into day as neatly concealed floodlights were turned on. A heat sensor that recorded the temperature emitted by a human being caused the closest camera to focus directly on the intruder. Looking completely surprised, the intruder shielded its eyes from the light, and with head down, started a hasty retreat.

Both the monitoring company in Johnstown and Wesley in his motel room in Youngstown watched the proceeding.

As the intruder made the retreat, the closest camera recorded the departure.

When the intruder had gone back across the two hundred yard line, the system shut down.

Wesley immediately called the monitoring company. When the person there answered, Wesley gave his password and said, "I see we had an intruder."

"That is correct," the person at the monitoring center said. "Would you like us to send someone out?"

"No, it looks like the system worked as designed," he said.

"Yep, it is a pretty reliable system. Sleep well, we will keep our eye on it."

"Thanks. I should be back in the area late tomorrow evening. I will check my tapes to see if the cameras operated properly and I will give you a call.

"Thank you," the person on the other end said and terminated the call.

Chapter 34

On Wednesday morning Jacob got up early to have breakfast with Sarah and Nathan before they left for school. When they had gone, Sylvie ate breakfast and they sat and chatted over a second pot of coffee. Normally he was an impatient person when he traveled and was in a hurry to get on the road. This morning he couldn't seem to extract himself from their conversation. It was nearly noon when Sylvie asked if he would stay for lunch. Suddenly realizing how late it was he told her he had better hit the road, that he had an appointment with his doctor on Thursday.

It was 12:10 when he exited Breckenridge Lane and pulled onto I-264.

Later in the afternoon when he had crossed the Tennessee-Alabama line, Jacob assessed the reality of the situation; he was not going to make it to Pensacola by nighttime. He had trouble keeping his eyes open and his left leg was completely numb. When he had stopped for gas at the Pulaski exit south of Nashville, he got out of the truck only to have his left leg completely fail him. Had he not been holding on to the seat with his left hand and the truck door with his right, he would surely have fallen to the pavement.

He felt that if he could make Birmingham, he would have enough time to get to Pensacola the next morning and still make his appointment. By the time he reached Cullman, Alabama, he knew he had been over optimistic. For the first time in his life, he became despondent about the encroaching end of years.

It was not a fear of death that overtook him, but just the realization that he may never again climb a hill. That he might not be able to travel and would become house bound. That perhaps he had for the last time sat on the edge of the valley and watched the sun set over the hills four valleys away. There were a few more things he was hoping to see his grandchildren do, and then he thought about Wesley. What puzzled him so much about this man? He still needed a little time, and he asked the good Lord for the same as he pulled off the interstate at Cullman, Alabama, and looked for a motel.

Before checking in, he called his doctor's office, hoping they were still there, to say that he might not make it for his Thursday appointment and could he reschedule for some time next week. The receptionist put him on hold to check the doctor's schedule.

The person that came back on the line was Dr Cantrell's nurse. Jacob could tell she was not happy.

"Mr. Grant," she said and Jacob noticed a bit of annoyance in her voice, "you have already rescheduled once and Dr. Cantrell is a bit concerned about your latest test. Why can't you make it?"

"Well, I was inadvertently delayed one day in Pennsylvania and I am now north of Birmingham, but stopped for the day as I am completely tuckered out."

"Well, based on what Dr. Cantrell says about your tests, that seems reasonable. How many hours are you away from Pensacola?"

"Birmingham to Pensacola is about four, so from here, probably another forty-five minutes," Jacob answered.

"Why don't we do this? You give us another call at about noon to see if you think you will make it."

"Okay," Jacob said. "That sounds like a good plan."

"Oh! And by the way," the nurse replied.

"Yes," Jacob answered.

"Drive careful, don't kill yourself getting here."

"Thanks," was Jacob's reply.

Jacob checked into the Days Inn, threw his over night bag and a change of clothes on to the bed and went to the Kentucky Fried Chicken restaurant across the street for a bite to eat. He felt a bit better. As he walked, he placed a call to Sylvie to let her know he had stopped for the night. He didn't tell her how tired he was, and she praised him for being concerned for his own well-being and thanked him for calling. Before going to bed, he took two Motrin in case his leg started to hurt once he laid down. He didn't turn on the TV, but read the front section of USA Today that he had purchased that morning after walking Sarah and Nathan to school.

He woke at about 2:30 a.m. to go to the bathroom. His leg was not bothering him now and when he crawled back into bed, he fell asleep almost immediately. At about 5:45 am, he again felt the need to go to the bathroom. This time he turned on the light by the bed and decided he would go ahead and take a shower and hit the road. That should put him into Pensacola in plenty of time for his appointment.

At 6:20, he threw his bag and dirty clothes into the back seat of the truck and walked to the front desk to check out. The night clerk was still on duty and was busy putting out the fixings for the continental breakfast. She stopped to take care of his bill and he pulled himself a cup of coffee and wrapped a sugar-covered donut in a napkin. The young lady behind the counter didn't seem too friendly, but he remembered having the midnight to seven duty many years ago when he was in the Navy. His memory still served him well and he recalled that by this time of the morning you were simply operating on rote. She stapled the credit card slip to the motel's bill, folded it neatly and handed it to him with the normal "Thank you for being our guest."

Jacob thanked her in return and then said, "Oh, one other thing."

"*Yes*"

Then Jacob smiled, "When you get off work here shortly, you go have a good sound sleep."

She also smiled now and answered, "Thank you, I intend to."

At 6:30, Jacob was again southbound on I-65 towards Birmingham. He hit the outskirts of the City just as the morning rush hour traffic was starting to build but it was flowing smoothly. He clicked the local traffic channel. I-20 east toward Atlanta was going slow due to construction at the I-459 intersection, but that would not affect him. On all other main arteries into and out of the city, traffic was flowing smoothly. There were no wrecks on the city streets so far this morning. He passed through without delay.

By 7:50 he was just north of Montgomery at Prattville and as on the way up a few days earlier, he decided it was too early for breakfast at his favorite Waffle House or Cracker Barrel. About fifty miles south of Montgomery at Greenville, Jacob decided that his stomach was telling him it was time to stop for breakfast. He knew that he would make Pensacola in plenty of time to make his appointment. He would eat breakfast and then call Dr. Cantrell's office to inform them he should be on time.

There were two restaurants here that he could use, Shoney's or Cracker Barrel. He decided he would use the Cracker Barrel so he could purchase some postcards and write them while he waited for his breakfast. He would send one card to his daughter Cheryl in Hawaii, and one to the other grandkids, David and Eliana.

The parking lot at the Cracker Barrel was quite full and he had to nearly circle the building before finding a parking space. He just started to get out of the truck when his cell phone chimed. He assumed it was his daughter Sylvie checking on his progress, but was completely surprised to hear Wesley's voice.

"Well, this is a complete surprise, Wesley. What is up?"

"Before I go into that, where are you now?"

"About an hour and a half north of Pensacola. Why?"

"Well, I may need your help. There seems to be some problems in country paradise. I sent you an e-mail explaining most of it, but I just called to make sure you read it as soon as you got home."

"You can't tell me now?" Jacob asked.

"It is a bit complicated and I spelled it out pretty well in my e-mail. It is not a life or death situation; well I don't think it is. And since you will be home in a couple of hours, just read it and give me a call," Wesley said.

"Well, okay. I have a doctor's appointment at 2:00 p.m., but I will get home in time to read it before going to see my Doc. Depending on what you are talking about, I may not get to call you back until after I am done with the doctor," Jacob replied.

"I understand that Jacob. Drive carefully for the remainder of your trip."

"Yeah, sure after you dump this on me, I am suppose to give the road one hundred percent of my attention."

"I am sorry Jacob, but it isn't worth jeopardizing your safety for."

"It's okay. Talk to you later. Goodbye."

Jacob ended the call, but decided he would not go into the restaurant now, he would go back by the McDonalds, get a sausage and egg McMuffin, a coffee, and eat while he drove.

At 11:45 he turned on to Blue Angel Parkway. His cell phone was in a bracket on the dash, and he punched the single digit for Sylvie's number and the speakerphone button. Sylvie answered on the second ring in her normal joyful voice. "Hi," Jacob said. "Just letting you know I am within a mile of home."

"You made good time," Sylvie replied.

"Yeah, nice weather and no traffic holdups. Pretty routine. Will talk to you later. I love you and give my grandkids a kiss," Jacob said with his normal way of ending his call to her.

Her reply was, "Love you too and will do."

He then hit the button for Dr. Cantrell's office. When the receptionist answered, he identified himself and said to tell Dr. Cantrell's nurse he was back in Pensacola and would make his appointment on time.

Chapter 35

When he arrived at the house, Jacob immediately went in, turned off the alarm and turned on his computer. While the computer was booting up, he headed to the bathroom. He took the computer remote with him and when he heard the chime, he hit the internet connect button.

When he came back to his desk, he immediately hit the mail button. The screen was full of mail. He used to take his laptop with him so he could check his mail, but lately considered that was just another rope tied to him that was not necessary. He scrolled down until he found the one from Wesley. He hit read and Wesley's message now filled the screen.

It began: "Jacob, I may need your help. Without a doubt I need your advice. Please read this carefully and give me a call regardless of the time of day."

Jacob hit the print button and then went to unload the truck. He put his toiletry items back in the bathroom. When he looked in the mirror he noticed he hadn't shaved his neck under his beard since leaving Pennsylvania. He did that and then took another shower. While he was toweling off in front of the mirror he saw that he had cut himself slightly on the neck while shaving. He started to take a napkin to dab away the blood, but then decided he would take a piece of gauze from the vanity drawer. After that he got dressed for his appointment. It was now a little less than an hour and a half until his appointment. It took him approximately 25 minutes to get to Dr. Cantrell's office, but he decided he would go early in case they were running ahead of schedule, but he had never heard of a Doctor running ahead of schedule unless someone didn't show up for his or her appointment because they had died. If not, then he would have time to carefully read Wesley's letter and consider an answer.

He took his old leather briefcase from beside his desk, put Wesley's letter inside and went back to the bedroom. He went through his dirty clothes from the trip and retrieved the gauze patch that Wesley had held on his cut. He then took the gauze patch he had used to swab the blood on his neck. He put both in a plastic sandwich bag and put them in his briefcase.

When Jacob arrived at Dr. Cantrell's office, a building shared by six other doctors associated with the same HMO, he went to the receptionist's window to sign in. He told the young woman sitting there his name and the doctor he was to see. She clicked a few keys on her computer keyboard, looked at Jacob and said, "You are early, and please have a seat."

"Yes, I am early," Jacob replied and then continued, "I thought the good Doctor might be running ahead of schedule."

The receptionist raised her eyebrows as if to say, "Are you joking?"

Jacob caught the raised eyebrows and replied, "Yes, I was joking."

The waiting room was nearly full and Jacob looked for a seat the greatest distance from the television. He sat down, opened his brief case, extracted Wesley's e-mail letter and started to read.

On the subject line, Wesley had put the same words he had said to him on the telephone earlier in the day. "Problems in Country Paradise."

Jacob read again the first two lines as they appeared on his computer screen before he had hit the print button an hour earlier. Wesley's letter continued: I was awakened in my hotel room on Monday evening at 10:32 p.m. when the security system at my home was activated. I was able to activate my notebook computer and watched the scene unfold. The monitoring company in Johnstown was also put on line by the security computer. When the floodlights came on we were able to see what looked like a male intruder just a few paces from the bottom of the steps on the lower side of the house. The person was taken completely by surprise but was able to shield his face from the cameras. The intruder recovered his composure very quickly and left the area.

At that moment I considered it could have been anybody, because anyone who read the Monday edition of the Somerset paper would have known I was out of town. It carried a short article about my award in Youngstown and said I was leaving on Monday to accept the award on Tuesday. Apparently the people at Holy Spirit Catholic Church in Somerset had notified the newspaper.

After awhile, my human weakness kicked in and overrode my priestly training, and I figured it must be my number one local adversary.

When I got home I immediately checked the tapes in my system. I knew the camera that was closest to the intruder when the lights came on so I scanned that tape first. I was able to take it sequence by sequence, but I could not get a clear picture of the intruder's face because he had his head down and was wearing a long visor cap that further concealed his face. However, I was able to identify the cap. It was not who I suspected, God forgive me; it belongs to young Jake Grayson. Naturally, I was totally deflated, and, as of this writing, uncertain of what action I should take. I did call the monitoring company and told them my tapes captured all the action and they could reuse theirs. I now have the only record.

That is the first dilemma, now for the second. While I was driving to Ohio, I mulled over what we were talking about the previous evening when we were sitting on the lower porch. It was my discussion about the Chautauqua Society of New York and Father McGinnis' experiment up on Lake Erie. What I didn't tell you about was that when Father Mac died several years later, the project fell through. When I got back to Youngstown, I tried to resurrect the idea because I had seen how much it had accomplished, but I couldn't raise any interest in the diocese. I had made an additional quest for the program about a year before I requested my Sabbatical, and again it received very little support. Only Father Broderick thought it was a good idea.

Then I remembered our second trip to the May homestead on Saturday and the fact that a 'For Sale' sign had been posted. I thought this would be an excellent place for a retreat facility and I would run it by Father Broderick in just a general way.

When I started to mention it to him, I noticed he smiled slightly and kept nodding his head. I assumed he was just being polite, but I continued to the end. When I finished he looked at me and said, "Still have that it the back of your mind, don't you, Wesley?"

I said, "Yes sir, at times."

Then he shocked me when he said, "Good. You see, ever since you left I have been trumpeting your cause. I am happy to tell you on the occasion of this special day when you are being recognized by the good citizens of this community, those in higher places within the Church feel you had a commendable idea. I caution you not to be too optimistic; the wheels often turn slow in the church hierarchy."

We discussed it a bit more, but he told me that when I got back, I should check the details and have the realty agency contact him and he would put them in touch with the appropriate authority. Father Broderick is a very persuasive man in his quiet way; one of God's best.

After I had reviewed the tape, I was naturally quite distraught and had to get out of the house. I drove back to the May place to get the information from the 'For Sale,' sign. I parked my truck at about the same place you and I had parked, and I went walking around and taking a few more pictures to send to Father Broderick. When I returned to my truck the lady that lives in the big new house that we had surveyed was walking out to check her mail and she said hello.

I walked over to her and introduced myself. She introduced herself as Brea Gable. I saw the name Gable on the mailbox. Apparently she doesn't get a lot of people to talk to back in there so she gave me a lot of unsolicited information about her and her husband. Again, I think we judged prematurely, as did Janet. I don't believe she is a woman who cheats on her husband. Before she and her husband moved back here, they lived in Pittsburgh where she worked for her father for over ten years. Her father owns a private investigation firm.

She then told me that she still dabbles in it on her own. A bell rang in my head, very loudly. So in my own sleuthful way I said, "Very interesting, but I suppose there is not much use for that here."

To which she replied, "Oh, you might be surprised."

She also told me that her husband sometimes worked for her father. I could have goofed up here, because I said, "I thought your husband drove truck."

To which she replied, "He does, but there is a lot of work in the trucking business for investigators. You know, insurance companies keeping track of drivers and their records, the government tracking illegal cargo, jealous wives wanting to know how hubby is spending his down time. There are all kinds of things."

I told her I guessed she was right; it was just that I never thought about it.

We chatted a bit about the property and she asked me if that was why you and I were back there last weekend. What she actually said was 'you and the older man.' I said that we did see the sign when we were here earlier. I then excused myself, saying that I had to get home as I needed to get on the computer and do some work. As I drove away, it dawned on me that Mr. Larkin might be her client.

I was trained as a Priest, not as a detective, so I am confounded as to what I should do. I would greatly appreciate hearing from you as soon as possible. I trust your advice."

Wesley.

PS: Violet and her son Zack did attend the presentation. Violet and I had an early dinner together on Tuesday evening. We had a wonderful conversation. I owe you one.

Jacob held the letter in his hand for a moment and then put it back in his briefcase. He shut his eyes and contemplated. He felt a great concern for Wesley pass over him. For five minutes he did not move, and then he heard the nurse call his name. "Jacob Grant, the Doctor will see you now."

He rose, took his briefcase and followed the nurse through the doors to where the examining rooms were located. She didn't stop at the scales to weigh him as she usually did, but went to the corner and took the hallway to the left. She stopped at the third door on the right.

Go right in there, Mr. Grant, the doctor will be with you shortly. Normally the nurse also went in and took his vital signs. Today she did not.

Jacob sat in the chair by the window. He did not pick up a magazine to read, but instead he peered out towards the forested area beyond the parking lot. It looked so peaceful, but suddenly so unobtainable. Somehow he sensed that Wesley's letter wasn't the only bad news he was going to receive today. He would probably have gone into a terrible funk if he had not noticed an albino squirrel cross the lawn and jump up on the privacy fence. Years ago there was one that lived close to their house. He and Monika would put out peanuts and pecans for it and its normal gray friends. They noticed that the squirrels always took the pecans first. They couldn't tell if it was male or female so they gave it a unisex name; they called it Taylor. About a month after the pecan season ended, Taylor ceased to come by. Jacob had watched everyday and continued to put out peanuts for the rest of the squirrels, but he never saw Taylor again. Albino squirrels are not that much of a rarity, but Jacob always thought that they were one of the most beautiful animals he had ever seen.

As he sat there and watched the squirrel move down the privacy fence and out of sight, his mind flashed back to some years before when he would come here for his annual physical. When he returned to the shop, Monika always asked him, "Well, what did the doctor say?"

To which he always answered, "He said I should live to be one hundred if you don't kill me first."

"Yeah, right," she would continue. "What was your blood pressure reading?"

"I don't remember. Not bad enough for him to chew me out, but not good enough to take me off the pills." And sometimes I would add, "He probably could take me off them with out endangering my well being, but then he would lose his pill royalty."

Monika wasn't as much against taking medication as Jacob was so she didn't think that was funny.

"Good afternoon, Jacob," Dr. Cantrell said pulling him out of his trance. "How are we doing?"

"Well, based on the few words I had with the nurse on the telephone, I assume you are going to tell me."

"Yes, I guess that is partly true. I am afraid some of it is not good news. I don't want you to get panicky. There are a lot of things we can do, but we need to get started."

"Dr. Cantrell, I am seventy years old. I have been coming to you for at least the last fifteen of those years. You should know me by now that I do not get panicky."

"Very well, Jacob. Then let me tell you bluntly, you have the big C. Fairly early stages, but it can move fast. We just have to move faster."

There was a short pause and again Jacob stared out of the window towards the trees, but this time it was as if his mind had left his body. He was entering the woods and there was a familiar path, but the path wasn't in Pensacola, it was somewhere in his boyhood memory. He had a stick in his hand; it served as his sword. He was barefooted and his beagle, whom he had named King, trailed close behind. They followed the small stream as it meandered its way down the valley. Then, just as in night dreams, it changed. The stick was now a cane, he was wearing shoes and they seemed very heavy. His beagle had deserted him and he was ascending a steep hill, the little river very far below. He was tired. He had to stop and catch his breath.

Dr. Cantrell's next words again brought him back to reality.

"Since this treatment will be mostly outpatient, we will first need to check with the Navy Hospital to see if they will provide the care. If not, then you will be under the care of Dr. Regina Anderson. She is very good. She has a great sense of humor, but I warn you, she is pretty fast on the uptake and can deflect most good-natured sarcasms. I think you will like her."

"In that case, why don't we just go with her and forget the Navy?" Jacob answered.

"Would if we could, but we can't. First, we need to get some blood work done so let me write the tests we will need. My nurse tells me you were up north for a few days."

"Yeah, I was in Ohio and Pennsylvania for a few days, came back via Kentucky and spent a couple days trying to spoil my grandkids. By the way, Dr. Cantrell, speaking of blood, I have a couple samples of dried blood that I want to have a DNA comparison test done on. Can you get that done for me?" Jacob asked.

"I can, but you can get it done yourself. I know you are somewhat computer literate. Go to any search engine and type in DNA. You will find all kinds of labs listed. Some charge as little as two hundred dollars for a two-blood comparison."

"Gosh, I don't know why I didn't think of that. Maybe I have brain cancer in addition to prostate."

"Jacob, don't test fate."

"You sound a lot like Monika, Doc. She couldn't take a joke either. Maybe that is why the two of you got along so well."

"You mean you and I don't get along well?"

"Of course not, you have always been my favorite pill pushing, prescription writer."

"Anyway, did you put a flower on Monika's grave on my behalf?"

"Yes I did, but I couldn't afford exotic orchids like you grow so I put a small geranium. I also told her that if you have your way, I would probably be joining her very soon."

311

Dr. Cantrell just laughed.

"If I may ask, why are you having a DNA comparison done?"

"Just some research curiosity," Jacob answered without offering any additional comments.

Dr. Cantrell, having known Jacob for many years, knew that he liked to expound on his research, but with this answer, he knew enough to drop the subject.

"Okay, Jacob, take this by the desk on your way out and the secretary will set you up with an appointment with the center close to your house to have the blood drawn. As soon as we get the results, we will get in touch with you."

"Thanks, Dr. Cantrell, and thanks for putting up with my cantankerous ways."

"I don't see them as cantankerous, but wouldn't want it any other way."

Chapter 36

When Jacob got home, he put the briefcase on the worktable by his computer. He extracted the e-mail from Wesley and the bag with the two blood samples. He removed the blood samples and took a piece of scrap paper that lay on his table and wrote DNA. That way he would remember to search for a lab the next time he signed on.

He took Wesley's e-mail, the blood samples, and his cell phone with him to the kitchen where he poured himself a large glass of water. He tossed the blood samples in on the top shelf of the freezer where he kept freezer bottles for the portable cooler he took along on trips. He then took the e-mail, his water, and cell phone out to the far corner of the back yard. The yard was in perfect condition, the grass had been mowed, the flowers trimmed and weeded, and new mulch had been added all around. He told himself, to call the lawn master people and tell them of the fine service they were providing.

He set his glass of water on the table along with the phone and the e-mail. He always kept a roll of paper towels tucked into the braces of the huge umbrella covering the table so he could wipe the table and the chairs when needed. As he set the items down, he noticed that the tabletop and the chair seats had also been taken care of.

Jacob sat down, read the e-mail one more time and then dialed Wesley's number.

Wesley answered on the second ring. "Hello, Jacob, I was just sitting here waiting for your call."

"Hello, Wesley. You know I wish Ma Bell, or whoever, had never invented caller ID."

"Why do you say that, Jacob?"

"I don't know. It just seems to take all the intrigue out of answering the phone and not know who might be calling."

"Perhaps, but just think of all the telemarketers you don't have to hang up on."

"Small satisfaction, but I guess it will have to do.

"I couldn't get an argument out of my doctor either, so let's talk about your problems," Jacob said.

"Okay, but before we do, tell me, how did it go with your doctor?"

"Oh, fine. He said I would probably live to be a hundred if I didn't fall asleep at the wheel going to or from Pennsylvania."

"I know you are not telling me the truth, Jacob, but I will let it slide," Wesley said in response. "I suppose you have had time to read my e-mail?"

"Yes, I have. Several times in fact. I will give you my thoughts, but take them as a grain of sand. You are more skilled in these matters than I am, and I don't think it requires the knowledge of a detective. Your counseling skills should do just fine. Let's take the last part of you letter first."

"The way I see it, you think that Mr. Larkin was just going back there to get his update on whoever she was shadowing for him. My question is; who would that be? From what I have heard, it would hardly be his wife. And your assumption doesn't jive with what Janet said. She said her brother was a scoundrel, Mrs. Larkin was a saint, and she apparently suspected, with cause, that he was seeing this woman for reasons other than as a private detective."

"I thought about that. She obviously knows her brother quite well, and because of that, she could be drawing a conclusion not supported by the facts. She apparently knew he went to this woman's house and just assumed it was for an illegitimate rendezvous. Also, I think she likes her sister-in-law, but I don't think she finds her to be a saint."

"Sorry about that, Wesley. I know you Catholics take your saints seriously. What I am looking at here is from what you have told me. Everyone thinks Mrs. Larkin is a fine and proper lady. And you confirmed to me that you saw her shortly after he beat her bad enough that she could not make the next Wednesday night church service two days later. He picked a fight with you for no other reason than being in, what he considered, his territory after this beating of his wife. Maybe I have been going to the Lutheran Church too long and it has made me stubborn, but I wouldn't let him throw the hook too soon and swim downstream unimpeded. And that is from a non-fisherman."

"Okay, Jacob, I see where you are coming from, but what do you propose I do. Remember this, I am still very much the outsider, regardless of how well it seems the locals may like me. One wrong move and I am an outsider forever."

"That is very true, Wesley, but there is a reverse side to that, you could come out the hero. I suppose you need to play it cautiously. My daughters always said I was the proverbial, 'bull in the china shop', and after I had wrecked havoc, I became the 'lamb of peace'. I never quite understood that, but I suppose they would say at this juncture, Wesley, do it your way.'"

"Okay, I will reevaluate the case with Mr. Larkin. Now what about Jake? I have prayed for guidance here, but so far I haven't received an answer. I am hoping that the good Lord will use you as a relay."

"Wow! You really do have faith Wesley. I haven't really been on good terms with the good Lord since I came back from the doctor, but that can wait. The thing with Jake also bothers me greatly. I don't know the young man, only having talked to him briefly the one time, but I knew his grandparents very well, and in my conversation with his mother, it just doesn't seem plausible. This would be my suggestion, if you can get in touch with Jake without his mother knowing, talk to him and tell him what you know. Personally, I believe that he will insist on telling his mother himself. From that point on, a good Priest should be able to control the situation."

"Permit me to reiterate your 'wow.' You certainly have a great deal of confidence in me, but I agree that what you said is a good course of action. I was going to call his mother as you had told her I would. Maybe I will ask her if Jake can come and help me with some things around the house. That will give me an opportunity to talk to him in private."

"Oh, wait a minute, Wesley. I forgot you were going to see her. See, another one of my senior moments. Why don't you call her and ask when you can talk with her. If Jake is there, you should be able to easily gauge his reaction. If he was the intruder, he will know he was caught on camera and will most likely be ill at ease. If he was not the intruder, he will probably act very normal. If he acts uneasy, or isn't there, don't say anything to his mother, but then go back to the plan I mentioned before."

"That makes a lot of sense, Jacob, and that is exactly how I will proceed."

"Sounds like a good plan, Wesley, I say go for it and keep me appraised. I am home for a spell and will check my e-mail daily. In case of an emergency, you know my cell number. I will talk to you later."

"Not so fast Jacob. What is this about you, God, and your doctor?"

"Oh, it is nothing, just some glib talk that slipped out."

"I know you had a doctor's appointment today. Did you get bad news?"

"Define bad news. That is an old turn of the century term, but to be honest, I have to go through some tests for something. I am not sure."

"There is another old saying, Jacob, 'You go to hell for lying.'"

"Wesley, you are as bad as my daughters, and that is why I don't tell them more than they need to know for their own good. I told you I would keep in touch."

"Okay, Jacob, I will let it go. Talk to you later."

Jacob sat at the table and finished his glass of water but something was bothering him about what Wesley had said concerning the private detective lady. Something didn't add up.

He went back in the house to refill his glass with iced tea and see if he could find something to eat. He had missed breakfast because of Wesley's call, and it was now a quarter past four, and he was starved. He opened the refrigerator and found exactly what he had expected, nothing to eat. He always cleaned out the refrigerator before he left, so he checked the pantry. He found a glass jar of Boston baked beans and decided that would have to do. He liked them cold so he unscrewed the lid, got a tablespoon from the drawer, filled his glass with iced tea and went back to the patio table.

He sat down, took two spoonfuls of the beans, and called Wesley back on the cell phone.

Again Wesley answered on the second ring. "Boy, you said you would get back to me, but I didn't think it would be this quick. What's up?"

"The thing with the private detective lady has been bothering me. Something is screwy. Okay, as Detective Columbo would say, 'Let's go over the situation one more time and see if I can discover what it is.' But before we do, I am glad the presentation in Youngstown went well and you had a good conversation with Violet."

"Yeah, she told me about a rather strange coincidence that happened on Monday morning."

"Oh," Jacob said, "you will have to tell me about it the next time I see you. Now back to the detective lady. You said she told you that her husband did drive truck, but it was in an investigative role for her father's company. Janet told us that he drove for Wal-Mart. I just don't see Wal-Mart giving permission to have one of their trucks being used for that type of service."

"She said he worked for her father sometimes, but you make a good point, Jacob. When the people from Old Bethel helped me move in, I met a man who also drives truck. If I get a chance, I could ask him about Mr. Gable as long as I am careful not to raise any suspicions."

"What time did you drive back to the May place?" Jacob asked.

"I guess it was about 9:30 a.m. Why?"

"Ah! Very interesting. What time do you normally get your mail delivered?"

"Normally between 1:30 and 3:30 pm depending upon the amount of mail the carrier has."

"Is the carrier headed toward Kingwood or toward Humbert when your mail is delivered?"

"Toward Humbert. I talked to him once. He goes down the Coke Oven Hollow, then retraces his route and goes in by Old Bethel. He told me that from my place, it takes him about one more hour to complete his route. It often takes him longer in the winter."

"So, again I ask you, Wesley, when did you talk to Mrs. Gable, and did she retrieve any mail from her box?"

"Okay, Jacob, the light just came on. She did not retrieve any mail. So she just came out to engage me in conversation and see what I was up to."

"That is how I would sum it up," Jacob said.

"Okay, that is not a hard game to play. I know it has just been a short time, but do you have any more thoughts about Jake?"

"I wish I did, but without seeing the tape, I have no suggestions. The only thing I can think of is that except for the autographed visor, it is just a regular Penguin hat that anyone going to a game might have. As a matter of fact, I have one just like it in my closet."

"That is the problem, Jacob. When you zoom in on the hat, the writing is visible. Not readable, but visible."

"Oh," Jacob said, "that may sound pretty convincing." Then he continued, "Do you make any intrusion tests of your system?"

"Not of a stealth type," Wesley said. "Why?"

I don't know your system, but I would guess your camera and your lights are not synchronized."

"What makes you think that?"

"Well, a person who is entering as this person did, would most likely have his head up and looking in all directions. You intruder had his head down, so the lights must have come on a second before the cameras started to record."

"No, Jacob, that didn't happen. I checked the computer records and the video records, and everything worked as programmed. The monitoring station in Johnstown agreed that the system worked perfectly. The cameras came on as soon as the intruder crossed the fifty-foot radius. The lights came on when he crossed the thirty-foot radius. There were no glitches."

"Well, I guess you have no choice but to try it as we previously mentioned. Let me know how it plays out. I will be here over the weekend, and then I will be out of town for a few days. Will take the laptop, so e-mail me."

"I will let you know how it goes. Where are you going out of town?"

"May go to Houston to see my brother, so I will talk to you later. Bye."

"Bye," Wesley responded in return.

Jacob went back into the house and put his glass in the dishwasher. He then returned to his room, turned on the computer and opened a file from the CD write drive. It was titled: Innocent Indiscretion, a novel by Jacob Grant. Muchi came in and jumped up on the table to be with him. As usual, she pushed papers out of the way so she could lie down.

Chapter 37

As soon as Wesley finished his second conversation with Jacob, he galled Gladys. When she answered, Wesley immediately identified himself. Gladys said she knew it was he by her caller ID. She sounded very relaxed, and Wesley took that as a good sign.

"I just spoke to our mutual friend Jacob and he was bemoaning caller ID. Said he liked it better when there was a bit of a mystery when you picked up and answered."

"I don't know Jacob that well, but I would guess he was just pulling your leg, as the saying goes."

Oh, I am sure that is the case, Jacob likes to sound like more of a curmudgeon than he really is. However, he is the reason I called you. He told me that you were a bit worried about Jake, and felt that because of my profession, perhaps I could help. So I am offering my help, but I hope it isn't needed."

"No one could wish that more than I," Gladys said. "For the first time in a very long time, I think things may work out. After Jacob and I had the conversation on Sunday, I took his advice. When Jake came home from work on Monday eve, he and I had a long talk. I started the conversation at the supper table, and at ten o'clock, the table wasn't cleared and we were still talking. There were tears on both sides from time to time, but when we finally stopped, cleared the table and went to bed, we both felt better than either of us had for a long time."

"That is reassuring," Wesley said. "So, maybe you don't need my help after all."

"I wouldn't write that off so soon, but even if we don't, Jake would like me to meet you. I know that he is very impressed with you."

"Jake is a fine young man, and I also do want to meet you Mrs. Grayson. Actually that is one of the reasons I called. I was wondering if you and Jake would like to come over this evening for supper?"

"That would be very nice, but I will have to call Jake first. I know he was going to umpire a ballgame at the prison, but with this rain, I feel sure they won't play. I will call him and then call you back if that is okay?"

"That will be just fine," Wesley said.

"What was the other reason you called?" Gladys asked.

She noted a slight pause from Wesley's end so she prompted him. "You said one of the reasons you called was to invite us over. What was the other reason?"

"Oh, yeah, too much on my mind recently; I am getting forgetful. I wanted to ask Jake if he could help me move some of my things into my ground floor office on Saturday. That is if he isn't busy."

"I am sure he will be glad to help, but he doesn't always keep me appraised of his plans so I will let him speak for himself."

"I understand that, so call me right back if Jake can make it," Wesley said.

"I will," Gladys said.

Although he had a lot of boxes and electronic equipment, he was sure he could handle it by himself, but by inviting Jake to help him, it would give him an opportunity to talk with him. Maybe he could get some answers to a few things that were bothering him. He went downstairs to the office area to await her call.

Earlier in the day, Wesley had received a call from Home Depot saying that all the materials for his bookshelves and other fixtures for his basement library had arrived, and they would like to know when he wanted the contractor to start. This was good news for him, so he told them he would like to start as soon as possible.

"We can start in the morning, if that is okay with you, Mr. Donaldson."

"Tomorrow morning will be just fine. What time should I expect them?"

"They should be there by 9 a.m."

"Do you have any idea how long it should take them?" Wesley asked.

"Looking at the spec sheet, they have allotted four hours, so provided there are no major glitches, they should be out of there by 1:00 at the latest."

"Does that include the electrical wiring and lighting?"

"Yeah, that includes the whole package."

When he had finished talking to the person at Home Depot, he called Office Depot to find out when they could deliver his file cabinets, desk, tables and other ancillary equipment. To his great pleasure, they said they could deliver by 2 p.m. after the other contractor had left. This was really good news, because he had been anxious to get back to work on some of his projects.

In less than five minutes, Gladys called back. When Wesley answered, Gladys said that she talked to Jake. The rain had caused the baseball game to be cancelled, and Jake was delighted that Wesley had invited them over for supper.

Gladys continued, "What time would you like us to come?"

"Feel free to come as soon as Jake gets home. I figured we would eat about 7:30 p.m., but if you come early, it gives us time to talk and I can give you the two-dollar tour as Jacob Grant called it."

"I would love to see the house. Jake told me that it was very nice. Now, before I hang up, is there anything I can bring? Perhaps a peach pie, that is Jake's favorite and I baked several pies for his lunch next week."

"I was going to say no to your offer, but since I am not a pie baker, and Giant Eagle's bakery is my normal source, I will accept and say, 'that a peach pie would be nice.' By the way, is there anything that you do not like?"

"We are not finicky eaters, Mr. Donaldson, and please do not go to a lot of trouble."

"I promise, I won't," he said, "and please call me Wesley."

"Okay, I will, if you call me Gladys."

"That is a deal."

"Then we will see you soon, Wesley."

'Okay, Gladys."

Wesley hadn't given much thought to what he would make for supper. He could do lemon chicken. Most people liked that, and it was easy to prepare. Maybe he could make a cucumber salad and some pasta with plain yogurt and Parmesan cheese. Pasta didn't take long to prepare, so he could wait and ask if that was okay, or, if they preferred a red sauce. If so, they would have to settle for some of Paul Newman's best.

At 5:55, Wesley heard the chime that told him someone had crossed the entrance to his driveway. He assumed it was his guest and went out onto the porch to await their arrival. From the top of the step, he watched as Jake pulled his truck into the parking space in front of the garage door. He descended the stairs and waited for his guests to get out of the vehicle.

When Gladys got out of the passenger side of the truck, Wesley was immediately struck by her beauty. She had dark brown hair and eyes the color of polished ebony. She was small, maybe five foot one and with a slim figure. In one millisecond after he saw her, he wondered if that was appropriate for a priest to make that appraisal. Immediately after that, he remembered something his father had once said about his mother: *God made roses, and then he improved upon it by making beautiful women like your mother.* Although Wesley knew that for some reason, his mother wasn't always sure about her beauty, and maybe Gladys felt the same way, at least he was sure that God was not admonishing him for recognizing beauty.

"Mr. Donaldson, I would like you to meet my mother."

Both extended their hand and Wesley acknowledged, "My definite pleasure in finally meeting you, Gladys."

"It is also my pleasure, Wesley."

Wesley then extended his hand to Jake and said, "Your mother and I buried the formalities when we spoke on the telephone this afternoon. I know I am older than you, but I would prefer if you also just called me Wesley."

"Of course," Jake said, "I thank you for extending me that privilege."

The trio then started toward the stairs.

"Explain to me why you consider that a privilege, Jake."

"I don't know," Jake said. "I just know you are a very learned man and I hold you in high esteem."

Wesley looked at Gladys and said, "That is a very polite young man you have raised." Then he looked at Jake and said, "My knowledge is one thing, although it is probably not as great as you envision. And I have had more years than you to work on it. As for high esteem, I have heard a lot about you, and I have witnessed a fair amount. I assume we may consider ourselves as equals."

"That is a great compliment, Wesley. What can I do but accept?"

When they were in the house, Wesley proposed the tour for the sake of Gladys. She was most impressed with the layout and surprised that a priest had such good taste in decorating. She did not know that Wesley had hired an interior decorator for that purpose. Jake on the other hand was very impressed by the electronics that Wesley had incorporated into the house, even though at this time most of it was still jury-rigged in a spare bedroom. When Jake saw the monitors and equipment for the exterior security system and started to express his fascination and understanding of the system, Wesley knew then that it was not Jake on the intrusion tapes. He did not mention it at this time.

When they had completed the tour of the house, including the ground level where Wesley's office furniture was to be installed the next day, they returned to the kitchen. Wesley took the pan containing the chicken he planned to roast for their dinner out of the refrigerator and placed it in the oven. He set the temperature controls and the timer.

"While that is in the oven, perhaps since the rain has stopped, you would like to take a walk around the premises," Wesley said.

"I would love that," Gladys replied.

They walked the path from the house out to the property line where it connected with the perpendicular path going up over and down over the hill. They engaged in small talk.

A the end of the path, Wesley said, "Let's go down the hill to the pond first."

When they reached the bottom where the pond was, Wesley motioned for them to sit down.

"You were talking about my security system up at the house," Wesley said looking at Jake. "Are you familiar with how they work?"

"I'm very familiar with them. We use some pretty sophisticated ones in the prison. And seeing the monitoring system you have in the house, I would guess yours is also pretty sophisticated."

"I think it is a pretty good system. It worked very well a couple of nights ago when I was in Ohio."

Both Jake and his mother looked at him in amazement.

"You mean that you had a break-in?" Jake asked.

"Well, the person never got to the house, but they did intrude far enough to activate the cameras and the flood lights."

"Do you know who it was?" Gladys asked.

"I don't know who it was, but they intended for me to believe it was you, Jake."

"What?" Jake asked.

"Yes. The intruder was wearing a Penguin hat just like yours. It is even autographed, although the writing is not readable from the tapes I have. I am sure it could be enhanced and read, but there is no need for that."

"You don't believe Jake did it, do you, Wesley?" Gladys asked.

"Now I don't, but the first time I ran the tape I did because of the hat. I have corresponded with Jacob since it happened and we are both convinced that it was a

setup. Your willingness to come over here with your mother, and the comments you made about the security system when you saw the equipment, proves to me, beyond a doubt, that it is not you on the tape. My question is who and why?"

"I would also like to know who and why," Jake said. Then he continued, "I knew when we were here to help you move in, that you had a security system installed. The number of strategically placed flood lights and the little box next to them is a dead

give away. There is nothing wrong with them being visible; it can serve as a deterrent."

"That is what the person who installed the system said. He said there is an up and a down side to that," Wesley added.

"There is always a way to beat the system, but yours is probably pretty hard to beat. Do you still have the tapes?" Jake then asked.

"Yes I do," Wesley said.

"Could we view them?"

"I was hoping that you would ask that. You may be able to throw some light on the matter. No pun intended."

Wesley rose and said, "Shall we continue back up over the hill? If my calculations are correct, we can take the upper trail and get back to the house just about the time our supper should be ready."

Gladys hadn't said much during the past few minutes, but as they approached the path to the house, she asked, "Jake do you know of anyone who might want to do something like this against you?"

"No one that I would care to name without more information to back me up. I suppose there are one or two that might do it, but I don't know what their reason would be," Jake said to his mother.

When they were at the top of the path that now turned to parallel the road, there was a series of beeps, like a cell phone. Jake looked at Wesley, Wesley looked at Jake, and Gladys looked at the two of them. It beeped again and this time Jake and Wesley both spied the instrument lying on the ground just a few feet off of the path. Wesley immediately reached for it, but Jake grabbed his hand.

"No," Jake said. "If your intruder dropped it, it may have their finger prints on it."

"Good quick thinking, Jake," Wesley replied. "Working in law enforcement helps, I see. So what do you suggest?"

"I suggest we call the police and let them come down and retrieve it. If you don't mind, I can call out to the Police Barracks and see who is on duty. I know all of the guys out there."

"Jake, you are now officially in charge. Let's head back to the house, and while I finish getting supper ready, you can call the police and see what they advise.

Gladys helped Wesley set the table and get the food ready while Jake went out on the lower porch and called the police. When he came back in, he said everything was taken care of. Jake knew one of the State Police Officers by the name of Vernon Shipley lived down by Whipkey's Dam. The man on duty at the desk called him, and he said he would be up as soon as he finished his own supper. Jake told the dispatcher to tell Vernon to take his time, as they were just about to have supper themselves.

The three of them had just finished their dessert when the chime sounded as a vehicle crossed the entrance to the driveway. They assumed that it was the policeman and went out onto the porch to await his arrival.

When the man got out of the car, Jake yelled from the top of the stairs, "Sorry to interrupt your off time, Vernon."

"That is okay, Jake. You now owe me one."

"I hear that, just as long as it not one of your late Sunday umpiring jobs," Jake said.

"Uh huh," was the policeman's answer. "I have been meaning to talk to you about your umpiring."

"How is that?" Jake asked.

"Them prisoners pay you off? The reason I ask is because that was a bad call on me at first base when we played them the last time."

"I call them like I see them, but you know you were out by a full stride. But," Jake continued, "they do pay better than you guys." They both laughed.

The state policeman was driving his personal vehicle, and popped the lid to the trunk to retrieve a small briefcase.

Wesley, Jake, and Gladys went down the steps. When they got to the car, Jake made the introductions.

"So, where is this mysterious cell phone?" the policeman asked.

"Just a few feet off of the upper path," Wesley said and started to lead the way.

When they got to the spot where the phone had been spotted, the policeman opened his briefcase and got out a pair of gloves and a plastic bag. He picked up the phone and looked at it. "I have one just like this, the new Kyocera, they have one of the longest lasting batteries of any cell phone on the market." He then placed it in the plastic bag and put the bag in his briefcase.

The policeman looked at Wesley. "According to what Jake told the dispatcher, you had someone broach your security system a couple of days ago, is that correct?"

"Yes, sir, that is correct. I was out in Ohio at the time."

"Did you notify the police?"

"No, the watch officer at the control center in Johnstown said they would take care of everything."

"I will check that when I get back to the station. I assume they did not get into the house."

"No, sir. When the flood lights came on, the intruder turned and fled."

"Your system has video cameras associated with it I presume?"

"It does, and the intruder was videotaped, but he has his head down so his face is concealed."

"Oh, that is interesting. Do you have a copy of the tape?"

"Yes, I do. We had planned to view the tape anyway, before we found the cell phone." Wesley then went on to tell the policeman how it was made to look like Jake was the intruder.

"What you say we go have a look at that video," the policeman said.

Wesley led everyone to the spare bedroom where the monitoring equipment was temporarily set up.

"The system has two night vision cameras, but they are positioned to cover points of entry into the house. They come on at the same time as the other cameras."

"And that is when?" the policeman asked.

"At the fifty-foot radius," Wesley said.

"And the lights?"

"At the thirty-foot radius. The system also uses heat sensors to detect human beings and direct the closest camera for close up."

"Wow! You have a very sophisticated system," the policeman said.

"The technology has been around for some time, but it is a good system. However, I do have a friend that calls me a techno junkie," Wesley said.

"Sorta like this guy sitting next to me here," he said nodding his head toward Jake. "Okay, let it roll."

The tape began and there was nothing but a nearly black screen. After less than a minute, the screen came to life and a figure, head down, came into view. The intruder was wearing a long, loose fitting shirt and a Pittsburgh Penguin hat.

"Looks to me like you are guilty, Jake," the policeman said. "I recognize the hat."

"Okay, you found me out. Get the cuffs. I won't go willingly," Jake said.

"Stop that, Jake. This is not funny," his mother said.

"Sorry, Mother."

"Rewind it and play it again Sam, and freeze frame it as soon as the lights come on," the policeman said.

Wesley did as he requested.

"Now back it up, step by step until the light goes out."

Again Wesley did as the policeman requested.

"His head is down before the lights come on, so whoever it is, he definitely knows your system. Go ahead and let it run."

When the tape had played through the second time to where the intruder was out of the picture and the system shut down, the policeman said, "Any comments?"

"It was a pretty warm night so why was the intruder wearing a long heavy shirt?" Wesley asked.

"Well, they knew they were going to be passing through some underbrush, so they may have done it to keep from getting their arms scratched," the policeman said.

"Or to hide their figure," Gladys cut in.

All three men looked at her with a questioning stare.

"You are all men, and even with respect to Wesley's profession, I can't believe that none of you recognize that as a woman."

"Play it one more time," the policeman said.

This time when it had finished, they all looked at Gladys and acknowledged that she was probably correct in her assessment.

"I will need that tape, Mr. Donaldson," the policeman said.

"It will only take me a minute to fast dub you a copy. Will that do?" Wesley asked.

"You may dub a copy for yourself, but I will need the original. You will get it back when we are finished."

"Fair enough," Wesley said as he inserted a tape into a second recorder and hit the fast record button.

The policeman gave Wesley his card, and Wesley gave him one in return.

"Somebody will be in touch with you soon, Mr. Donaldson."

"Okay. I appreciate you coming by on your off time."

"It's okay. There is no such thing as off time for a policeman, but I'll get Jake to make the compensation," and he winked.

"I will make the compensation for you helping to exonerate my son," Gladys said.

"You are the one that helped to exonerate him, I was ready to cuff him and haul him back to Somerset."

Chapter 38

On Friday, Jacob got up at 6:45 and followed his normal routine. He made coffee, put some bread in the toaster, poured a glass of orange juice and took his pills. While waiting for the coffee and toast to finish, he went outside and retrieved his newspaper from the driveway. It always took him about one hour to read the paper, give or take a little depending upon the amount of news that attracted his interest. When he was finished, he hit the mail button on his computer. Except for a couple of jokes relayed to him from an old Navy buddy, his box was empty.

At about 10:30 a.m., Jacob received a call from Dr. Cantrell's nurse telling him that Medicare and TRICARE For Life had approved him for treatment at West Florida Hospital. She then gave him a number to call for Dr. Regina Anderson's office assistant. When he got in touch with her, she said that Dr. Anderson would like to see him in her office at 7:00 am on Monday morning.

"Gosh, the good doctor must get up at a very early hour," Jacob said.

"I guess so," the assistant said. "She is always here when I get in."

"You might warn her that I can be a bit grouchy when I have to break my normal morning routine," Jacob said.

"If you desire, I will tell her that, but I am sure she has heard it all before."

"Okay then, see you on Monday at 8 a.m.

"That is 7:a.m., Mr. Grant."

"Okay, whatever you say. By the way, you know I am Mr. Grant, but I don't know who you are."

"My name is Lavina Kapanski."

"See you on Monday, Lavina Kapanski.

"Goodbye, Mr. Grant," she said and hung up the phone.

Chapter 39

On Monday morning at exactly 9 a.m., Wesley received a call from State Policeman Vernon Shipley.

"Mr. Donaldson, this is Vernon Shipley. Would it be convenient for you to come out to my office sometime today? There are a few questions I need to ask you."

"I have something scheduled for this afternoon, but I could come now, if that is okay."

"That would be fine. So I can expect you, say in forty-five minutes?"

"Yes, or less," Wesley said.

"Take your time, no need to speed."

When Wesley arrived at the police barracks about thirty-five minutes later, a secretary showed him into Vernon Shipley's office.

"Have a chair, Mr. Donaldson."

"Thank you."

"Okay, we have had an opportunity to check out a few things starting with the cell phone, and we came up with some pretty good information. Of course you know, finding the owner of the cell phone only took a minute, but that doesn't mean the owner was the intruder.

"I understand that you haven't lived here very long, but have you made any enemies in that time?"

"I did have a minor run in with one individual shortly after I moved into the house."

"Who might that be?"

"His name is Larkins. He and his wife live up the valley from where the town of Humbert was located."

"Yes, I know where they live. So tell me what happened."

"I had taken a walk one morning. I went in past my neighbors, the Lannings, and worked my way down the valley on an old trail. It comes out on a dirt road that goes up over the hill and also down toward Humbert and past the Larkins' home. Before I got to their house, I heard a lot of yelling by Mr. Larkins. I didn't want to intrude so I held my position. A minute later I saw Mr. Larkins back his truck out of the driveway and speed away; his tires kicking up gravel. I then continued my walk, but when I came along side of the Larkins' house, I saw Mrs. Larkin sitting on the step crying. I had met Mrs. Larkins when the people from Old Bethel helped me move in, so I asked her if I could help. She seemed very embarrassed, but asked me not to come in. I honored her wishes."

"I continued my walk. When I got to the end of the dirt road, I saw Mr. Larkins' truck come down the hill of the hard top road and turned in toward his house. When he saw me he stopped his truck and asked in a very belligerent tone what I was doing there. I had never met him, and he had never met me, so I was a bit taken back. He then got out of his truck, and it was obvious to me that he intended to engage me in a fight. He did attack me and I defended myself. I was able to subdue him quite easily with out hurting him. I did have him pinned on the ground, and we played a little bit of 'school yard uncle' if you are familiar with that."

"I know it very well," the policeman said. "And then what happened?"

"Well, it took several times before he completely understood the rules, but eventually he just said 'uncle' and I let him up. He got in his truck and continued on home. He even drove at a reasonable speed."

"Did you have any more encounters with him after that?"

"No direct encounters, and we never spoke again, but you might say that our paths crossed. Perhaps close and parallel would be a better description," Wesley said.

"You are going to have to explain that one, Mr. Donaldson."

Wesley then told the policeman about the two times he and Jacob had visual contact with him back at the May place. He didn't really want to tell him about the second time, but there was no way to get around it without lying, and he wouldn't do that.

"So, were you harassing Mr. Larkins the second time you went back to the May Place?"

"No, sir, we didn't do it to harass him."

"What would you call it, Mr. Donaldson?"

"Well, I suppose he might construe it as harassing, but Mr. Grant only wanted to confirm if Mr. Larkins' sister's suspicions were correct."

"Just to set the record straight, Mr. Donaldson, the fact that your friend intentionally waited until he saw Mr. Larkins start up the hill so he would have to back up, is harassment. However, since Mr. Grant isn't here, let's move on.

"Since you were back at the old May Place, tell me what you know of the Gables?"

"Nothing."

"Have you ever met either Mr. Gable, or Mrs. Gable?"

"I met Mrs. Gable once."

"When was that?"

"The next day after I came back from Ohio."

"What reason did you have to go back there?"

"The May property is for sale, and Father Broderick of my former parish asked me to check it out for a project that he and I have been trying to get started for some years. I was still a bit upset because at that time, I saw Jake as my intruder. I had to get out of the house and do some thinking."

"So that is when you met Mrs. Gable?"

"Yes, sir."

"The Gable house sits a little ways from the access road, did you go back to her house?"

"No, sir. I parked my truck by the fence and walked back to where the old May house once sat. I took a few pictures to send to Father Broderick, and when I came back I saw Mrs. Gable walking out toward her mailbox. She opened the box but there was no mail. She said hello to me and walked toward me. We talked for a few minutes. She said she saw me back there earlier with an older man, that being Mr. Grant. I told her that Mr. Grant was showing me around the area and relating some of the history to me. She did not know of Mr. Grant or his family, and I did not give any more information. Then she asked why I was there today, and again I told her. She then told me that her father had an investigative service in Pittsburgh and that both she and her husband still helped him at times. I wasn't sure why she told me this, other than she seems like a person that likes to talk."

Wesley didn't give all the details of their conversation, but he didn't feel that under the circumstance any more was necessary. If the policeman wanted to know more, he would answer his question truthfully.

"I think that is about all the questions I have, Mr. Donaldson, but I do need to ask you, if we determine for certain who broached your security system, do you wish to press charges?"

"I do not. As a matter of fact, unless you feel it is in my best interest or the best interest of others, I do not even wish to know who it was."

"Understood," the policeman said. Then he raised his left hand and motioned with his index finger, "There is one thing I almost forgot. You said earlier that your friend Mr. Grant wanted to confirm Mr. Larkin's sister's suspicions. What are her suspicions, if I may ask?"

"Since you phrased it that way, may I say, 'no you may not ask?' Wesley asked with a smile.

"Poor choice of words on my part Mr. Donaldson, please explain."

"The same day that we first went back to the May farm, we later went down to find the old Sam and Priscilla Rugg homestead. We parked close to the large old stone house just before you get to route 281. We met the lady who lives there. Her husband is an airline pilot. Their name is Snyder."

"Okay, I know the Snyders."

Well, Janet Snyder is the sister of Mr. Larkins. Apparently she feels her brother is a cad. She likes her sister-in-law and thinks he is cheating on her. She thinks the lady of his indiscretions is Mrs. Gable."

"That is very interesting," the policeman said.

Wesley got up to leave, then turned to the policeman, "Sergeant Shipley, I was wondering…"

"Yes?" the policeman picked up quickly.

"Well, Mrs. Snyder did say that what she told us was in confidence. If it is at all possible, I would like to not betray her confidence. She seems like a very nice person, and although I haven't yet met her husband, I would like to have them as friends."

"Don't worry, Mr. Donaldson, I will not betray your confidence. You have been very helpful, and I appreciate your coming by. And, by the way, the next time you speak to your friend, Mr. Grant, tell him I am waiting to meet him. Seventy year old men should not be playing harassment games with very athletic twenty somethings."

Wesley laughed, "I will certainly do that. He will get a kick out of that and I am sure he will come to see you. However, after we had left the scene that day, Mr. Grant also realized it could be construed as harassment and that it was childish on his part to suggest that we bait and trap. He asked me to delete the photos I had taken and I was very glad to just that."

"Well, I guess you two are not as bad as I had first imagined," Sergeant Shipley said with a slight smile.

When Wesley got back to the house, he had a message on his voice mail from Janet Snyder.

He listened: *"Wesley, this is Janet Snyder. You are a very difficult person to locate. If you had several unresponsive calls on your voice mail, they were probably mine. I hate to leave messages, but since this is the fourth time, you leave me no choice. I had a call from Nellie and she said she has your painting of Goat Lady finished. She even had her son take it and have it framed. Also, Marshall has your new wristwatch and cell phone, so we would like to invite you down for supper on Friday. I was thinking that we could do it at Nellie's house. I know she is very excited about presenting you with the painting, but since it is difficult for her to get out, I thought I would make dinner and we would just take it to her house to eat. If you can't make it then, please call me as soon as possible. Bye. Janet."*

This was the first opportunity Wesley had to use the facilities in his new ground level office, so he hit the button for contacts "S" and got Janet's number. He hit the button and on the second ring, Janet answered. "Helloooo," was all she said.

"Hi, Janet, this is Wesley. I just got back and listened to your message."

"Oh, hi, Wesley, I thought it was Marshall."

"So that would explain the cooing melodic voice," Wesley said.

"Perhaps, but I didn't think a priest would pick up on that," she said.

"Priest, are supposed to be celibate, but not one hundred percent desensitized. I know cooing when I hear cooing, Janet."

"Forgive me, Father, I know not what I say. And I hope the Good Lord doesn't find that to be sacrilegious."

"I can see where you and Jacob would get along very well."

"You are probably right, Wesley, we were born down here in the same spirit."

"Well, the reason I am calling is to say that I can make the Friday get-together, and I really appreciate the invitation. Also, I know I will never convince Nellie to take anything for the painting, but would you be so kind as to tell her I would appreciate paying for the framing."

"I will tell her, but I am sure your offer will be carried away in the wind. I imagine Curtis paid for it, and since he and Rosalie will be there for supper, you can tell him, but I must warn you, he is a lot like his mother, so don't expect too much. They are proud people; so if I can give you a little advice, just graciously accept their hospitality."

"I appreciate your advice, Janet. What time should I be there?"

"Why don't you be at our house by 6 p.m., if that is okay."

"Six it is," Wesley said.

Chapter 40

At exactly 6 p.m. on Friday evening, Wesley rang the doorbell at the old John C. King stone house. The man who answered the door was Janet's husband, Marshall.

"Come on in. I assume you are Wesley?"

"I am Wesley, and am I safe in assuming that you are Marshall?"

"No, I am not, but Janet often gets her dates mixed up. He won't be back until tomorrow."

Wesley was a bit taken back, until he saw Janet approach from within, and she quickly said, "Pay my husband no mind. He learned the practical joking in the Navy and has never been able to completely shed it."

Marshall had extended his hand when he first opened the door, and the two men were still grasping hands when Janet spoke.

"Just kidding. Come on in, Wesley."

Wesley entered and handed Janet two yellow roses.

"My wife has no appreciation for practical humor. I hope you were not offended."

"Certainly not, but I have a feeling that your wife has a great sense of humor. However, before we go into that, I hope you are not offended that I gave your lovely wife two roses?"

"Not at all," Marshall said, "but may I ask why two?"

"Oh, very good, I have one on you. Well, one of my old parishioners in Youngstown who owns a florist shop once told me, husbands either bought one rose or a dozen roses for their wife. His theory was that if they bought one rose, it was just to tell her that he still loved her. If he bought a dozen roses, he might still love her, but had perhaps done something that she didn't approve of, or at least he had a bit of a guilty conscience from something. He told me I was the only one he mentioned that to. I guess he assumed that as a priest, I would pass it on to the other parishioners, many of who were also his customers."

"You mean like they might have been unfaithful?"

"Oh, no," Wesley was quick to reply, "it could be something as simple as buying some expensive electronic 'boy toy' that his wife felt was extravagant."

Janet smiled and Marshall looked at Wesley and also smiled, then he said, "Five deuce."

"It has been a long time since I played tennis, but I was second team at Notre Dame," Wesley said.

"Really, I love tennis," Marshall quickly replied. "It is okay though, Janet won't let us play on her courts."

"That is correct, and I expect at least marginal adult conversation. Now if you two gentlemen would be so kind as to assist, we will load the food in the SUV and head for Nellie's house."

"Please wait while I get something from my vehicle," Wesley said.

When Wesley got into their SUV carrying a package wrapped in tissue paper, Janet looked at him with skepticism. "If that is for Nellie, I warn you that she may not accept it," Janet said.

"Oh! I think she will," Wesley said quite assuredly.

When they arrived at Nellie's house a few minutes later, Curtis and Rosalie were already there. From Nellie's living room you could see a car as it pulled into her driveway. When they stopped the car, Curtis and Rosalie had both come out onto the porch waiting for them. Janet made the introductions, and the customary pleasantries were exchanged. Janet followed Rosalie into the house while Curtis helped Marshall and Wesley get the food from the car and bring it into the kitchen.

"I really hate having you do all this cooking, Janet," Rosalie said.

"Janet?" Marshall exclaimed. "I will have you know I did the cooking, Rosalie."

Knowing Marshall quite well and his inclination to tell stories, she looked at Janet with a sideward glance.

"I confess, it is true, he did everything except for the dessert. But before Wesley gets the wrong impression that I make my husband do the cooking, I will tell him that he does it by choice."

"Well, Janet and I will handle it from here," Rosalie said, "so why don't we go into the living room and see Mother Nell. She is excited, but I gather a bit nervous about presenting the painting to Wesley."

Nellie was in her wheelchair, and close by was her easel. It held the painting of the goat lady and her house, but it was draped with a red velvet cloth. In her lap lay a book that she had been reading. She inserted a bookmarker, closed it and laid it on the table by her side. A radiant smile crossed her face as the group entered from the kitchen. Janet and Marshall went immediately to her side and gave her a hug and a kiss on the cheek. Wesley, a bit hesitant about the proper procedure, stood where he was for a second until Nellie said, "Good evening, Wesley. Do I rate a hug from you?"

"You certainly do, Nellie," and he walked to her side, gave her a hug and a kiss on the cheek. Then he held her hand and continued, "It is so very good to see you again. Also I might add, that when I talked to my friend Jacob the other day, he said to be sure and tell you hello for him."

"That is so nice of him. Please convey my greeting to him also."

"I will," Wesley said.

Then Curtis spoke, addressing his comments to Wesley. "Mother would like to know if you prefer she unveil the painting before we eat or afterwards?"

"I would defer to her wishes, but since she has been so gracious as to permit me to make the choice, I will go with before. I am very anxious to see her work, so if I had to wait until after we ate, I might be inclined to rush through the meal. I don't want to do that because I wish to honestly evaluate Marshall's culinary skills."

Everyone laughed, and Marshall said, "I am sure you will not be disappointed."

"Such egotism," Janet said.

"Why don't you all find a place to sit and I will have Curtis remove the drape."

When they were all seated, Nellie said, "Curtis is the only one who has seen the finished work. That was necessary because he did the framing for me."

339

Curtis went and stood in front of the easel. Grasping the top corners of the velvet cloth, he removed it and stepped aside. Not a word was said, and then Wesley rose and walked to the painting. He said nothing, but shook his head in what was apparent unbelief, but approval. Two female goats stood close by the side of the porch eating grass, while a completely white billy stood precariously on the roof of the shed and reached for green apples. Several chickens were on the porch pecking at several ears of corn in a wire mesh bucket, undoubtedly left there by Sarah Jane for just that purpose. The door leading into the kitchen stood ajar, but all that was not what caught Wesley's attention, because he had seen most of this when he, Jacob, and Janet had been here earlier. What caught his attention now was the figure of a young lad, perhaps thirteen or fourteen years of age, walking on the road close to the house. He also saw that the position of Sarah Jane had been changed. Previously, she had been kneeling in her garden with her back completely toward the road, but now she was slightly turned and her head was cocked a bit to the right, as if someone had just spoken to her.

Wesley had a slight smile on his face and turned towards Nellie, "Is that my friend Jacob?" he asked.

"It is intended as our friend Jacob," was her reply.

"Yes, our friend. You have done a magnificent job here Nellie. I can't wait until Jacob can see it. I would take a photo of it and e-mail it to him, but that wouldn't do it justice. He will just have to wait until he returns to the hills," Wesley said.

"I am very pleased that you like it, and I hope that Jacob will approve of my putting him in the picture. I had to do a bit of searching to find a picture of him when he was a young boy."

"Nellie, you do not know how much this means to me. I have been assured many times that you would not accept any thing for this beautiful painting, and so what I have for you is not in payment for the painting, I have just borrowed a page from Sarah Jane's protocol. My grandfather was a bit of an artist himself. He was what is often known as a 'whittler.'"

Wesley removed the paper from the object in his hands to show a beautiful

Hand-carved wooden vase. "My grandfather carved this for my grandmother one time when he was laid up with a broken leg. When she died, it passed to my mother and then of course to me. It is carved from a piece of chestnut that was once a part of an old rail fence. I notice that you put your paintbrushes in an empty coffee can. Such artesian tools would probably look good in this old chestnut vase. Sara Jane could not accept unencumbered gifts for reasons we do not understand, but you and I can exchange gifts as newfound friends."

"Wesley, you are a wonderful, thoughtful person, a true friend. I accept your gift."

Wesley looked at Janet with a sideways glance.

Janet just nodded her head very slightly and smiled.

After everyone had taken a good close up look at the painting and the vase which now held Nellie's bushes and bestowed their praises on the artist, Janet and Rosalie went to put the food on the table. Marshall also went along to carve the roasted leg of lamb that he had prepared. Curtis and Wesley stayed and chatted with Nellie.

"I must give you credit, Marshall, this lamb is excellent," Wesley said.

"Thank you. I generally buy it fresh from the neighbor up the hollow. He uses his own stock for his restaurant. Lamb is one of their specialties."

"Marshall is just being modest now," Rosalie said. "The owner of that restaurant has offered him a job as their lamb chef."

"When I stop flying, I may take him up on that," Marshall said as he smiled and raised his eyebrows.

Just as everyone was finishing their dessert, Janet's cell phone-watch vibrated. She punched a button on the side, and then said, "It is Beth, let me take this in the kitchen."

She listened intently for a few seconds and then everyone at the dining room table heard her say, "Oh, my God, what happened?"

Marshall immediately excused himself and went to the kitchen where Janet was again listening.

"What is it Janet?" Marshall asked.

Janet shook her head and raised her right hand to indicate for Marshall to be still for a second.

"Would you like us to come by?" Janet asked.

Then after a second she continued, "Okay, Beth, just stay calm, we will be there in a few minutes."

"Okay, bye."

"So, what is the matter?" Marshall asked again.

"She is okay, but my brother is in the hospital. I will tell you on the way. Rosalie, I am so sorry to leave you with this mess but we will have to go."

"Don't worry about it," Rosalie said. "I just hope everything is okay."

"Me too. I will call you first thing in the morning."

"Wesley, I would like it if you could come with us."

"Of course," was his reply.

I don't know what is going on here," Wesley said to Nellie, "but I will come by tomorrow for the painting."

"Janet needs you so don't worry, it will be right here waiting for you."

Chapter 41

When the three of them were in the car, Marshall said, "Okay, Janet, what is going on?"

"Beth didn't know all of the details, but she had a call from the police. Apparently Derek Gable came home unexpectedly and caught my brother in bed with his wife. He beat him to within an inch of his life. He is in the Somerset Hospital in serious condition."

"Oh, gosh," was all Marshall could say.

"I just knew something like this was going to happen. How many times have I told him to stop cheating on Beth, but you can't talk to him. He just denies it, when everyone in the valley knows what is going on."

They were close to the house when Wesley said, "Let me out and I will follow you in my truck. Are you going to Beth's house or to the hospital?"

"Yeah, you can follow us. We are going to pick Beth up and take her to the hospital. I guess the police want to talk to her after she has a chance to see Carl."

At the hospital, they all went directly to the emergency room area. Beth went directly to the nursing station where a policeman was interviewing one of the nurses on duty. Janet followed close behind Beth while Marshall and Wesley stayed a few paces back. They couldn't hear what was said, but when the policeman turned toward them, Wesley immediately recognized him as Officer Shipley.

"Fancy us meeting twice in such a short period of time, Mr. Donaldson," the policeman said.

A nurse led Beth and Janet back to the emergency room where Carl Larkins lay.

"Don't go far, Mr. Donaldson, I may want to ask you a few questions after I have had a chance to talk to the wife and sister of the patient."

"I will remain right here."

"Well, it may be a long night, so if you and Mr. Snyder would like to wait in the coffee shop, it is okay. If I need you before that, I will have them page you."

"Thank you officer, perhaps we will do that."

An hour and a half, and several cups of coffee later, Marshall and Wesley saw Beth, Janet, and Officer Shipley enter the coffee shop. Shipley sat down at a table close to the entrance and motioned for Wesley to join him.

When Wesley was seated, the officer began, "There is possibly a connection, at least as far as some of the parties involved, between what has just happened and the matter of your intruder. We are still working on it so I just want to caution you to restrict your discussion of the matter concerning the intruder. Okay?"

"That is okay. I understand and will comply."

"Okay, You can rejoin the others."

When Wesley got back to the table where the others were seated, Janet gave him the same brief update she had just given Marshall. "It appears that Carl is going to be okay. He has some cuts and bruises and a couple of broken ribs. No spleen damage. He has a bad bump on his head, but no concussion. Right now they have him very heavily sedated, so he will be out of it for a while. However, Beth and I are going to stay here for the night so would you mind taking Marshall back to the house?"

"Well, that is good news, I guess. As for taking your husband home, after that great supper he prepared, how could I refuse?"

As they drove back toward Hexie, Marshall asked Wesley what the policeman wanted with him. Wesley told him as much as he dared, then he asked Marshall if Janet had given him any more information on what happened.

"Janet and Beth said that he gave them very little information. He interviewed them separately. He did say that Mr. Gable was incarcerated, and that Mrs. Gable had been treated for a minor cut and some bruises. He did not say if they were intentionally inflicted. The ladies are going to spend the night in a motel so I assume they will compare notes."

"He didn't tell them not to do that?" Wesley asked.

"I guess not. He is smart enough to know that you can't put two women together and not have them compare notes."

"Right," was all Wesley said.

"I assume they did interview both Mr. and Mrs. Gable, and it may be pretty cut and dry. The only question will be if Carl wants to press charges."

"Do you think he will?"

"I think he is a fool if he does. I know Janet is very upset with Carl's shenanigans, but she will handle it; it is Bethany that I feel sorry for. She is such a nice young lady. He is my brother-in-law, but how she ever got tangled up with him, sure beats me."

"Officer Shipley sort of swore me to silence concerning another matter, but I have had an encounter with both Carl and Mrs. Gable. I have never met Mr. Gable. I will tell you and Janet of the details as soon as I can."

"Interesting. May I ask you, were they together at the time?"

"No."

"Okay, I won't press you any further, but when it is permissible, we would like to hear about it," Marshall said.

"Well, this I can tell you, my direct encounter with Carl had nothing to do with Mrs. Gable. That was not what Officer Shipley was referring to. I just never mentioned it because I didn't want to upset Janet."

"Believe me, Wesley, there is nothing you can tell Janet about her brother that will surprise her, or upset her more."

"I won't go into the details, but I will say that I can confirm Janet's suspicions that he did, at least on one occasion, mistreat Bethany."

"By mistreat, do you mean he beat her?"

"I did not see him actually lay a hand on her, but I saw her on the steps of their house immediately after he left in his truck in great haste. Her dress was badly torn, one sleeve was out, the side of her face seemed all red and she was crying. I was going to assist her, but she begged me not to come closer. After offering a second time, and her refusing, I respected her wishes and walked on. Later when I reached the Humbert area, her husband was returning. He stopped his truck and picked a fight with me."

"Really. What happened then?"

"I have trained a bit in the martial arts and was able to subdue him quite easily."

"How did it end?" Marshall asked.

"When I let him up, he drove off, a bit embarrassed because I used the 'say uncle' technique that young kids like to use. He also probably held a lot of anger."

"Wow! Remind me to remain your friend."

"I certainly hope that I can count both you and Janet as friends," Wesley replied.

"I am sure you can."

Chapter 42

On Saturday afternoon Wesley drove back down to Nellie's house to get his painting.

Marshall had been standing by the window and saw Wesley's truck pass by. "Wesley just drove by," he said to Janet.

"He is probably going to see Nellie and get the painting. Why don't you call her in a minute. I want to talk to him."

"What do you want to talk to him about?" Marshall asked.

"Actually, Beth wants to talk to him."

"Oh! I would think she would talk to Reverend Pritts."

"I asked her about that, and she said she would just feel more comfortable talking to Wesley. The way she explained it, I guess I can see her point," Janet said.

About a half hour later, Wesley pulled into their driveway. When he rang the doorbell, Marshall greeted him.

"Come on in, Wesley, Janet is making some coffee."

"You drink your coffee black, do you not, Wesley?"

"Good memory, Janet," Wesley said as confirmation.

"Why don't you two come out here to the kitchen," Janet said.

"I love these big old country kitchens," Wesley said. "They are so gemutlich."

"What does that mean?" Janet asked.

"May I tell her?" Marshall asked.

"Be my guest," Wesley said.

"It is German and there is no literal meaning, but it is kinda like sitting by the fireplace with your sweetie on a cold winter evening, wearing comfortable pajamas and drinking a cup of hot chocolate. Is that about right?"

"I think it is probably right on, but I would not have used the 'sweetie' portion," Wesley said.

"So aren't you the smart one," Janet said talking to her husband.

"I learned a few things flying into Hamburg and Frankfurt."

"I just hope you didn't learn it sitting by a fireplace with some Fraulein by your side," Janet said smiling and looking at her husband out of the corner of her eye.

"No way," Marshall said. "I know if you ever caught me, I would be in much worse shape than Carl is."

"We had better terminate this conversation, or Wesley is going to get the wrong impression of us," Janet said.

"I think I can recognize friendly jesting," Wesley said.

"On a more serious note, I asked you to stop by because Beth wants to talk to you," Janet said.

"I see," Wesley said. Then after a long hesitation, he continued, "Do you know what about?"

"I guess I do, but I would rather she tell you herself."

"I will go see her, of course, but it is just that I feel a bit awkward. I don't want to infringe upon Reverend Pritts's counseling territory."

"She told me why she wanted to talk to you. She said she had mentioned it to you the first time she met you."

"Yes, she did, but she never said why. In retrospect, I suppose I was remiss in not seeking her out after I had the run-in with your brother."

Wesley paused, then continued, "Did Marshall tell you about that?"

"Yes, he did. I only wish that you had told me."

"I am sorry about that too."

"Don't worry about it," Janet said.

"Well then, would you mind calling her and asking when it would be convenient for me to stop by?"

"I'll do it now."

Janet picked up the phone and called. Beth apparently picked up immediately and Janet explained that Wesley was at their house. Janet looked at Wesley and asked, "Is now okay?"

"It is fine with me. Please tell her I will be by in ten minutes."

Chapter 43

Beth was waiting by the door when Wesley pulled into the driveway. She opened the door before he had a chance to ring the bell. She was not wearing any makeup and she looked very tired. He could tell that she had been crying.

"Come on in, Mr. Donaldson. You don't know how thankful I am that you agreed to talk to me. Can I get you some coffee or something else to drink?" she asked.

"No thanks, I already had two cups with Janet and Marshall."

"They are such great people. If only Carl were more like his sister, things would be so wonderful," Beth said.

"Yeah, but things aren't always as we would hope. Sometimes we just have to accept things as they are and try to determine what is the best thing to do."

"That is so true. I suppose I have known for a long time that Carl was cheating on me, but until something like this happens, you are always hoping that there is a remote chance you are wrong. You think, maybe tomorrow this person that you love will realize how much they love you and will stop what they are doing that hurts you so much. I love Carl, but I don't know how much more of this I can put up with."

Beth stopped talking and she began to sob. Wesley knew he had to say something, but he knew from his own counseling experience, it was better to let the person speak as much as possible. Bad feelings, or feelings of hurt, are like poison; you must get them out of the system.

"Bethany, I am not too familiar with the circumstance in the situation between you and your husband, but I have encountered similar cases in my role as a priest, so I will be glad to help you as much as I can. Perhaps the best thing I can do at the moment is to be a good listener."

Beth took several paper tissues from a box on the end table by her chair. She wiped her eyes and tried to regain her composure, and then she spoke again. "Mr. Donaldson, I do not believe in divorce, but I do not believe that Carl is going to change. I would love to have children, but I know what Jake Grayson told me he went through with his father. I will not bring a child into this world to go through that. I come from a very religious family, and many of my friends here are conservative and pious. What will they say? I know that is part of our problem: the church has always been part of my life, but it has no meaning for Carl. Because of that, we have very few common friends. I see now that our marriage was a mistake, but what can I do? I just don't know where to go from here. I do not know how to face tomorrow." Again she stopped talking and started to cry.

"Bethany, your family and your friends will understand. They become your strength at a time like this, and also you call on the principles you learned as a child and when you were growing up. Right now is a time for crying. I am a firm believer in the therapy of crying, because when the crying is done, you see what is before you with clearer vision. I do not feel I am the one who should counsel you about divorce, but I do not believe that one stays in a marriage at any cost. I am not cognizant of Reverend Pritts' beliefs concerning divorce, but I do believe that you should talk to him as soon as possible. When things like this happen, you are not the only one who may not know what to say or do; your friends and neighbors will feel the same way. They won't know what to say to you, should they offer condolences or angry words against your husband. So that is where Reverend Pritts can probably help. Since you were raised as a conservative Lutheran, it might be advisable to talk to a minister of that denomination concerning divorce. It may help to relieve feelings of guilt that you are sure to encounter in your mind from time to time. If you don't know any Lutheran ministers, I can give you the name of one who I think would be a good choice. He serves a Lutheran Church out in Friedens.

"That would be helpful," Beth said.

Her eyes were red, but the tears had stopped for the time being. Wesley knew they would return, but like he had told her, that was okay.

"I just knew if anyone could help me see the way to start, it would be you, Mr. Donaldson. I don't know how to thank you."

"Well, you certainly don't owe me any thanks, I am elated that you trust me enough to take me into your confidence and ask for my help. I believe you are a strong person, and I also believe that your faith will see you through this time of trouble. You feel free to call on me at any time."

"I will."

"Remember the old cliché," Wesley said as he opened the door to leave.

"What is that?" Beth asked.

"The sun will rise tomorrow."

"Yes, I think I can face it," was all she said as she waved to him and closed the door.

Chapter 44

On Sunday morning, Beth rose at 6:20 to view a beautiful cloudless day. She took her bath, dressed and drove into Somerset to visit her husband.

Later at 10:33 she walked through the portal of the Old Bethel Church just as the congregation was singing the opening hymn. She walked down the center isle to the sixth pew; she did not take her normal place with the choir. Two pews in front of her she saw Jake Grayson and standing next to him was his mother. She opened her hymnal and started to sing in that beautiful melodic voice.

Reverend Pritts said above the singing, "The Lord truly blesses us," and continued singing.

Chapter 45

On the Monday edition of the Somerset Daily American there appeared a short article under the byline: Police Blotter.

Love triangle lands one man in jail and one in the hospital. Derek Gable of Hexie came home unexpectedly on Friday evening to find his wife and another man from Hexie, Carl Larkins in a compromising situation. A fight ensued with Mr. Larkins receiving the worst of it. He suffered various cuts on the face, bruises on his body and several broken ribs. According to the police report, Mrs. Gable received a minor cut on the chin and several bruises when she intervened to stop the fight and prevent more serious injuries. It is expected that Mr. Larkins will be released from the hospital by mid-week. Mr. Gable is still incarcerated pending any charges that may be filed. Mrs. Gable could not be reached for comment.

On Wednesday morning, Wesley was working on translating one of his training programs into French. It was intended for missionary schools. He had just completed the first segment and was satisfied with the results. Just as he hit the save button to copy it on a CD, he heard the doorbell ring from the porch entrance. He looked at the monitor and was surprised to see Carl Larkins standing there. He could have gone out the door from the lower level, but decided it was better to open it from the upstairs level.

He opened the door to see Carl. His face was badly bruised with a number of stitches below his left eye, but beyond that he seemed quite normal.

"Good morning, Mr. Donaldson. I suppose you are surprised to see me," he said.

"A little bit, but won't you please come in Mr. Larkins," Wesley answered.

"Thanks! Nice place you have here," he continued as he looked around.

"I like it. How are you feeling?"

"Oh, you know, a little bit sore, but I will make it. Derek did a pretty good number on me, but then he had an unfair advantage."

"From what I heard and read, he had some motivation."

Carl winced his mouth slightly and said, "Yeah, I guess so. But I suppose you know that is not why I stopped by."

"I welcome all the people in the area to stop by so I can meet them, but I do reason that your visit is other than just social, Mr. Larkins."

"Yes it is, and could I ask you to call me Carl?"

"Certainly, Carl, and I prefer Wesley."

"Okay, Wesley it is. You have only been here a few months, but already some people think you are a knight in shining armor. At least Beth and my sister think so."

"I am sure you are reading that wrong, Carl, but please continue."

"Maybe a little bit, but don't get me wrong. I don't know much about you, but I do respect you. You beat my butt once, but you didn't gloat about it to anyone else."

"Carl, I did not beat your butt. I subdued you in a conflict between two different defense disciplines. I also had no reason to gloat or tell anyone else at the time. However, Mr. Gable did beat your butt."

"Yeah, but he cheated."

"How is that?" Wesley asked.

"He caught me by surprise."

"I would imagine that almost anyone caught in bed with another man's wife would be taken by surprise," Wesley replied.

"What I mean was, we were monitoring his GPS unit. He wasn't where it was; his truck was, but he staged it and had another driver take his run."

Wesley thought about the intruder who had set off his security system and said, "Well, I guess technology is not always foolproof."

Carl looked down his nose at Wesley concerning his last comment, but decided to let it pass. He continued, "Yeah, whatever, but that 'say uncle bit' was a little childish."

Wesley just smiled, "You mean you never used that Carl?"

"Not since I was maybe twelve."

"It still works though, huh, Carl." This time Wesley said it with an open smile. He hoped he was putting Carl at ease and perhaps could establish some rapport. It would be good to try and understand where Carl was coming from, for although he greatly disapproved of Carl's actions, he held no animosity toward him on a personal level.

"I just wish Derek had used it," Carl said and he also smiled.

"Listen, Carl, can I get you something to drink?"

"Sure, a beer would be nice, but I don't suppose priests keep that in the frige, so a pop will suffice."

"Sprite or Coke?"

"Sprite."

Wesley brought the Sprite, along with a glass containing several ice cubes and sat it on the end table next to Carl. He brought a glass of iced tea for himself.

"Why don't you continue, Carl?"

"Okay. Excuse me if I ramble a bit, but just hear me out. I think you will understand."

"I am going to ask Beth for a divorce and I need your help. I know that you know some of the unsavory aspects of my life. I do not deny them, but I am not sure I am at that point in my life where I will expend a lot of energy in changing. Believe me when I say that I love Bethany. I think that she is a wonderful person, but our marriage was a mistake. I knew she was very conservative and religious when I met her, but I had this grand opinion of myself as being the person that could convert her to my idea of 'the good times.' I was wrong.

"I could tell you more about our life, and how I justified some of it in my own mind, but when I say it out loud, I realize there is no justification. Beth was never a person to nag. She never held bad feelings. For me it would have been so much better if she had.

"You know Beth has a beautiful voice and loves to sing. Music is her one great passion. She wanted to teach music at one of the schools, but I said no. There was no reason for not allowing her to teach, other than the control factor. Ironically, it was a song that helped me make the decision to ask Beth for a divorce. Although heaven knows, she should be telling me in no uncertain terms that she wants a divorce, but Beth will never do that."

"What was the song that you referred to?" Wesley asked.

"Do you listen to any country and western music?" Carl asked.

"Occasionally. I listen to a little bit of everything. If I am driving and I get bored, I will often look for some of that type of music."

"That type of music," Carl said with a bit of a sarcastic inflection. "That type of music is often popular with my type of character. Anyway, when I left the hospital about an hour ago, I stuck an old Waylon Jennings CD in the slot. One of the songs on there is called Amanda. Have you ever heard it?"

"I can't say that I remember it," Wesley said.

Carl continued, "I think he recorded it back in the 70s. In two verses it tells the story about a carousing country boy, a lot like me, but it is the chorus that is my story. It goes like this: 'Amanda, light of my life. Fate should have made you a gentleman's wife.' Just substitute Beth for Amanda."

Wesley thought he saw a tear form on Carl's cheek just as he moved his stare to the window on the lower side of the house.

"Do I understand you correctly. You were just released from the hospital and you stopped to see me before you even went home?"

"That is correct."

"But why?"

"Why you ask? I thought you were a priest. Haven't you ever counseled in cases like this?"

"Yes, I have, but not exactly under these circumstances. I have never had the abuser come to me first. Don't get me wrong, I think it is great that you have, but can you still tell me why.

"Because I want you to go tell her I plan to ask her for a divorce."

"Excuse me."

"Listen, Wesley, if I go there now and ask her, she is not going to go along with it. She won't even hear me out. Then I will get upset and you know what will happen."

"We sure don't want that to happen, but I am still not convinced this is the way to proceed."

"Believe me, Wesley, this is the only way."

"What about your sister Janet?" Wesley asked.

"No good. Janet and I get along best when we are not together. We are not good at giving each other advice."

"You don't think that in this case she might think it was a good idea?"

"With Janet it is hard to tell, but if she didn't approve, she would take her posture as the oldest sibling and lecture me. Wesley, I am asking you a favor. I realize it is a big favor, but I will not waste your time if you don't want to do it."

"Carl, I did not say I wouldn't do it. I want to help you, and I want to help Beth. Just give me a minute to formulate some things in my own mind."

"Like what things?" Carl asked.

"Well, for one thing, what do I say if Beth asks about Mrs. Gable?"

"Tell her you don't know."

"That won't work. She is the other woman in this case, so that is not going to be the correct answer. Let me put it another way. What do you think is going to happen between you and Mrs. Gable?"

"Truthfully, I don't know. I like her, but it may be more passion than love."

"And what about her feelings toward you?"

"Oh, she said she would divorce Derek if I divorced Beth. As for her husband, she would probably have to plead and say she is sorry for him to take her back."

"Do you believe her?"

" I guess I do, but with LeAnn one can never be sure."

"What about her relationship with her husband?" Wesley asked.

"That is a problem for her. She would have to plead with Derek and say she is sorry for him to take her back, and she just isn't going to do that."

"Not even after what she did?"

"The two of us did," Carl interjected.

"Right, what the two of you did."

"No. She may be wrong, but I bet she would never in her life succumb to saying 'uncle.' She was a street kid who grew up in a rough section of Pittsburgh, so saying sorry was a form of weakness and the weak didn't survive. By the same token, Derek has a form of pride that is blinding; he will never take her back without the apology."

"A street kid. You mean she was a poor kid?"

"Yeah, a poor kid, kinda like a street urchin, if you will."

"She told me her father owned a private investigative service in Pittsburgh."

Carl laughed. "I never heard that one before, but she is good at telling stories for her own survival. Her father works as a forklift operator in a warehouse on the south side. Derek was loading freight there once, and LeAnn worked at the coffee shop across the street from where her father worked. That is how they met."

"Is she still back at the house?"

"Of course not. She called me at the hospital. Said she was back in Pittsburgh staying at her sister's house. She said Derek told her to never come back. I guess she is going to try and wait until he is on a trip and sneak back for her things.

"Are you going to press charges against him?"

"For what? Interrupting sleeping with his wife. That would certainly be a no win situation, now wouldn't it?"

"I suppose you are right. Tell me, what am I to tell Beth your plans are?"

"I am planning to tell the school here that I will not be returning. Of course, after all the publicity, I probably wouldn't have a job anyway. Tell her she can stay in the house. I will talk to LeAnn. If she plans to stay in Pittsburgh, maybe I will try to get a teaching and coaching job there."

"Do you think it will work out?" Wesley asked.

"Who knows. I will hope for the best. One thing about it, if it should happen that we do get married and there is cheating, the one who gets caught first will probably be dead."

Wesley didn't acknowledge Carl's last statement, but said, "Okay, Carl, as much as I dislike this, I will go talk to Beth."

"Thanks, Wes, I owe you one."

"When you leave here, where are you going?"

"That depends on you. When are you going to talk to Beth?"

"I will call to see if she is home, and if so, I will go immediately," Wesley said.

"In that case, I will be at Janet and Marshall's house until you call. After that, I will decide and let Janet know. She can tell you and Beth."

"I thought you said your were leery of Janet's response."

"Not with you as the negotiator. Remember the knight in shining armor."

"The only thing ..., well not the only thing, but one thing that bothers me about this, Carl, is that you seem to take it rather lightly."

"Not nearly as light as you might expect there, Father. It is all about saving face."

Wesley did not respond, but he walked with Carl to the door and extended his hand. When Carl grasped it, Wesley said, "Carl, I don't know if I will ever talk with you again, but as a priest I will say, my prayers go with you."

"Can't ask for more than that, now can I," Carl said as he started down the steps toward his car.

Chapter 46

The treatment that Jacob was going through didn't make him extremely sick, but he felt a bit lethargic. Mostly he would come home and sleep for several hours and then read. Occasionally he would watch a bit of television, something on one of the history or discovery channels. He liked the National Geographic specials. He would also call his daughters from time to time to let them know he was fine. Normally he would call from his cell phone so if he had to, he could say he was going here or there. He had planned to call Wesley once, very early on in his treatment. He intended to say he was outside of New Orleans, headed for Houston, when in fact he was outside a small restaurant in the historical district. He deemed that only the last part of that would be a lie; after all, the restaurant was, "Taste of New Orleans." However, it didn't matter, he decided not to make the call.

He seldom did any research or writing during this time and about the only time he went near the computer was on Monday when he would pay his bills for that week. And it was at this time during the second week of his treatment that he found the note he had written to himself several weeks previous when he had returned from Pennsylvania. It was in the bottom drawer of the two-drawer file cabinet where he kept his bills to be paid. All it said was, "DNA," and then he remembered. Apparently Muchi had pushed it off the table and it landed in the bottom drawer. He had forgotten all about it. He hit a button for the Google search engine and typed in blood test labs. He got over two thousand hits and decided to narrow it down by going regional to western Florida. He found several in Pensacola, but finally decided on one from Ft. Walton Beach. He completed the on-screen form and printed a label with both addresses. He went to the refrigerator and retrieved the plastic bag with the samples. He stuck the samples in a brown shipping envelope and laid it aside to take to the post office later in the morning.

While the computer was still on, he decided he would also check his e-mail. He had finally put a block on to eliminate all spam, or at least as much as the software could recognize. He saw the indicator said he had one message. That was more than he had hoped for, but he opened it. It was from Wesley.

The letter began:

Jacob,

I have been calling your cell phone number for almost a week, but with no success, so I thought I would write you an e-mail in hopes that you turn on your computer. Quite a lot has happened here since I spoke with you last. Some not so good, but things seem to be turning out okay. I won't bother you in advance with the details, but if you wish to know more, please return a line, or give me a call.

Wesley

Jacob read the e-mail and thought for a few minutes about what he wanted to say. For a moment he just stared at the large electronic eye in front of him, then his eyes went upward and he saw the framed items that decorated the wall over his computer desk. The first page from the Book of John, printed on an exact replica of the Gutenberg press. A needlepoint of the name, PITTSBURGH with some of the cities most recognizable features included. A family coat of arms and a gold depiction of the hemispheres of the world also hung there. To his right the wall was covered with pictures of the grandchildren, some dating from birth to their late teens. Back of him, he knew without looking, hung one framed picture, a pencil sketch of two young ladies in their teens, the daughters. On the top shelf of his desk was a small silver frame in an oval shape; it held a picture of Monika and him taken many years before.

He looked back to his keyboard and began to type.

Wesley,

I apologize for being so unresponsive and not staying in closer contact. I am now going to tell you something, but you must treat it as though you heard it in a confessional booth, if you Catholics still use that procedure. Also, I do not wish to talk about it when next we meet. I am being treated for cancer, nothing too serious, but it is something that I do not wish to worry the rest of my family about.

That having been said, I most certainly want to hear what has been going on since I was last there. You see, I leave you in charge and the whole place erupts. Ha! Ha!

Jacob

That evening as he was watching Fox News, his phone rang. He looked at the viewing area and saw that it was Wesley.

"Hello, Wesley, glad to see you are at home for once."

"I will ignore that comment, Jacob. In three words or less, tell me how you are."

"I AM FINE," Jacob said with emphasis.

"I am glad to hear that, but knowing you, that may or may not be the truth."

"In this case, it is the truth. At no time have I been feeling real bad, just a bit lethargic and blah. I assume you received my e-mail and are calling to tell me what all has been happening."

"I am calling to tell you that I sent it all to you in an e-mail. I know you don't always check your computer so I am simply calling to tell you, 'You Have Mail'."

"Okay, I will read it and call you back if there is anything I don't understand."

"Before you say goodbye, Jacob, I know I am stepping over the line here, but on that unmentionable matter, you could have told me."

"I know I could have, Wesley, I just wanted to play some of it out first. I hope you understand."

"I suppose I do. Goodbye, Jacob."

"Goodbye, Wesley."

Chapter 47

By the Labor Day weekend, Jacob had finished all the treatments Dr. Anderson had prescribed. She said it was now a wait and see situation, but she seemed fairly confident that the treatment was a success.

On Sunday, Jacob went to the early church service. It was a beautiful morning, a cloudless sky and not as suffocating with heat and humidity as it had been the last two weeks of August. The merchants at the beach would be ecstatic with this fine weekend because they knew it would keep the cash registers churning. He decided he would add his small portion to the money flow by having breakfast on the beach. Hemingway's was one of his favorites, but he thought one overlooking the gulf would be nicer on this day.

He went to the Garden Hilton and decided on their buffet breakfast. Even when he made his own breakfast on Sunday, it was generally quite ample so it would sustain him all day. He would then have a light snack in the evening, watch 60 Minutes, and then read until bedtime.

As he ate his breakfast this morning, his thoughts went back to Hexie. Except for a couple of weeks of strange and hectic activity after his last visit, Wesley told him in the e-mail he received on the previous Saturday that everything was pretty normal. "Serene" was Wesley's word for the current state of affairs. He had been a bit shocked when Wesley told him that he was considering a request to be relieved of his priestly vows. He was as equally surprised when Wesley told him that he and Gladys had gone to dinner twice. Once they went to Confluence and sat on the porch of the restaurant and watched the fishermen. Their waitress was very nice, but not as talkative as Celeste. She did know Celeste, however, and said that she was back at the University of Pittsburgh.

Jacob was about to call Wesley and tell him he planned to come up, but thought he had better talk to Dr. Anderson about it first.

When he called Dr. Anderson on Monday morning, she said she thought it was a great idea; it could even be good therapy. She said he should not try and drive more than three hundred miles a day. At that rate it would take him over three days to get there; he didn't think he would take her advice on that, but he would not tell her.

When he finished talking to Dr. Anderson, he immediately called Wesley. He was a bit disappointed to get Wesley's voice mail, but left a message saying to call him on his cell phone. If he were going to make the trip, he would go to the library and check out a couple of audio books. The last time he was there, he saw they had a copy of War and Peace in their classics section. He had never felt courageous enough to start reading it, but maybe this would be a good time to listen to it.

He had just pulled into the parking lot at the library when his phone rang. He looked at the display and saw that it was Wesley. He pressed the receive button and said, "Sorry I can't take your call now, but if you leave your number and a short message I will be glad to call you back."

"Hello, Jacob," Wesley said.

"Didn't fool you for a second did I?"

"Not for a second. You should have let it ring more than once, but with this new phone Janet's husband got for me it wouldn't make any difference. As soon as you hit the receive button, I get a green light."

"Ah, you techno junkies, you take all the fun out of it. Anyway, I was calling to tell you I might come up that way sometime next week. Need to bring Monika some nice fall flowers."

"Well, that is great news. I have a few things to tell you that I am pretty excited about."

"Don't tell me that you have already been relieved of your vows, and you are getting married," Jacob said with enough levity in his voice that Wesley could tell he was joking.

"Not really. I haven't submitted that request yet, but if I do and anything like that should happen, you will be the first person I tell. One thing is, I am going to be teaching several foreign languages through the Somerset County School's web site. They have a great setup where it is interactive. Also, I wanted to tell you that Bethany is going to be teaching music at Somerset High School, and the large Lutheran Church there is trying to get her to be their choir director. When I talked to her last week, she still hadn't made a decision on that, but she is getting an apartment in Somerset. And according to Janet, she and Carl sold the house and split the profits. Janet said Carl did get a job in Pittsburgh working in the athletic department of Pitt University. The thing with LeAnn Gable did not work out. Apparently by the time he got to Pittsburgh, she was already living with someone else. Her husband filed for a divorce, but it is not final yet. Gladys told me that LeAnn came with a rental truck to haul off everything while Derek was on the road, but he had hired a security guard and posted him in the house. He had packed all her belonging in boxes and stored them in his truck garage. That is all she left with."

"That is great news, and some great gossip, Wesley. We will talk more about it when I get there. I will let you know my itinerary later, but I do know I want to put one day in Richmond at the Virginia State Library. There is an old chancery record that I want them to pull for me. You have to give them five days advance notice, so I couldn't make Richmond before next Monday."

The following Friday evening, Jacob called both daughters to tell them that he was planning to go to Pennsylvania for a few days. Also, that he was planning to stop in Richmond, Virginia, to do a few hours research in the State Library. He received the same lecture from both of them, be careful and don't try to make it to Richmond in one day. He assured them that he would take two days. He would probably stop the first night somewhere close to Charlotte. He still had not told them that he had gone through the cancer treatment. The treatment hadn't been too rough on him and Dr. Anderson was pleased with the results, so why worry them, he reasoned.

The only thing that put a bit of a cloud over this trip was that he would not have to have someone take care of the cat. Muchi had passed away. It had just been a week after he came back from Pennsylvania the last time, and shortly after she had pushed papers off of his desk onto the floor for the last time.

He got up at about 3 a.m. to go to the bathroom, and when he lay back down, he felt her jump onto the bed. She walked up alongside of him and nuzzled at his neck, then she turned and went back down and lay next to his thighs. She was still lying there when he went back to sleep, but sometime during the rest of the morning she had left.

He got up on Sunday morning and as he walked by the door to his study, he saw her in her favorite place, the hickory rocking chair. He knew immediately what was wrong. Her mouth was slightly open and her tongue protruded from one side. She had died in her sleep, but she had come to him earlier to tell him goodbye.

He knelt by the side of the rocker, brushed his hand across her fur several times, and then with tears filling his eyes, he said, "You can go see Monika now."

He left her lying there and went to the garage and got a shovel. Close to the back patio by a rose bush that Monika had planted many years ago, he dug a grave. He took an empty office file box from a shelf in the garage and went back to the room where she lay. He picked her up, with the blanket still under her, and placed her in the box. He wrapped the blanket over her. On the way out of the kitchen to the garage he saw her food and water dish. He set the box on the floor, picked up both dishes, emptied their contents into the garbage disposal and put both dishes in the box with her. He placed the lid on the box and went into the garage. He secured the lid with packaging tape, carried it to the back yard, and placed it in the grave he had dug. He covered the box with the dirt and heaped it slightly, and then he wept unashamedly.

After he ate supper on Friday evening, he busied himself with putting things about the house in order. He had never been able to sleep well before leaving on a trip, and he knew this night would be no different. However, he would keep busy and go to bed an hour later than normal hoping that would help him sleep until at least 3 a.m. when he would have to answer to his bladder. He didn't plan on being gone too long so he saw no reason to call the cleaning lady; nevertheless, he liked for everything to be in order. It was something that Monika had always insisted upon, and over the years it had rubbed off on him. He had washed a load of clothes earlier, and now he would put them in the dryer so they would be finished before he went to bed.

His office was the most disorganized, especially the folding table to the left of his chair that sat in front of his computer terminal. Most of his records and reference material he kept in file cabinets and on shelves that completely filled the large walk-in closet. When he was working on projects, he would pull a lot of the material and put it on the folding table for easy reference. There it would normally stay until he had finished that project, or it got so crowded that he had no place to put additionally material, thus forcing him to re-file some of it. Of course, in the past he had to always leave one corner of the table clear. Again his thoughts went back to the cat. When Muchi came to be with him, she would often jump up on the table and lie down. If she didn't have adequate space, she was not above taking her nose and pushing some of the things on to the floor. She didn't mind walking over top of papers and books; she did it quite often when she would come close to nuzzle for just a moment. But when she was ready to lie down, she wanted a cleared space. She wouldn't lie on the table for long periods, generally opting to jump on to the hickory rocker where her blanket was always kept.

It took him almost an hour to clear the table and stow everything back to its rightful place. It wasn't that there was actually that much lying on the table, but he had a bad habit of picking something up and then starting to read it again. More than once, he would go and pull another record to check something that he had just read.

When he had the table nearly cleared, he came to a couple of magazines that he still hadn't read. There was a National Geographic, a Biblical Archeology Review, and a Smithsonian. He picked them up and placed them on their respective stacks in the closet. Underneath was a letter from a DNA testing Laboratory that he had received more than a week ago. It was still unopened. He picked it up, thought about throwing it away, then decided to file it somewhere. He laid it on top of the file cabinet and opened the top drawer. He removed a file folder marked Donaldson, Wesley, and removed two CDs that he had planned to take to Pennsylvania for Wesley. He placed them in his old leather briefcase along with some pens and pencils, his telephone/address binder, and a legal pad. He placed the folder back in the drawer, and not thinking, picked up the lab report envelope and put it in the Donaldson file.

At 9:15 p.m. he turned on the television to get the weather report for the area he would be traveling through, and to catch the headline news. At 9:25 p.m., he turned the television back off and went to bed.

Chapter 48

Jacob left Pensacola at about six in the morning on Saturday. By three in the afternoon he was at Spartanburg, South Carolina. He had gassed up just south of Greenville, but hadn't gone to the rest room. A mistake, because now just twenty miles up the road he had to go.

He exited and pulled in to a Chevron station, it was the first one on the right off of the exit ramp. He pulled in to park alongside of a red Camaro, and just as he did, a young girl of nine or ten opened her door without looking and stepped right into his path. Jacob was paying close attention and was able to stop without endangering the young girl. Realizing what she had done, the young girl looked at Jacob and made a wide-eyed expression and pushed her shoulders up around her neck and mouthed something that he read on her lips as "I am sorry." Jacob just smiled at her, waited until she had closed the door and pulled in along side of the red car.

Before he left the service plaza, he purchased a bottle of water and a Snickers bar. He was standing by his truck opening the water when the same young girl and her mother approached. The mother was talking, and Jacob assumed she was talking to him because she said, "I wish they would give instruction manuals when you have kid; they just never listen." Jacob couldn't open the door to his truck because the young girl was opening hers to get in. She didn't seem too happy, so Jacob reasoned there must have been a slight mother-daughter disagreement. Thinking quickly, he sought to defuse the situation.

"You're right," Jacob said, and he sensed that the young girl was now giving him the evil eye, but he did not make eye contact with her. He just continued. "I have two daughters, and a long time ago I asked them to make me a promise that they would never leave me, but they didn't listen either. They both met young men, got married and moved away, but there is one good thing," and Jacob left it hang there forcing the mother to say something.

"What is that?" she asked.

"After that, when they do come to visit me, they bring my grandchildren, and that is really nice."

"I guess so," the woman said with a slight laugh.

Jacob then made eye contact with the young girl and he winked. He saw a smile as big as Texas cross her face. He backed out before the mother and daughter did, caught the light just before it turned red, and was back on the entrance ramp for I 85 North.

He had planned to stop some where in this vicinity, so he decided to go a few more miles to Gastonia in North Carolina and call it a day. When he had gone to the rest room back there, he noticed that he was really tired. He had promised his doctor and both daughters that he would take it easy, and so he would. Besides, it was a very hot day, so maybe he would check in to a motel and take a dive in their pool, then read the Pensacola News Journal that he had thrown on the back seat of the truck when he left this morning.

Just before he got to the Kings Mountain exit, he heard a car horn beep. He looked to his left and saw the red Camaro as it started to pass him. The young girl looked up at him with the same big smile, and she waved and winked. The mother pulled back in front of him and took the exit for Kings Mountain. As he passed the exit by, he saw a small hand come out of the passenger side window and wave. Jacob beeped his horn in response.

He just knew that some day, that young girl would relate the events of this day, maybe even today to her grandmother, or perhaps some time later to her own daughter, maybe not until she had grandchildren, but some day. She would remember an old Bald-headed man with a white beard who made her smile. It had certainly made his day.

Eight miles later he was at Gastonia. He pulled off the highway for the day.

At about six o'clock, he was hungry and went across the street to an Italian restaurant. He had never heard of the name so assumed that it was a local ownership. The food was excellent and he ate more of the pasta and rich tomato sauce that he should have; of course he always did. Now he would have to walk some of it off before he went back to the motel. Two blocks from the restaurant, he saw a catholic church and people were entering for the evening Mass. He knew he would not get a chance to go to church tomorrow so he decided to attend the Mass.

He received a copy of the order of service when he entered. When he sat down and opened the bulletin, he saw that it was the fifteenth Sunday after Pentecost. He knew the scripture readings would be the same as what would be read in the Lutheran Church tomorrow so he removed the Missal from the rack on the pew in front of him and turned to the appropriate page. The first reading was from Deuteronomy, the second from Ephesians, and the Gospel from Mark 7:1-8, 14-15, and 21-23. The Gospel writer is talking about a confrontation between Jesus and the Pharisees. According to the writer, Jesus quotes from Isaiah where that prophet tells the people of his day of God's lament when he said: "This people pay me lip service but their heart is far from me. Empty is the reverence they do me because they teach as dogmas mere human precepts."

Jacob had hoped the Priest would use this as the text for his sermon, or homily as the Catholics referred to it. It was the deacon who gave the homily, although Jacob didn't know it at the time, and he used the reading from Ephesians as his text. That reading has to do with Christian warfare against the forces of darkness and evil. Unlike Islamic warfare, or jihad, the Pauline epistle says specifically that the battle is not against human forces.

The service was not that much different from the Lutherans. He would not receive communion, although if the sermon had been based on the Gospel, he might have considered it depending upon what would have been said about dogmas based on mere human concepts. He would mention it to Wesley later and get his reaction.

When Jacob left the sanctuary, he shook the hand of the person who had given the homily and said, "It was a good sermon, Father, but I was hoping you would use the Gospel as the basis for your sermon."

"Well, thank you, but actually I am only the deacon."

"My mistake," Jacob said, "but that doesn't detract from the sermon. Besides, although I attend Lutheran worship services, I do know the amount of time and work that is required to become a deacon in the Catholic Church, so when you say 'only the deacon' it is an understatement."

Then the deacon surprised Jacob and said, "I would love to converse with you for a minute, Can you wait until the parishioners have departed?"

"Of course," Jacob said, "I will wait outside the door."

There were only about thirty or forty people at the Mass, so Jacob's wait was not long. In a few minutes he was joined by the deacon who again extended his hand and introduced himself as Deacon Erickson.

Jacob accepted the man's extended hand and said, "My pleasure, the name is Jacob Grant."

"My pleasure also, Mr. Grant," the deacon said. Then he continued, "We naturally welcome anyone to our service, but if I may ask, what brings a Lutheran here on this beautiful, but hot evening?"

"The answer to your question is travel. I am on my way further north and stopped here for the night. I had dinner at Devinci's Fine Italian Foods, where I was a bit of a glutton, and was trying to walk some of it off when I came to this piece of impressive architecture.

I was interested in your comment when you said you wished I had used the Gospel lesson for the text of the sermon, or homily as we say. Why?"

"Perhaps we shouldn't go there with so little time to explain our mutual beliefs, Deacon, but you understand that there are human dogmas, similar to those mentioned by the old prophet that separate us."

"I do indeed, but it was Luther and his followers who made the break."

"I am not justifying the Lutheran's beliefs or pitting them against those of Catholicism. I am just saying that both, along with all the other denominations, have these human dogmas that both Isaiah and Jesus preached against. Dogmas that indirectly pit one group against another because of their difference in belief, even in trying to reach the same goal."

"I understand what you are saying," the deacon responded, "but I am not sure of your specific point."

"Okay, I did not take communion, not because I believe there is anything in the Bible I would be erring against, but because it would be against the Catholic belief of who is justified to receive the sacraments. Knowing I was not a Catholic, would you have given me the bread and wine?"

"The body and blood; I am not sure. I might have."

"That is good to hear." He had heard that before, but it didn't exactly square with the guidelines as written in the missal. There were two paragraphs; one addressed 'our fellow Christians' and the other addressed 'members of those churches with whom we are not yet fully united,' Jacob wasn't sure under which paragraph he fit, but it didn't seem the time or place to pursue it further, so he continued, "I am aware of the difference of the bread and wine, or body and blood issue as subscribed to by most major denominations. Based on my reading of the Bible, and how I come to understand the teaching of Jesus, I would be comfortable in taking communion in the church of most of the denominations. That doesn't say I would do it without first talking to the person administering the rite. Now I must be going," Jacob continued, "and I hope it does not seem like I called you to task. I truly did get a blessing from the service."

"That is all that is important," Deacon Erickson said. "I didn't recognize any confrontation on your part. As a matter of fact, if you are ever through this way again and want to stop in, please feel welcome. I would enjoy talking with you some more."

"Thanks, Deacon, I would feel welcome in returning. Next time I might talk to you before the service," Jacob said with a smile and started to walk back to the motel.

The mass and his conversation with the deacon had only lasted a little over one hour. He was back at the motel by 8:15 p.m., but that was late enough to go to bed after he turned on the weather channel to get tomorrow's forecast. He would get an early start in the morning and make Richmond by early afternoon.

Chapter 49

The audio book of War and Peace had been checked out of the Pensacola library before he got there on Friday, so he decided on a book by Dean Koontz, "One Door Away From Heaven." He owned a copy of the book and had read it five or six years earlier, but couldn't recall all the details. Koontz was great at developing strange characters and suspenseful situations. Jacob reasoned that is what he might need to help him get through the boring miles of interstate highway.

It helped, but the trip from Gastonia to Petersburg, Virginia, was still a drag. I-85 ended at Petersburg and he got on I-95 to take him into Richmond. He had hoped to make it to a motel before he gassed up again, but the empty light came on just as he got on I-95 so he took the first exit where he saw a BP sign. There was a Days Inn just across the street, but he wanted to get closer to downtown Richmond before he stopped.

After he had gassed up, he got back on the interstate and continued north. Several miles up the road, he saw a billboard advertising the Downtown Radisson Motel. That was where he would spend the night, and he would be within walking distance to the library in the morning.

It was 3:45 p.m. when Jacob checked into the Radisson Motel. At about the same time, a severe storm spawning several tornados was crossing southwestern Pennsylvania. One tornado had touched down in Somerset County causing a great deal of damage. It made the six o'clock evening news in the Virginia capitol city, but Jacob would not know about it until late the next morning, because he almost never turned on the television set when he stayed in motels. It was one of the things he and Monika never agreed on when they traveled. Monika liked to turn on the TV and find some movie, but inevitably she would fall asleep without turning it off. Hours later, Jacob would wake up and have to turn off the TV.

After he had checked into his room, Jacob left to find a restaurant. He wasn't especially hungry, and it was a good thing, because although there were a lot of small restaurants in the downtown area, most were closed on Sunday. Not finding a place to eat, he walked down Broad Street until he came to the library. He walked to the front doors to confirm the hours of operation. It did open at 9 a.m. on weekdays.

Jacob was at the library the next morning about two minutes before the doors were unlocked. He had been here several times before, but it had been four or five years since his last visit. He knew that when he went in to the archives portion of the library, he would have to check his briefcase and any pens he carried, so he left them in the truck. He brought only a legal pad and a mechanical lead pencil. He went through the security checkpoint on the first floor and asked the person behind the desk exactly where the archives section was. He produced the e-mail the library had sent him stating when the requested record he sought would be available. The lady told him second floor, turn right and he would see the sign at the end of the hall.

He entered through the glass door to confront a receptionist behind a desk that blocked further access. There was a turnstile by the side of the desk, but the receptionist asked him what he wanted to see in this section. Jacob handed her the e-mail. She looked at it and typed a few strokes on the keyboard of her computer. "Okay, Mr. Grant, that record has been pulled. If you will enter and go to the first counter, someone will bring the record to you."

Jacob thanked her and went through the turnstile. When he got to the counter, another lady greeted him and explained how things worked. The original was available and he could see it if he so desired, but actual research of the document was done through microfilm records, which in this case, had recently been converted to a compact disc. Jacob knew for certain that he would not be using the original, but the computer and compact disc would probably prove to be a big advance over the old microfilm records.

Jacob told her that he would indeed like to see the original before he left, but would complete his perusal of the record first. She pointed to a table with a computer terminal. "I assume you know how to use a computer," she said.

"I get by," was Jacob's answer.

"It is permissible to print excerpts from this document, but the printers are behind the counter here. If you have a library debit card, the cost for printed pages will automatically be deducted from your balance. If you do not have a card, you can pay by cash or credit card when you are finished," she continued.

"I will pay by cash when I finish," Jacob said.

"Okay, Mr. Grant, you may go to the terminal. I have already inserted the disc."

"Thank you," Jacob said and walked to the computer terminal and sat down.

He clicked on the "open record" icon and watched as the first page appeared.

From the bill filed in the cause Thornton, &c. vs. Taliaferro. &c. Bill filed at Rules holden August, 1790, in High Court of Chancery.

Jacob was familiar with much of this old record, having previously read in this same library an account by William Clayton-Torrence entitled, "Rootes of Rosewall. Mr. Torrence cited may excerpts from the record, but Jacob had found a couple of errors, none of which were problematic. He was more concerned about what was contained in the pages that Mr. Torrence did not cite. Especially any references to Priscilla Rootes Grymes and her brother George Rootes. George was a lawyer and real estate broker who had made a lot of trips in to Pennsylvania, although at that time, the areas in which he did business were considered by many to be part of Virginia.

Anthony Thornton, the husband of Mary Rootes, instituted the lawsuit to recover a legacy left to her by her father, Philip Rootes. Mary was a sister of Priscilla and George. She and Priscilla were next to each other in age. Philip Rootes died in 1756, and Mary's husband brought the suit in 1773. Not much was done on it for about six years, and then a ruling was made in favor of Mr. Thornton, but by this time most of the original executors and trustees were dead, and much of the money and other estate items were unaccounted for. To say the least, it was a mess. In 1806, or fifty years after the death of Philip Rootes, the Court of Appeals of Virginia was still considering the case. To Jacob, the case itself, although very interesting, was not his main interest. He was looking for names.

Jacob scanned several pages and then moved to page 12 because of an oddity in Mr. Torrence's record. He found it very interesting and continued to rapidly peruse pages 13 through 15, because he had not included any of these pages in his account. What he read almost made him shout 'eureka,' but this being a library, he just silently said an emphatic 'yes.' He looked at his watch and saw it was already 10:15. There was no way he was going to get through this entire record.

He scrolled back to the second page, and then went to the counter to speak with the lady who had waited on him. "This record is much more than I am going to get through as there are over one hundred pages. I have to be in Pennsylvania by this evening, so I was wondering if I can just print the entire thing?"

"You may. Just remember the library charges twenty-five cents per printed page," she said.

"No problem," Jacob said, "a bargain at twice the price."

He returned to the computer and hit, "Print document" then sat down facing the counter and waited. Within a few minutes, he saw the lady at the counter motion to him that the print job had ended. He went to the counter to pick up the copies.

"Would you like me to punch those and bind them with an ECCO fastener?" the lady asked.

"Yes, that would be nice," Jacob said.

As he rode down the escalator, he reveled in his find. He was sure that this document would provide the proof to confirm his theory about his old progenitor. The only down side of the whole episode was that the one person he wanted to prove it to was now deceased, and that he was getting to old to write their story. But Wesley was a great writer; perhaps he could enlist his help. He would see. As he walked across the lobby, it suddenly dawned on him that he had not requested to see the original. He almost turned around, but decided against it.

Chapter 50

Jacob walked back to the motel where he had left his truck parked. It was now 10:50 a.m. He opened the door and placed the document on the passenger seat and then retrieved his Virginia map from the door pocket to review his route. From Richmond, he would take I-95 to north of Fredericksburg. There he would get old national route 17 that would connect with I-66, then west to I-81. From there he would go north to Hagerstown and pick up route I-70, which would take him to Somerset. From Breezewood to New Stanton I-70 and the Pennsylvania Turnpike was the same road.

Jacob did not like to listen to his audio books when he was in congested traffic, or when he needed to watch for road signs, so as he got ready to exit the motel parking lot, he ejected the audio disc. He hit the scan button on the radio and immediately got a radio station playing music that he found to be acceptable. He turned down Broad street and toward the I-95 North entrance ramp. At his time of day, traffic was moving smoothly and within minutes he was again on his way.

At 11:00 a.m., the music on the radio stopped and the announcer cut in. "Now for a review of the top stories making the news this morning. At least seven deaths have now been attributed to the terrible storm that moved across southwestern Pennsylvania and Western Maryland late yesterday afternoon." Jacob immediately reached for the radio and turned up the volume. The announcer continued, " According to the weather service, at least two tornados touched down in Somerset County, Pennsylvania, and one in Garrett County, Maryland. Luckily, there were no direct hits on any of the small towns along the paths of the tornados, although the small villages of Scullton, Kingwood, and Ursina, Pennsylvania all reported very close misses. The tornado that touched down in Maryland, may have been a continuation of the one in Pennsylvania. It crossed north of Keysers Ridge and south of Grantsville."

Jacob saw a sign for the next exit, one mile; he decided to take it. The announcer gave a few more comments about the storm and then started on the next headline. Jacob turned down the volume, and as he reached the end of the exit ramp, he turned left into a Shell gas plaza. He immediately hit the button for Wesley's home phone. It rang and Wesley picked it up on the third ring. "Hello," he said.

"Man, I am glad to hear you pick up that phone," Jacob said. Continuing, he said, "I just heard about the storm. Fill me in."

"Well, it was pretty scary, and it could have been an awful lot worse. The weather service had passed severe storm warnings on both radio and television, but I was reading so I didn't know anything about it. At about 3:45 it got so dark that the lights in my study came on. I got up and walked out on the porch, and I heard this terrible noise. I knew immediately it was the proverbial freight train that people always mention when a tornado approaches. The tree branches were whipping around wildly, and I immediately went down the steps and into the basement. The noise got louder and louder, almost deafening, and I could feel the house shudder. I expected at any minute to see the entire structure disappear from above my head, but then in a moment the noise lessened and the house was still. I waited for a few seconds, and then opened the door. It had cut a large swath just a hundred yards north of the house and along the ridge above where Smith Run begins. It did get pretty close to the house because it took the major branch from your old walnut tree. It may now have to be cut."

"That is sad," Jacob said, "but it had a long and productive life. Thank God you are safe. I did hear there were three deaths in Somerset County, and two in Garrett County, Maryland."

"It made a direct hit on a house close to Scullton, and it is believed the couple who lived there were inside. It also hit a house close to Chicken Bone Hollow.

"In Maryland, it flattened two barns owned by Amish farmers. There were two men killed in each barn. Apparently they were getting ready to do their evening milking when the tornado hit."

"Where are you now, Jacob?" Wesley asked.

"I am still in Richmond. I had just started to head north when I heard the news. You know I never turn on the television in the motel. Actually, I guess you might not know that, and if I had left a little later after 11, I would probably still not know. Anyway, I will get back on the road and should get into Somerset later this afternoon.

"Why Somerset? You are going to stay here, aren't you?"

"Well, I hadn't planned on it. I hate to impose."

"Jacob, don't give me that imposing garbage. You are staying here, that is final."

"Okay, okay. I will change my route and get on I-68 instead of taking 70 to the turnpike at Breezewood," Jacob said. "So I should see you later this afternoon."

"Before you sign off, was your endeavor at the library a success?"

"I think, very much so. I copied it all down to read later," Jacob said. "I will tell you more about it when I get there."

Jacob put the phone back in the holder and drove back toward the interstate. As he approached the exits for Fredericksburg, he thought about his plan this morning to visit the Civil War cemetery where his great-great-grandfather, Peter Growall, was buried. He had served in Company C of the 142 Pennsylvania Regiment. He was felled on December 16, 1862, not by an enemy's bullet, but by the effects of typhoid fever. He decided he would not stop today.

As he drove, he also thought about the old walnut tree. It was almost as if it were a human being. He was sure it must be over a hundred years old, and its demise was like marking the end of an era. He was now feeling a bit melancholy; going back was no longer as enjoyable as it once was. The trip, without Monika sitting in the seat next to him, was much, much longer. A lot of old friends and relatives had since passed on. It was a new generation that now inhabited the hills and valleys of Hexie. He knew almost none of them, and had it not been for meeting Wesley and his returning to put flowers on Monika's grave, he might never again return until he was ready to make the final ride. Wesley had taken good care of Monika's grave, and he could converse with Wesley by phone and the internet. Wesley had even suggested he install a video camera with his computer, but he wasn't comfortable with that. He would discuss it with Wesley.

He drove on 1-68 until he came to the Grantsville exit. He drove the one block from the exit to old route 40 that was the main street of the town. Since he was going to check in at Wesley's "motel," he turned left toward Keysers Ridge and Addison as opposed to right toward Salisbury and Meyersdale.

Two blocks up the road there was a barricade across the road that went in where Yoder's country store used to be. "Closed to thru traffic," the sign read. Jacob assumed that was due to the effects of the tornado. He could have taken that road and came out at the little village of Listonburg, although he seldom did. Two miles outside of Grantsville, coming up the hill toward Keysers Ridge, Jacob saw the devastation the tornado had caused yesterday afternoon. A path approximately three hundred yards wide stretched as far as he could see. The trees in the center had been completely smashed to the ground like a giant bulldozer had come through. Trees on the edge of the path had tops broken off and limbs twisted and hanging. Other cars in front of him had slowed to a crawl as people stared at the destruction. There were cars parked all along the road, and people were just staring. Some were taking pictures. Luckily, the tornado had missed the McDonalds that sat atop the ridge. On a Sunday afternoon there most likely were diners therein. A few hundred yards further up the road, where a large metal utility building once stood, there was nothing but a few twisted metal girders.

When Jacob got beyond the path the tornado followed by Keysers Ridge, he didn't see any more effects until he came through Ursina and had turned off of 281 onto the Humbert road. Just before he got to the stone house where Janet and her husband lived, he saw again the destruction up on the slope, crossing almost exactly where Sam and Priscilla's old house once stood, and exactly where Mrs. Colburn's house stood just yesterday morning. Jacob pulled the truck off to the right shoulder of the road, turned off the engine and dropped his head to the steering wheel in disbelief. He sat like that for several minutes before he could again look up on the ridge at the destruction. Wesley had said it was close to the Chickenbone Hollow. Did he not know? Or was it that he didn't want to tell him on the phone. Of course he must know. He was sure that Janet would have called him, and by now it was certainly known in the entire region. It would have been on radio, television and in the newspaper.

Chapter 51

It was 3:20 when Jacob started the engine of the truck and pulled back onto the road. He was in a complete daze.

At the same time, a little over a mile further up the road, the crew of an electric utilities pole setter truck with cable carriage had stowed all their tools and climbed into the cab to depart.

The five-man crew had been on the job since 5:00 this morning replacing a pole and large transformer that had been taken out by the storm. The pole with the transformer sat close to the road on the hill as you left the area once known as Humbert. They had arrived coming through Kingwood where another crew was working on some downed power lines, but there was no place here to turn the large truck around so they would continue down the road and pick up route 281 north of Ursina.

Jacob followed the road that was so familiar to him that he always felt he could walk it with his eyes shut. He had walked it many times. He had driven it many times. From the old stone house, the road was straight for a few hundred yards to the first ninety-degree left turn. From here the road went directly across the valley to the river. At one time, a long ways back, this portion of the road marked the boundary between two brother's properties. When it met the river, it made another ninety-degree turn, this time to the right. Here, one of those brothers of another era had operated a gristmill. It was also here, over one hundred years ago that the covered bridge was built. The road then followed the river for about three-quarters of a mile. At the entrance to Chicken Bone Hollow, there was another turn of greater than ninety-degrees and the road went up along the side of the hill. This was his corner as his grand kids often called it "his corner" because of a childhood bicycle crash.

Rose Hill. Levi Rose once lived in a little stone house at the top. It was said that he made very good shine. Roses, Ruggs and Trimpeys lived up Chicken Bone Hollow.

As Jacob rounded the bend, he saw a mound of dirt was partially blocking the right side of the road. The stumps of several fallen trees, apparently brought down by the tornado, hung precariously above the pile of dirt. A road crew had apparently cut up the fallen trees, and now a front loader would have to come and remove the dirt. There was another blind corner at the top of this, the Rose Hill, and Jacob had to pull to the left to get around the pile of dirt. He leaned heavily on his horn.

The driver of the electric utility truck heard the horn blast just as he rounded the blind curve at the top of the hill. He hit the brakes and swerved the truck hard to the right taking out the first guardrail in the process, but it was too late. The driver's side bumper and fender of the much larger truck caught the driver's side fender of the pickup. The larger truck continued to take out guardrails as it traveled down the hill. The initial impact spun the pickup truck sideways to where it was perpendicular with the larger truck and then it was pointed back down the hill. The driver of the large truck finally was able to steer his vehicle away from the guardrails. In the process of getting back to the center of the road, the cable carriage, still carrying the spool and over half of its contents, caught the back end of the pickup, pushing the front into the pile of dirt brought down by the fallen trees, and flipped the pickup truck end over end. The driver of the larger truck, apparently believing he could not make the right turn at the bottom of the hill without smashing into the log house that sat at the bottom, now turned the truck hard left and onto the Chicken Bone Hollow road. The pickup truck flipped endwise once and then rolled sideways coming to rest with all four wheels on the roadbed. The cab was flattened almost to the height of the bed. The driver's door had been knocked open and was twisted and nearly off it hinges. The airbag had deployed. The driver's seat belt had held, but it had not saved the driver. Jacob's neck was broken.

The crew of the utility truck alighted from the cab through the left side doors and rushed toward the pickup. The smell of gas was heavy in the air and gas was pouring from the tank. Knowing that it could explode at any minute, there was no time to take precautions concerning the welfare of the driver. One man reached in and unbuckled the driver's seatbelt while two others grabbed him under the arms and dragged him free of the cab. Each man took one of Jacob's arms and draped it around their neck, then circled his back with their other arm. With the toes of his shoes dragging, they carried him away. Another member of the crew had approached them carrying a fire extinguisher, but they motioned him back. They had reached a point just beyond their own vehicle when the gas tank on Jacob's truck exploded with a loud boom and was instantly a roaring inferno.

Wesley sat on the lower porch of his house, waiting for Jacob to arrive, or at least to call. By five-thirty he was a bit concerned and decided to call Jacob's cell phone number. He reached for the phone that he kept in a holder on the swing just as it began to ring. He assumed it was Jacob calling him. He picked it up and said, a bit elated, "Hello."

It was Gladys' voice he heard on the other end. She was crying and Wesley could barely understand her when she asked, "Have you heard?"

"Have I heard what, Gladys?"

There was a long silence as Gladys tried to regain her composure.

"Please, Gladys, tell me what is the matter?"

"Jake just called me. Jacob was just killed"

"What?" was all Wesley could say.

Then from a long ways off he thought he heard himself say, "How?"

Gladys did not answer, and then Wesley repeated, "How?"

Gladys said in a low voice between sobs, "Jake said there was a bad wreck... on the Rose Hill... head on with a large truck. A power company truck he thinks. It is going to be on the six o'clock news." There was a long pause and then Gladys continued, "Oh, Wesley, say a prayer for him. Remember me in it for him. I gotta hang up."

"Yes, a prayer," he said as he heard Gladys hang up the phone. But a prayer did not emanate from Wesley's lips. He sat in stunned disbelief, still holding the phone in his hand. All he could manage was: No, no, no. Some questions not answered, so much not said. The phone dropped from his hand onto the porch floor. He lowered his head into the curled fingers of hands and sobbed uncontrollably.

PART III

The Funeral

Chapter 52

esley was suddenly pulled out of his remembrances by the sound of vehicle traffic approaching. It was more than one vehicle, and they were not moving as fast as most traffic did on this road. He looked at his watch and knew it was the funeral procession. As he stood and turned to face the road, he saw the Gray hearse that bore the body, followed by a string of cars. Their lights were on and a small flag fluttered from the front windows on the driver's side. His mother had always been a bit superstitious and said you should never count the number of cars in a funeral procession. Wesley never asked why, and never gave it much consideration, but he dropped his head so he would not be tempted to count. It was an appropriate time for a silent prayer.

He didn't know Jacob's point of view concerning intercession, but Wesley was sure that this once he would understand. In his own mind, Wesley phrased this prayer to their Lord. *"Dear Heavenly Father, you have seen fit to call your servant Jacob from our midst. We let go with reluctance but know it is thy will. On his behalf, we thank you for calling him home on his hill, in these hills and valleys he always called home. May his spirit now reside in peace. In the name of the Father, and the Son, and the Holy Spirit, Amen.*

After he heard the last car pass and the sound fade away as they descended the hill, he left his bench and walked back toward his car.

When he got to where he had parked his car earlier, he was surprised that he did not see any of the procession on the road that went to the church from the foot of the hill. Then it became completely clear to him and he wondered why he was even surprised; they were taking him one last time past the old home place.

He remembered one of Jacob's stories and in just a split second, as if watching a movie in extremely fast motion he saw the whole thing, a young boy of fourteen helping a young girl who was only a year older. They hauled a bucket of water from the run and were about to carry it up the hill to the road where the girl's mother had stopped the horse so it could rest. It was not a conscious thought, but it might have continued had it not been that he saw the funeral procession as it rounded a right angle turn in the road about a quarter of a mile from the church. It was time for him to also leave.

He decided he would go the same way the cortege had gone. He knew the casket would not be opened in the church, but it would be moved in and placed before the chancel after all the people were seated. He wanted to time his arrival after all this had taken place and to be as unobtrusive as possible. Jacob had told him a fair amount about his daughters and his grandchildren, but he had never met them and so he felt it better to remain out of the picture at this time of their mourning.

He pulled the car onto the road and started to descend the hill. His thoughts went back to the previous day when he went to the funeral home early in the morning.

True to form of not wanting to cut flowers, Jacob must have, at some previous time, made it known to his family that there should be no baskets of flowers or wreaths. The obituary column in the newspaper had said that those desiring to offer a remembrance should make a donation to their favorite charity, or his, which had to do with underprivileged children. Wesley chose that one, and a particular one in Youngstown, Ohio, because he had worked with many of those children and knew their needs. He had also made a substantial donation to the same charity in his mother's name.

He had talked to the funeral director and asked if he could pay his respects before the first official viewing. When he had explained his reason, the funeral director reluctantly agreed.

The first viewing had been scheduled for 2:00 p.m. on Monday afternoon. Wesley was there at 1:00 p.m. and Mr. Braden, the funeral director, had let him in. There were no flower baskets, but Jacob thought it so nice that pots of live flowers had been strategically placed. He wondered if the family had perhaps requested that.

Wesley had approached the open coffin, made the sign of the cross and said a silent prayer. Then he looked at the still face of his departed new friend. He was certainly a friend, but he was much more. The face looked very natural. It almost had a smile, but a smile would have been wrong. Jacob was often jovial, and he could laugh freely, but his normal face did not show a smile. It was more one of contemplation, as if he were listening and about to give a slightly "tongue-in-cheek" answer. That is what the mortician had captured; he had done an excellent job.

The body was dressed in a suit, and for Wesley that was different. He had never seen Jacob in a suit. Jacob had told him that he had retired from the Navy and the hat of a Master Chief Petty Officer rested against his left thigh. The left hand lay across the hat with the fingers curled around the edge of the white cover. The right arm had been bent at the elbow and the forearm lay across his chest. Stuck into his curled fingers were perhaps the only cut flowers that would be present, six yellow roses, and a small card that read: "For you, Monika."

Wesley bit his lip, then held them firmly between the thumb and index finger of his left hand, but some tears that he could not squelch rolled down his cheek. He stood for what seemed a long time, and when he had again gained his composure, he said another silent prayer, gave the sign of the cross, turned and walked toward the front door. The guest book had already been placed on the small table at the entrance to the chapel area. He picked up the pen to sign the book, thought a minute, laid the pen down and left the book unsigned.

When Wesley rounded the same curve in the road where he had spotted the funeral cortege a few minutes earlier, he saw that the people had already entered the church, and the coffin was being wheeled up the handicapped ramp and into the church.

Old Bethel Church. A beautiful church, but not much like the little old wooden structure the author knew as a youth.

He pulled into the parking lot and took one of the few remaining slots. Jacob hadn't lived here for many years, but he had a lot of cousins in these hills, and a lot of friends. He never forgot them in all his years of absence and would see as many as he could when he made a sojourn back home. Today, they had not forgotten him.

Wesley entered the foyer of the church and then entered the main sanctuary via the first door that led to the left isle. He sat in the back pew. He had never met Jacob's daughters or grandchildren, but he guessed they were the ones on the front pew closest to the center isle. The bier with the coffin was positioned in front of the altar. It was covered with the flag of the United States.

Reverend Pritts had taken his place behind the pulpit, and except for him, no one else was aware of Wesley's entrance.

Reverend Pritts began. "Let us pray." When the prayer was ended, he continued.

"Sometime ago, our departed brother wrote a letter to both of his daughters in which he described what his funeral service should be. The letters to both daughters were identical. As soon as they received notice of his tragic passing, they opened the letters he had given them and sent me a copy immediately. He requested four scripture readings, one to be read by each of his four grandchildren. He listed what they should be. He wanted three songs to be sung, one by the congregation before the first and second reading, and another before the third and fourth reading. He named those songs. After the second song, the sermon would follow. After the sermon was ended, he requested the person of my choice sing a solo and that person could pick the song. He also requested the final prayer be said by a young member of the church, male or female. You may be interested to know that he left me a short note. I will read it at this time: 'Reverend Daniel,' he always called me Reverend and then my first name; I guess he was showing respect but didn't want it to go to my head, but let me continue, 'I know you will render a fine sermon, but I ask, please do not over praise me and embarrass me before my God, and don't keep the congregation too long. Remember, it is a funeral and not a revival.'"

Again there was slight laughter, and Wesley noticed that even his daughters and grandchildren smiled.

When Reverend Pritts ended his sermon, he said, "I have asked a young lady that you all know very well to render the solo that Jacob had requested. Although Bethany and Jacob never met each other, they knew of each other through their mutual friend, Wesley Donaldson. When Bethany is finished, Jake Grayson will give the closing prayer."

When Jake Grayson finished with the final prayer, Reverend Pritts announced the order of departure from the church. The pallbearers would await the bier at the front door. The funeral home personnel would move the bier from the altar area to the front door. The immediate family would follow the coffin, and the rest of the congregation would file in behind them from the front pews to the back pews and follow to the place of interment.

As the pallbearers rose, Wesley silently left his seat and walked to a place in the graveyard, about twenty paces from the tent that covered the open grave. On the opposite side of the tent was a ceremonial burial squad from the United States Navy in immaculate dress blue uniforms. They had arrived after everyone, including Wesley, had gone into the church. The person in charge, Wesley saw, was a Master Chief, and there were five other enlisted people. Four had rifles and stood now at parade rest. The fifth person, a young woman, stood a bit apart from the others and toward the head of the grave. She held a bugle in her right hand and under her arm. He was so glad to see that his cousin had come through. He didn't know how, but he had.

When the bier was outside the church and down the ramp, Wesley watched as the pallbearers took their place on each side of the bier and lifted the coffin away. As they started to walk toward the grave, the person in charge of the military detail called a quiet, 'attention'. The four riflemen snapped smartly to attention and shouldered their rifles. The bugler also came to attention but held the bugle in the same position.

As the people followed the coffin and moved toward the graveside, Wesley saw someone, who he assumed was a granddaughter and an older lady, probably her mother, look in his direction. A few people whom he knew, and who also knew him, made very slight nods of their head in recognition. He responded in kind. He also noticed that a small stand stood at the head of the grave and it contained a vase of perhaps a dozen red carnations. Other than the roses now sealed inside the coffin, these were the only flowers.

When everybody was close in toward the grave, Reverend Pritts said, "Also, per our departed brother's request, I will read from Psalms 118, verse 24: 'This is the day which our Lord hath made; we will rejoice and be glad in it.'" He then said a prayer committing the body to the earth from whence it came. From the birth of his great- grandfather, who was buried not more than two hundred feet away; they spanned one hundred and sixty years.

When Reverend Pritts finished his prayer, the man in charge of the burial party gave the command, and the riflemen fired three rounds in quick succession. When the sound of the last volley had faded away, the young woman raised her bugle and sounded taps. It is a beautiful, but very sad tune arising out of that most dreadful war we know as the insurrection, or Civil War. Wesley knew that if he shed a tear, he was certainly not alone.

There was a brief silence when the bugler sounded the last note, almost as if to say, " The spirit of the deceased has now departed," but Wesley knew, as most likely did his family, that the spirit of Jacob would never leave these hills until the day the Lord called everyone forth.

The bugler placed her instrument on the end of a staff placed in the ground for just that purpose, and then she and the Master Chief in Charge came forward, removed the flag from the coffin and ceremoniously folded it. It was folded in half across the length, and then again in half. After that the corner was folded in a diagonal and that procedure repeated until the end. The last corner was tucked inside so that it would not unfold and the Master Chief then presented it to the family. The oldest grandson rose to accept it. The Master Chief saluted, did an about face, marched back to the rifle party and the bugler, and they marched away.

Then Reverend Pritts announced, "The family of our deceased brother has asked that you join them in a time of remembrance at the fellowship hall where the ladies of the church have provided some food for our earthly bodies."

The family that was seated, rose, and a lady who Wesley assumed was Jacob's oldest daughter, took a flower from the vase and laid it on the lid of the coffin. A gentleman, probably her husband, did likewise, followed by their children and then the second daughter and family. Then Wesley saw Jacob's one sister whom he had met, two other ladies and two gentleman followed suit and place the last of the flowers on the coffin. Thirteen flowers in all. Wesley felt a bit of lightheartedness and wondered if Jacob had planned it as thirteen. Probably not, because it was something he couldn't control, but then again…

Wesley did not follow the crowd to the fellowship hall, but stood and watched as the coffin was lowered into the ground.

PART IV

A Time of Reckoning

Chapter 53

The congregation filed into the fellowship hall where some of the ladies of the church were busy putting the final touches on a long buffet table filled with food that different members had prepared. Four rows of banquet tables were set up and covered with white tablecloths. The smell of the food and the fresh brewing coffee permeated the large fellowship hall. Reverend Pritts seemed to keep eyeing the door as if waiting for someone else to enter, but when it looked like everybody was inside, he asked for attention and said, "Let us bow our heads and say grace."

When Reverend Pritts finished, Helen King spoke up and said, "You can form two lines, one on each side of the table. You will find coffee, iced tea, and pop on the table over by the wall. And in case there is anyone here who likes dessert, it is also on a table next to the drinks." Everyone laughed at the last comment.

Sylvie, Jacob's oldest daughter, whispered to her aunt Maxine who was standing beside her, "Dad would have approved of that because he always thought there should be a bit of levity at such occasions. My mother would also have liked it, because the dessert table was the first place she tried to locate. She would go look at all the great desserts before she went through the main line, that way she knew how little other food to take so she would still have room for dessert.

Jacob's youngest daughter, Cheryl, was behind her sister and her aunt talking to her great-aunt Jean. "Who was the gentleman standing off to the side at the gravesite?" Cheryl asked.

"Oh! You haven't met him? That was Wesley Donaldson. he and your dad had become very good friends in the short time they knew each other. Your Dad was teaching him all the history about this area," Jean said.

"No, we haven't met him, but we certainly want to. Do you think he will be coming down to eat?" Cheryl asked.

"Maybe, but possibly not. He still feels a bit like a stranger here I guess, but just about everybody likes him so I don't know why."

Cheryl looked around and saw her son David, got his attention and motioned for him to come over. When he got there she said, "David, go up to the graveyard and see if the gentleman we saw standing off by himself is still there. If so, tell him we would like very much for him to join us."

David left to do his mother's bidding, and Cheryl went back to talking to her great-aunt Jean. "Well, my dad wasn't a great socializer, but he loved to tell his stories of people and places to anyone who would listen. I just hope he didn't bore the poor man too much."

"I am sure he didn't. I think Wesley encouraged him to tell him everything he knew of the area, and your dad knew a lot."

"Oh, that he did. I have read some of his articles. I think my daughter Eliana has read more of them than I have. He would often send them to her to proof read, always telling her to be honest. Nevertheless, she was always a bit hesitant to correct him on anything, unless it was a major mistake. So who is this Wesley Donaldson?" Cheryl asked.

Jean started to explain as they inched closer to the beginning of the food line.

Meanwhile, Sylvie and Maxine, who were almost through the food line, were having almost the exact same conversation. They set their plates down at one of the first tables and were going back to the beverage table when Sylvie spotted her daughter, Sarah, talking to some other kids about the same age as her. They didn't seem to be in any great hurry to get in the food line so Sylvie went over to her. "Sarah, there was a man standing by himself close to the grave site."

Before her mother could finish, Sarah said, "Yeah, I saw him. Why didn't he join us?"

"I don't know, Sarah, but listen to me."

"Okay."

"I want you to run up to the graveyard and if he is still there, ask him to come down and join us. Have you got that?"

"Of course. What is so hard about getting that?" Sarah said a bit too sarcastically, but under the circumstances her mother let it slide.

"Okay, just go." Sylvie said.

Old Bethel Church Cemetery. Many Hexie families stories end here, still untold. Mary and Bolish lived nearby, but their stories did not end here.

The workers from the funeral home were just finishing taking the tent down and storing it on a truck when Wesley saw a tall young man approach from the direction of the fellowship hall. It was the same young man who had accepted the flag at the gravesite. When David was about three steps away from Wesley, he extended his right hand and said, "Hello, I am David O'Reilly. That was my grandfather."

Wesley took the extended hand and replied, "So nice to meet you David. My name is Wesley Donaldson. Your grandfather was a remarkable man," he continued.

"I thought so too," David said. "I will miss him a lot."

Wesley could see that the young man was about to cry, but he held back, and continued. "Did you know my grandfather well?"

405

"I only met him about six months ago, but if I think about your question and give it my best answer, I would have to say, I think I got to know him as well as anyone could in such a short period of time. Through him, I even know a fair amount about you David. I know your parents are Cheryl and Patrick. I know you have a sister whose name is Eliana, and attends the Naval Academy, and I know you are studying law at the University of Florida. Am I right?"

"Yes, on all accounts, but before we pursue this any further, I came with orders. My mother said you are to come join us."

"I really don't think I should, David. Please extend my gratitude to your mother and all the family, but this is a time for family and friends. Not outsiders."

"Mr. Donaldson, I am in my fourth year of law school, but I could have made a convincing case against that reasoning when I was in Law 101."

Wesley did not respond immediately and both men watched as the truck bearing the tent departed and the three men who would close up the grave prepared to do their job. One man went to get a tractor that had a front-end loader attached. It had been parked by the edge of the graveyard. The other two men stood by with shovels.

David then looked down over the hill toward the fellowship building and saw the curly haired head of his cousin Sarah come up over the bank.

As she got closer, she saw David, stopped and said, "David! What are you doing up here?"

"Probably the same thing you are coming up for, to ask Mr. Donaldson to come join us," David answered.

"And?"

"And, what?"

"And is he coming?"

David didn't answer, but instead made an introduction. "Mr. Donaldson, I would like you to meet my cousin, sweet and lovely, but at times a bit obnoxious, Sarah Kelly.

Sarah immediately extended her hand and said, "A pleasure to meet you, Mr. Donaldson."

To which Wesley replied, "I am certain the pleasure is going to be mine."

"And contrary to what my cousin David said, I am always sweet and lovely," and she raised her eyebrows.

"But you did have a courtesy lapse there, Sarah. Mr. Donaldson is your senior so you should have let him speak first," David jokingly chided her.

"David, go get something to eat," Sarah said in her best commanding voice. "And you didn't answer my question," she continued.

"What question was that?"

"Is Mr. Donaldson coming down?"

"He said it was for family and friends, but since you are here, you may ask him yourself."

"Mr. Donaldson, I beg your forgiveness, but I leave you in the hands of my unmerciful assistant. Please reconsider my request." David turned and walked back toward the fellowship hall.

"What was David's request?" Sarah asked.

"He asked if I would come and have some food and join you," Wesley said.

"Oh! That is what he just said. And, are you coming?"

"I don't think so," Wesley replied.

"Why?"

"Well, like I told your cousin David, these things are more for family and friends. I am a bit of an outsider," Wesley said in a way of extending his reason.

"Did you know my Pappap?"

"Yes, I did."

"Did you like him?"

"As I told your cousin David, he was a remarkable man. I liked him very much.

"So he was a friend, am I correct?"

"Yes, he was a friend, you are correct."

"And you just said, these things are for family and friends, correct?"

"Correct again," Wesley answered rather meekly.

"Then I don't understand," Sarah said.

Wesley was about to attempt another answer, when Sarah took his hand. She had been watching as the dirt was spilled into the open grave and it was now full. The tractor operator had completed his portion of filling the grave, and the three men were using shovels to smooth and heap the ground on the top. The dirt that was left over would be loaded onto the bucket of the front loader and hauled away.

"Can we go closer to the grave?" Sarah asked.

Wesley said nothing, but followed, hand in hand where the young lady led him.

When they were at the side of the grave, Sarah stopped and picked up a clump of dirt that lay close by. She removed her hand from Wesley's and with both hands, she crumbled the dirt onto the raised mound. "Goodbye, Pappap," she said. Then with tears in her eyes, she turned and hugged the man she had just met.

It was a bit more than Wesley could stand. Taking Sarah's lead, he too bent down and picked up a clump of wet earth, but before he crumpled it, he made the sign of the cross and said, "Goodbye ---- Friend," and let the dirt fall between his fingers.

Then Sarah said, "Come on, Mr. Donaldson. Let's go get something to eat."

"Okay," Wesley said as he grasped the hand of this young girl and she led the way.

As they walked toward the fellowship hall, Wesley wanted to break the silence so he asked, "What do you plan to study when you grow up and go to college?"

Without hesitation, Sarah said, "The male species."

"I think you are too young for that," Wesley said with a laugh. But he was glad to see her sorrow had subsided and she was again, the sweet and lovely child.

"But you said college, and by then I wouldn't be too young. I just want to find out why they are so weird, but maybe I will study nursing, or I will write stories," Sarah then said.

Wesley had to laugh inside about having misconstrued her reason for studying the male species, but he let it pass. "Nursing is a great profession, but I was thinking you should follow your cousin's lead and go into law. Give him some competition and keep him on his toes. On the other hand, if you are anything like your grandfather, Pappap as you call him, writing stories might not be a bad idea."

When David went back into the fellowship hall he saw his mother, sister, aunt Sylvie, and a great-aunt at one table. When he got close to the table, his mother Cheryl asked, "So is he coming?"

"Oh, I am sure he will," David said with a smile.

"And what is that supposed to mean?" his mother asked.

"I mean, I left him with Sarah. You should have sent her in the first place."

"Who sent Sarah?" Cheryl asked.

"I did," Sylvie said. "I didn't know you had already sent David."

"Well, David is right, yours was the better choice. But have you no mercy. We don't even know the man yet," Cheryl said, and they all laughed.

"We may not know much about him, but apparently Pappap told him a bit about us. I think you will like him," David said.

"They have some great food here, David," his sister Eliana said.

"Better than the Academy's mess hall?" David asked.

"Yes, and I am sure it is better than that slop you get at Florida State," Eliana said, intentionally naming the wrong school.

David ignored her and went to the buffet tables.

He was about at the end of the line when the door to the outside opened and Sarah and Wesley entered.

Sylvie and Cheryl just looked at each other and shook their heads.

"Are you going to take me over and introduce me to your family?" Wesley asked.

"Yeah, but let's get something to eat first," Sarah answered.

Wesley saw that everyone at her table was watching, so he just raised his hand in the open, palms up position, as if to say, "I am following her lead."

When they had approached the end of the line, Sarah said, "We will set our plates down and then I will introduce you. Okay?"

"That works for me," Wesley said.

As discussed, they set their plates down and then Sarah, commanding the floor, exclaimed "Okay, everyone, this is Mr. Wesley Donaldson!"

Then taking full command of the situation as if she were the most authoritative person there, she continued, "When I am finished, you may shake his hand."

Wesley again smiled slightly and raised his eyebrows slightly.

"Mr. Donaldson and Pappap were friends. Mr. Donaldson this is my cousin Eliana; next to her is my mother, her name is Sylvie; my great-aunt Maxine; my father, his name is Kevin; and my cousin David whom you already met. Over there is my aunt Cheryl aaand," she paused not knowing for sure the name or relationship.

"I know her," Wesley said. "I think she would be your great-great-aunt Jean."

"Oh, yes, I am sorry great-great-aunt Jean. I forgot your name."

"That is quite alright," Jean said with a smile.

"Continuing, that is my uncle Patrick, he is married to my aunt Cheryl. So did I miss anyone?" Sarah said, intentionally looking away from her brother Nathan.

"Me, you missed me," Nathan said, but knowing his sister and not to be out done, he stood and was the first to extended his hand to Wesley. "Hello, Mr. Donaldson, my name is Nathan. I am my parent's only normal child," he said with a bit of glee.

Wesley shook the young boy's hand and said, "Really."

"From what you have just seen and heard, you are probably sorry you ever made an acquaintance with our father," Cheryl said.

"Quite the contrary, the last ten minutes have been stupendous - pleasurable and memorable beyond my wildest expectations. I just don't know what to say, but then why am I surprised, because within ten minutes after meeting Jacob for the first time, he had me laughing, confused, and spellbound among other things, so what else would I expect of his children and grandchildren. Of course, I am being unfair to his wife, your mother and grandmother," Wesley said. "I don't know how much influence she had on you all."

"We called grandma, Oma," Nathan said.

"How nice and proper. I know that German usage," Wesley said.

"You really missed something in not meeting her," Patrick said. "She didn't take any guff."

"Jacob was a bit of a rolling stone. Monika was the force that kept him from rolling too far or too fast," Kevin added.

"I understand that you are a Priest," Cheryl said.

"Yes, I am. But I have been on an extended sabbatical for about a year."

"What is a sabbatical?" Nathan asked.

"It is like a long vacation," Wesley answered.

"You mean like when school is out?" Nathan asked.

"That is a very good analogy, Nathan," Wesley said.

"What is an analogy?" Nathan asked again.

"It is a comparison," Sylvie said curtly to her son, "Now be quiet."

"Never dampen the spirit of the inquisitive child, Aunt Sylvie," Eliana said.

"Sorry, I forgot you are studying to be a psychologist. That would come under 'Child Psychology 101,' I guess," Sylvie said.

"Actually, 'Human Development,'" Eliana said, "but I didn't mean to be rude, Aunt Sylvie."

" Don't fret Eliana, no offense taken. I have known you since you were less than one hour old, and your Pappap, now lying up there, and I watched you do pushups under the heat lamp in the nursery. We both knew then you weren't going to be just some ordinary kid," Sylvie said.

"I don't want to overrule my older sister, and super-child, but I think we may be boring Mr. Donaldson," Cheryl said.

"No, please, quite the contrary. As I just said, you are such an interesting family, and I have been thinking, how tragic it would have been for me, if David and his able assistant, Sarah, had not convinced me to come down and meet you all. But I know there are a lot of people here who want to offer condolences and other words of comfort fitting the occasion, and I would like to step aside so they can do just that. But I would really like the opportunity to talk with you all some more. I have many questions I would like to ask about Jacob and your family. I know that you all live some distance from here, but I was hoping that if you were going to be in town for tonight, maybe we could all get together at my house later on. Jacob loved the place, even made me feel guilty for having it instead of him," Wesley said.

"Yep, that sounds like our dad," Sylvie said. "I think that is a great idea. We may be in town until Saturday, and I think Cheryl and Pat will be here until, when?"

"Thursday," Cheryl said. "We will take Eliana back to the Academy and David back to Gainesville. And, yes, we would love to stop by. Have some questions we would like to ask you too about our father.

"It may be an hour or more," Sylvie said. "I remember my father at funerals. He liked to put people at ease, and so he would always start to say something about the deceased. First he would almost make you cry, and then he would make you laugh. When he had everyone in good spirits, he would ask others to give some of their light hearted remembrances of the deceased. It was good tonic, so I think we will follow suit.

"Are you going to start it?" Wesley asked.

"Oh, not me. Being the oldest member of the family, I am going to volunteer my dear brother-in-law, Patrick O'Reilly. Have you ever heard of a half Irishman/Italian who couldn't find a word to say?" Sylvie said.

"Moi?" Patrick retorted.

Before Patrick could start, Cheryl cut in, "Patrick can go second. Sylvie, I think you should relate the story of the plastic flowers that our cousin Kimberly mentioned one time."

"Oh, yeah!" Sylvie said with glee. "This is really great. Our mother once asked our father if she died first, would he re-marry? Before I go further, I suppose I should lay some groundwork. As you saw today, there were no large baskets of cut flowers, which was per our father's request. He did not believe in cutting flowers. His reason being that you could enjoy them as they grew and that the birds and bees depended on them.

"Back to the story. He said he wasn't sure, but he didn't think he would. Then he said, 'Of course I don't think that should affect your decision to re-marry. All I would ask is that you not do it before the flowers on my grave wilt' (of which there were none). Our cousin who was visiting at the time said, 'Since he doesn't want cut flowers, what if the people place plastic flowers on the grave?' Since our mother preceded him in death, I guess we will never know.

"Okay, Patrick, it is all yours."

"Okay, Mr. Donaldson, we will let you finish eating and I will get this thing rolling, especially since my sister-in-law has so graciously set the stage.

"Please call me Wesley."

"Okay, 'Wes', you got it."

In a fairly booming tone, Patrick started. "If I might have your attention. I know some of you are still eating and please go on. There is some really great food and dessert here, so if you want to get more, please go ahead while I continue to prattle. My sister-in-law volunteered me for this starting role, but I don't know why. However, to keep peace and harmony in the family, I accepted. By now most of you probably know who I am, but I will quickly mention the particulars. My name is Patrick

O'Reilly. Jacob Grant was my father-in-law, and Cheryl Grant O'Reilly is my wife.

As Patrick continued to speak, Cheryl and Sylvie asked their great-aunt Jean to introduce them to the young lady who sang the solo and to the young man who offered the prayer. They were seated at a table across from them and they acknowledged each other, but hadn't been introduced. They noticed that Wesley Donaldson had said hello to the group at that table before he sat down.

When they got to the table, and Jean had made all the introductions, Gladys was the first to speak. "It is so nice to meet you," she said. "Your father and my parents were real close friends when they were growing up here. I met him a couple months ago when he was visiting. It was the first time I had seen him since I was a very young girl, but he helped me on a matter during that time."

Cheryl and Sylvie almost said in unison, "That is so nice to hear."

Then Sylvie continued speaking to Jake and Beth, "We were all so emotionally moved by the beautiful solo, Bethany, and by your prayer of remembrance, Jake. It is something that we will never forget."

"I only had the pleasure of meeting your father one time," Jake said, "and I don't think that Bethany ever met him, but between my mom, and Mr. Donaldson, we feel like we knew him very well."

"We are just thankful that we could be part of the service," said Bethany. I know him a little bit through his writing that Mr. Donaldson let me borrow. I was raised as a Missouri Synod Lutheran, so it was interesting when he wrote of his association with that denomination."

"You will have to talk to my daughter before you leave," Cheryl said. "She has read many of his writings. Maybe you can compare notes."

"I would love that," Bethany said.

"Perhaps even better," Cheryl continued. "It is this part of the service that he felt was the most positive. The time when friends and family would stand and say a few words about the deceased. To him, it meant that the mourning should end and the good remembrances help carry you forward. I don't want to put anyone on the spot, but maybe when my husband stops, someone here would like to continue. I know his grandchildren would love to hear what you say."

"That is nice of you to ask, eh…" and Gladys sought for the name.

"Cheryl."

"Yes, Cheryl. I would love to say a few words."

This is not my first time here. We attended service here a couple of times with Jacob and my mother-in-law, Monika. According to my wife and sister-in-law, Jacob liked to try and put people at ease at funerals. His theory was that the deceased has gone to a better place, or at least he hoped they had, and therefore funerals should not be a time of sadness. Now I know if my father-in-law could respond, this is what he would say 'Good grief, you are letting Patrick lead this off. He and I never agreed on much of anything.' But then he would say, 'Granted he helped give us two wonderful grandchildren, and he was always good to our daughter.' Patrick looked at Cheryl and said, "Right?"

"Sometimes," Cheryl responded and the people laughed. "Continue," she said.

"Okay. Well, like I was saying, we didn't agree on a lot of things, but in time we came to disagree more amicably. Our religion was different, but that was never a problem with him. Our political philosophies were different and we could never discuss that for any extended period of time. He was a person who I never heard say he disliked anyone. He disliked Republicans as a group, but on a one-on-one, they were all okay. So all I can say is this, the family has experienced a great loss. He left very little as far as material things, but I believe he did leave a great legacy."

When Patrick sat down, it was Gladys who stood to speak. For Jacob's family, this was nothing out of the ordinary, but for the people who attended the Old Bethel Church, it was a great moment. She gave a wonderful account of the early years of her parents and Jacob. Then she stunned everybody, except her son, when she told of the meeting with Jacob that she had just a few weeks earlier in the summer. No, all knew why she had "returned to the fold," so to speak.

Reverend Pritts leaned toward his wife and whispered, "They told me that Jake got his speaking ability from his grandfather. I would say he got a lot of it from his mother." Mrs. Pritts just nodded her head in agreement.

When it seemed as though everyone who had anything to say had finished, Wesley stood up. "Most of you who live in this area, and especially those who attend church here at Old Bethel Church, know me, but this is the first time I have had the privilege of meeting Jacob's immediate family. In the short time I knew Jacob, we became great friends, actually more than friends. I learned an awful lot from him, not just about this area we call Hexie, but about life. Life! For twenty-two years I was a Priest, but Jacob taught me many things without ever knowing it, things that will be a great asset if I ever return to that calling. As I sat on the stone bench above my house this morning waiting for the funeral cortege to pass, I reflected on the time since I first met this man we just interred on the top of the hill. I was very sad, even despondent. I stood in the graveyard and watched the graveside ceremony unfold. The song by Bethany, the prayers by Reverend Pritts and Jake, taps by the bugler, and the family laying one last flower on the casket as they departed. I have never questioned my God, but I could not reconcile it. I found him, and he had meant so much to me without ever knowing it. Perhaps he did, but how could I lose him now? And then a young person, who her cousin jokingly called obnoxious, showed me the way. I remember an old saying that my mother told me when I was still a child. She said, 'What God takes away, he returns many fold.' I have met Jacob's family and now I know that my mother was right. I will always miss him, but now there is less sadness, and no despondency. May God bless you all."

When Wesley sat down, Reverend Pritts stood up and spoke. " I don't know how to follow such and eloquent expression of love and friendship, so before we depart, I would like to ask Father Wesley Donaldson to dismiss us in prayer. Father Donaldson!"

After the prayer, Great-Aunt Jean saw Sylvie and Cheryl together and went over to talk to them.

"We won't be going to Wesley's house, but why don't you take some of the food and dessert along in case you get hungry later. You can just leave the dishes with Wesley and he will see that we get them all back. And again I want to say, I understand your great loss."

"Aunt Jean, I know exactly what my father would say if he were here, he would say, 'Aunt Jean, thanks, you did it again.'"

"You are so kind. I know you have lot to take care of before you leave, but if you have time, please stop by."

"No promises, but we will try," both Sylvie and Cheryl said.

Janice, Francis, Vadna, Andrew, and Perry all came by to say goodbye to their nieces, Sylvie and Cheryl, and to say that they too would not stop by Wesley's house, as they thought it ought to be a time for just them. Many of their own cousins stopped by to say goodbye.

415

Wesley then came by and said he would wait for them at the house. "I want to make sure all the dirty dishes are in the dishwasher and my bed is made," he said jokingly.

"Yep, two things our mother would have demanded of our father," Cheryl said. "So you may depart, take care of those matters and await our arrival."

Cheryl looked around and spotted the kids. "Hey you guys, Great-Aunt Jean said we should take some of the food so why don't each of you grab a plate and fill it up."

"Big mistake," Sylvie said.

"Why?" Cheryl asked.

"Because you are going to end up with four plates of dessert, that is why," Sylvie said.

"You are probably right. Nathan, you can get the dessert. The rest of you get real food," Cheryl said.

Eliana looked at her brother and her cousin Sarah and then said, "None of us are crazy about veggies, so, David, you get ham, Sarah, you get meat balls, and I will get chicken.'

Then she looked at Nathan and said, "Take the peach pie and the brownies."

"But I want the chocolate chip cookies," Nathan said.

"Okay, take them too," Eliana said.

"Bring that fruity stuff with the whipped cream," Sarah said.

"I can't carry that much," Nathan said.

"Okay. I will come and help you. Here, Eliana, take these meatballs, I will help Nathan."

"Right," Eliana said.

When they were outside in the parking lot by the church and had loaded the food into the SUV that Cheryl and Patrick had rented, Cheryl said, "Why don't you all ride with Patrick, so you can hold the food, and Sylvie and I will follow you. You know where we are going right?"

"The Days Inn," Kevin said just to be contrary.

"Right. But those going to the Days Inn don't get any food," Cheryl said.

"Okay, top of the hill it is," Kevin replied.

Sylvie and Cheryl waved to a few people still in the parking lot, and then Sylvie pulled out to the road. She saw that Patrick had taken the shortcut that would bring them out at the foot of the hill below Wesley's house. "Shall we take the long route by the old homestead?" Sylvie asked.

"Why not?" Cheryl said.

Chapter 54

For a minute, the two sisters rode in silence, then Cheryl asked, "So what do you think?"

"About what?" Sylvie asked.

"About Wesley."

"I don't know. What about Wesley?"

"Well, I don't know either," Cheryl said, "but I get a funny feeling."

"Like what?" Sylvie asked.

"That's just it. I don't know. He seems like a very nice person and apparently he and Dad hit it off. Maybe he will enlighten us," Cheryl said.

"And if not?" Sylvie asked again.

"Then I will just have to ask some nosy question, I guess."

"How old do you guess he is?" Sylvie asked.

"I am not very good at guessing people's age," Cheryl said, "but I would say he is a few years older than you."

"Yeah, that is what I was thinking. I did notice that he had pretty blue eyes," Sylvie said.

They were now passing where their grandparent's old house had stood, and for a moment the two sisters said nothing. Then Sylvie spoke. "Except for the outhouse, I really liked that old place. I can still remember the smell of grandma's kitchen floating upstairs in the mornings when we would visit. Do you remember that?"

"Yes, I remember it very well, but what I remember most was on Saturday when she would bake all those pies and a cake. One time I counted the pies and there were twelve. I said, 'Grandma, we will have pies for two weeks.' And do you know what she said?"

"No," Sylvie said.

"She said they will be gone by Monday, and they were. Of course she had a lot of people for dinner on Sunday."

They were now at the top of the Barney Kreger Hill and saw the driveway going down to Wesley's house. It was not paved, but both sides were neatly lined with newly planted shrubs.

"I wonder why he didn't pave the driveway?" Sylvie asked.

"I don't know, but before I ask him the nosy questions, you can ask him about his driveway," Cheryl said.

When they reached the house, Patrick, Kevin and the kids had already taken the food out of the car and were walking toward the steps that went up to the lower porch.

Wesley stood at the top of the steps.

Patrick turned to the two ladies and asked, "What took you so long? We thought you got lost."

"Hush, Pat, Sylvie answered. "We took the long way, but it looks like we are only a minute or so behind you all."

"Uncle Patrick missed the turn-off so we had to go up the road and turn around," Nathan said.

"What a blabber mouth you are, Nathan," Patrick said. "It is all Wesley's fault. He didn't make the entrance at the right place."

"We didn't have any problem," his wife said.

Patrick decided he would let the subject die.

When the children, along with Kevin and Patrick were on the porch, Wesley told them to just set the food on the table in the kitchen.

Sylvie and Cheryl were still standing at the bottom surveying the surroundings.

"I can see why our father tried to make you feel guilty about having this place. I might just pick up his cause," Cheryl said with a laugh. "I bet our cousin Liz would love it," she continued.

"It really is beautiful," Sylvie added, "but I always thought Dad wanted something more rustic."

The others had returned from the kitchen to the porch and Kevin said, "If your father had built something like this, your mother might have moved."

"Yeah, for the warm months at least," Sylvie said.

"Where does the path go?" Cheryl asked.

"It goes out to that old hickory tree and splits," Wesley said. "To the right it goes down over the hill to where the little stream begins. Your dad told me the first day we met that it was called Smith Run, and of course it is. To the left, the path goes up above the house and back out to the driveway.

"There is your opening," Cheryl said.

Only Sylvie knew what she was talking about, but she picked up on it immediately before anyone could ask.

"Speaking of driveway," Sylvie said. "If I am not being too nosy already, why did you decide on dirt and not blacktop?"

"Money," Wesley said and winked.

"OOOH, now I feel bad," Sylvie said.

"That is a 'gotcha,'" Wesley said. "See, I did learn something from your father. Actually, it had nothing to do with money; as a matter of fact I think it cost more than a blacktop driveway. I had suggested a blacktop driveway, but the guy I contracted with who builds these log houses in the tri-state area said he didn't like blacktop going up to a log house. He said it wasn't aesthetically correct. I asked him if that meant I couldn't have electricity, running water, air conditioning, and so on. He just laughed, but didn't answer. He told me I should have a WPA stone pike road and that is what I got. Of course, speaking of aesthetically correct, your father said I needed to build an outhouse."

"I know of that," Eliana said.

"Now that you mention it Eliana, I remember he told me a story about a house in West Virginia that had an outhouse, which he thought was for show. He said you didn't much like the idea."

"Gosh, he remembered that. It was probably, lets see, at least twelve years ago," Eliana said.

"Back to your driveway. When it rains real hard isn't it going to wash out?" Sylvie asked.

"The builder said it wouldn't. We have had several very hard rainfalls, and as you see it is still in great shape. One, the trees act as an umbrella, especially when they have their leaves. Beside that, it is slightly crowned with drainage pipes on each side. The bed is ten inches of crushed rock held together with a form of epoxy cement and then covered with a heavy type of coarse sand. I am sure it is a bit more advanced than what the WPA used," Wesley said.

"What is the WPA?" David asked.

"It would take too long to explain it, and then you would probably not remember it because it isn't all that interesting. When you get back to Florida State, no, University of Florida…"

"Thank you," David Interjected.

"Your sister's fault there. But anyway, Google it and it will mean much more to you. I will say that it was before my time, and even your grandfather's time, although he remembers his grandfather working on WPA roads."

"I like your teaching style," Cheryl said.

"Yeah, you sound like my teachers, 'look it up, look it up,'" Sarah said.

"Thanks for the compliment, Cheryl. Twenty years of helping poor kids in poor neighborhood helped some. And Sarah, do you think your teachers are right?"

"Yes, I guess they are right," Sarah acknowledged.

"Good," Wesley said with a smile. "I could have given you the old line of, 'back when I was your age…'"

"Meaning what?" Sarah asked rather hesitantly.

"Meaning that, even your mother would had to have gone go to the encyclopedia, but all you have to do is get on the computer and "Google it.""

"So, I say to my self, 'Sarah, leave well enough alone.'"

"So, why did you leave the priesthood?" Eliana asked.

"Hold that thought for a bit later because I want to tell you something about the first meeting between your grandfather and me. I will include that because he asked me the same question," Wesley said.

Everyone was now standing on the wide lower porch, except for Kevin and Patrick. They were seated in two spring style rocking chairs that you find on patios.

"Boy, you two guys look comfortable," Sylvie said.

"We are," Patrick said. "I could spend all afternoon sitting here."

"You may prop your feet up on the railing," Wesley said. "I always do it when I sit out here in the evening and read."

"Well, while you guys are so comfortable, I would like to see more of the place. Do you mind if we walk one of the paths?" Cheryl asked.

"I was just going to suggest that," Wesley said. "We'll let the guys relax and I will show you the upper trail."

"Mom and Aunt Sylvie, I know you want to talk to Mr. Donaldson about Pappap, so Eliana, Sarah and Nathan and I will take the lower path down to the run, if that is okay, Mr. Donaldson?" David asked.

"It is certainly okay with me. The run at that point is only a trickle, but I have cleared a little spot where I put a picnic table and there is a small frog pond. Sometimes when I sit down there in the evening, I will see some deer come up through. I assume they pay an unsolicited visit to the salt block that David's sons have placed there for the cows. The walk back up is pretty steep so perhaps you would like to take a bottle of pop with you?"

Sarah and Nathan both stared at him not knowing what he had meant.

"Ah! Ha! I see you don't understand this northern lingo. Pop is what they say for soda or soft drinks around here," Wesley said.

"Thanks for offering it, Wesley, but I think they had enough at the church, Sylvie said.

"Sorry, mothers know best," Wesley said. "Shall we go then?"

They started down the steps and Kevin yelled from his comfortable chair, where he had taken Wesley's advice and propped his feet on the railing, "See you in a little bit."

When they were on the path alongside of the hill heading to where it split, Wesley started the conversation. "Based on what Reverend Pritts said, I gather that your father had previously picked the scripture readings and the two songs prior to his death?"

"Yes, he did," Sylvie said. "After we had buried our mother, he took Cheryl and me aside and gave us each an envelope. It was sealed, but on the front it said, 'Open immediately upon notification of my death,' and he had signed it Jacob S. Grant. We were still a bit grief stricken having just buried our mother, so we protested to the extent of saying something like, 'Oh, Dad,' but he told us not to worry, it was just something that had to be done now that our mother was gone."

"From your point of view, would you say your father was a very religious man?" Wesley asked.

"I think he was religious, but I am not sure how you mean 'very,'" Cheryl said.

"May I say something?" Eliana asked.

"Please do, Eliana," Wesley said.

"I haven't had much personal time, that is to say, one-on-one contact, with my grandfather for the past seven years because of where we lived, and then going to the Academy, but I have read much of what he has written. I also remember a couple of instances when I was Sarah's age or a little older. I think Pappap was 'very religious' in his own way. He was just never very conventional. I don't think he ever had conflicts with his concept of God, but he often had a lot of problems with Pastors and Priests of the denominations telling him what they thought God had meant to say. God in this case, includes the Trinity. I know it always bothered him that he could not take communion with his grandchildren. I also know he could never understand all the fuss about grace and works. To him it was just a moot point. He felt that the people, including the leaders of the churches and the denominations, simply do not understand their own concept of Christianity. I vaguely remember one article he wrote a long time ago. It was what you might call a position paper. It contained a lengthy prologue where he debated these points and then told the story of a very poor family that moved to this area. I think my great- grandparents and a farmer hereabouts befriended them. The farmer was not a religious man, but he had helped the family in the way they needed most, with food. His point was, how was the farmer's good deed reconciled? I remember he listed several Biblical references, both Old and New Testament. So, as far as my Pappap's religiosity, I think in what he did, he tried to be truly Christian, but his beliefs short-circuited a lot of denominational dogma." Eliana said in finality.

Eliana's reference to the article about the poor family caught Wesley's attention, but when she had finished, he said, "Well, thank you, Eliana, for getting me out of that hole. I agree with your observations whole-heartedly, but I think you said it more succinctly than I could have."

"Sue-sinkly what?? Sarah asked.

"Suc-cinct-ly," David said. It means, saying exactly what you want to say with the minimum number of words. Something unknown to lawyers, politicians, some preachers, priests, and you, of course."

"Ha! Ha! Ha! David, I am going to get you," Sarah responded.

"I wasn't including you, Father Donaldson," David was quick to add.

"Thanks, but you have never heard me speak. I think sometimes I am a bit windy," Wesley said.

"My other grandfather would probably say if your sermon went over fifteen minutes, you weren't being succinct," David added.

"Then I fit into your first discourse," Wesley said.

They had now come to the divide in the path. To the right, went down over the hill to the run and pond, and to the left, went up the hill a short distance and then paralleled this path and the road above.

"David, I think I will go with Mom, Aunt Sylvie and Mr. Donaldson," Eliana said.

"No problem. I can control these two munchkins. Maybe we will find a snake and bring it back for you," David said.

"Don't even think it David," his Aunt Sylvie said.

"Not that you will encounter any on the path, but you do know how to recognize rattlesnakes don't you?" Wesley asked.

"The boy is a natural science whiz," Cheryl said. "So we don't scare Sylvie to death, he has taken scouts on outings and is very conscientious of his responsibilities, and aware of the dangers. Now if he just remembers what poison ivy looks like," Cheryl said with a laugh.

"Not funny, Cheryl," Sylvie said, "but Nathan is also very familiar with the outdoors through the scouting programs."

As David, Sarah and Nathan started down the path, Sarah asked, "David, "why did you call Mr. Donaldson, Father?"

"Because he is a priest. Don't you remember at the church when my mother mentioned it and he said he was on a sabbatical, then Nathan wanted to know what a sabbatical was?"

"Oh, yeah, I remember now. But where is his church?" Sarah continued.

"He is on a sabbatical. He doesn't have a church." David replied.

"I don't see how he can be a priest if he doesn't have a church."

"Well, believe it," David said, "once a Priest, always a Priest, or something close to that."

"I am still just going to call him Mr. Donaldson," Sarah said. "I like him, but you know what?"

"What?"

"He uses too many big words I don't understand," Sarah said.

David laughed and then said, "I will tell him you said that, and I am sure he will watch it, henceforth, but you know what Sarah?"

"What?"

"I listen to you. You have a great vocabulary. You articulate well and are very observant. I think you are just bluffing to see if I make a mistake; a hustler so to speak."

"See, you are just as bad. Maybe you should be sue-sinkly."

"Suc-cinct-ly," David said.

"Whatever," Sarah said.

"But why did you mention that?" David asked.

"Because you said, 'henceforth'. Why didn't you just say 'next time?'"

"Point well taken, and that is what I will do henceforth," he said a bit mockingly.

"Sarah kicked at him, not intending to make contact, but David jumped away knowing that was what she was going to do.

Nathan was several paces ahead and was standing by a plant with small flowers. Most of the flowers had bloomed earlier and in their stead was a seedpod. Nathan touched it and it sprung apart causing him to jump back. He noticed the pod had curled up and the seed fell to the ground.

"Come here, Sarah," Nathan called to his sister.

"What do you want?" Sarah asked.

"Here, touch this," Nathan said.

"Touch what?" Sarah asked.

"This little green pod."

"Why?"

"Just touch it and you will see. It isn't going to hurt you," Nathan said.

Cautiously, Sarah touched the pod and like the one Nathan had touched, it sprung apart. And like her brother, she quickly moved her hand, and then laughed.

"What kind of flower is this David?" Nathan asked.

"Beats me," David said. "I guess we can ask Wesley, or I can look it up when I get back to school. Or, as Wesley said previously, we should all look it up and then we will remember it."

"I think you should look it up and send us an e-mail," Sarah said. "We will remember it. Huh! Nathan?"

"No, I will look it up myself," Nathan said.

"Okay, David, you don't have to send me an e-mail, Nathan will tell me," Sarah said.

"No, I won't," was Nathan's reply.

On the path above, it was Eliana who was asking the questions and not her mother Cheryl. "If I may be so bold, why did you ask if we thought Pappap was very religious?"

"That is a bit difficult to answer because in retrospect, my original question was not one that I really thought about. It just seemed to pop out, but there must have been a reason. I suppose it was a contrast between my preconceived notion of what Jacob's religious character was and what I had to reconsider after hearing the funeral service.

"In our conversations, matters of religion did come up, but they were never topics that we delved upon in depth. I knew he was very ethical, but one can be very ethical without being religious. I also know that he went to church regularly, but attendance doesn't always equate to piety. Gosh! I think I am digging myself into a hole again. I am not putting into words what I really want to say," Wesley said.

"I don't see where you are saying anything wrong, Wesley, but perhaps it would help you to start from a different point. What did you mean when you said you had to reconsider after hearing the funeral service?" Sylvie asked.

"Yes, that may help," Wesley said. "Reverend Pritts said that your father/grandfather picked all the scripture readings and the songs. Is that not correct?" Wesley asked.

"Yes," said Cheryl.

"Did you know what they were before the service?" Wesley asked.

"Of course, we knew as soon as we opened his letter upon hearing of his death. We immediately faxed a copy to Reverend Pritts," Cheryl said.

They had now come to the stone bench that Wesley had the stonemason build, and where he had sat waiting for the procession earlier in the day. "Would you like to sit down for a minute?" Wesley asked.

"This is really nice, Wesley," Sylvie said.

"It is one of my favorite places to come when I want to enjoy the solitude. If I want to read, or work on something on the laptop, I generally go the lower path to the little river. It is here that I was sitting the first time Jacob drove by, stopped, and our friendship began. I was also sitting here early this morning, remembering our conversations and meetings as I waited for the funeral cortege to go by.

Sylvie, Cheryl and Eliana all sat on the stone bench, while Wesley leaned against a small locust tree a few feet away.

"So where were we?" Sylvie asked.

"Cheryl had just mentioned about faxing a copy of Jacob's letter to Reverend Pritts," Wesley said.

"We didn't fax everything in the letter, just what pertained to the funeral that Reverend Pritts would need," Sylvie said. "He called us back and said he had two problems. He said, the song, 'Where the Soul Never Dies' was not in the Old Bethel hymnal, and that one scripture reading was from the Book of Sirach, which is not in the Protestant Bible. I told him that since the grandchildren were doing all the readings except for the sermon reading, the last thing would cause no problem as they all had Catholic Bibles. He said, 'he guessed that was okay.' As for the song, we felt confident we could find it somewhere on the Internet, and Kevin did find it almost immediately on a web page called the Pentecostal Online Hymnal. It had all the words and the music. We gave him the web page address so the organist could download it."

"And he really did tell Reverend Pritts to not make the sermon too long?" Wesley asked.

"Oh, yeah he said it," Cheryl replied, "but he said it in a way that that was not offensive. Apparently you got to know him fairly well in a short period of time, at least well enough to know he was a bit of a walking paradox. I never asked Sylvie about her thoughts on his sealed letter, but I assume they were the same as mine; something sad and depressing, but it was quite the contrary. I mean I just got the word that my father had been involved in a fatal accident, so I immediately went to my dresser drawer and retrieved his letter. I was crying when I opened it, but as I started to read what he had written, my tears stopped and I started to smile. It was lighthearted and even a bit amusing. I have a copy of it back at the motel, if you would like to have a copy. I would be glad to give you one before we leave."

"Yes, I would love to have a copy," Wesley said.

"The reading from Sirach might have caused more of a problem sometime earlier," Wesley continued. "I might have softened the way, but in retrospect, I now think I might have been duped."

"How is that?" Cheryl asked.

Wesley continued, "Let me ask you this, after your father gave you the letter when your mother died, has he ever changed it?"

"Yes, as a matter of fact he did," Sylvie said. Then looking at her sister Cheryl she continued, "I think about the first of May he sent us a letter containing a new sealed envelope. He said we were to return the first one to him unopened, and that is what we did."

"I assumed he had us return it because he didn't trust us to destroy it without reading it first," Cheryl said.

"I hadn't thought of that, but I bet you are right," Sylvie said. Then she continued, "So would you have read it before you destroyed it, Cheryl?"

"Naaaah," Cheryl said with a laugh.

"Well that 'son of a gun,'" Wesley also said with a laugh. "This is just a guess, but I bet that is when he included the reading from Sirach.

"You may be absolutely right about that, Wesley, because when he lists the reading from Sirach, he has a note in parens that says, 'I hope the foundation has been laid for this reading.' I just dismissed it," Sylvie said. "What about you, Cheryl?

"Yeah, I did too," Cheryl answered. "So what does it mean?"

"It is really pretty simple," Wesley said. "It goes back to our very first meeting. After I had showed him about the house, and when he was ready to depart for the cemetery, he gave me some advice. He said I was to get to know the people and because of my religious background, maybe I should attend service at Old Bethel Church sometime, maybe on Wednesday when they had Bible study. 'Play it slow and cautious,'" he said.

"The first time I did as he had said, and then I sent him an e-mail asking for advice. He was a bit elusive, but now I gather that he wanted me to gradually explain Catholicism to them as I absorbed their Protestantism. That is very evident now in light of what Eliana has just previously said about his religious philosophy. I hate to put those two words together, but sometimes they fit," Wesley concluded.

Then Eliana spoke. "You know, I am much more of a conformist in my religious thinking than my grandfather, and perhaps more than my mother."

"Well, that is for sure, Eliana, but that is also quite okay," Cheryl said.

"I understand that mother, but let me continue. I read Pappap's letter about how he wanted his funeral to be carried out, and although I could never do that for myself, I think he handled it so well. Maybe I am prejudiced because he was my grandfather, but I don't think so. I just can't believe that God would let me talk that way, but somehow, I think God expected that from Pappap, the man we knew as Jacob. Maybe like his Biblical namesake of many generations ago, he wrestled with God and won a compromise. As a Priest, I think you will find his letter very worthwhile reading. I will give you my e-mail address at the Academy, and when you have had a opportunity to read his letter, I would appreciate it if you would drop me a line and let me know your thoughts on the matter." Eliana said.

"I certainly will," Wesley said.

Then Cheryl said, "You know, my daughter's religious thinking may not be the same as his, but in other ways she is very much like him. She will probably make a great Naval Officer, because she never breaks the rules. Dad was also pretty much like that. We would have buried him in his Navy Master Chief's uniform, but he was emphatic in his letter that we should not do that. When he retired, beards were authorized. Today's Navy men are not authorized to wear beards, but he did not want to have his beard shaved off and he did not want to be out of uniform. That is why he requested that only his hat be included. He said, 'Perhaps Saint Peter's Navy, if I go that way, will permit beards,' and then he followed it with a, Ha! Ha!"

"So you followed his instructions to the letter?" Wesley asked.

"Well, almost," Sylvie said. "He requested that friends not send flowers. He did ask that six yellow roses be included in the casket. 'I want to take six yellow roses to your mother so she will remember our first date,' he had said in his letter."

"And the flowers you placed on his coffin?" Wesley asked.

"That was our decision, but we are all a bit afraid to go to sleep tonight, lest he chastise us for that in our dreams," Cheryl said.

"Oh! I doubt that," Wesley said.

"There is one thing we would like to ask you, Wesley," Sylvie said.

"Oh, what is that?"

"How did you manage to get the color guard?"

"Who said I did?" Wesley asked.

"The funeral director," Sylvie continued. "Dad had said in his letter, it would be nice, but he didn't think it would be possible. However, it was in the instructions we faxed to the funeral director."

"Well, I knew which funeral home was involved and I was calling for another matter. The Director mentioned the color guard request but said he wouldn't be able to get that taken care of since there was no military installation in the immediate area. I then called my cousin who is a Navy Captain, and he called a friend who is a three-star admiral. This friend was also an acquaintance of your father's through the Blue Angels. It got taken care of.

"We certainly thank you for that," Sylvie and Cheryl both said.

Just then they heard voices and saw David, Sarah and Nathan coming along the path. As usual, Nathan was walking behind and gazing about as if in deep thought. When they got close enough, Sylvie could see that Nathan's pants were wet up to his knees.

"Nathan, what did you do?" Sylvie asked.

"I was trying to catch a frog," Nathan said.

"Well, why didn't you roll up your pant legs?"

"I don't know. I took my shoes off," he said.

"Yeah, I guess you did one thing right," Sylvie said.

"David, why didn't you stop him?" Cheryl asked.

"Because I was getting ready to take my shoes off to help him. Besides, someday he may be a great zoologist, and I didn't want to impede his research," David said with a laugh.

"Did you go in too, Sarah?" Cheryl asked.

"No way, I do not like slimy things," Sarah said. Then she continued, "We are rather hungry."

"Who is 'we?'" Sylvie asked.

"David, Nathan and I."

"Why did you include me in that?" David asked giving a wink to the others.

"Because you said it first," Sarah said.

"I said it first?" David asked.

"Who said it first, Nathan?" Sarah asked.

"David did," was his reply.

"Okay, two against one. I admit, I said it first, but we men have to learn to stick together Nathan, because women form a natural conspiracy against us," David said with a laugh.

"That is not true Nathan. Don't believe everything that your cousin David tells you," Cheryl said.

"Okay," was Nathan's only response.

"Besides David, we just ate at the church less than three hours ago," his mother said.

"I know, but you try and keep track of these two and see if it doesn't make you hungry," David said.

"He has a valid point there, Cheryl. I know that for a fact," Sylvie said.

"Ever the peacemaker," Wesley said, "I suppose I am also a bit hungry. I only went through the line once and there was some really good food there. Come on all of you. On the way down to the house, I will tell you what happened when I went to Ohio to get my belongings."

Wesley then told them about coming back and finding a lot of the people from the church waiting to help unload the truck. About the food the ladies had set out and about Bethany's song.

When they got back to the house, Patrick was sleeping on the porch swing and Kevin was reading.

"Why don't you all make yourselves comfortable and I will see about setting the food out," Wesley said.

Cheryl cut in immediately, "Our father was not a male chauvinist. As a matter of fact, he championed women's rights, and so if you don't mind us rummaging around in your kitchen, Sylvie, Eliana and I will take care of that. At the church I was talking to my Great-Aunt Jean and she told me a bit about this place. Maybe Nathan and Sarah would like to see and hear about the old house and how you preserved the springhouse."

"Hey, I would like to hear about that myself, " Eliana said.

"Go ahead, Eliana, I will help Mom and Aunt Sylvie," David said.

"You can be such a sweet brother at times," Eliana said and kissed him on the cheek.

"Before you go, where do you keep the paper plates, etc.?" Cheryl asked.

"I don't like eating off of paper plates so I don't have any," Wesley said. "Just use what you find in the cupboards. I was thinking, maybe it would be nice if we ate at the picnic table under the old walnut tree," Wesley said.

"That was our plan," Sylvie answered.

"Okay, I see everything is in good hands. Shall we start the historic tour?" Wesley said, and Eliana, Sarah and Nathan started to follow him down the steps to the basement.

"Setting the food out won't take us too long so don't let them get you too involved," Sylvie said, but the door had already closed and there was no response.

Chapter 55

The stairwell going to the basement was circular and ended facing the length of the basement, almost in the middle between the wall on the upper side of the house and the lower side. At the far end, the wall was completely covered by bookshelves from the floor to the ceiling. All of the shelves were very nearly filled. Along the upper wall were five, four drawer file cabinets, next to them was a two door cabinet of the supply type, and next to that was a beautiful wooden cabinet with two glass doors. It was lighted. In the center of the room was a long worktable. There were some papers in several neat stacks, and a couple of loose-leaf notebooks lay open next to a large map of the world. The map was held in place by paperweights that were replicas of famous cathedrals. On the lower side of the room were two large windows. There was a large executive desk facing the windows so that the person working here could look out over the valley from under the porch that also served as a "rainy day" patio. Next to the desk was an equipment console that contained two computer processors, and an array of other peripheral equipment.

"This is a really nice office, Mr. Donaldson. You wouldn't mind sending some of it down to the Naval Academy, would you?" Eliana asked laughingly.

"I don't know about the Naval Academy, but I was just out to Notre Dame to see a good friend of mine. He teaches foreign languages. Anyway, he took me through some of the living quarters. I found them to be pretty well wired," Wesley said.

"Actually, I can't complain now. It was a bit crowded the first two years though."

Sarah had moved over to the table and was admiring the miniature cathedrals that were holding the map in place. Nathan had taken a seat in the large chair by the desk.

"Nathan, since you are sitting there, punch the yellow button on the telephone, and then punch the one labeled Kitchen. Tell your mother than they can find tablecloths in the linen closet at the end of the hall," Wesley said.

"Okay," Nathan said now feeling important. He did as Wesley had instructed and then said, "Mom, this is Nathan down in Mr. Donaldson's office. He said you can find tablecloths in the linen closet at the end of the hall."

"Tell her she can answer by punching the yellow button by any telephone and then punch basement."

"Mr. Donaldson said you can talk to us by punching the yellow button by any telephone and then punch basement," Nathan said.

There was a short pause, and then Cheryl's voice came through on hidden speakers. "Thanks for that information. As of now, you have five minutes and counting, after that we eat without you. Out."

"Well, I guess we had better get a move on," Wesley said. But he saw that Sarah was still admiring the miniature cathedrals, so he asked, "Can you identify any of them, Sarah?"

"Only two," she said. "This is Saint Peter's in Vatican City and this is Notre Dame in Paris."

"That is very good," Wesley said.

"Well, not really, because we have each of them in our school library."

"Well, I still think it is good that you remember and recognize these great examples of man's attempt to glorify God," Wesley said as words of encouragement.

"Now that was a line that could have been taken out of Pappap's rhetoric," Eliana said.

"It was," Wesley said. "Glad that you recognized it. Can you name the other two cathedrals?"

"I think so," Eliana said. "This one I know is St. Basils in Moscow, and because of the minarets, the one on the far corner, I think is, or was, St Sophia's in Istanbul, then Constantinople. It was converted to a mosques after the Muslims victory there."

"I am very impressed. Jacob has very intelligent grandchildren," Wesley said.

"Can we see the springhouse now?" Nathan asked.

"My thoughts exactly, Nathan, otherwise we are going to miss out on the food. Perhaps you can call your mother and plead for a couple more minutes," Wesley said.

"Good idea," Nathan said with a smile and punched the necessary two buttons on the telephone. "Mom, this is Nathan. Sarah and Eliana asked a lot of questions so we are running behind. Can we have five more minutes?"

"This is your lucky day, Nathan. This is your Aunt Cheryl and I grant you your request because we just woke your Uncle Patrick and it will take him that long to gain his wits and equilibrium. But no longer, do you understand?"

"Yes, Aunt Cheryl, I'll tell them."

"Good job Nathan," Eliana said.

"But you didn't need to blame Eliana and me," Sarah said in protest.

"Uncle David said it is always good to front load your argument."

They started to walk toward the opposite end of the basement toward the old stonewall.

"I thought mom told you not to believe everything that Uncle David tells you," Eliana said.

"But it got us the extra time," Nathan said with conviction.

"Well, Sarah, I guess your objection is overruled," Eliana said.

Wesley began to explain about what they were going to see. "Much of what I am going to tell you was told to me by your grandfather, but he also told me of some other people I could talk to and get additional information. The stones in this wall, and the wall on the other side, are the same stones used in the walls of the original old log house built here in the middle 1800s by a man named, Barnhardt Kreger. The name Kreger has been anglicized in several ways, but in the original German, it was probably Kruger. The builder tore down the original walls but he marked every stone and replaced them as close as possible to their original position."

"Why did he do that?" Nathan asked.

"Good question, Nathan. He noticed that the walls, especially the outside one, the one that would bear much of the weight of the new house, canted inward. Also, the original wall was built using straw and mud as the mortar"

"What is canted, Mr. Donaldson?" Sarah asked.

"That means it was leaning," Wesley said.

"Oh!" was all Sarah said. Surprisingly she didn't tell him to use more common words.

"You see," Wesley continued, "the builder wanted to make sure that the walls were on a solid footing. Now about this door, since we were retaining the original walls, going back well over one hundred and fifty years, the builder thought it would be nice if this door also reflected the same time era. The boards come from an old barn that was being torn down and he fabricated it, that is to say he built it," Wesley said, sensing that Sarah might ask for a definition of fabricated, "and he used the common Z method to hold it together. He could not find the hinges and latches that you see here, so he went to an Amish blacksmith close to the small town of Springs and had him make them."

When Wesley opened the door, the lights came on automatically.

"There are no windows in here because the original house had none. It had a door there at the lower end, and the one where we just came in.

"Whose idea was it to use the old lanterns as lights?" Eliana asked.

"That, too, was the builder's idea. Now we come to the center of the old cellar. Here on the upper wall is the original spring. Some of the stones were repositioned, but it is for the most part the same as it was when originally built. The water for the house comes from here through a pipe and filter system installed by the plumber to be inconspicuous.

"The original old log house was much smaller than my house, but even so, the cellar and spring house didn't go under the entire length of the house. The door we came through went out under a porch that was on the upper side of the house, and then via a path to the old barn that was a couple of hundred feet away. Your grandfather remembered the upper porch. He was not sure if there was a lower porch, but I found out from an original descendant of old Barney Kreger that there was none.

"When the builder rebuilt the walls and the spring house, he did not do the water trough that you see. The first time your grandfather and I went driving around, he showed me a trough back on the old May farm, and explained the purpose of the three depths. I later called my builder to see if he could construct a similar trough here. He did. It was going to be one of my surprises for your grandfather."

"Mr. Donaldson, **would you mind telling me what you mean by a spring house?**" Sarah asked with articulation.

"Sarah, I sincerely apologize, and I certainly will. As a matter of fact, your grandfather had to explain it to me," Wesley said.

"It seems that in this part of the country and I imagine many places, the early settlers and farmers would look for a good natural water source, or spring. They would then build their house on one side and the barn on the other. They would also build a small building at the location of the spring, and thus it became known as a springhouse. Now the springhouse served several functions. It was the source of your drinking water, and the excess runoff normally went into a water trough that was used by the livestock. But it served another purpose, long before electricity and refrigeration; it was your means for keeping food cool. Come on over here and I will show you what I mean.

"You see, as the water flows out of the pipe from the spring, it flows into this long trough that has three levels. The first level is only a few inches deep, the second level is about nine inches deep and the third level is about two feet deep. The third level could often be controlled as to how much water you wanted it to contain. So, let's take a hypothetical case," Wesley said.

"Suppose it is 1890, and you have just finished the evening meal on a hot summer day like today, although it is now autumn. The butter in a crock dish is starting to melt and there are some leftover cucumbers in a sweet cream sauce. Your mother says, 'Sarah, put the butter and leftover cucumbers away'. There is no refrigerator, so what do you do?"

"Ah! I see," Sarah says with delight, "I bring them down to the spring house and set them here where the water is not very deep."

"You catch on very quickly, Sarah. Your mother would be proud of you."

"Now, Nathan, you are helping your daddy milk the cows."

"I don't think daddy knows how to milk cows," Nathan said.

"Well, maybe not, but in 1890, and living out here in the country, I am sure he would have known how. So, he says to you, 'Nathan, take this bucket of milk into the springhouse so Eliana can separate it.'"

"What do you mean, 'separate it?'" Nathan asked.

Eliana was glad that Nathan had asked because she also didn't know, but her relief was short-lived.

"Eliana," Wesley said quizzingly.

Eliana raised her eyebrows and said, "Mr. Donaldson, I am a city girl. I have no idea."

"Now I don't feel so bad, because I didn't know either what it meant when your grandfather was telling me about it and I also had to ask," Wesley said. "But if you think about it, it make sense. If you let whole milk set for a while, the cream will rise to the top, because the milk and the cream have different specific gravities. In very early days, that is exactly what the farmers would do. But by 1890, there was a thing called a separator. You would pour the milk into the upper bowl, generally through a straining cloth that filtered out any foreign objects like flies, or dirt, and then you would turn a large handle that caused this bowl to spin. When you got it spinning at a good rate, the lighter cream would rise to the upper outer wall of the bowl and be fed through a spout into a large crock. The rest of the liquid was heavier and would go to the bottom where it went out through another spout to a second crock."

"Oh! We learned about that in third grade science," Sarah said. "I think it is called a centrifuge, but we didn't use milk. We used salad oil and vinegar."

"Exactly," Wesley said, "The farmers just said separator instead of centrifuge."

"I feel so stupid," Eliana said.

"No need for that," Wesley assured her. "But you can now see the process and the purpose for the different depths in the trough."

"So where does the water go from here?" Nathan asked.

"From the overflow in the deepest part of the trough, it goes down into that grate and a large pipe takes it down to the pond where you tried to catch the frog. With the original house, it probably went further down the hill and into a watering trough for the livestock. And from there it worked its way down to the bottom of the hill and the little stream know as Smith Run," Wesley said.

Wesley had left the door leading from the office area to the spring area open, and they all heard Cheryl come on the intercom: "Your five minute extension is up. The food is on the table. Grace will be said in 60 seconds, 59, 58, 57," and then the intercom clicked off.

"Knowing my mother, I suggest we make our presence known," Eliana said.

The party of four left the basement area via the door leading from the office and out under the porch. The other party of five was standing by the table. Sylvie spoke, "Father Donaldson, we await your words of Grace."

"Perhaps we can all join hands," he said and then began a common prayer that they all knew. "Bless us oh Lord for these Thy gifts which we are about to receive from Thy bounty, through Christ our Lord. Amen. In the name of the Father, and of the Son, and the Holy Spirit."

When they had all finished eating, Wesley said, "If you are interested, I will tell you about the first meeting between Jacob and me. As I said a little bit earlier, I was going over it in my mind this morning as I waited for the funeral procession."

"We weren't planning on leaving until you filled us in on your meeting and subsequent friendship with our father," Cheryl said.

"Yes, we are dying to hear," Sylvie added.

"Sarah and Nathan, if you think you might get bored by this, you are welcome to go into my library and turn on the computer marked fun and games. I write software for games that the church uses in some of their outreach programs. You might find them interesting," Wesley said.

"Thanks, Mr. Donaldson, but I think I would like to hear about Pappap," Sarah said.

"Me too," was Nathan's reply.

"Well, I am so glad to hear that," Wesley said. "To keep it simple in the telling, I won't refer to him as your father or grandfather, but just as Jacob, the man I met and, and …I guess learned to love as a great friend.

"He normally just called me Wesley, but if he wanted to make me feel a bit guilty about something, he would use my clerical title, mostly Father, or Padre, for some reason. If he wanted me to give deference to his age or greater wisdom, he would say, 'boy or son,' but mostly he just said Wesley. He never argued with me or chastised me, but if he did disagree, he had this way of looking at you as if to say, 'you can't be serious,' or 'I don't think so,' and then he would start to talk about something slightly different and eventually wend his way back to the original subject."

"I assume he changed with age," Patrick said, "because when Cheryl and I first got married, he wasn't a bit hesitant about arguing with me"

"I remember that," Eliana said. "They use to get really loud."

"He chewed me out a time or two also," Kevin said.

"Okay, we all will agree that Wesley got to meet the older, more mellow Jacob Grant, but let him continue and maybe we will see a side of our father and grandfather that we overlooked, or did not recognize," Sylvie said.

"I think that is it," Wesley said. "When I had a Parrish, and I would talk to families after a funeral, in circumstances very similar to this, there were often cases of seeing the different sides of an individual. I guess, that like a beautifully cut gemstone, we are all multi-faceted, and the light at any given moment and from any given angle will show different colors, but that doesn't necessarily detract from the subject."

"Well said, Mr. Donaldson. Won't you please continue, and let the gallery be silent," David interjected in his best rendition of a courtroom voice.

Wesley then gave them a complete rundown of his first meeting with Jacob Grant including much of their conversations. He did not expound on most of his personal thoughts. He also gave them a brief rundown of Jacob's second visit when they toured all the back roads and talked about some of the earlier inhabitants of Hexie.

"So he gave you a copy of all of his writings and articles?" Eliana asked.

"I don't know if he gave me everything, but he gave me a lot."

"I talked to that young lady who sang the solo. She said you let her read some of his writings."

"That would be Bethany. I asked your father if he cared, and he said it was a great idea."

"She told me that she learned a lot about the history of the area from reading them. She especially liked the article about the old log house and the feistiness of Elizabeth Growall," Eliana said. Then she continued, "I assume we are going to go back to the house in Pensacola at some point, so if you e-mail me a list of what he did give you, I will see if there is anything else you might be interested in," Eliana said. "In fact, I can probably hack into his computer. He has been using the same password for years."

"That would be nice. I don't mean hacking into his computer, but having access to anymore of his writings. Of course, I don't want things he might not have intended for me to have," Wesley replied.

"I doubt that he had much that would fit into that category,." Cheryl said.

"We do have to go back to have the will read, or talk with his lawyer and take care of legal matters related to his estate," Sylvie said. "Is there anything of his you would like to have as a personal reminder of him?"

"Well, I don't know what he had, but if you find something among his effects that you think he might not have intended for any of the family, yes, I would be delighted to have it.

"I don't know if you are aware of why Jacob went to Richmond," Wesley continued. "He was hoping to find the answer to the identity of your old progenitor, Priscilla Rugg."

"Yeah, that bothered him for many years," Sylvie said. "I don't know why he just couldn't accept that it was the proverbial lost piece of the puzzle, or accept what others accepted about her."

"Maybe the lost piece wasn't a finality. As soon as your father heard about the tornados on the radio, he called me from right outside of Richmond. Before he hung up, I asked him if his endeavor at the library had been a success, and he said, 'Very much so. I copied it all down to read later.'"

"That is very interesting," David said. "The insurance company let us go through the burned wreckage of the truck. Everything was pretty much totally consumed, but we did find his leather briefcase in recognizable condition. It had slid under the front seat and was somewhat protected. There was nothing in it except for some pens, a folder with names and address, and a couple of badly warped CDs. However, on the floor in front were the recognizable remains of a legal pad. Also there were the remains of some type of a binder. There didn't seem to be a cover to it, just a bunch of papers between metal fasteners. That could have been what he copied. Also, the remote control for his garage door, and an audio book container had been thrown out of the truck. They were found by the crew of the electric company and given to the police who investigated the wreck."

"You are probably correct in that assumption, David. I do know that the record he was researching was a very old one because he had to give the library advance notice so they could pull it for him."

"In that case, it being the Virginia State Library, I am sure they would have a record of his request and visit. Anyone interested should be able to contact them and get the same record," David said.

"That legal 'gopher' job of yours has really made you an acute observer," Eliana said with a smile as she looked at her brother.

"Why do you say he is a cute observer?" Sarah asked.

"No, Sarah, it is not 'a cute' but 'an acute', meaning I have very good observational skills. My sister is bestowing a compliment on me, you see."

"Oh, I missed the indefinite article," Sarah said. "At least I learned another new word."

David looked at his sister and just raised his eyebrows, and then Nathan said in his sheepish monotone, "Keep going Sarah, and you may someday be as smart as me."

Sarah looked at her brother with a bit of a scowl, but apparently felt the comment unworthy of a reply.

"Okay, it is getting late and I think enough has been said for today," Cheryl cut in. "Time we let Wesley have his solitude back, and we need to get back to the motel and discuss what and when and how to settle Dad's affairs."

Chapter 56

Back at the motel in Somerset, Sarah and Nathan pestered their mother to go swimming in the motel's pool.

"You can't go by yourself unless you are sixteen, and I do not feel like going," her mother said.

Sarah turned her head toward Eliana but didn't say a word.

"Okay, go get your suit on. David and I will go down with you."

"Thanks for volunteering me," David said. "What makes you think I want to go?"

"For one thing, I know you don't want to disappoint your cousins, and second, we have something to talk about."

"We do?" David said as he raised his eyebrows and twisted his mouth in an expression of uncertainty.

David and Eliana waited while Sarah and Nathan put on their swimsuits and both took a towel from the bathroom. The four of them then walked to the enclosed pool area.

Sarah and Nathan went immediately to the water, while David and Eliana found chairs close by, but not close enough to get splashed by the rambunctious children doing cannonball jumps in to the pool.

"Would you like a soda, or as they say here, 'a pop'?" David asked his sister.

"You buying?" Eliana asked.

"Sure."

"Then bring me a Sprite."

When David came back, he noticed his sister seemed to be in a bit of a trance, but he said nothing. He handed her the Sprite. She took it and thanked him but continued to stare off at nothing in particular. David sat down and after a short time he broke the silence. "Space station to Eliana, we see you but we do not copy. Please come in Eliana."

Eliana slapped her brother's hand, smiled and said, "Sorry about that, I was just trying to organize some things in my mind."

"Well, you did say we had something to talk about. Did your trance and mind organizing concern that matter, and if so, please bring me up to speed," David said.

"Actually it did. I was just trying to determine how to mention it without sounding like a kook. Maybe I am seeing more than is actually there."

"Okay," David said, "let me ask you the big question. What are you talking about?"

"What do you think about Father Donaldson?"

"Wow! That is a big question in itself. Can you narrow it down?"

"I am not sure I can. I am not even sure I know what I want to ask. I suppose I want to ask you if you got the feeling that he didn't tell us everything about the relationship between him and Pappap."

"Are you saying you think he didn't tell us the truth?" David asked.

"No, I think he was truthful in what he said, I just don't think he told us everything. I get the feeling that he knew something about Pappap that he didn't tell us."

"Like what?"

"That is what troubles me. I do not know what that might be."

"Was it something he said that I didn't hear? Like when I went with Sarah and Nathan down the path and you all went the other way."

"No, it was more of what he said at the fellowship hall."

"I remember that was very touching, but I can't recall specifics that would make me ask questions."

"David, you are forever the sentimentalist. As a lawyer, you are going to have get over that."

"I don't plan to be a trial lawyer, but you can chastise me later. What do you remember from his words that I apparently missed?"

"At one point he said, referring to Pappap, 'he was a friend, more than a friend.'"

"Okay, and you take that to mean…"

"What is more than a friend, David?"

"Well, I think that was just an expression. He was speaking extemporaneously and probably didn't realize he had said something like that. We all do it at times. Lawyers will often go for it, and certainly learn to recognize it."

"Okay, so much for your legal take on it, but then he also said, 'I found him.'" David, you meet new friends, you don't find them."

"You can find old friends."

"That is true, but did you hear anything in the conversation to suggest they were old friends?"

"No, you got me there, Eliana. So let me see what I am hearing. Am I correct in assuming that your studies in psychology make you believe those comments were Freudian slips?"

"Freudian slips? I don't know that I would go that far, but yes, maybe Freudian slips. At least they make me wonder."

"And what are you suggesting, might I ask?" David replied.

"I am not suggesting anything, but I think we should get some background information on Wesley."

"Eliana, before we go down that path, let's say specifically what I think you are thinking and analyze it."

"Okay, David, what do you think I am thinking?"

"I think you believe that Pappap may have fooled around in his younger days and fathered a son, albeit one that he never knew about. Am I close to the target?"

"Bull's-eye. It is quite possible. I mean, I would like to think that he married Oma as a chaste individual, but I think that is unrealistic, and in no way reflects on their long marriage. He was, after all, a sailor, although this would had to have happened long before he was a sailor."

"I guess going to the Academy you would know about those Navy guys."

"Not in that way dear brother."

"I apologize, if you misconstrued that last comment. That was not what I meant."

"I know it wasn't, but getting back to the subject, don't you think it is possible?"

"Possible, yes of course it is possible, but I don't see it being probable."

"Why not?" Eliana asked in a voice that required a specific answer.

"Well, for one thing his age. How old would you say that Mr. Donaldson is?"

"I am not good at guessing ages, but I would say fifty-two, maybe fifty-three."

"I know you will call me a sexist for bringing this up, but I read an article recently that said young women generally see older men as being younger then they actually are. I say he is at least fifty-five."

"So how does that impact my theory?" Eliana asked.

"Well, as they say, do the math. That means he would have been about fourteen."

"Still possible," Eliana again countered.

"Very possible, but consider, this is a country area where everyone pretty much knows everyone else's business. Add to that, the fact that our great-grandparents were conservative and moralists and it poses a problem."

"I see what you are saying, but I think we are missing something."

"I say you are trying to create another uncle, and I say we have enough. I am getting tired, so what you say we see if we can get Sarah and Nathan out of the pool."

"Okay," Eliana said with reluctance. "It has been a long day and tomorrow is going to be another one. But just one thing."

"What?" David asked with a bit of skepticism in his voice.

"Could we still do a little bit of background investigation so to speak?"

"Have at it," David said.

"Well, I was sort of hoping you would do that," Eliana said holding her left index finger in front of her mouth and smiling.

"Me! Why me?"

"Because it would be difficult for me to do it from the Academy, and because lawyers do that sort of thing."

"Lawyers may do that, or at least have someone do it for them, but I am not a lawyer, I am a law student, and one with some really tough courses this semester."

"Ooookay," Eliana said, sounding rather resigned. David didn't say anything, but she knew he would at least do a token search.

They walked to the end of the pool where Nathan was still swimming and splashing around with some other boys his age. Sarah was sitting on the edge of the pool having a conversation with a young boy close to her own age.

"You two ready to go?" David asked as he and Eliana neared the end of the pool.

Nathan didn't answer. Either he didn't hear David or he chose not to hear him. Selective hearing was an art form with Nathan. Sarah on the other hand gave a resounding, "No."

"Well, too bad," David continued, "the proctors are leaving the arena and their 'subjectees' must follow."

When David and Eliana got to where Sarah was sitting, she stood up and said, "This is my new friend 'Toby,' and these two older people are my cousins."

Toby was apparently well mannered, because he stood and extended his hand, first to Eliana, who took it, and then to David who did likewise.

Sarah made no more objections, and then in a harsh voice, yelled to her brother, "NATHAN, come on, we're going."

Nathan well understood the meaning, or at least the inflection of the last call; he got out of the pool and fell in line.

As they started to leave, Toby turned to Sarah and said, "Nice talking to you, Sarah."

"It was nice talking to you too, Toby," Sarah said in a lady like fashion.

"I think it is time we get Sarah out of town," David said to Eliana with a wink.

"Why?" Sarah asked.

"Because I see a budding romance coming on," David continued.

"Oh, don't be silly, David," Sarah said and kicked at him intentionally missing. Then she continued, "But you don't need to tell my mom."

"We won't," Eliana said, but I don't think your mom would care, seeing as you had two of the best chaperones and Toby seemed like a very nice young man."

"Yes, he is. His mom works here and she sometime lets him swim for an hour after she gets off work," Sarah said.

"That is nice," Eliana continued.

"Yes, it is. His mom and dad are divorced. He doesn't get to see his father, but he didn't tell me why."

"That is sad then," Eliana continued.

"Yes, that too," Sarah said with a sigh.

They walked the rest of the way back to their rooms in silence. Nathan was bringing up the rear and dragging his towel behind him. David turned to wait for him, and guessed that two minutes after he got back to his room, Nathan would be zonked out.

He gave him one minute too much.

While the kids were at the pool, Sylvie and Cheryl discussed how to go about settling their father's estate. They didn't anticipate any problems since there were no major assets besides the house, and they knew their father had left a will. The state police investigating the accident had not released their findings yet, but indications were that it was mutual fault, brought on by natural cause, meaning the effects of the tornado.

They decided to change their original plans and head back as soon as possible. Cheryl would take Eliana and David back to their respective schools, and Patrick would go ahead and fly home. Sylvie and Kevin would go back to Kentucky, and then Sylvie would continue on to Pensacola where Cheryl would meet her after dropping David off at Gainesville. Sylvie said that on the way home, she would contact the lawyer who was the executor of their father's will and see what was the earliest she could set up a meeting for reading the will.

Kevin reminded them that it was possible she couldn't do it on such short notice, and they might want to confirm it before they both headed to Pensacola. Until the will was read, nothing could be removed from the premises. Sylvie agreed with her husband, but said there were other matters that need to be attended to that might require immediate attention. For one thing, they would need to contact a realtor to handle the sale of the house when the time came. Also, since an inventory of belongings would have to be made, perhaps they could get a key and put things in order.

Kevin said he wasn't sure what she meant by putting things in order because Jacob was generally quite organized.

"Don't worry Kevin, Cheryl and I are not going to go there and get into a fight over who gets what. After he took care of all of mother's things with us, he said he would make a list of what personal items of his he wanted each of us to have, and what each grandchild should have. He has nothing of great value, and never put much personal value on any of his possessions, except for a few things the grandkids gave him over the years, and those should go back to the giver. To that we all agree, I believe," Sylvie said in finality.

"Yeah, I don't think there will be any difficulties," Cheryl agreed.

"I will call Wesley first thing in the morning and tell him of our revised plans," Sylvie said.

"Yeah, that is a great idea." Cheryl said.

Chapter 57

At about 10:30 a.m. the next morning, just southwest of Columbus, Ohio, Kevin pulled off of I-71 to gas up. Sylvie took the time to place a call to Cynthia Pappas, Jacob's attorney and the administrator of his will. Her secretary answered on the first ring. She said that Mrs. Pappas was out of the office at the present time, but if she would give her a telephone number where she could be reached and the purpose for her call, Mrs. Pappas would return her call as soon as possible when she returned.

Sylvie told her it had to do with her father's will, and she gave her both her cell phone number and her home number, just in case they got home before Mrs. Pappas had a chance to return the call.

The secretary offered Sylvie her condolences and said they had received a copy of the death certificate from the director of the funeral home.

They had just crossed the Ohio River at Cincinnati, and were now in Kentucky when Sylvie's cell phone beeped. It was Cynthia Pappas.

After Sylvie had said hello, the lawyer identified herself. "Hello, This is Cynthia Pappas. My secretary told me what this is about, so permit me to say that I was greatly saddened by the news of your father's tragic death."

"Thank you," Sylvie said.

"Your father and I go back quite a ways. We were a bit more than just attorney-client. He made me some Navy uniforms just before he sold the business. He started making uniforms for me about fifteen years ago when

I was on active duty. I stayed in the Navy Reserves, thus the need for more uniforms several years ago."

"That is very interesting," Sylvie said. "I guess he chose you as his administrator to give you a chance to get some of your money back."

"It is so interesting that you should say that. When I went to his shop several years ago to order the last set of uniforms, I told him he had made uniforms for me a long time ago. He asked me my name, and I said, 'Pappas, but it was Dixon back then'. And he said, 'Oh yeah, Cynthia, is that right?' I was dumbfounded that he remembered after so many years. He went to his file cabinet and pulled out my sheet from all those years previous. Anyway, how can I help you today?" she asked.

"Well," Sylvie began, "my sister Cheryl and I were wondering what would be the soonest we could meet with you to have a reading of the will, or what ever the normal procedure is in matters like this. Both of us live quite a ways from Pensacola."

"Your father's will is pretty simple, so you tell me when you can both be here, and I will see if I can fit you in."

"We were hoping for Friday," Sylvie said.

"Ouch! Friday is not a good day. I have court on Friday morning and was hoping to go to Tallahassee in the afternoon to see my son's high school football game. Tell you what, could you make it Saturday morning?"

"Sure, Saturday would be fine. We just didn't want to inconvenience you."

"It is no inconvenience for me, and I seem to feel I owe it to your father in some way. If I recall, he did my uniforms on short notice. How about, say 10:00 a.m. That will give you a chance to have breakfast without rushing. Do you know where my office is?"

"Yes, your secretary gave it to us. I am sure we can find you."

"Okay then, I will be looking to meet you and your sister on Saturday."

Sylvie thanked her, terminated the call, and punched the button for Cheryl's cell phone.

When she reached Cheryl by cell phone, they had already dropped Eliana off at the Naval Academy and were headed south on Old National Highway 301. They would stay on 301 to just south of Fredericksburg where they would pick up I-95 and head toward Jacksonville, Florida.

Sylvie told Cheryl about her discussion with Cynthia Pappas and the arrangement to have the will read on Saturday morning.

They agreed to travel to Pensacola on Thursday as they had previously planned. The tourist season would be over and the snowbirds wouldn't be arriving for several weeks, so perhaps they could get a good rate at a Motel on the beach. They could track each other's travel progress by cell phone, and the first one there would select the motel. Friday they could relax a bit and check out realtors and temporary storage facilities.

Chapter 58

When Cheryl got to Fort Walton, she gave her sister a call. Sylvie was just north of Montgomery, Alabama, which meant Cheryl would get to Pensacola Beach first by at least an hour and a half.

"Okay," Cheryl said, " I'll get us a room. Call me when you get to Cantonment and I will tell you where we are staying."

"I will do that. By the time I get there, I should be starting to get really hungry. I thought maybe we could go to McGuire's."

"I was thinking seafood, but we can do that on Friday. Old Catholic tradition," Cheryl said with a laugh.

"See you in a little bit."

"Okay."

A half hour later, Cheryl crossed the bridge onto Santa Rosa Island at Navarre. It had been quite a few years since she had traveled that part of Highway 98, and she couldn't believe the amount of development. The same was true as she looked towards where the Gulf of Mexico should have been on the far end of the bridge. The view of the beach was completely blocked by high-rise condominiums and motels. She knew the same would probably be true at Pensacola Beach; the only respite would be a few miles through the National Seashore Park.

When she got to Pensacola Beach, she saw a sign for the Hilton and decided that would do for their stay, but when she made the left turn, she saw she had passed the entrance for that motel and as was now in front of the Hampton Inn. "What the heck," she thought to herself, "it didn't make any difference, and so the Hampton Inn it would be."

Cheryl checked in and told the young man who waited on her that her sister would be joining her in about an hour. He gave her two key cards and asked if she needed assistance with her bags. She told him she wouldn't be bringing her bags in until later, and if she needed assistance she would call at the desk at that time.

As she started to leave the check-in counter, she turned back to the young man and said in a questioningly manner, "This room is Gulf side?"

"Yes, ma'am," the young man replied.

"Thanks, good work," she replied.

"Thanks, and you are welcome," was his reply.

The lobby area in front of the elevators was empty. Cheryl punched the up button and the doors to the elevator slid open immediately. She entered and punched the button for the seventh floor. Once inside the room, she threw her purse on the bed and went to the balcony. The view of the Gulf was spectacular. She went back inside and opened the door of the small refrigerator. She took out a can of Sprite, retrieved a glass from the stand, and went back out on the balcony to await Sylvie's call. So much had happened in the past week, and she knew that it wasn't over yet, but for now, she would just sit here and savor the quiet and the warm breeze wafting in off the gulf waters. She looked down the beach to her right and saw the fishing pier. She remembered the times when her parents brought her and her sister here to frolic in the surf. It was a long time ago, but only a moment ago in the back recesses of her mind. She took a drink of the soda, set the can and the glass on the small table by her chair, closed her eyes, and for a short time, escaped into joyous oblivion.

She was brought out of that state of oblivion by the sound of soft chimes. It took her a moment to recognize what it was and where she was. It was her cell phone and she was sitting on the balcony of a motel a long way from home. She checked her watch as she reached for her cell phone; she had dozed off for forty-five minutes. She was sure this would be Sylvie calling. She punched the button and said, "Hello."

"Hi. I assume you got there," was Sylvie's reply.

"Yes, about an hour ago. We are staying at the Hampton Inn with a beautiful view of the Gulf."

"Great. I am ready to kick back and just relax."

"I know what you mean sister. Where are you?"

"Right now I am at the light in Cantonment by the paper mill. The light has just changed to green so I am proceeding south."

"Listen, Sylvie, instead of coming out to the beach and then going back to McGuire's, why don't I just leave here now and meet you there?"

"That makes a lot of sense. See you there."

It being a Thursday, and most of the tourist crowd having departed the area, there was no waiting line outside of McGuire's restaurant. However, Cheryl waited outside on one of the benches for Sylvie to arrive. She sat there no more than five minutes when she saw Sylvie come off the I-110 ramp and turn north for two blocks on 9th Avenue.

Although they had just seen each other the day before, the two sisters embraced and then entered the bistro. They were seated immediately.

The hostess seated them, placed menus on the table in front of them and said their waiter person would be along momentarily. And as promised, a young lady came with two glasses of water and introduced herself as Brea.

"Can I get you something to drink while you peruse the menu?" Brea asked.

"It has been a long boring day, and I think I can have one glass of wine and still drive the remaining four miles, so yes, I would like a grass of chardonnay," Sylvie said.

"Make that two glasses of chardonnay," Cheryl said.

" I will do that posthaste," Brea answered.

"We are in no big hurry, so at your leisure will be just fine," Sylvie said to the waitress with a smile.

"Yeah, that will give us time to look over the menu, although I think I know what I want," Cheryl commented.

"Right," Brea said as she departed towards the bar to get their wine order.

"So what are you thinking of having?" Sylvie asked.

"If we are going to a seafood restaurant tomorrow, I thought I would have McGuire's prime rib."

"That sounds like an excellent idea."

The waitress returned in a short time with their drink order. "Have you had sufficient time to make your selection?" Brea asked.

"We have. We will both have the prime rib. I would like mine medium well," Cheryl said.

"I will have mine medium rare," Sylvie continued.

"And what size portion?" Brea asked.

"The king cut," Cheryl said in all seriousness.

Brea looked at her with a surprised expression, then Cheryl laughed and said, "Just kidding of course. I remember that this restaurant is famous for it's large portions. I am sure the twelve ounce cut will be more than sufficient, especially if I am to have room for the bread pudding with the Irish whiskey sauce."

"And you, madam?"

"The same. Before you go, may I ask you something?" Sylvie asked.

"Most certainly. What is it you would like to ask?"

"Are you taking a communication or journalism course in college at this time?"

Brea smiled, "Yes, but why do you ask?"

"Oh, just your choice of words like peruse and posthaste. Most waitresses would not use those words."

"That is a very astute observation on your part. My professors said we should practice using other than the common forms. I hope I didn't sound too ostentatious."

"Only if you had said perspicacious instead of astute," Sylvie said.

To which Brea just replied, "Touché."

"Don't mind my sister," Cheryl said "We each have a daughter with similar traits. We are used to it."

"That is very interesting," Brea said as she left to turn in their order.

As they waited for their dinner to be served, Cheryl and Sylvie planned their itinerary for Friday and Saturday. On Friday they would need to contact a realtor, rent a temporary storage facility, and then go to the house and start some form of appraisal of what to do with their father's possessions. First they would have to call Cynthia and see if she knew where they could get a key.

They saw Brea returning with their dinner, so they cut the conversation off at that point.

They ate in silence and Brea checked back from time to time to see if she could be of assistance. A thing good servers do if they hope to deserve a good tip.

When they had finished, Brea asked if they would like to have their bread pudding with whiskey sauce and coffee.

Both decided they were too full for dessert at this time, but each would take an order of the famous bread pudding to go. Brea obliged and went to bring the dessert order and their bill.

Back at the motel on the beach, Cheryl and Sylvie took their clothes bag and overnight bag from their respective vehicles and went to their room. Once inside, Sylvie looked around and then went out onto the balcony. The sun had set and it was nearly dark, but the lights from the high-rise motels cast enough light to see the surf roll in and break up into foamy white suds, recede and then be met by the next wave.

"I am tired, but a bit too wound up to go to sleep. Not to mention still too full from dinner. What do you say, we go down and sit on the deck by the edge of the sand, have a glass of wine, and listen to the waves break on the beach," Sylvie asked.

"That sounds like an excellent idea," Cheryl said.

They went by the outside bar and each ordered a glass of chardonnay. Then they found a small table at the edge of the deck closest to the sand and sat down.

"So how was the trip from Pennsylvania back to Louisville?" Cheryl asked her sister.

"Long and boring, but I should not complain, seeing that yours was twice as long," Sylvie said.

"Yeah, it was a pretty long trip. I suppose the fact of losing their Pappap finally set in with David and Eliana as they were both unusually quiet on the way back. Eliana especially. I asked her if anything was bothering her that she wanted to talk about, and she said, 'No, perhaps later.'"

"David did open up a little a couple of hours down the road after we had dropped Eliana off at the Academy. He asked what I thought about Father Donaldson, but the thing was he didn't say Father Donaldson, he said Wesley. I didn't think much about that at the time, but on my way over here this morning, I kept rolling it around in my mind, but I couldn't come up with any particular reason why that would seem strange to me."

"So what did you say to him?" Sylvie asked.

"About the same thing you said to me when I asked you the same question when we left the church after the funeral. I said I didn't know. He seemed like a very nice person, and apparently he and Dad became good friends in a short amount of time. As a priest, he was probably a good listener and Dad found someone to listen to his tales about Hexie and the hills. Then I asked him what he thought about him."

"And."

"And, he said he found him to be very likable, but a bit evasive. Especially when he first talked to him in the cemetery. I asked him to explain, and he said it was nothing he could put his finger on, just a feeling. Then he said he and Eliana talked about it when they were watching Sarah and Nathan at the pool. He said Eliana had picked up on some things that Wesley had said at the church and she had formed some opinions. He said he told her he thought she was reading too much into it. I asked him to be more specific, and he said he couldn't, it was something Eliana would have to tell me when and if she was ready. I said, 'Come on David, tell me'. He said he couldn't, and asked me to please accept his position on this. Sensing he did not want to betray his sister's trust, I dropped the subject, and nothing more was said about it for the rest of the trip. However, I did remember when we had the similar conversation. I had said that maybe he would enlighten us, to which you said…"

"I said, 'And if not,'" Sylvie cut in.

"Exactly, and I said, 'I will have to ask some nosy questions, but the only nosy question I asked was why he hadn't blacktopped his driveway. Some great sleuth I am.

"Well, I am a bit like David I guess, I think we are making too much of a good thing. You know that Dad was a loner in many respects, but he loved to expound on his own favorite subjects. I think he just found a listener who liked to hear what Dad liked to talk about."

"You are probably right, Sylvie."

"Good. Now that you accept that, I will tell you that Sarah had her own suspicions."

Oh, great!" Cheryl said, "Please do tell."

"Well, when we stopped at a rest area in Ohio, she and I were walking to the rest room and she said to me, 'Mommy, I think Pappap and Father Donaldson must have been very good friends.' I told her that I thought that was probably true, but why did she say that. She said, 'Well, when the men had put the last of the dirt on Pappap's grave, I walked over and picked up some dirt and sprinkled it on his grave. I saw that in a movie one time, and I thought it was nice.' It was very nice, but please go on.

Then she said, 'Then Father Donaldson came over and did the same thing. He did the sign of the cross, and said, 'Goodbye Friend,' but he didn't say it quite like that. I asked her how he did say it and she said, 'Well he said that, but he said goodbye, and then he waited for a long time to say friend. It was as if he was searching for another word besides friend, but could not find it. Anyway, he had tears on his cheeks, so I told him to come along with me and he did.'"

"What did you say to Sarah then?" Cheryl asked.

"I said that he and Pappap had become very good friends, so if he had tears on his cheeks, he was probably a bit emotional and had to control his voice before he said friend."

"And she accepted that?"

"For the most part. She did say that it was the first time she had ever seen a priest cry. I told her that I thought Father Donaldson was a very sensitive man. He was shedding a tear as a man, not necessarily as a priest."

"So then she accepted that?"

"She said, 'Whatever,' and we left it at that."

"Would you like another glass of wine?" Cheryl asked.

"I don't think so, but I could probably eat that bread pudding by now. Why don't we see if the coffee shop is still open and get some coffee."

"No need to do that, the room has a well-stocked little pantry with plenty of coffee and the fixings. They even have a microwave oven so we can heat it up."

Chapter 59

By 11:00 a.m. on Friday, the sisters had discussed business with a realtor, talked with a temporary storage facility manager, and located a key to the house. They had the garage door opener that had been found at the wreck, but once inside the garage, they found the door leading into the kitchen was also locked. It took them another forty-five minutes to contact the security service and get authorization to enter the house. Their father had left very specific instructions relating to procedures to follow after his death, but he neglected to tell them who had a spare key to the house, and what the security code and password was.

Once inside, they walked through the entire house and found it to be immaculate, just like when their mother was living. Although they knew that their father liked everything to be orderly and clean, he was not so thorough in dusting and vacuuming. From all indications, the house-cleaning lady had been there not long before he left or perhaps even after he had left.

Seeing that the rest of the house was in good order, they determined the place they needed to start was his office. They needed to see if he had left any specific instructions. They also needed copies of any of his insurance policies and the deed to the property.

He had left the folding table set up, but it was cleared of all papers. Eventually they would also have to get onto his computer. There may be bills that would have to be paid, and they would have to see what his financial status was. He had given them the password to his computer, but they could have guessed it. He hadn't changed it in many years. It was an acronym formed by letters from his grandchildren's names. They knew that he paid most of his bills online, so what they did not have were the passwords for these accounts. He might have set them up through PayPal or through NFCU, but in either case they did not know the password. These were matters that probably would have to be handled by the administrator of his will.

Most of the books and personal items they would box and put into temporary storage, but they couldn't do anything until the will had been read and they saw what he had designated for any of them.

Cheryl sat in front of his computer and opened the two-drawer file cabinet by the side of his desk. The top drawer contained hanging files and a quick view through them showed they were mostly correspondence and research related files. In the bottom drawer were two accordion folders, each with twelve slots that were marked with different colored tabs. They contained the receipts of paid bills, but upon inspecting them they found no current receipts. Apparently, he was paying everything online. Back of this was a small metal box that contained his checkbook. It, too, showed that no checks were being written for normal reoccurring bills. There was a calendar on the wall by his desk that showed the date when bills were to be paid. She assumed he did this so he could check his balance online and make payments that varied from month-to-month, such as his cell phone bill.

Sylvie had gone into the walk-in closet that he had converted to a library storage area. She stood and surveyed the contents and thought to herself, "Oh, where to begin." One wall contained five shelves. The top three held loose leaf note books, all related to family research. The fourth shelf contained mostly stacks of newspapers, and magazines. The bottom shelf contained an assortment of books, even some old textbooks going back to his college days. Under the bottom shelf were two office file boxes containing many years of unsorted photographs.

A large bookcase, over six feet tall, covered most of the back wall. On top of the bookcase was an assortment of framed photographs, and actually hanging on the wall, just below the ceiling, were senior high school pictures of both her and Cheryl.

The first two shelves on the left-hand side of the bookcase contained books dealing with Islam, including a copy of the Koran and a nine-volume set of the Hadith of Bukhari. There were perhaps thirty or more books by a variety of authors who expounded on the dangers of this religion and the militant Muslims. After the events of September 11, 2001, he started to study the religion and the Muslim culture in depth. He saw the religion as a problem mostly because most non-Muslims knew almost nothing about the religion; the Muslims themselves were very good at presenting a distorted image that put non-Muslims at ease. He had written many letters to the opinion editors of the newspapers trying to alert people to the dangers and get them interested in reading for their own good. Mostly, to no avail.

The third shelf contained mostly books about Christianity. The bottom shelf and the top two on the right contained books about history and current political views, both liberal and conservative. The remainder of the bookcase contained mostly works of fiction.

Just inside the door on the left was a four-drawer file cabinet and above that were two shelves that extended the length of the wall. These were filled with many years of National Geographic Magazines. They would later find many more in the garage, he had started collecting them in 1964. Also on one of the shelves were two regular usage Bibles, one Catholic, one Protestant. There were three other Bibles, one a large print version that belonged to his father before his death. If you looked very carefully, you could see silver hairs protruding from the pages. In the years before his death when his eyesight was failing, his father would sit at the table and read with his face almost touching the page, and on occasion, he would fall asleep with his head resting on the Bible, thus the silver hairs. His mother had given him the Bible after his father's funeral, and when he brought it back and looked at it, he found the silver hairs extending from the closed pages. Inside, at several places he found an array of bookmarkers. In II Kings, Chapter 7, he also found an unfinished crossword puzzle from the Sunday paper of September 14, 1988. His father didn't die until July 11, 1989. He left it where he had found it.

There were also two songbooks and several books of poetry on the back shelf. There was also a book entitled, "Coal Dust on the Fiddle," and on the inside cover in his handwriting was a post-it that read, "Maxine's book."

467

Below the two shelves and to the right of the file cabinet hung a framed bulletin board. The top portion contained various size frames for photographs. It was filled with photos of the grandkids. Below that he had tacked an old 1860's map of the area where he was born and raised, and it was partially covered with the street plan of the old coal mine town of Humbert. The wall also held the early art work of the grandkids, and one charcoal sketch done by Eliana in her early teen years.

Just inside the door to the left, at the height of the top shelf, hung an antique oak frame, which caught Sylvie's attention. The white oak wood had been stained a very dark color. The glass was broken and the top portion had been removed. It contained a poem that had been copied in a nice calligraphic hand. The poem itself was placed behind a dark bronze, heavy paper with an oval cut out to show only the words of the poem. A gold gilded border surrounded the cut out. Cheryl heard her sister exclaim, "Oh, my gosh."

"What?" was Cheryl's reply.

"Here is a framed poem that I gave dad for Christmas many years ago. I think it was after I got out of the Air Force and was finishing my degree. I didn't have much money, so knowing our father was sentimental; I thought he might like it. I envisioned it might someday fit his thoughts, and I think I was right.

"Read it," came Cheryl's reply.

"It is entitled, "Simplicity" and goes like this:
I've walked along this road for a long time now
I know I'll have to turn somewhere
Or perhaps, to turn back to my beginnings
Along the way the leaves have fallen off of me
So I walk this road with only the bare bark of my own winter
It's the last that is left of me and, the best.

"I guess you are right," Cheryl said. "I can see a lot of him in that also. But back to our task at hand. I don't find anything of importance in this small file cabinet so it must be in there."

"His main briefcase is here on the floor, so why don't you go through it and I will go check out this file cabinet," Sylvie said.

"Okay, bring it here."

Sylvie took the briefcase and set it on the folding table where Cheryl sat. She returned to the closet library and pulled out the top drawer. She started to go through the contents, which looked like it contained mostly the copies and research records for articles he had written.

Cheryl had opened the briefcase, which was not locked and almost immediately realized this was what they were looking for. "I think we have it here," she said to her sister.

"Good," Sylvie answered. "You sort it out and I will continue to check for anything of importance here. With that, she opened the second drawer. "This could be interesting," she said.

"What did you find?" Cheryl asked.

"There are folders here for each of us and for our children. There is also one here marked for Wesley Donaldson."

"Oh," Cheryl said, "let me see mine," as she rose from her place at the table and joined her sister in front of the file cabinet.

Sylvie had already pulled her folder out and opened it to look through the contents. The first thing she saw was a short letter addressed directly to her.

It started:

Dear daughter Sylvie,

Since the day of your birth, I have saved a few things that relate specifically to you. They are not of any value, but they have always been priceless to me, as was your birth. I thank the Good Lord for sending you my way. These bits of memorabilia were simply my way of tagging different stages of your life for my own post recollections. A lot has been lost or misplaced along the way, but I wanted you to have these scraps of paper. Perhaps they will remind you of some of the good times we had together, or God forbid, the lectures. HA! HA! Use them to tell my grandkids a good tale about me; some embellishment is permitted. But most important, know always that I love you.

Your father

Cheryl opened her folder and found the exact same letter addressed to her.

"It looks like it contains mostly memorabilia that applied to us when we were younger," Sylvie said.

"Yeah, here is something I may want to hide from David and Eliana," Cheryl said.

"What is that?"

"Some old report cards. Oh and look at this, a report I had to write for him one time when I didn't do something I was supposed to."

"Really," Sylvie said. "I have one of those also. I will let you read mine, it you let me read yours."

"Okay, here," Cheryl said as they swapped papers.

The two sisters read in silence and then Sylvie said, "I think we had to write these at about the same time. It sounds like you had some candy or donuts to sell as a class project. Also you must have been told to watch something on the stove and went outside to play instead."

Cheryl didn't say anything as she continued to read. Cheryl's letter was one page, whereas Sylvie had written three pages. She included a cover page, and a blank back page. The pages were punched for insertion into a loose-leaf binder. Two red ribbons, neatly tied, ran through holes at the side to hold it all together. When Cheryl had finished reading, she said, "Boy, you were a bit obstinate. Did he accept it when you gave it to him?"

"I don't remember everything exactly, in fact I will have to re-read it to see what I did say."

"Here, have at it while I re-read mine."

Cheryl laughed as she read what she had written many years before. "I assume they were written at about the same time, as yours is much better composed than mine. You were probably in eight grade and I was in fourth."

"Boy," Sylvie finally said, "That sounds exactly like something my daughter Sarah might write. I suppose I was too old, or I might have gotten a spanking."

"I doubt that, as Dad didn't do too much of that. Read your next to last paragraph about receiving a lecture, and it will bear that out. Remember, we used to say; we would rather have the spanking than the lecture."

"I don't remember saying I would rather have the spanking, but I do remember the lectures," Sylvie said.

"You probably don't remember it, because you never got into as much trouble as I did, but that is the past, and of course, you and I have never lectured our children thusly," Cheryl said.

Both sisters laughed.

"Why don't you check out the folder marked for Wesley, while I go through the rest of the briefcase," Cheryl said.

"Okay."

The folder marked Wesley Donaldson was fairly thick, actually thicker than any of theirs. Sylvie laid it on top of the file cabinet and started to look through the contents. On the top of the stack was an unfolded letter similar to that in their own folders and the ones he had for his grandchildren, except it was dated, theirs were not. It was dated just three weeks previous.

It began:

Dear Wesley,

If you are reading this, it means that I have gone to call upon my maker and I assume my daughters will ensure you receive it.

I consider finding you as a real miracle, and the fact that you have taken an interest in the area that I love has been especially gratifying. I hope that I haven't bored you or caused you to express an interest in things, just because they were of interest to me.

I am compiling a list of my papers and research notebooks that I would like you to have. These are mostly working papers that I have compiled over the years. I have already given you copies of most of my stories and reports, so these papers represent the who, when and where of those reports. If you find no use for them, sort out anything you think the local historical societies might like to peruse and pass them along. They can use them or dispose of them as they see fit.

I am enclosing a rough table of contents, but I am not sure how much of a help that will be. As you know from doing all your own research, the person doing the hunting and recording simply knows where it is located. Although in recent times, I seem to have more difficulty in finding things that I was sure I had placed in a specific folder. Age has its price to pay, I suppose. Ha! Ha!

Jacob

Under the letter, Sylvie found three pages listing the binders that were placed on the opposite shelves along with a brief rundown of their contents. Next there were several plastic protectors for three-ring binders that contained two CD disc each. At the bottom of the stack was a letter. It was addressed to her father, Jacob Grant. The return address was from a DNA laboratory in Ft Walton Beach, Florida. The postmark was just three weeks previous.

"Come here, Cheryl. See what you make of this."

Sylvie handed her sister the letter and she looked at it. "So what do you make of it?" Cheryl asked.

"I don't know. Do you think we should open it?"

"Your call. Do you think he put it in here by mistake?" Cheryl asked again.

"I don't know that either," was Sylvie's reply.

" Let me grab my cell phone from my purse."

"Who are you going to call?" Sylvie asked.

"My daughter. I want to ask her what she picked up on at the funeral that the rest of us missed.

"You think she will tell you."

"She has to. She is my daughter."

"Uh huh," was all Sylvie said as she watched Cheryl punch the button for Eliana's cell phone.

Eliana's phone rang three times and then Cheryl heard the following message: "I cannot answer your call at this time. If you wish to leave me a message or have me return your call, please so indicate." Then Cheryl heard another recording before the beep prompt. "Note for Friday. I will be out of touch until approximately 10:30 p.m."

"Dang," Cheryl exclaimed. "Okay, I will just have to put some pressure on David and see if he will give me more information."

"Ah!" Cheryl said as David picked up on the second ring.

She explained the situation and what she and Sylvie had found. Then she heard David's reply. "Mom, I am sorry I can't tell you anymore until I speak to Eliana. I gave her my word, and you always told us to honor our promises. However, there are some things you might try. First, can you access his computer?"

"I don't know. We haven't tried, but I would assume so, but why?" his mother asked.

"You said the return address was from a lab in Fort Walton Beach. It is possible that he found it through the internet, so if you can access his computer, check out his history and see if he contacted the web page of that lab."

"Your are so smart, son. I am glad to see that money your father and I contribute to your higher education is showing results," Cheryl said.

"Mom."

"Yes, son."

"The money you and dad send me I generally use for partying. I pay my tuition with money I make from my part time jobs."

"Right. Goodbye, son."

"Bye, Mom. I love you."

"Love you too," Sylvie heard Cheryl say as she closed out the call.

"So what did he say, for you to pay him such a compliment?" Sylvie asked.

"Let me turn on the computer and I will show you."

Cheryl hit the power button and the computer started to boot up. When the password box opened up, she typed in, 'daelsana.' There were chimes and the desktop opened up.

He had configured his opening screen to show a flashing icon if he had mail in his box. She was sure it would probably be pretty full, but she decided to open it before she checked the history. She reasoned that going through the history might be a bit time consuming because they didn't know how far back they might have to check. Cheryl clicked the blinking mailbox and was surprised to get less than a full page of e-mails.

The very first letter caught her attention. The subject line was, further tests, and the sender was a Dr. Anderson. Who was Dr. Anderson? She knew that his regular doctor was Dr. Cantrell. She clicked on the button marked, 'read,' and then started to do just that. Sylvie was looking over her shoulder, and neither said a word as they read the two paragraphs in amazement. When Cheryl had finished, she twisted in the chair, looked at Sylvie, and then said, "He didn't tell us that he had cancer. I can't believe it."

"Oh, knowing our father, I can believe it," Sylvie said. "He probably figured that if he told us, we would worry, which of course we would have."

"That may be true, but I still feel we had a right to know."

"Well, our feelings may be hurt, but at this point I can't say I am surprised. You know he never complained much and didn't always tell mother about his aches and pains.

"Okay," Cheryl continued, "we will just have to contact Dr. Anderson and see what the story is. In the meantime, since we are in his mailbox, lets see if there is anything else of interest."

She scrolled down through all the entries and saw nothing else that caught their attention.

"We might as well go ahead and do a history search," Sylvie said. "His having cancer would have nothing to do with a DNA testing lab. But I have been thinking, the last time he came back from Pennsylvania and stopped in Louisville, he did say he was working on an idea for a book. He didn't say what it was about, but he may have been doing research, and contacted them for information."

"That is plausible, I suppose," Cheryl said. "When was that, because it might give us a start date for checking his computer history?"

"Let me see. I don't remember the exact date, but it must have been at least two months ago," Sylvie said.

"Two months," Cheryl exclaimed. "I doubt if his computer will let me access history that far back." And she was right. When she got to where she wanted to be, she could only access the last four weeks. She clicked on that anyway. "Okay, as our waitress said, let's peruse what we have here."

As they read down the screen, there wasn't anything that indicated a pattern for research. And when Cheryl started to scroll down, they were surprised to find that there was only half of a second screen remaining on the history file.

"Doesn't seem like he was doing much searching on the internet during the past month," Sylvie said.

"You are right. I wonder if it may have had something to do with his cancer treatment."

"Maybe so. Just per chance, why don't you click on his documents file and see what comes up."

Cheryl did as her sister had instructed. There was nothing on the main window that appeared of interest so she clicked on the drop down box in My Documents that showed the different drives. On the CD write drive she saw a title, Innocent Indiscretions. She clicked on it and it opened in Word. The first page showed the title close to the top and several lines below that was typed, "A novel by Jacob Grant." The bottom information bar showed they were on page 1 of an 88-page document.

"This must have been the last project he was working on," Cheryl said.

"I wonder what the indiscretion was?" Sylvie asked.

"If he was like most authors, you probably don't find that out until the very end, but it could have to do with something that required he know something about DNA." Then Cheryl continued, "Should we print this off and give it a quick review when we get back to the motel?"

"Might as well," Sylvie said.

As soon as David and his mother had finished their conversation, he went to his computer and sent Eliana an e-mail. "Dear Sister," he wrote. "Good news and bad news. Good news is that a friend of a friend is from Youngstown, Ohio, and his mother is a historical and genealogical nut. He took the little bit of information I could give him and sent it to his mother. He assures me that if there is anything there, she will find it. Now for the bad news, Mom is trying to get in touch with you to pressure you in to telling her of your suspicions. She and Aunt Sylvie are in Pensacola and were going through Pappap's papers. They found an unopened letter from a DNA testing lab in Ft Walton. It had been placed in a folder marked for Wesley Donaldson. So you can either try to evade her for a few days, which is not going to be easy, or you can prepare an answer for when she does get in touch with you. I didn't get to talk to Aunt Sylvie, but it may just be that they have a suspicion similar to yours. Based on what I just told you, you might want to call her first. If it were I, I would call her very early in the morning just to get her attention. Don't tell her I said that, and check in with me when you can.

David."

Before Cheryl and Sylvie left their father's house, they packed the personal folders into an empty office storage box that he had in the closet. "Should we take the one that belongs to Wesley?" Sylvie asked.

"Sure, why not? We can bring it back tomorrow so it is here when we send him the things that Dad wanted him to have."

They set the alarm system and left via the front door. They planned to go to Fisherman's Cove Restaurant at the Innerarity Point Bridge for dinner.

When they got back to the motel, they each took a soda from the small refrigerator in their room and went out on the balcony to read the pages from their father's uncompleted manuscript.

You go ahead and start scanning the novel and I will go through the papers in Wesley's folder more thoroughly," Cheryl said.

They both pursued their own task for a few minutes and then Cheryl interrupted the silence. "Look here," she said.

"What is it?" Sylvie asked.

"On the list of things he either sent or intended to send to Wesley is, *Innocent Indiscretions*. Doesn't that seem strange to you? I mean the book is only in the early stages of development. Even if he were going to have Wesley edit and proofread it, it seems strange he would give it to him at such an early stage. Don't you agree?"

"Yeah, when I think about it, it seems a bit strange, but our father would often do the unconventional. Besides, we don't know if he gave it to him," was Sylvie's answer.

"But it is on this list in Wesley's file."

Sylvie said nothing to this and then after a log pause, Cheryl continued, " But then again, you may be right. If this list is in the file, and based on the cover letter, it means that he hasn't given any of this to Wesley at this point in time."

"Meaning?"

"Meaning, this was something he wanted Wesley to have, even if it was unfinished at the time of his death," Cheryl said.

"I think you are recalling your Nancy Drew days," Sylvie said with a smile.

"I never read Nancy Drew stories," Cheryl said, "but I still have this feeling. So how does the book start out?"

"It starts out with a young boy, age not yet determined, living in the country. It takes place apparently some years ago and perhaps his family is poor, but too early to say. It could be autobiographical but he could just be calling on things he knew well.

"It starts out pretty interesting. I was just going to scan it, but it drew my interest so I started to read instead of scan. I say we go down by the pool and find more comfortable chairs. That way we can also have the benefit of the hotel staff to bring us a drink."

"Sounds like a good idea to me," Cheryl said.

They left their unfinished sodas sitting on the table and took the elevator down to the pool area. Now comfortably seated by the pool, the two sisters asked the waiter to bring them each a sprite with a twist of lime.

"I have read the first three pages, so you can have them. If you come across anything that strikes your sleuthful mind, don't be afraid to mention it to me."

"Agreed," Cheryl said and started to read: *Dog days it was; that period in early September when the first light frost had not caused the leaves on the sugar maples to turn, the grass to go dormant, or harm the green tomatoes still hanging on the vines. At that time of the year in our part of Southwestern Pennsylvania, the mornings normally start out cool, but by early afternoon they can turn very sultry, and so it was this day where my story begins when I was in my tenth year.*

Cheryl was going to ask her sister if she thought the reference to his tenth year meant his age, or his school year, but felt herself that it was probably intended to mean his age and so she let it pass.

Sylvie would read a page and lay it on the table next to Cheryl. They both read in silence and stayed about two pages apart. A few minutes passed and then Sylvie said, "Ah ha."

"What?" Cheryl asked.

"A young girl enters the picture,' Sylvie said.

"Okay, you stop right there. Let me catch up and then we will take turns reading out loud to each other."

"And what if someone comes and sits at the next table," Sylvie wanted to know.

"We won't be reading that loud, or we could do as my friend Carla would probably say, 'Would y'all mind not sitting there?'"

When Cheryl had finished reading page twelve, she lay the page down and said, "Okay begin."

"Okay, at the beginning of the page he is completing the task his father had told his mother to have him do. He continues: *...I looked up toward the road and saw a horse-drawn wagon approaching the entrance to the path that came down to our house.*

"That could definitely be the old homestead," Cheryl said. "Please continue. Sorry for interrupting."

Sylvie continued reading: *The wagon appeared to be laden with the contents of someone's house; it seemed to me a big load for one horse to pull.*

A woman was leading the horse; she was not riding, perhaps because she, too, felt it was enough of a very heavy load for the animal. A few paces behind the wagon walked a young girl and a boy. The boy seemed to be about my younger brother's age, and I assumed the girl might be my age. The woman stopped the horse and yelled at me.

"Can we get some water for the horse?" she asked.

From the road she could see the small run that meandered down the valley, but I guess she didn't want to cross someone's property without asking. It wasn't our property she would be crossing, but since the path lead to our house, she must have assumed it was our property.

"I'll get my mom," I replied.

"Mom, there is someone here," I yelled as I jumped the banister onto the upper porch.

"Well, who is it?" she asked.

"I don't know. She wants to know if she can get some water for her horse," I answered.

By this time Mom was out on the upper porch and walking toward the yard.

Again the woman called out, "Hello Missus, can we get some water for the horse?"

"Of course," Mom replied. "Do you need a bucket?"

"No we have a bucket. Every time we see water, we get him some. I don't let him drink too much at a time, 'fraid he'll get sick," the woman said.

"How about you and the kids? That run water is okay for the horse, but you better let us get you some from the well," Mom told her without waiting for her to answer the question.

By this time Mom was standing by the bars that were part of the fence separating our property from Chal's. Chal never tilled this land, but he did use it to graze his cattle, thus the fence was necessary.

"You can probably tie the horse to the fence post there and come on down to get some water for yourself," Mom said.

"I'll be okay," she said. "The horse gets pretty skittish when a car passes, so I want to hold on to him."

"Okay, I'll get Jason here to get a bucket and bring some up to you," Mom told her.

"It may be autobiographical, but at least he changed his name," Cheryl cut in.

Sylvie kept on reading.

"It's not necessary. We'll be okay," the woman answered.

"The kids there look like they could stand some," Mom said after taking note of the boy and girl.

By this time the boy and girl were on their way down to the run to get water for the horse. Both were barefooted, but that was normal here in the country at this time of the year. Except for going to church on Sunday, we never wore shoes from the time school was out until we started back in September. So it wasn't the lack of shoes that got mom's attention, but their appearance. They were both pretty fair skinned, but she could tell by the redness of their faces that it wasn't entirely from the effects of sunburn. They looked exhausted; their hair was wet from sweating, and their clothes were pretty ragged and dirty. She didn't know how far they had come, and although their clothes were dirty, they could have been clean this morning. The dirt road by our house was pretty dusty when it hasn't rained recently, so if you are really sweating and several cars pass you throwing up a dust storm, you can look like a mud pie in no time.

"You get a bucket of water and a couple of glasses from the house," mom told me, "I am going up to the road."

By the time I pumped a bucket of water, got glasses and toted it up to the road, the woman was telling mom about their plight. I wasn't much interested in listening, and learned most of it when mom was telling the story to dad at the supper table. I was watching the girl hold the bucket so the horse could drink, but I didn't say anything. Mostly she kept her head down, but once or twice she did glance at me. Once I thought I saw a small twitch of her mouth, but she never said a word.

Mom tried to get more information from the woman, but as she would later tell dad at the supper table, she thought the woman was a bit ashamed of their plight. There was no reason for her to be ashamed, bad fortune can befall anyone. It wasn't as if they had done anything wrong. Her husband had broken his leg and as a result had lost his job. They had been renting the house from the man he worked for, but when he broke his leg, it not being in the line of his work, they had to move. His employer had to hire a new man and his family needed the house. At least the man was considerate enough to let them get most of the remaining things from their garden, and he was going to use his truck to bring the rest of their things up on Saturday. Because her husband's leg was in a splint, he would also ride up with the man on Saturday along with their two older children who had stayed to glean the garden and help load the rest of the stuff on the truck.

Mom asked her if she had any food on the wagon. She said, "Not now, but they had stopped a couple of hours ago down by the covered bridge to eat the sandwiches she had packed. Not to worry," she continued, "all the fruit *and vegetables she had canned would be coming on the truck tomorrow, Saturday."*

"And what about these little ones?" mom asked.

With that, I thought I saw the young girl give mom a bit of a raised eyebrow at being referred to as a 'little ones.' Her dress was too big for her and loose fitting, but like me, she probably wore hand-me-downs. But I noticed that she had breasts; a thing that only recently caught my attention.

"Hold it right there for a second," Cheryl said as she reached for the pages they had already read. She took the first page and read the first paragraph out loud to Sylvie. So what does he mean when he says, 'I was in my tenth year?'"

"He was ten years old," Sylvie said.

"No. Ten-year-old boys, at least back then, did not notice breasts on girls. Besides, he said the girl was probably his age, and ten-year-old girls do not …"

"Okay, I see what you are saying there, Nancy," Sylvie said as a joke, "But what do you think it means?"

"I think he was referring to his tenth year in school. It is probably something that he would have corrected when he re-read his work."

"Continue reading," Cheryl said.

"Would you like to read for awhile?" Sylvie asked.

"No, you read better, I listen better," Cheryl said.

Sylvie just shrugged her shoulders and began to read.

Their name was Nelson, and Mrs. Nelson still had some pride as she was reluctant to accept charity, but with a bit of perseverance, mom convinced her to accept a loaf of fresh baked bread, a half pound of white oleomargarine, and a jar of strawberry preserves.

When mom told dad that they were going to move into the old house below the road at the top of the Barney Kregar Hill, I remember him saying, "That old log house is nearly falling down."

"Okay, I have heard enough for tonight," Cheryl said. "That is exactly where Wesley has built his house."

"You are right again, Nancy. I agree, let us call it a night and sleep on it."

"Just one more thing," Cheryl said.

"Yes."

"You can dispense with the Nancy thing any time."

"Okay, but I thought it was sort of a compliment."

"Compliment accepted. Lets pay the bill and go upstairs."

At ten past five the next morning, Cheryl's cell phone chirped. Somewhat disoriented in the strange room, she had to get her bearings and then find where the chirping was coming from.

Sylvie heard the chirping and said, "Turn off the alarm."

"It is not the alarm. It is my cell phone if I can find it," Cheryl said. When she finally found it, she hit the button and said a very groggy, "Hello."

"Hi, Mom," came a joyful greeting from the other end. "I didn't wake you, did I?"

"Of course not. I just came back from a three-mile walk on the beach."

"Oh, how nice."

"I was being sarcastic Eliana, of course you woke me; it is only a little after five o'clock."

"Oops, sorry. I forgot Pensacola is central time. You want me to call you back later?" Eliana asked.

"Nooooo. I am awake now. Just let me see if I can roust your Aunt Sylvie to make us some coffee."

In the background, Eliana heard a faint, "Forget it" emanating from her aunt Sylvie.

"Tell you what, hang on until I call room service and order some coffee and toast."

Again Eliana heard the faint words from her aunt, "Tell them to make it two orders of toast and some orange juice."

Then she heard her mother say, "Since you are now awake, why don't you call?"

"Okay, I'll call, but put Eliana on the speaker phone. I want to hear what she has to say. And just pass niceties until I finish with room service."

Cheryl pressed the speaker button on her phone and then asked, "So why did you call me?"

"David dropped me an e-mail and said you were trying to get in touch with me."

"I never told him I was trying to get in touch with you,"

Realizing that she had made a slight error, she quickly covered her tracks and said, "Maybe he said you would probably try and get in touch with me." Then she threw in a distracter, "He was the one that said I should call you very early."

"He did, did he? I am going to get that boy."

"He is not a boy anymore Mom."

"I am his mother, he will be a boy as long as I say he is a boy," Cheryl said.

Eliana knew her mother was joking, but said with all seriousness, "Yes, ma'am."

Eliana then heard her aunt say, "Our order is in, go ahead and light the fire."

"What does Aunt Sylvie mean, 'light the fire'?"

Sylvie heard Eliana's question and just smiled.

Cheryl said, "You know your aunt, she speaks in metaphors, this time it must have to do with, Little House on the Prairie. It could have come from Star Trek in which case she would probably have said, 'fire the rockets' or something related."

"So what did you want to talk to me about?" Eliana asked.

"See, there you go again. You called me. What do you want to talk about?"

"Okay, mother, I know when I have been bested. David said you and Aunt Sylvie found a letter at Pappap's from a DNA testing laboratory in Ft Walton, and that he had placed it in a folder for Father Donaldson. What did it say?"

"It was unopened, and we left it that way, but before we go on, you tell me what made you suspicious about Mr. Donaldson. What you and David discussed before we left Somerset."

"I would rather not at this time, mom, if you don't mind. David is trying to get some additional information about Father Donaldson through a contact in Ohio. I would like to see what he gets before I say anything. Please, please, please."

"Okay, I will go along with that, but I will hold off on telling you the theory that Sylvie and I came up with."

"What theory did you and I come up with?" Eliana heard Aunt Sylvie ask.

Cheryl ignored her sister's comment. Then she updated Eliana about what they had discovered in her grandfather's house; the fact of his treatment for cancer and the unfinished novel. After she had briefed Eliana on the portion of the novel she and Sylvie had read the night before, Eliana interrupted her.

"I am familiar with that story, or at least part of it. He must have recently decided to expand on the story and present it as a novel, but he wrote a personal position paper on it about ten or twelve years ago. Did you get to a place where a farmer who lived close by let them pick a couple of rows of potatoes?"

"No," was her mother's reply.

"Well, you will. Pappap didn't necessarily believe you could get to Heaven because of your good works, but he did believe that God would show mercy on whom he wished to show mercy, and any dogma created by man wouldn't change that. He wrote about this family and the farmer to show his position."

"And how old was he at the time?" her mother asked.

"I couldn't say that he recorded that information. It wasn't important to his position paper. The farmer was the focus of his story."

"Do you remember the name of the family?" Cheryl asked.

"It was Nelson, but I remember it only because you mentioned it."

"I see," Cheryl said to her daughter and then continued. "I don't know what is going to happen later on this morning when we meet with dad's estate lawyer, but I will let you know where we go from here. If there are no problems, I will probably go back to Hawaii on Sunday or Monday and let Sylvie take care of the rest. It looks like it is going to be simple enough. Let me know what you hear from David's source."

"I will, but don't hang up just yet. Are you going to finish reading the remainder of his novel before you leave?"

"It depends upon how much time we have. We will take it with us when we go to breakfast. We will try and scan it before we meet with the lawyer."

"Will you give me a call and let me know if you find anything else?" Eliana asked.

"Okay, I can do that. Where can I contact you?"

"Call my cell phone number. I have to supervise some plebes who are working off demerits, and I will be with them until noon. It wasn't my turn; I am just filling in for a friend who is going to the Navy-Pitt football game. Her boyfriend is on the team, but I suppose you know that our team is not very good. Pray for us that we may at least beat Army later on."

"I'll give it a try, but I don't think God has favorites when it comes to football. Of course when you play Notre Dame, you might watch out. So, gotta run hon, take it easy."

"Okay, Mom, I'll do that. And Mom?"

"Yes?"

"What if it turns out that you have a half brother?"

Cheryl hesitated for a long moment and then replied, " I guess I can live with that. Just think, a priest in the family."

"Yeah," Eliana said and then continued with, "Goodbye."

Cheryl turned off her phone and the two sisters looked at each other, but neither said a word.

It was only 6:30 a.m. when Cheryl and Sylvie had showered and dressed.

"We have a lot of time to kill before we meet with attorney Pappas," Cheryl said as they got into the car. "Why don't we head over to the mainland and have breakfast at that place we saw at the foot of Palafox Street. Maybe we can get a table outside and scan the rest of dad's novel," Cheryl said, and then added, "I think Eliana is very eager to see what else he had to say."

"That sounds like a good idea for breakfast," Sylvie said as she got into the passenger's side of the car. " But I think you were a bit cruel in not telling her your theory, or 'our theory' as you put it. And just what is 'our theory'?"

"The same as her's. I just assumed you had the same theory."

"Well, okay, I can go along with that. It is just that..." and Sylvie trailed off.

"Just that, what?" Cheryl asked.

"I don't know, it is hard for me to imagine our father having a..." and again she couldn't finish her thought.

"You mean having sex before he met mother?"

"Of course not. He was a sailor after all. I am not a prude or so naive to believe that he never had sex before marriage, but I just can't see him fathering a child."

"In the first place, dear sister, we don't know for sure that he did, and in the second place, even if he did we do not know the circumstance. I always thought I was the conservative-minded one of the two of us, but I know this, when I die, there are some things in my life that I would rather that my children never knew, but if it is revealed, I would hope that I have raised them with enough gumption so that they would understand."

"Of course you are right," Sylvie said. "But let me ask you this question. If Wesley was his illegitimate son, do you think he knew?"

Cheryl took a deep breath, let it all out and then answered her sister's question. "Until he met Wesley, I don't think he had the slightest idea. After that, he may have come to suspect, or perhaps even know for sure, but he wasn't convinced on how to proceed."

"And what about Wesley, do you think he knew?"

"I think he knew, perhaps from almost the very beginning. I am speculating on that, of course."

"Then why didn't he say anything?" Sylvie asked.

"I don't know, other than perhaps he knew, or at least assumed that dad didn't know."

"Okay, let me speculate some more here. Somewhere along the line Dad became suspicious and was successful in getting a sample of Wesley's blood. He then took a sample of his own and sent them away to be analyzed, but he never opened the envelope to find out for sure. Why?"

"Good question, Sylvie. It is just that I don't have the slightest idea why."

Cheryl and Sylvie did get a table outside overlooking the port side of Pensacola facing the Royal Front condominiums. The hostess seated them and gave them menus. Their waiter, a young man with curly black hair, brought them water, a basket with warm honey bread and three types of flavored butter. The ladies ordered coffee and scanned the menu.

"So, why don't we scan the rest of dad's document real quick while we wait," Sylvie said.

"Good idea," Cheryl said. "Any suggestions of what we are scanning for?"

"I guess any-thing that might cast some light on a more than casual relationship."

While they waited for the waiter to bring their coffee and take their order, the two sisters divided the remaining seventy pages of Jacob's manuscript in half. Sylvie gave Cheryl the first half and she kept the second half.

By the time the waiter had brought their coffee, took their order and later returned with their breakfast, neither one had found anything of specific interest. They ate their breakfast in relative silence, paid their bill and then walked to some benches along the tree-lined street that marked the foot of Palafox. They sat down and continued to scan their respective pages of the manuscript. After about twenty-five minutes, Sylvie finished and said, "So I found nothing other than he and the girl Karin had formed a good friendship. How about you?"

"Same here," Cheryl said, "just the rudiments of how that friendship was formed."

Later that morning at the appointed time, the two sisters met with Cynthia Pappas and heard the reading of their father's will. It was simple and to the point. Neither they nor the attorney anticipated any problems in accomplishing what their father had stated as his last wishes.

Cheryl had bought an open-end ticket, and so she called the airlines to find out what was the earliest she could depart. Luck was with her; she was able to get booked on a 7:45 a.m. flight out on Sunday morning.

Sylvie said she would also drive back to Kentucky sometime tomorrow. She would keep in touch with the attorney, the realtor, and the temporary storage people. The attorney had already discussed with them the closing of the bank accounts, paying bills that had accrued, and stopping his Navy retirement payments and his Social Security payments.

When they left Cynthia Pappas' office, the two decided to go back to the house one more time. They would collect all the material that their father had designated for Wesley Donaldson. None of it had been delineated in his will. He had just said they could dispose of his writings and research as they saw fit, but based on things in his office, they knew there were some things he probably intended for Wesley to have. Sylvie said she would load them into her car and send them from Louisville.

Chapter 59

On the following Wednesday, after the return from the funeral, Eliana came from her early class and checked her e-mail. She had some free time before going to the mess hall for the noon meal. She had an e-mail from David. She saw it was a forward, but he had entered a new subject line that read: Theory is correct.

She opened the letter and David had started it with a reiteration of the subject line. "Dear sister, From the following e-mail that my friend forwarded to me, it appears that your theory may be correct. After you read this, I will let you forward it to Mom and Aunt Sylvie, or you may paraphrase it as you see fit. Let me know what you think. David."

The original e-mail was addressed to the researcher's son. It began:

Dear son, Please pass this information on to your friend. It is all I could find about one Wesley Donaldson. I hope it is sufficient. Please note that for the most part I used public sources. I talked to some other people, but the individual's legal privacy was in no way violated.

He was born September 19, 1953 in Warren, Ohio. His mother bore him out of wedlock. Her name was Karin Nelson, and she was only sixteen at the time of his birth, having been born in 1937. Karin was born in Confluence, Somerset County, Pennsylvania. Her parents moved to Warren, Ohio, in December 1952. Wesley was baptized in the Methodist religion, but three years after his birth, Karin met and married Stephen Donaldson. Stephen

487

Donaldson worked in the steel mills at Youngstown and he adopted young Wesley shortly after he and Karin were married. He was fourteen years Karin's senior, but apparently they got along very well as husband and wife. They had no children of their own. The Donaldsons were Catholic, and Karin changed to her husband's religion, thus Wesley was raised as a Catholic. Apparently he was a very intelligent young man, completing high school in three years and even so, was valedictorian of his class. He was accepted at Notre Dame and completed the four-year program also in three years with a double major, one in languages, and one in history, finishing in the top five percent of his class. He continued his studies at the theological seminary. He served a vicarage at a church in Arkansas. Then after he was ordained, he went to Missouri for three years. After that, his old parish priest got him assigned as assistant at his home church.

According to a parishioner I talked to, he was very involved in the community, especially as related to the very poor and disadvantaged youth, but apparently there were some disagreements within the catholic hierarchy, but I couldn't find out exactly what. If your friend is interested, I can pursue it further. However, the people I talked with were reluctant to talk about it, but some did say it was a shame he couldn't do what he had wanted to. One lady said a bit hesitantly that he wanted to build people and not edifices. Whatever that meant. After his mother's death about a year and a half ago, he requested an indefinite sabbatical. One person I talked to said she heard that he was thinking about being released from his vows, but she couldn't say that was a fact. I did not find one person that spoke ill of him. Karin Nelson had four siblings, an older sister who stayed in Confluence, Pennsylvania, now deceased, an older brother and sister who moved to Ohio along with a younger brother. I located two older ones in Ohio, but I did not contact any of them as requested. Apparently the younger brother lives in Mobile, Alabama.

The e-mail simply ended with: *Your mother.*

At the end of the letter, David inserted, "I would go for it sister, and by the way, if I ever do decide to go into criminal law, I want you as one of my investigators. HA! HA!"

Eliana read the letter several times; she deleted David's comment and added a query of her own at the bottom of the page: "So who is going to welcome Wesley into the family?" Then she clicked on the forward button of her computer and the address entries for her mother and her Aunt Sylvie.

She clicked, send. She sat for a moment and then said to herself, "Will wait and see." She pulled some study notes and a text book from her bag and started to read.

On that same Wednesday in the late afternoon, Wesley Donaldson received a large package from Sylvie Kelly. She had called him on Monday to say that she was sending a lot of her father's writing. They exchanged pleasantries and she had told him how things went with the reading of the will. She did not give any indication of what he might expect to find in the package.

Anytime a vehicle entered the driveway at the top of the hill, it triggered an alarm, so Wesley was waiting when the driver pulled in. The UPS driver parked his truck by the door that led into Wesley's lower level office and library. He went into the truck and moved the large box toward the front.

"Wesley, now standing by the truck, greeted the driver, whom he knew from a lot of previous deliveries, with a friendly, "Good afternoon Thad."

"Good afternoon, Wesley," the driver responded. "I got two real heavy ones for you today."

"Yeah, I have been expecting them. A lot of books and writing from a dear departed friend," Wesley said.

"Sorry to hear that," the driver said.

"Thanks. I appreciate that."

The driver took the packages off of the truck and carried them into Wesley's office and set them on the long table in the center of the room. He handed Wesley the electronic signature pad, and Wesley signed by his name.

The driver thanked him and said, "See you next time, Wesley."

"Right. See you next time, Thaddeus."

When the UPS truck started out of the driveway and up the hill to the main road, Wesley turned and went back into his office. He looked at the boxes for a long time; he then went upstairs to get a large glass of lemonade from the refrigerator.

When he returned downstairs with his drink, he took a box cutter from the middle desk drawer and cut along both ends of the box marked one of two that the driver had set on the table. He then carefully cut though the tape that held the two cardboard flaps together. When he opened all four flaps, he saw a one-inch thick rectangular piece of foam. He removed the foam. On the very top was a folder in Jacob's handwriting. On the cut out tab it read: "Wesley Donaldson."

He removed the folder and placed it on the table by the box. Immediately under that was another folder with a "2 by 4" label on the face, it read: "Innocent Indiscretions." Wesley removed it and laid it beside the first folder. He looked at the rest of the contents and it appeared to be a large number of loose-leaf binders. He decided these could wait; he would start with the two folders that were on top. He assumed that Sylvie Kelly had probably looked through these, and perhaps put them on top for a specific reason.

He opened the first folder and saw the letter from the DNA testing laboratory addressed to Jacob Grant. It was unopened. The rest of the folder was simply a compilation of books and papers he had given to Wesley in the past or intended for him to have.

He now opened the second folder and started to read. By the time he had finished the first page he closed the folder and took it upstairs along with the unopened letter. He went to the bedroom that contained his mother's belongings. He opened the closet door and retrieved the box from the top shelf. He placed it on the bed, opened the four flaps, and removed the Bible that he had put back in there right after he had moved into the house. He took it back downstairs and picked up the folder and the unopened letter. He retrieved a letter opener from his desk along with the glass of lemonade, and started to walk down the path to the table by the frog pond.

When he had seated himself, he opened the folder that contained the unfinished manuscript titled, "Innocent Indiscretions." He started to read.

After page twelve, he stopped reading. Those twelve pages were the detailed account of the first time that Jacob and his mother had ever met.

Tears filled his eyes, but he then took his mother's old Bible, the one given to her by the Methodist Minister, Reverend Whitmire in 1953. He turned to Psalms 68 and removed the letter that his mother had written many years ago to Jacob Grant. Jacob was now deceased so he saw no reason why he should not open the letter.

Stuck in the pages of the Bible and away from the light, the envelope had yellowed very little. He took the point of the letter opener, inserted it under the corner of the top flap, and opened the letter. He extracted two sheets of plain white bond paper from the envelope. They had been tri-folded and then the end folded again so it would fit in a 3 ½ by 6 ¾ envelope.

Wesley unfolded it and read:

Dear Jacob,

I am writing you a letter that you will never read because I will not send it. I have asked my self why, but I have not come up with a good reason. I just know that I have to write it.

I want to tell you that you have a son. He is a beautiful baby who even at birth has exhibited a strong will. He has the most beautiful blue eyes, but some tell me that might change. I hope not.

He lays in his crib whining softly as I write this letter. I think he realizes I am writing to his father, at least I told him that when I placed him down for the night.

I know it was so wrong of me to encourage you on that last night we were together to do something that you would not ordinarily have done. When I received your first letter, I knew that you cared for me more than just as a friend, but at the time in December, I wasn't sure of that. You had been the first person who ever treated me with such kindness, but because of a lack of confidence in myself, I could not see it as anything more than you feeling sorry for me. It was very hard for me to see that you could care in any other way, so I had to show you in the ultimate way, that I loved you.

I was also very dumb. I did not think that I could get pregnant the very first time. I thought it would be something we could remember and write about. Something we could keep in our memory even though we were a long way apart. I was wrong, but later I could not get the courage to write and tell you. You will never know how difficult it was for me to keep from answering your second and third letter, but by then I had already missed my period and I knew that something was wrong.

I thought about writing to you and telling you, but then I thought, what if you were only being a friend. I knew pretty much how you felt. I knew you had deep moral and ethical feelings, and so you would feel obligated to do what you would consider right. I did not want that. I confided in my mother and my sister. We cried a lot, but felt that this was best.

I was able to finish the school year at my regular high school, but will have to go to a private school this year. We go to the Methodist church, but they do not have a parochial high school; however, Reverend Whitmire thinks he can get me accepted in the Catholic High school. I want to finish my education so that I can raise Wesley. Did I tell you that I named him Wesley, in a proper manner. He may never know his father, but I want to raise him to be the same caring type person that his father was.

I was not raised with a strong religious background, some of it my fault, but I know you were, so I have tried to learn some things about religion since I have been here. Reverend Whitmire has been a great help. He has been a shoulder to lean on. I need that right now. It was he who said that maybe I should write this letter. He said that I did not need mail it, 'just write it,' he said. 'When you have said what you want to say, it will make you feel better,' he told me.

I hope he is right, Jacob. I hope that some how this letter will cross aspects of time and space that you and I cannot even imagine. Maybe sometime, somewhere, somehow, without you ever knowing it, our paths will cross.

I now kiss our son for you. I ask that God's blessings always be upon you. You were the first person to show me that I, too, walk in God's light; that I am a person who can also walk with dignity.

I loved you and will always remember you,
Karin

Wesley folded the letter, put it back in the envelope and placed it back in the Bible at Psalm 68 where his mother had placed it over fifty years ago. He then took the letter that Jacob had received from the DNA laboratory and was going to open it in the same manner. He looked at it for a few seconds and decided against it. "Why?" he reasoned. He would place it the shredder.

The sun had already dropped below the level of the trees so it would be dark in a few minutes. He picked up the Bible and the two folders and started to walk toward the house. He felt fairly at ease with himself. He really liked Jacob's family, and he also felt that his mother would have approved of how things had turned out so far. But there were at least two things he had to do immediately. He had to make some phone calls and then he had a most difficult letter to write. He hoped, no he prayed, that all recipients would understand.

When Wesley entered the house through the ground level office, he saw the light on one of his computers blinking to indicate he had mail. He sat down and opened his mailbox. There was an e-mail from Sylvie, with a subject line that just read, "welcome."

He opened the e-mail and read the short message. He paused for a long time, almost not trusting his eyes. He read it again, this time out loud: "Dear Brother Wesley,

On behalf of my sister Cheryl and your new nephews and nieces, welcome to the family. After what you saw following the funeral, I just hope you don't come to regret it. 'joke, joke.'"

It was signed, "Love, your sisters Sylvie and Cheryl, nephews and nieces, David, Elania, Sarah and Nathan."

Wesley stared at the screen for a long time and then hit the print button on his computer. He then picked up the phone and made a three-way call to two of the people he had planned to call anyway, but now there was no apprehension.

He spoke only briefly with them, but said he knew there would be a lot of talking when it all settled in.

When he hung up with his two newfound sisters, he made one more call.

She answered on the second ring. Glancing at the caller ID, she said, "Hello Wesley, I am glad to hear from you."

"Gladys, I just had the most wonderful news and I have to tell someone, and you are my first choice. Would you join me for dinner at the Riverside Café? I can be at your house in twenty minutes."

"Twenty minutes doesn't give a lady very much time," Gladys said, "but seeing as I am anxious to hear your good news, twenty minutes will do fine."

As Wesley entered the Township road at the top of his driveway, he thought to himself, just one letter to write. Then a second thought that passed as a silent message, *"But I will always be your servant."*

The End